D.J. Taylor's novels
winner of a 1999 C
(1998). His biograph
1999 and he is curren
He lives in Norfolk w

What the critics said:

'Impressive and to be applauded … Taylor doesn't do trans-
ports of delight. But he is the novelist-laureate of sadness,
regret and a very English melancholy. … This is nostalgia, in
its best, purest sense.'

Christopher Hart, *Literary Review*

'"All comedy," Eric Morecambe once suggested, "is based
on fear." Taylor finds in King's voice the truth of that statement and, in exposing his neuroses, analyses the frailty and
innocence of what once made us laugh.'

Tim Adams, *Observer*

'Sweeping the English past, re-examining it from the present
… *The Comedy Man* gradually, and thoroughly, is a rather
successful modern novel, showing, with Orwellian precision,
where our overvaunted modernity came from … precious
little proof that we have more fun now than we did then.'

Julian Evans, *New Statesman*

'Taylor's fictive metaphor is at once satisfying and dis-
quieting … the many, varied and richly done Norfolk scenes
are what give Taylor's novel its special distinction.'

Paul Binding, *Independent on Sunday*

'D.J. Taylor's artful re-creations of different times and ways
of living never sink into nostalgia. Instead, they convey a
sense of a whole world changing, of something lost, and only
partly retrieved in the act of remembrance.'

David Horspool, *Times Literary Supplement*

'He's wonderfully good at places … but even better at
people. Taylor does people like the admirer of Victorian and
Edwardian fiction that he is renowned for being. Ted King …

is a real triumph of character-drawing, his story one of the most intimate growing-up narrations around, and as good as anything in this line Taylor has managed so far.'

Valentine Cunningham, *Independent*

' ... this book is a nuanced and unflattering portrait of post-war England, shrewdly judged and ambitious in scope. With his scrupulous observation and his ability to evoke a landscape and a mood, Taylor is marking out a territory as distinct and as disturbing as Greeneland, with the same imperative towards moral inquisition and a flatlands melancholy that is all his own.'

Hilary Mantel, *Sunday Times*

'It reads so easily that it is only when one puts it down, with a purr of satisfaction, that one realises how much ground it has covered. From post-war Yarmouth to modern Plumstead, via the Soho of the Sixties and Seventies, Taylor has animated very different worlds with equal panache.'

David Robson, *Sunday Telegraph*

' ... vivid evocations of the places and personalities ... his portrayal of the Fifties Norfolk landscape rings powerfully true.'

Michael Arditti, *The Times*

'Upward is a penetratingly observed funny-man who is as alarming as he is amusing ... The pin-sharp and painful evocation of a youth spent aimlessly in the grey austerity of 1950s Norfolk never falters ... Taylor is utterly enthralling in memoir mode ... a rhapsody.'

Bob Monkhouse, *Guardian*

' ... while *The Comedy Man* is not funny, it is quietly unsettling, even devastating ... the narrative has a slow-burning charm and power ... You probably had to be there. You probably ought to read it.'

Robert Hanks, *Daily Telegraph*

' ... a masterly reconstruction of a vanished age. ... it probably throws more light on what it is like to be a comedian than any work of fiction or non-fiction published in living memory.'

Andrew Barrow, *Spectator*

'This highly original novel is both a vivid meditation on post-war English life and a poignant tribute to a lost generation of English comedians.'
East Anglian Daily Times

' ... accessible and bitter-sweet.'

Eastern Daily Press

'Taylor has written a quirky, affectionate, often funny, very English novel; bitter-sweet, flirting with sentimentality but shying away at the last minute. There's a touch of Orwell in his attitude to England, critical but loving. He is a nicely evocative writer, with an acute awareness of the passing of time ... Taylor ... has found his own unmistakeable voice.'

Allan Massie, *The Scotsman*

'Taylor paints an evocative picture of postwar Britain ... With great invention, humour and feeling, he deconstructs what goes into creating a comedy act and the melancholy that has a large part to play.'

The Times

' ... abrasively intelligent ... Taylor sketches the tat and tinsel of small-time showbiz with a loving touch ... Ravishing in its historic sweep, restrained in its attention to the tedium of everyday life, the book is too grimly real to be an uplifting read. ... But as a state of the nation novel, it is state of the art.'

Christopher Bray, *Mail On Sunday*

'The quietness and isolation of Norfolk are caught beautifully ...'
Time Out

The Comedy Man

The Comedy Man

D.J. Taylor

Duckbacks

Published in 2002 by
Duckbacks, a paperback imprint of
Duckworth Media Group Ltd.

First published in 2001 by
Duckworth Literary Entertainments, Ltd.
61 Frith Street, London W1D 3JL
Tel: 020 7434 4242
Fax: 020 7434 4420
email:DuckEd@duckworth-publishers.co.uk
www.ducknet.co.uk

A CIP catalogue record for this book is available
from the British Library

ISBN 0 7156 3157 8

Typeset by Derek Doyle & Associates, Liverpool
Printed in Great Britain by
BOOKMARQUE Ltd, Croydon, Surrey

For Leo David Alexander Taylor
born 13 April 2000
and not forgetting
'T.T. Taylor' (1882–1951)
'the popular comedian'

By the same author:

Fiction

Great Eastern Land
Real Life
English Settlement
After Bathing at Baxter's: Stories
Trespass

Non-fiction

A Vain Conceit: British Fiction in the 1980s
Other People: Portraits from the Nineties (with Marcus Berkmann)
After The War: The Novel and England Since 1945
Thackeray

The greater a comedian is, the more gruesomely and helplessly he reduces our stupidity to the comic formula, the more we have to laugh! How people love to laugh! They flock from the suburbs in the bitter cold, they stand in line, pay money, and stay out until past midnight, only in order to laugh a while.

HERMANN HESSE – *Reflections*

To exhibit themselves, perform before a crowd, is the keenest pleasure many people know, yet self-presentation without a basis in art is liable to crumble to dust and ashes.

ANTHONY POWELL – *Temporary Kings*

You can take the boy out of Norfolk, but you can't take Norfolk out of the boy.

ANON

Contents

UPWARD & KING

Arthur Upward (b. 1938) and Edward 'Ted' King (b. 1940) originally met as National Service conscripts. Upward came from Salford, Greater Manchester; his partner was born in Great Yarmouth, Norfolk. Although they were on the road as a comedy act by the mid 1960s – their earliest engagements were in Soho cabaret – the duo's breakthrough came several years later, when ITV commissioned the first series of *The Upward & King Show* (1972). The pair had previously built up a reputation in BBC radio. Several more series followed, and for the rest of the 1970s they were rarely absent from the nation's screens.

With roots deep in the routines of the old-style Variety halls, Upward & King were essentially a cross-talk act updated to suit the modern taste: Upward short, red-haired and combative; King tall, reflective and lugubrious. Though initially seen as 'Northern comedians' – a consequence both of Upward's origins and their long apprenticeship on the working men's club circuit – they quickly adapted their act to a wider audience. Often compared to Morecambe & Wise (q.v.) and, less usefully, to Mike and Bernie Winters (q.v.), Upward & King were perhaps a more abrasive proposition than some of their television material (collected in *An Audience With Upward & King*, 1984) might suggest. Unusually for the period, they were not afraid to tackle political issues, while their odd, if slightly old-fashioned, brand of surrealist slapstick drew comparisons with The Crazy Gang (q.v.).

Off-stage, Upward & King's lives seemed uncannily straightforward projections of their professional guises: Upward extrovert and a staple of newspaper gossip colums; King more thoughtful and retiring. Almost uniquely for their time, they succeeded in attracting the attention of both the mass audience and more highbrow critics – including, at the start of their career, Kenneth Tynan – who cherished their links to inter-war Variety.

In 1980 ITV declined to renew their contract. There were several ill-advised film ventures, notably *It's Nicer Lying Down* (1981), in which the pair's familiar bantering – a curious mixture of genuine affection and apparent contempt – is ruined by a creaking script (in general they wrote most of their material themselves). They formally separated in 1982, citing Upward's ill-health – he had suffered a minor heart-attack while filming the final TV series – although their popularity had for some time been in decline. There have been sporadic reunion concerts, and low-key, and mostly unremarkable, solo work. Upward's autobiography, *Solo Performance* (1984), provides a somewhat self-serving account of their boom years.

[From *Heroes of Comedy: An A-Z of British Comedy Acts,
1900-1985*, 1987]

Prologue

It was only when they started clearing away the plates from the first course that I realised the thin man was Tracy Jacks.

Until then I hadn't taken much interest in my surroundings. The two old girls on either side of me, each of whom had peered suspiciously at the menu card arranged against my napkin, had been rebuffed after a sentence or two. A woman I'd known in TV twenty years ago had come and pecked me on the cheek, but she was seated three tables away so there was no chance to talk even if I'd wanted to. In any case, I was too busy thinking. Paula's face propped up against the pillows, Shena's voice on the phone, what you gave a ten-year-old boy to eat and how you got him to swallow it. All the time, though, I'd been faintly aware of the thin man sitting at the top of the table two rows away, picking wretchedly at his food and taking tiny sips of water from a tumbler one of the waiters had brought.

Outside it was raining quite hard, so the tops of the buses moving down the Strand were streaked with water. Inside the low rasp of conversation – occasional whoops of laughter as somebody cracked a joke – blended with the street noise. It was difficult to tell where individual sounds came from. Twenty feet away arc-lights burned over the top table. Here half a dozen instantly recognisable faces – an ex-prime minister, an ex-prime minister's husband – bent over their food. I'd been staring at them for a bit in that vague, disinterested way you stare at famous people, still thinking of the trip back from Charing Cross and what I'd say to Daniel, when once again my eye caught the thin man. He was coughing a bit over his glass now and clawing at his raggedy moustache with the fingers of one hand. It was then that recognition clicked in. Something else, too. Voices from far back in time.

An Irishman walks into a pub with a parrot on his shoulder. The barman looks at him and says, 'Where did you get that then?' And the parrot says, 'There's hundreds of them on the boat from Sligo.' Twenty-five years ago, in a studio somewhere in the rafters of Broadcasting House, Tracy Jacks had roared over that.

I was staring across the table to get a better look when I felt a pressure on my arm. The old girl on my left-hand side, prawn cocktail neatly disposed of, was wheeling in for conversation.

'Ai have a feeling,' she pronounced, 'that Ai ought to know you.'

She was one of those beak-nosed, aristocratic types, face sinking away into jowls and dewlaps, with sharp blue eyes and what people call 'good bones': the kind of cheekbones that allow you to live till ninety and still look impossibly haughty.

I muttered something about having a good face for memories, but she wasn't going to be put off.

'Have Ai perhaps seen you on the television?'

Tracy Jacks had seen me now: I could tell. He was making odd little gestures with his hands.

'I suppose you could have done.'

'And what is your connection' (*con-nex-ion*) 'with the magazine?'

'The magazine?'

'With *Senior Citizen*. With this *luncheon*?'

I was saved by the intervention of a waiter, who plonked down a wodge of scarlet beef immediately under beak-nose's chin and waved a mustard pot in her face. Hearing the little-old-lady shrieks as she fended him off, and called for 'Anthea' – apparently the name of the other old girl on my right – to pass the horse-radish, I was reminded, of all people, of Father and the genuflexions he'd have made if anyone with a voice like that had ever come into the shop. That brought me back to Dan again, and the look on his face when I'd left him outside the school gates that morning. Happy? Sad? Confident? Petrified? It had been hard to tell.

Outside the autumn afternoon was drawing in. I'd have to leave early if I wanted to meet Dan. In the far corner of the room beneath the high windows a TV camera was roving silently round the tables. The old lady had a point, of course. What was my connection with *Senior Citizen* magazine? I'd been invited and I'd turned up. Upward always used to say – even in his days of fame and prosperity – that you never turned down a lunch.

Beak-nose, who was struggling gamely with the bloody beef, drew my attention to the camera.

'Quite' (*qui-ate*) 'an occasion. Ai believe Ai heard somebody say that Peter O'Toole had won the award. Ai must say Ai've never really *cared* for him as an Ack Tor.'

Already the waiters were hovering again to whisk the plates away. Peter O'Toole. Ronnie Barker. Bruce Forsyth. Denis Thatcher. On the top table somebody tapped a microphone experimentally with a finger, making a dull, thudding sound like a chair being sharply drawn back. Men – oldish, red-faced men in overlarge suits – were getting to their feet, anxious to have a smoke and a chat before the speeches began. I walked away towards a long, white-cloth-covered table in the corner where there were ice-buckets and piles of stacked-up coffee cups.

'How've you been, Ted?'

Tracy Jacks' voice sounded completely anguished – worn down, tragic. Turning round to shake hands, I saw that he looked even worse than the glance across the table had suggested: skin drawn back over his face, desperately thin. He couldn't have weighed seven stone.

'Are you all right?'

'Nothing you'd want to know about,' Tracy Jacks said – not angrily, but a bit sadly, as if he'd somehow forgotten how to deal with questions about his health. The noise of the rain droned on. It would have been ten years since I'd last seen him – back in the sports hall at Witham, perhaps, or at the funeral – but there was nothing I could think of to say to connect him with what had happened in the interval. Tracy looked as if he understood something of this. He waved his hand back over the throng.

'Don't ever remember seeing you at this before.'

'Never got asked.' To which could be added phrases like *wasn't here* and *couldn't have gone anyway*.

'Celebrity like you. I'm surprised.'

I let that pass. 'What happens next?'

'There'll be a speech or two. Then they hand out the awards. "Perkiest pensioner", that kind of thing. Then if you like you can get pissed in the bar.'

'I've got Dan to collect.'

Tracy Jacks nodded sadly. I was on the point of asking him if he intended on getting pissed in the bar, but pulled up. Tracy Jacks, I could see, would be going home to bed, to a doctor's surgery or a hospital.

'I was sorry to hear,' he said. 'Sorry to hear. About Paula.'

There was more tapping on the microphone. Around us the waiters were starting to shoo people back into their seats. Tracy Jacks took a small, uncertain step forward, tottered a bit and then regained his balance. He looked out of place among these large, fat, old people, as if he'd got in under false pretences, might soon have his cover blown, be chivvied out into the street again.

'Thanks, Tracy,' I said. 'Thanks for that.'

We stared at each other for a while longer – me in the double-breasted suit in which I could just about pass for an old-style company director or soccer chairman, Tracy Jacks an angry, soured little fifty-year-old furious at being surrounded by health and appetite – but there wasn't much more to say and we knew it. Back at the table I got a sharp look from beak-nose for holding up the proceedings and sat down in my seat just as the first speech began.

The rain was starting to ease off now, and you could see sunlight glinting off the church spire directly opposite the window. I watched it for a moment as the words of the editor of *Senior Citizen*, a gnarled-looking bloke in a corduroy jacket, echoed above my head.

'Distinguished fellow-guests … Delighted to welcome … Barbara Castle sadly unable … Generous sponsorship …'

Seeing Tracy Jacks had badly upset me. There was no question about that, Tracy Jacks who, when I'd first met him, must have weighed thirteen stone. Looking up across the tablecloths, I noticed his place was empty, which made me jump a bit. For some reason, though, there were other things moving into the mental space he'd abruptly colonised: Paula, Upward, Father and Mother, even Mary and the woods beyond the Parmenters' farm.

'Pleased that we could come together in this way ... As young as you feel ... Age cannot wither, or custom stale ...'

It was the usual kind of rubbish you get on these occasions. In normal circumstances I might have put up with it. Now, though, it was all too much to bear. At my side beak-nose was staring furiously at the top table through a pair of lorgnettes. It was half-past two. An hour to meeting Daniel. Taking a last look over to where Tracy Jacks had been – there was still no sign – I stood up, murmured something that the nearest half-dozen guests might just have taken for an apology and hurried out, narrowly missing a collision on the stairs with an old woman who, memory insisted, might just have been the Duchess of Devonshire.

Waterfront

Practically the first thing I remember is the smoke billowing across the wheatfields.

They were burning stubble on one of the big farms alongside the Acle Strait, which means it would have been a Sunday morning in September 1945, say, or maybe 1946. In those days stubble-burning was a kind of social ritual, like Easter or the Whit Monday holiday – all the people in Yarmouth and the nearby villages knew when a farmer was going to let his fields blow, and the whole population would turn out armed with fire-irons and hockey-sticks to see if they could get a rabbit. There were never enough rabbits to go round. It's not exaggerating to say that the whole thing sticks in my mind like a painting: a huge, flat field, perhaps half a dozen acres square, the farm-lads pouring trails of white spirit round the edges, the farmer waiting on his big horse by the incline where the two fields met, the crowd of people stirring expectantly by the drainage ditches, like a gang of marathon runners waiting for the off. Then, at a signal from the farmer, one of the farmhands would chuck a lit match into the straw and immediately the flames would take and go rushing over the field in a wall four feet high with the people following behind. The trick was to be there when two lines of flame converged and the rabbits – it was usually rabbits, though once or twice you'd see a fox or even a badger – came leaping back towards you.

But the thing I recall most is the noise: the crack of shot-guns that one or two of the farmhands and the lesser gentry had, an extraordinary hubbub of raised voices and drumming feet, the odd whistling noise that a newly-harvested cornfield makes when you run over it. A dozen times since that day I've dreamed of this scene: the smoke rolling in monstrous black plumes (woodsmoke is pearly grey in colour, but stubble burns black because of the spirit), the lurcher dogs loping in pursuit, the panic whenever a gust of wind from the sea threatened to blow the flames back in your face. Above all, that tremendous, unrepeatable, *buoyant* feeling of running through a field in late summer, not caring about the smoke watering your eyes or the voices of your parents twenty yards behind yelling at you to be careful, your eyes fixed on the shrinking patch of straw where the flames hadn't yet met. Sometimes as you got nearer, if there was a gap in the smoke, you could see a rabbit frozen with terror at the dead centre of the square. Mother and Father were too slow to catch anything, of course, but hanging around a gang of bigger boys who were banging at a smouldering tarpaulin that someone had left out in the field I once turned up a hare that more or less flung itself into my lap and managed to catch it, which everyone said was a splendid bit of beginner's luck. I remember wanting to keep the hare – it was hardly more than a baby and had enormous floppy ears hanging down over its eyes – and being sharply over-ruled by my parents. No one was sentimental about animals in Norfolk, especially in 1946 with meat still on the ration. I can remember Father breaking its neck with a stick – a bit miserably, as he hated inflicting pain – and the odd thud the hare's body made as it fell back onto the ground. That sort of thing hits you when you're six years old.

Most of my early memories, though, are to do with the war: the sound of bombs exploding out beyond the harbour, and Mother's face framed in the doorway of the Anderson shelter; a group of black soldiers – the first negroes anyone had seen – from the American army base loafing in the market square (people talked about 'these here niggers' and said it was a shame the US government couldn't find white troops to send); Father taking me to see the bones of a Dornier that had come down on the beach near Gorleston. Yarmouth had the guts knocked out of it in World War Two. Most of the bigger streets had gaps where bombs had hit. One night in 1942 an incendiary came down

on the grocer's shop on the far side of the square, and
Father, who was out fire-watching on the roof of St
Nicholas' church, said it went up like a blow-torch. My
parents had mixed feelings about the war. Father used to
say that it was a necessary evil as it taught 'that there Hitler'
a lesson. Mother wasn't so sure. I think that at bottom she
thought it was a costly conspiracy dreamed up by a gang of
men with the aim of inconveniencing their wives. Certainly
I think the idea of war being expensive worried her more
than anything, and I can remember her being very cross
once when Father read out a newspaper article saying that
it took a gallon of petrol to move a tank a mile. 'But who's
going to pay for it, I'd like to know?' I can remember her
saying once or twice in a vague, frightened way. Sometimes,
thinking about this twenty years later, I used to wonder
whether it wasn't one of those rare instances of a simple
person making a genuinely prophetic remark. In the end I
decided that it was simply the small tradesman's inability to
see the world as anything other than a gigantic shop. And
perhaps, when you think about it, this wasn't such a stupid
idea at all. Poor Mother! God knows what she'd have made
of my life if she'd lived to see it. Father, too, if it comes to
that. I can still hear their voices sometimes – Mother's slow
and faintly querulous, Father's more patient and with a
deference that came from standing in the shop all day –
blending in with the noise of the gulls, the sea booming and
the endless rush of the wind. Loud voices in small rooms,
wind pouring over the high dunes. That was my childhood,
more or less.

*

To get to the shop from the sea front you headed south
past St Nicholas' church, turned left across the market
square, took a sharp right through one of the sidestreets
that bordered the quay and went over the bridge that led
to Southtown. Here the road fetched up in a longish, grey-
stone square with a few beech trees fenced round with a
railing. There were about a dozen shops and small busi-

nesses ranging in size from Wedderbury's, the gentleman's outfitter, which extended over two floors and had a frontage ten yards long, to a bicycle shop run by an old man in a collarless shirt and a muffler, who opened up when he felt like it and was cut dead by the other tradesmen out of sheer snobbery.

Father's shop was on the far side, squeezed up between the sub-post-office and a tiny baker's. In terms of the square's complex commercial hierarchies it was a small affair. Wedderbury's employed half a dozen shopwalkers, chivvied about by an overseer in a black coat, but Father made do with just himself and an occasional errand boy, although sometimes Mother could be got to 'mind the counter' if he had to go out. There was a dusty shopfront – the paint on the window-frames had originally been green but it had cracked away to nothing – with a plate glass window displaying a few fake boxes of chocolates and cigarette packets (the stuff you see in a confectioner's window is always fake) and a line of chipped white lettering that read S. LUTTERWORTH. This wasn't my father's name. In fact it belonged to Mother's father, from whom he'd bought the business, but the shop was known in the area as 'Lutterworth's' and my parents had got it into their heads that it would be a bad idea to change it.

To get into the shop you made as if to enter the wide porch of the sub-post-office and then veered left through a second, smaller vestibule past a miniature grenadier guardsman that advertised some tobacco or other and a quarter-size model of a blind boy holding up a charity box, into which I never in all Father's time at the shop saw anyone put so much as a halfpenny. The first thing that struck you was an incredibly strong smell of pipe tobacco from the big jars of Erinmore and Latakia that Father kept on top of the shelf next to the door. To the left, at knee height, level with the window, were trays of sweets of the kind that have more or less disappeared: sherbet fountains, pink sugar pigs, rosebuds, fruit salad, candy bananas. Sweets were cheap when I was a kid. Fruit salad were a dozen a penny, candy bananas were a farthing, and you could make yourself sick for fourpence. Beyond the sweet trays came the counter proper, with its piled bars of Bourneville and Caley's Marching Chocolate that came from the big factory in Norwich, covering two sides of the room and ending up in rows of cigarette packets. Ardath. Woodbines. Player's Navy Cut. Gold Flake. People said Woodbines were made of horse manure. Most of those brands have simply disappeared. At head height and beyond ran a line of confectionery jars: Mint Imperials, Fruit Thins, Sugared Almonds and a queer kind of shiny coconut squares which I think were called Jap Desserts – and above these huge two- and three-pound boxes of chocolates, which people hardly ever bought except at Christmas.

It doesn't take much to imagine myself back in the shop. The sight of a row of lemonade bottles in an off-licence – the old jars of Vimto that Father used to sell forty years ago that are making a comeback – an old-fashioned cornershop of the kind you still occasionally see in northern towns, even a chocolate-wrapper face up on the pavement, and I'm back there, on a grey autumn after-noon, say, in the early 50s, with the lights going on across the square in Wedderbury's huge plate-glass windows, rain blowing in with the wind, and Father's head bobbing up from behind the till at the sound of the doorbell. The shop is where I best remember Father, and if I want to think about him I have to start by conjuring up the smell of tobacco and sweet stuff (confectionery has a distinctive, faintly sickly smell) that hung around him like scent. He was a small, spareish man, with a lot of brindled hair going yellow-grey at the sides like old piano keys, and a perma-nently cricked back from lifting boxes. At this time Father would have been in his late forties – he was born in 1904 – but he already had that faintly pinched, worried look that I associated with older people. This, of course, was standard for the time. People were matter of fact about growing old in those days. Father and Mother would have been scan-dalised by the idea of a woman dyeing her hair or jogging to keep herself looking young. They would have thought it

'against nature' or – one of Mother's favourite phrases –
'making an exhibition of yourself'.

Even now I'm not quite sure what Mother meant by
'making an exhibition of yourself'. On the one hand, from
my own point of view, it described simple bad behaviour –
making a noise in the square, putting more food on your
plate than you could eat (there was a terrible fuss once
when we went to tea at an aunt's house and I couldn't finish
a piece of fancy cake someone had given me). At the same
time, there was a huge selection of sub-meanings that
usually, but not always, reduced themselves to questions of
social propriety or (another of Mother's pet phrases)
'knowing how to behave'. Adding a couple of rooms to the
back of your house, which meant having builders' lorries in
the street and men in overalls unloading bags of cement,
was 'making an exhibition of yourself', but so, oddly
enough, was ekeing out your income by taking in lodgers
over the summer months when the town was crammed with
holidaymakers. There was no logic in Mother's pronounce-
ments. To her a plain girl who refused to have her hair set
or 'tidy herself up' was as bad as a pretty one who put on
make-up and came to church in high heels. Each was
somehow an affront to her odd sense of decorum, rules
which it was impossible to avoid transgressing because, in
the majority of cases, you didn't know what they were.

And yet by the standards of Great Yarmouth both my
parents would have been judged dangerously emotional
and volatile types – I've seen Father cry more than once,
and Mother, too, was prone to extraordinary public sulks
and offence-takings. At bottom, I suppose, they were
simply self-conscious. In Father's case this deep personal
unease had a social origin; he was a fisherman's son from
along the coast at Gorleston who had married a tobacconist's daughter, and the awareness of this transit
weighed him down and coloured everything he did. With
Mother it was more fundamental, a kind of aloofness and
detachment from life that concealed a deep and hugely
embarrassing wistfulness. Half a dozen times I can
remember her turning down some social invitation –

joining a group of other women for coffee in one of the big department stores near the front, which she always disparaged as 'a nice thing for people with no work to do' – and then brooding endlessly about the refusal. What was Mother scared of? What upset her so much about the idea of three or four shopkeepers' wives trading scandal in a teashop? Well, I never found out, and now I never will.

If my chief memories of Father are from the shop – bowing out a customer, perhaps, or standing in the doorway with a copy of the *Yarmouth Mercury* pressed against his midriff peering diffidently out across the square – then I associate Mother with the room that lay immediately behind it. Along with at least half the shops in the square, Lutterworth's had been converted from the front room of an ordinary house. Walking down the passage that began behind the till, consequently, you came first to a parlour, with a fireplace and peculiarly yellow-papered walls, and then a kind of kitchen-cum-sitting room, with the cooker and a row of cupboards at the back and the foreground taken up by a big deal table and half a dozen chairs. Like the shop, the first thing that struck you was the smell, in this case a compound of cooking, damp and eau de cologne (Mother thought women who wore perfume were 'cheap', but she wasn't above sousing herself in eau de cologne). She was a big, untidy woman with a scallop of ash-blonde hair that was flattened down into waves in the week after she'd visited Madame Melos's salon on the far side of the square and then sprang shaggily over her head for the month before her next appointment. Sometimes she'd be doing something vaguely culinary in the tiny scullery that backed onto the kitchen, but mostly she sat in an armchair at the side of the deal table nearest the door doing what she called 'getting on with things': knitting, or re-stitching the stiff white shirts Father wore in the shop, having what was always described as 'a nice cup of tea' or damping down what even as a small child I could deduce was a pretty relentless appetite (she wasn't above pilfering handfuls of sweets out of the trays although nothing was ever said about this).

About five o'clock, if trade was slack, and with one ear

cocked for the jangle of the shop bell, Father would leave
the counter and we'd have tea together. If you asked me
which times I remembered them best as a couple it would
be here in the back kitchen, Father hunched up in the big
armchair with his spectacles balanced on the bridge of his
nose, reading out paragraphs from the local paper, while
Mother cut slices off a loaf of bread (she did this in the
traditional Yarmouth way, holding the bread against her
hipbone with her left hand and cutting it with her right) or
nagged at Betty, my foster-sister, to stoke the fire. Mother
had an inexhaustible appetite for the kind of thing that got
printed in the *Yarmouth Mercury*: disasters at sea ('all
hands missing' is a phrase I remember from early on), fish
prices, visit of the Lord Lieutenant, assault cases from the
council estates. I can see the two of them sitting there now,
Father flicking the pages out in front of his face in a way he
had, Mother looking up from her work in a vague and
somehow querulous way as they discussed a shoplifting
case or the Lowestoft bigamist who was discovered to have
three wives living within ten miles of each other. National
events completely baffled them, of course. Mother had
been to London once or twice and Father, I think, had
spent some time in the Midlands during the war, but the
world beyond Great Yarmouth might have been the
Borneo jungle for all they understood about it. Neither, for
example, could have told you the name of any capital city
outside Europe, and I don't think Mother knew the name
of a politician beyond Churchill, Attlee and Aneurin
Bevan. Later, when I was nearly grown up, I can remember
them being furious about Suez and 'this here Nasser', as
Father put it, without having the least idea of who Nasser
was and what he stood for. But this kind of insularity was
standard for the time. Most of the tradesmen Father knew
in the square were proud of the fact that they'd never left
England except for war service, and in some of the nearby
villages, even in the 50s, you could still turn up old people
who'd barely been out of the county.

    If this makes it sound as if I disliked my parents, thought
them timid and narrow-minded, then it isn't meant to. In

fact there are times when I'd willingly swap what I have now
to be back in that room in Yarmouth, a mile from the North
Sea, with the daylight fading across the square and Mother
singing quietly to herself – she liked those tremendously
gloomy Victorian ballads where the heroine always dies of
consumption a week before the wedding – or drowsing over
Ethel M. Dell's *Silver Wedding*, waiting for the last of the
late-afternoon customers to drift away and Father to come
in from the shop to read her a story about a girl who'd been
sent to jail for drowning her illegitimate baby. They were
decent, modest-living, God-fearing people of a type you
don't come across these days: unambitious, sharp in small
matters, easily deceived in large ones. I think they loved me,
and I'm certain I loved them, admired them too, or at any
rate accepted them and their foibles in a way that's now
quite beyond my comprehension. When I remember their
faces, which I do with surprising regularity, it's for their
fundamental incuriousness, the way they'd look at me when
I came into a room with an odd and almost bovine disinter-
estedness. They were my parents, I was their son, and that
was it. What would Mother have said, I wonder, if I'd asked
what went through her head? Probably told me to stop
making an exhibition of myself and left it at that.

It's 1950, maybe, or 1951, and I'm ten years old, sitting
in the small armchair on the right-hand side of the deal
table with my forehead creased over my geography homework, which involves memorising the English county
towns. King George is at Buckingham Palace, and Mr
Attlee – of whom Father and Mother heartily disapprove –
is at Number Ten. Outside the gulls are soaring over the
square. Mother is thumbing through Warwick Deeping's
Sorrell and Son, while Father reads her a piece about a
dead whale washed ashore on Hemsby beach. God knows,
there were worse places to grow up.

*

Though Father used sometimes to say – without the least
hint of irony – that 'we' (meaning himself, Mother and me)

were 'a big enough unit', this wasn't by any means the limit
of the family circle. Father had tribes of relatives living
along the coast – red-faced fishermen from Cromer and
Sheringham who appeared unexpectedly in the shop at
tea-time and antagonised Mother by saying 'bloody' and
dropping cigarette ash on the grey drugget carpet.
Grandpa Lutterworth, who for some reason was known as
'Grancher', lived with us for a couple of years after the
war, although I don't remember much more than an old
man wrapped up in a blanket lolling in front of the fire
with his mouth open, and there was an odd cousin of my
Mother's with some queer job connected with electrical
parts who came intermittently to stay, and who I think
Mother and Father regarded as a bit of a black sheep.

By far the oddest addition to the row of faces round the
kitchen, though, was the arrival of my foster-sister Betty.
This must have happened in 1951 and took place literally
overnight, which is to say that I woke up one morning to
find a strange girl in a print frock eating breakfast while
Mother fussed about with packets of cereal and tea-cups
and Father fluttered in the shop doorway, running his hand
nervously through his brindled hair. This, of course, was
standard Southtown practice. Parents didn't tell their children things in those days, and it was quite usual for a girl
to be taken out of school and set to work in a shop at a
couple of days' notice. Even Mother, though, must have
realised that some kind of explanation was called for, and
an hour or so after breakfast, when Father had taken Betty
into the shop, she summoned me into the parlour and shut
the door behind us.

'Now then young Ted,' she said – I was a big, butter-
haired boy, tall for my age, and Mother and Father had
stopped calling me 'Edward' about the time I went to
infants' school – 'who do you think that is then?'

Curiously enough, I was less interested in Mother's
explanation of the strange girl in the kitchen than by the
fact that she'd dragged me into the parlour to deliver it. It
was a dreary, dingy room with a big horsehair sofa and a
couple of armchairs and a faded picture of Grancher

wearing a frock coat and a pair of spats, which was scarcely ever used except at Christmas or on occasional Sunday afternoons when there was 'company'. The symbolic significance of entering it at ten o'clock on a Monday morning impressed me no end. Perhaps Mother saw something of this uneasiness, for she waited a minute or two before starting off on a slightly different tack.

'I daresay you're wondering who that girl might be,' she resumed. 'The one that's in the shop just now with Father?'

I nodded. It seemed important, all of a sudden, to propitiate Mother. 'Is that what she's here for? To help Father in the shop?'

Mother laughed. 'Help Father in the shop? Not her. Not likely. She's your foster-sister, Ted.'

I thought about this for a bit, skimming over the pictures on top of the teak sideboard next to the fireplace: Father and Mother on their wedding day in 1936, aunts with gleaming teeth, a brood of windblown children staring out of the back of a charabanc.

'How old is she?'

'Fourteen, I think. Fifteen.'

There was a slightly forced jollity about Mother as she said this, which even then I diagnosed as someone attempting to make the best of a bad job.

'Anyway,' she went on, 'her name's Betty – Elizabeth, I should say – and she's coming to live with us. I don't expect she'll bother you much, but you've to try and be a friend and not aggravate her.'

'Will she be staying long?'

'That's for us all to see,' Mother said enigmatically. 'But just remember she's your sister and you've to be kind to her.'

'All right.'

'She seems a nice, decent girl,' Mother went on, without much conviction, 'but I don't suppose some of her ways will be our ways. Would be surprising if they were, wouldn't it? Just remember that, and we won't go far wrong.'

As if to demonstrate that the interview was at an end, she picked up the fire-irons, gave them an almighty clatter, and then began to take a furious interest in a sepia photograph of an old gentleman with a spade beard stooping benevolently over an outsize vegetable marrow.

Even today I can't begin to fathom the motives that led Father and Mother to import Betty into our household. She was a big, square-hipped, curiously wooden-looking girl – the kind that always look as if they're about to burst out of their clothes – with a habit of chewing on her underlip that made her seem faintly simple, which she wasn't in the least. At this point she would still have been at school – she was fourteen and a half as it turned out – at a backstreet secondary where the local social services sent their 'difficult' cases, but within a month or so the school business was mysteriously thrown over and she simply lay around the house eating enormous meals, chewing on her underlip and cheeking Father and Mother. I used to watch her doing it sometimes, with a sort of awe that was mixed with admiration, because it was carried out with such enormous subtlety. Listening to her getting out of making a cup of tea or helping Father bring boxes in from the yard, you could never put your finger on the precise word or phrase in her reply that was meant to annoy, while at the same time never doubting the absolute hatred and contempt she felt for whoever was doing the asking.

From an early stage it was clear to everybody – Father, Mother, me and Betty – that her arrival had been the most tremendous mistake. Beyond this, though, any attempt to deal with her was hamstrung by my parents' inability to agree a united front. Father said that she was a 'poor girl' who'd been 'dealt a bad hand in life', and after a few feeble attempts to get her to help in the shop sensibly kept out of her way. Mother, on the other hand, on whom most of the business of supervising Betty naturally devolved, merely disliked her. She was forever chivvying her around the kitchen, or devising futile little tasks which would 'help her to manage a house', or simply nagging at her. I can see the two of them now, standing there in the back room, with Mother doling out instructions in that faintly querulous way she had and Betty making things worse by getting her to repeat everything or pretending she didn't understand. Looking back, I think Mother was just embarrassed – by Betty herself, Betty's cheek, the situation she'd unwittingly brought about – and also slightly fearful, as if there were some even thornier problem looming up on the horizon which only she could foresee.

Quite what benefit Father and Mother thought they'd derive from having Betty on the premises I can't imagine. It can't have been financial – I think the council paid them twenty-five shillings a week for fostering, which given the amount she ate meant they were almost certainly losing money on her. Probably they'd gone into the business thinking they could procure a quiet eleven- or twelve-year-old who'd be a companion for me and perhaps a bit later could help out in the shop, only somehow to end up with Betty, who smoked cigarettes out in the yard and rolled her eyes at anything in trousers.

To do Father and Mother justice, they did make an effort with Betty. Father brought home girls' comics like *Treasure* and *Princess* which he'd gravely present her with, and Mother occasionally took her out to visit friends. It never worked, though. The magazines, with their curly-haired, fresh-faced girls smiling on the cover, stayed unread; installed at some tea party across the square with half a dozen shopkeepers' wives, Betty simply sulked. I can see now that my parents were quite baffled by Betty, that they couldn't understand why she wasn't grateful to them for 'taking her in', as Mother put it, or wouldn't lift a finger around the house. They used to sit in the kitchen after she'd gone up to bed having long, mournful conversations about her various delinquencies, but the thought that she might not have liked living in their house, and resented the entire social process that had brought her there, never occurred to them. For my own part, I don't suppose I had more than a dozen conversations with her. You know how you can be in a house with someone for a year – that was about the time Betty stayed in the square – and never really come to terms with them or determine who they are? Well, that was me with Betty. She had a trick of proposing more or less unanswerable riddles. Catching hold of me early in the morning in the passage, she'd suddenly demand:

'What's a thing the cleverest man in the world couldn't do?'

'I don't know.'

'Eat two dinners off the same plate.'

At other times she'd go on about her family – she came from the East End and talked about 'the Smoke' and 'fellers' – and her mother, whom she claimed had given her up for adoption at three. This was another thing my parents had against Betty, the fact that she came from London – Mother, in particular, regarded cockneys as not much better than plague-rats, and shivered whenever she saw a London coach making its way along the sea front.

The only real conversation I recall having with Betty was one time when she'd been with us nine or ten months. It was a grey autumn Sunday afternoon, with the rain coming in across the square, and Father and Mother had gone out somewhere leaving us alone in the house. Betty, I remember, was in a worse mood than usual because Mother had finally begun to lose patience with her and was talking about getting her a job in a shop or even – this was a mark of the depths of despair to which she'd been plunged – making enquiries about cleaning work at the Northgate Hospital. I don't suppose I'd ever been on my own with Betty before, and I wasn't much looking forward to it – there was a grisly 'tea' of ham sandwiches and Bath buns laid out on the table – but no sooner had my parents disappeared than Betty lumbered up from her chair next to the radiogram, fixed me with a look that was kind of calculating and enticing at the same time, and said:

'Here, young Ted. Let's go into the shop.'

There was an absolute prohibition on going into the shop when Father and Mother weren't there. Oddly, though, this didn't bother me. In fact a part of me wanted very much to stand on my own under the gaze of a couple of hundred cigarette packets. There was also the thought that somehow I wasn't responsible for this breach of regulations, that if any trouble came of it I could always put it down to malign exterior influence. Betty seemed to know this, for she said rather meaningfully:

'I won't tell. That's if you won't.'

'All right.'

Together we stole through the passage into the space behind the counter. The Venetian blinds that hung across the front windows had been pulled down, and there was a dust-sheet lying over the sweet trays by the door. When I went to turn on the electric light, Betty whipped my hand up from the switch.

'Don't put the light on. Someone might see.'

There was a stool under the lip of the doorside counter which Father used when he was restocking the shelves. I dragged this out into the middle of the floor, while Betty – who'd clearly occupied herself in planning this excursion – roved around the sweet jars for a bit and drummed her fingers on the till. There was a look of animation on her face that I hadn't seen before. All the same I knew that I didn't really trust her, and was already wanting the adventure to end. Finally Betty flicked a packet of Woodbines off the counter, flipped one out and lit it with a sulphur match that she produced from her shirt pocket and scratched on the sole of her shoe.

'Well, this is bloody boring. Come upstairs and I'll show you something.'

Halfway along the passage between shop and living quarters a wooden staircase led up to a tiny landing, where there was a greeny-grey oilcloth carpet and an aspidistra standing on top of a bamboo occasional table. Father and Mother's bedroom lay directly behind, the door thrown open so that you could see the picture of the two carthorses in a field that hung on the far wall. Further along the corridor was my room, the bathroom and a kind of box room that they'd done out as Betty's bedroom, basically by dragging in a cheap bed bought from the second-hand shop on the far side of the square and filling the rest of the space with various knick-knacks brought down from the loft that Mother thought would 'do'. It was here that we ended up, sitting on the pink satinette bedspread, kicking our legs back and forth, and staring at the room's only ornament – a picture of a man with slicked-back hair and a moustache that Betty had cut out of *Film Fun* and stuck on the far wall.

'Who's that?'

'He's an actor, stupid. Gregory Peck. I've seen him at the pictures. Your dad hasn't got a moustache, has he? I like men with moustaches.'

The idea of liking men with moustaches seemed so alien to any of the notions I'd conceived about the world, any of the preferences that seemed to govern the way in which things were ordered and arranged, that I simply kept quiet. Betty, meanwhile, was rummaging under the bed.

'You can look at these if you like. As long as you don't tell.'

She arranged the objects carefully on the bed. There were a couple of large, two pound boxes of Milk Tray, a dozen or so bars of chocolate, several packets of cigarettes, two copies of *The Woman's Home Companion*, one or two other things. Betty sat staring at them for a bit, running her hand gently along the edge of one of the boxes.

'You shouldn't take things from the shop.'

'Go on. *She* does. Always sneaking in there when she thinks there's no one looking. I've seen her.' One of the Milk Tray boxes was half open. 'Go on. You can have one if you like.'

They were expensive chocolates, probably the most expensive that Father sold. I got given them occasionally as a treat at Christmas or birthdays. I shook my head.

'Soft, you are,' Betty said, not unkindly. 'Take a box then, and have it later. Go on.'

With the box under my arm, reasoning that I could slip it back into the shop at some future point, I walked downstairs with Betty following. Half of me, I think, was a bit frightened at the sight of Betty's contraband; the other half was faintly exalted. I was twelve years old, and such rebellions as I'd engineered against Mother and Father had been of the most trumpery kind: not eating my tea, say, or pissing in the wash-basin in my bedroom when I couldn't be bothered to go to the bathroom. In the kitchen the fire had gone out, and the plate of ham sandwiches lay fraying on the tablecloth. Betty stood in the doorway, arms akimbo, one leg hooked over the other, smoking another cigarette. She had a look on her face that I later came to recognise: a kind of end-of-tether, don't-care-what-happens look, altogether alien and remote.

'I've a good mind to smash this bloody place up,' she said suddenly.

After that I can't recall the exact order in which things happened. I can remember Betty throwing one of the plates of ham sandwiches on the floor and grinding it with her foot, and finding a tray of eggs in the scullery – fine, brown eggs they were, too – which we smashed against the wall next to the cooking stove. There was a quart of milk in the cold box that Betty wanted to pour over the carpet, but in the end we compromised by throwing flour at each other and smearing jam over the covers of Mother's library book – it was a copy of J.B. Priestley's *Festival at Farbridge*. That's what children are like, sometimes, when they're sat on by their parents, and never allowed to kick over the traces. To this day I don't know why we did it – or rather I know why she did it, but I don't know why I joined in. I can remember feeling faintly sick and excited at the same time, and also a bit awed at Betty's brazenness. There was a moment towards the end when she stripped off her skirt and paraded around the kitchen in her slip pretending to be Diana Dors, and I stood there looking at her marching up and down between the clouds of flour, with the spilled jam sticking my fingers together and the glass from the smashed jar crunching under my feet, thinking that what we'd done was simple wickedness.

I daresay that if we'd been modern kids we'd have finished the job properly, smashed the shop windows, poured creosote over the floor and been found stark naked in Father and Mother's bed clutching an empty bottle of brandy.

But this was 1952, the kitchen clock had marched round

to half-past four and old Mr Hargraves who kept the sub-post-office next door was out in his yard casting interested glances through the back window. We calmed down a bit then, and sat on either side of the deal table staring at the mess and at each other. I'd got jam all over my white Sunday shirt, and Betty's hair was grey with descending flour. We were crying, too – me out of genuine shock and contrition, Betty more or less out of surprise.

Somehow we cleaned it all up in time, swept up the flour and the smashed plates, scraped the eggs off the wall and wiped it down. The library book was beyond saving, but we concocted a story about Betty spreading a slice of bread and jam and tripping over the lino. For some reason Father and Mother, when they got back, accepted all this, although I can remember Mother being very suspicious about the missing eggs and asking us several times what we'd got up to in their absence.

In normal circumstances, I suppose, this would have been the start of something between Betty and me – some complicity, even some vague alliance. As it happened, though, it didn't turn out like that, and I don't suppose we ever exchanged more than a few sentences (I remember her once stopping me in the street and telling me that she'd got a 'feller', and me asking who it was and being told to mind my own business). But the only thing that really troubled me about the afternoon was the box of chocolates, which I forgot about in the rush of tidying up and then found I'd left on my pillow, of all places. Slipping it into the shop when Father's back was turned, which had been my original idea, turned out to be more difficult than I'd imagined. For a time I wondered about hiding the box under my coat when I went for a walk and chucking it into a waste-paper bin, but it was nearly a foot long and Mother had sharp eyes for that kind of thing. In the end I simply put it in the big store cupboard at the back of my old bedroom, hidden under a pile of Father's old shirts, which I knew nobody ever disturbed. But for some reason I was always on thorns to make sure it was still there, turning it over in my hands like a fetish, a perpetual reminder of something which in other circumstances I might have forgotten – that queer, otherworldly afternoon when, like Tom Thumb and Hunca-Munca, the two bad mice in the story book, Betty and I had deliberately smashed up my parents' kitchen. But that was the kind of thing that a place like Yarmouth did to you, back in the old black-and-white world of gulls and factory smoke and bicycling old men – turned you in on yourself, made you sour, unable to yield things up and put them aside. Father and Mother never forgot a bounced cheque or a customer who'd 'done them wrong', and they weren't vindictive people, it was just a kind of elemental reckoning up of the profit and loss account by which they lived. I daresay a kid of twelve worrying about a box of pilfered sweets sounds odd to you, but people took things like that very seriously fifty years ago, and certainly I'd never have dared to tell Father and Mother what had really happened. I knew that they'd never believe me, that it would mean months of awful silences and festering resentments. Poor Father! I can see the look he would have given me – a sort of incredulity mixed with bitter disappointment – and I knew even then that I wouldn't have been able to live with it. Would you?

*

Beyond the dunes the coastal path tracked north to the seaside villages: Happisburgh, Hemsby and Eccles. Here on a good day you could see as far as Scroby Sands, mysteriously reclaimed from the sea in the 20s, where great herds of seals basked along the shoreline and the boatmen sometimes dropped holiday trippers. Southwards, not more than a few miles took you past Gorleston and Hopton over the county border into Suffolk. Even then people still talked about 'Silly Suffolk' and told jokes about the Suffolk farmer sent to market to find a wife who came back with his sister. Father had an uncle in Lowestoft, which I can only remember as a cluster of old houses and the fish market, but I don't think we went there more than three or four times. Westward lay the Acle

Strait, with the Norwich road running through the middle,
and the flat fields – so flat that you could look five miles in
either direction and not see anything except the windmills
dotting the horizon like enormous scissor blades. I haven't
thought much about Norfolk in the past thirty years, but
there's a confused impression of long, low acres of sedge
and drainage ditches running on endlessly into the
distance, knife-edged winds, billowing space and silence.
Set down at Yarmouth railway station, disgorged from
charabancs in front of the Britannia Pier, the tourists
sometimes took fright at what they found. In my teens,
once, I was hanging around near the marina when a
middle-aged man in an open-necked shirt with the collar
pressed back over his jacket and one of those old-fashioned cameras with a saucer-shaped flashbulb hanging
round his neck came up and, after a minute or two's
conversation, asked what there was to see. It was a good
question. How were you supposed to convey the immen-
sity of the Norfolk flat, the extraordinary sensation you got
walking back over the marshes that nothing had changed
in a thousand years, to a man who worked in an engineering shop in Dudley? In the end I simply pointed him
in the direction of the pleasure beach and the theatres, and
then watched him go off, camera banging against his collar-
bone, reassured by the horse-drawn carriages along the
front and the old men playing bowls on the Marrams.

By this time, of course, the herring trade had been and
gone, and Yarmouth was a holiday town pure and simple.
Thirty years before the trains had still shipped hundreds of
fisher girls down from Scotland every autumn to work the
quaysides, they'd unloaded eight tons of cod on South
Quay in one month in the 20s, but now the seas were fished
out and the great days were over. Everybody over forty in
the town had their memories of the herring trade. Even
Father and Mother, who weren't at all poetically minded,
used to talk sometimes about the forests of ships' masts
clogging up the quayside near Lords' Quay. Everywhere
you looked, too, there were memorials to this vanished life:
shop-window prints of ships crossing the bar of the town

harbour; plaques for trawler boats lost in the heavy seas beyond Scroby. It struck me sometimes, even then, that Yarmouth was really only a kind of ghost-town. The heart had been knocked out of it when the herring boats left, Hitler's bombs had done the rest, and only the sun-cured old blokes who stumped round the place in wading boots wearing bosun's caps and taking little skiffs out in the rough water under the pier had any real connection with what had gone. The rest was simply modern rubbish – marinas and pleasure gardens and candy floss – got up to entice the trippers.

The holiday season in Yarmouth lasted from about mid-May to early September, and began literally overnight. One day the front would be virtually deserted, with all the kiosks shut up and the guesthouses slumbering behind pulled-down blinds; the next the hotels would be sprouting a rash of VACANCY signs and everywhere was a riot of popcorn and Kiss-Me-Quick hats. The local people had horribly mixed feelings about 'trippers'. On the one hand, there wasn't a shop in Great Yarmouth, or the surrounding area, that didn't make half its profits in the summer: even in the square, which was a mile from the front, we'd sell a freezer-ful of ice-cream a week in July and August. On the other, the tradesmen regarded the Lancastrian mill-workers who thronged onto the beach on summer afternoons and got rowdily drunk on Saturday nights in the streets near the marina with an unutterable contempt. No one, for instance, would eat in a restaurant that was known to be patronised by tourists, and I've seen a shopkeeper spit in the till after serving a gang of apprentices with Yorkshire accents.

Mother was particularly 'down' on holidaymakers. At some point in their lives her parents had kept a guest-house, and she used to tell ghastly tales of defiled bathrooms and general misbehaviour, which even as a child I never really believed. Thinking about it now, of course, I can see my parents' point. Relying on the holiday trade meant that the place was dead eight months of the year, and – for any grown-up person – more or less unin-habitable for the other four. All through the summer

season they had a special magistrate's court that sat on
Monday mornings to try the drunks.

I don't need anybody to tell me that life went at a
slower pace in those days. I know it did. This was before
television, before rock and roll. I've stood in the doorway
of the shop some afternoons, late on a summer Sunday, and
not seen a thing stir for half an hour, unless it was a dog
moving from the shade of one awning to another, or a child
on a bike nosing through the strewn ice-cream cartons and
the torn news-papers flapping in the breeze. The things that
really stick about those early days aren't to do with the
front in summer and the thousands of people turning
lobster-coloured in the sun. They tend to take in the older
places here and there that hadn't quite been swamped by
the ROOMS TO LET signs, the hot dogs and the threepenny arcades: shrimpboats moored on the Bure just above
the north-west tower; crab-pots piled on the quayside; old
women on bicycles moving purposefully through the mist
to early service at St Nicholas'. And above all, the solitude.
In those days you could walk along South Denes, beyond
the power station with its monster chimney, and not see a
soul except an occasional fisherman with his dog, or a
schoolboy with his swimming things in a rolled up towel
under his arm, wheeling his bike out of the dunes. Even the
courting couples, whom you were always liable to come
upon in out-of-the-way places, didn't get that far. Twenty
years later, on TV sometimes or with Upward somewhere,
I used to find myself thinking about Yarmouth, and it was
always the same thoughts: the shrimp-boats, and the quayside, and the queer little shops that sold ships in bottles and
pink Yarmouth rock, Father and Mother and what they'd
think of me. The last thought was the most futile of all. I was
a Yarmouth boy, you see, and I knew they wouldn't have
approved in a hundred years.

*

Northwards, beyond the point where the river Yare flowed
into the grey expanse of the Breydon water, lay the

marshes: flat-bottomed row-boats upturned on the mud like giant woodlice; strange, smoky huts where old men sat making lobster creels; sandpipers scuttling over the creek beds. Further away, in sight of the sea, the landscape flattened out into a carpet of grey-green marsh grass, broken up by criss-crossing inlets and pools of stagnant water: a kind of lost world of marauding herons, smoke rising from the distant huts, sedge bent backwards by the breeze. In the distance, yachts floated sluggishly down the Bure or performed complicated manoeuvres against the upstream tide.

At this point in my life I spent enormous tracts of time at the marshes. Quite what attracted me to them I couldn't begin to put into words, but I know that I got a terrific kick out of the eeriness of the landscape. Coming back over the wet grass on a winter afternoon, for instance, with the mist rising up around you like ghostly cotton-wool, you got an indescribable sense of time having stopped, that it wouldn't seem extraordinary to see a pterodactyl taking wing out of the sedge. Even in summer, sprawled full length in a dry ditch with the midges eating you alive, this feeling never quite disappeared. In the holidays from school I'd spend whole days out there with a packet of sandwiches for my lunch and the *Observer Book of British Birds* in my jacket pocket (the marshes were a great place for birds – coming back at dusk once towards the river I saw an osprey swoop down over one of the ponds) idling through the tall grass or picking handfuls of samphire, which Father sometimes liked to eat with salad for his tea. It had an odd, woody flavour but wasn't bad if you cooked it with butter. And yet the times I liked best were in autumn – late autumn, say, fading into winter, with the pale afternoon sun sinking into half-light, the chill stealing up from the reed beds and the noise of the birds gradually falling away to nothing. God knows I'm not a wide-open-spacer, or one of those people who'll tell you they're 'at one with nature', but I can see that landscape as if it were yesterday: the twilight coming down over the sea, odd bits of timber that caught your eye by the river's edge, the silhouettes of solitary walkers wandering back along the coast road.

That particular Sunday for some reason I came home earlier than usual. Fine, wind-blown rain was falling over the square, and the streetlamps were going on. None of the shops were open, of course – Sunday opening was unheard of in Yarmouth except for the kiosks along the front – but, oddly enough, the light was on behind our drawn-down blinds, and Father was standing in the doorway gazing vaguely down the street. For a moment I thought he was looking out for me – like most people in Yarmouth Father and Mother had a thing about children 'spending their time at home', which essentially meant sitting quietly with a book while your parents prosed on over your head – but when he caught sight of me in the murk he just nodded matter-of-factly.

'That you, young Ted?'

Father had got thinner in the last couple of years, and his hair was starting to go. Caught in the flaring light from the shop – he'd forgotten to put his teeth in, too, which gave his mouth a fallen-in look – dressed in his usual Sunday afternoon get-up of shirt, shabby waistcoat and a pair of old corduroy trousers, he looked a bit parched and dried-up. Something in my stare must have alerted him to this strange feeling of dereliction, because he pulled at the space below his gums where the upper teeth should have been and passed his hand over his face.

'Nasty, cold day,' he said.

No climatic conditions had ever existed that appealed to my parents. Mother 'couldn't abide' the cold, and said the crisp autumn mornings made her joints ache. Summer heat, Father complained, left him 'malted'. They watched the rain clouds assembling over the North Sea like a couple of masochists.

'Perishing,' Father said again.

It was actually quite a mild day. I wandered into the kitchen, hearing the sounds of him locking up behind me. Mother was out somewhere in town. On a plate in the scullery lay the kind of meal she thought appropriate for a growing boy on an autumn afternoon – two slices of luncheon meat, a quartered radish and several lumps of cucumber. While I got through this, Father pottered nervously round the kitchen, straightening the slant of the yellowing envelopes on the dresser – some of these were years old, going back as far as the war – picking up towels and putting them down again. There was something worrying him, I could see, that went beyond the usual anxieties of a wet Sunday afternoon.

'P'raps I'll do some sticking,' he said.

Mother had no hobbies, unless you counted library books. She said flatly that such things were 'a waste of time', and was highly satirical of shopkeepers' wives who sowed fourpenny packets of seed in their flowerbeds or went to raffia work classes at the Southtown W.I. Father, though, did have a solitary relaxation. He was mildly fixated on the Royal Family, and kept a scrapbook in which he pasted photographs cut out of the newspapers. One of these books was lying on a chair by the kitchen table, I noticed, underneath a pile of clippings from the *Daily Sketch*. I squinnied at the topmost one, which showed the Queen Mother offering Princess Anne what looked like a plate of rock cakes.

'You seen Betty at all?'

So that was it. Every so often – it might be once or month, or once a fortnight, always, though, at times calculated to cause maximum inconvenience – Betty staged what Father and Mother referred to, with no humour at all, as 'vanishing acts'. Duration varied: three hours, once; half a day another time. Once, I remember, they were called to fetch her from a pub near South Quay where she was being stood drinks by a gang of American servicemen. Father's antennae were finely tuned to these disappearances.

There was absolutely no knowing where Betty might be: this much was accepted. Gorleston. Lowestoft. Hopton. Anywhere along a bus route. Several times she'd come back claiming to have gone as far as Norwich, a thirty-minute train-ride away, but no one was quite sure whether to believe this.

'Perhaps she's at a friend's?'

'No,' Father said decisively, and with what for him was a kind of paralysing bitterness. 'She ain't *got* any friends.'

There was something awful about the way he said this, which even as a child of twelve I think I caught something of – not so much in the anger, of which the dropped aitch was a symbol (Father and Mother normally managed to 'talk proper' as they put it unless they were especially upset), as in the dreadful glimpse it conjured up of the life Betty led, or that Father thought she led. Had Betty got any friends? I don't suppose she had. I don't suppose, if it came to that, that anyone cared either way.

Father looked a bit shocked after he'd said this, and muttered something about Betty probably being along in a minute, but it was no good. It never was. Betty's absences irked Father, jangled his nerves, offended his sense of personal security, in a way that I could never understand. The afternoon wore on, and the light faded into darkness. I can remember the rain sluicing down into the yard from the cracked gutter, and Father sitting hunched up in his chair, sunk in misery, as he tried to take an interest in a photograph of the Duke of Edinburgh inspecting a dead grouse. It was in this condition that Mother found us at a quarter to six, coming back in a bad temper because of the weather, with her newly-marcelled hair piled up under a rain-bonnet.

After that things happened very quickly. It took Mother five minutes to establish – something we hadn't thought of doing – that Betty's clothes were gone from her bedroom, and that she'd forced open the tin cash box hidden in the airing cupboard and walked off with three weeks' house-keeping money – about £15, I think. The enormity of what had happened – particularly the money going – calmed Father and Mother down a bit. I can remember them sitting there in the kitchen gloomily discussing whether or not they ought to send for the police, and in the end Father being sent into town to make enquiries at the railway station, which even I could have told them was a bad idea, but was typical of the way my parents went about things. It was no good though, no one had seen her, and in the morning – I think they had a vague idea that despite the £15 and the vanished clothes she'd somehow re-materialise during the night – Father had to put his best suit on and go and explain to the council what had happened, which now I think about it must have taken some doing.

To give them their due, Father and Mother were hugely upset about Betty. The official line was that they'd been let down, and for months afterwards they used to talk in a puzzled kind of way about how they'd tried to 'give her a home', only to have it all (Mother's phrase) 'thrown back in their faces'. Secretly, though, once they'd got over the theft of the money, which on the Yarmouth scale of things was at about the same level as adultery, I think they were faintly ashamed. Eventually, when Betty turned up again – in Skegness, of all places, together with the lorry driver who'd given her the lift there – there was talk of her coming back, but everyone knew it would never happen. It was all too far gone for that, broken up and irreclaimable. In a way I think I sympathised with Father and Mother about Betty. It was as if some mysterious agency whose existence they barely knew about had decided to judge them, and found them badly wanting. At the same time I realised that the whole business had done something fundamental to how I thought about them and our lives together in the Southtown square; had diminished them somehow and left them feebler and less confident. There were other things happening by this stage, of course, which I've yet to tell you about, but even then I had an inkling that the old world, that sedate landscape of back-to-back houses and flyblown tobacconists, was on the way out, there in a Yarmouth back kitchen with Father biting his nails over his scrapbook and the rain falling over the murky glass.

Q: Why did the lion get lost in the jungle?
A: Jungle's massive isn't it?

Actually, I'm still trying to work that one out.

Outside the sky is turning grey on blue. In the distance, over towards Millwall, a pair of police helicopters are buzzing over the clusters of towerblocks. Nearer at hand, between the warehouses and the tumbledown wharves, the river runs into view. Its surface is the colour of gravy. Apart from the helicopters and my hand inching over the page, nothing moves. All comedy, Eric Morecambe once suggested, is based on fear. There are times when I could almost agree with that. Now isn't one of them. Comedy of the kind I propose to inflict on tonight's meeting of the Plumstead Over Sixties is based on comfort, recognition, pleasurable re-encounters – a kind of light-entertainment plane-spotting involving outsize insignia, friendly silhouettes and not a bomb port in sight.

My wife, she's so thin that when she drinks tomato juice she looks like a thermometer.

Actually you have to be careful with a joke like that. Anything too funny just exhausts the audience. I ink a neat little line through *tomato juice*, which is one of the jokes that's made it to the prompt card, and go back to the window, where there are gulls hovering in mid-stream and lights going on in the houses by the shore. It's barely half-past four but already the place is settling down, turning in on itself. The newsagents shut at five round here. Later you can walk for hours round the tide walls and the lock-ups near Woolwich and not see a soul. Two floors below there's the faint hum of a TV. *Playdays*, *Kidscene* or something. The boy gets back from school at quarter to four, but he doesn't come up when he knows I'm working.

Working. It was Lennie who fixed tonight's gig (they all call them gigs now, even the sixty-year-olds). *Now you're back in the smoke you want to be earning a few quid?* God knows how Lennie survives, in his two rooms up the flight of stairs in Old Compton Street with the old *Carry On* posters still stuck on the walls like it was 1965. Lennie still talks about his great days populating the cast of the Black and White Minstrel Show (*Course, some of 'em didn't want to do it, but I told 'em, 'Who's going to see you under the fucking boot polish eh?'*). Perhaps Lennie is one of the Plumstead Over Sixties. It wouldn't surprise me. Nothing surprises me now.

Replaying Lennie's advice on audience requirements (*Arf an hour'll do it, and not too blue mind*) I do another trawl through the memory store. What does 'not too blue' mean these days anyway? Thirty years ago it meant they didn't like you saying 'fuck'. These days it probably means no incest jokes. I once saw Roy 'Chubby' Brown go on stage somewhere in the north where they were having a big child abuse enquiry and greet the audience with 'I'm surprised any of you lot are here. I thought you'd all be at home fucking your children.' Of course they all *roared*.

I asked my wife the other night, 'What do you think about sex on the TV?' She said: 'I don't know. I've always found it a bit uncomfortable.'

That'll do.

*

I bought this place back in 1972, around the time we did the first TV series, before Lennie, 'alternatives' and jokes about hurting children. It cost £3,000. Everyone else was going for West End flats and Surrey mock-Tudor; I wanted a bolt-hole. I remember Upward coming down here once not long after, parking himself in the front room and saying 'What the hell are you up to, Ted?'

You could never explain anything like that to Upward. Women, for some reason, used to like it. Coming back in a taxi, late at night, they detected romance in the curve of the Thames, the lights moving away downriver. Only in the morning would the illusion fracture.

'Why didn't you tell me you lived in the bloody Far East?' a girl once snapped at me from the bedroom door.

To me, though, it was London: grey streets, the river, the petrol smell mixing in the raw air. Coming back a couple of months ago I was surprised to find how much of myself I'd left behind: the blown-up TV stills on the wall, a pile of comic postcards twenty years old sent back by Upward from holidays in the north. ('*Has that vicar any children?*' '*No, they say his stipend's too small.*') In a box in the cellar, hidden amongst old bikes and petrol cans, there were sheaves of photos, professional ones with agents' stamps on the back: Upward and me in the middle of a dance routine involving a file of statues; in the presentation line at a Royal Variety Show; at some bottle-strewn dinner table stuck between a couple of fellow diners. I had to look at them closely before I could work out quite what was going on, and who was who – that the fat chap with the gurning smile was Les Dawson, that the younger man in the tuxedo with the ambrosial hair was me.

*

Later I go out for a packet of fags and an evening paper. The streets round here are sharply segregated now: old dockland terraces and the new estates put up in the last property boom. The new estates have names like 'Heron's Quay' and 'Kingfisher's Rest'. God knows who lives in them. There are men in suits out on the pavement in the early mornings, as vague and rootless as tourists. The real inhabitants – vixens wheeling pushchairs, skinny boys in white T-shirts, burly crop-headed dads – don't come out till noon. Not having lived here properly for a quarter of a century, the first thing that struck me was how fat the women have grown. You see them on the street corners, stabbing the air with their cigarettes as they gesture, elephant legs splayed under micro-skirts or bulging out of shellsuits, with the shaven-headed child in the buggy looking on. Do they like looking this way? Do they aspire to what the newspapers call an acceptable body image? The talk is always of men. Always. *Cunt wanted to do me up the bum, but I wasn't having any*, I heard one say to her mate the other day. Seriously, too.

Half the houses in the street are empty, I gradually worked out in my first month back. Looking through their upper windows you can see the twilight settling like ink. Officially this is a 'regeneration area', and there are posters in the shop windows to this effect, but I don't think it cuts much ice with the flotsam of the streets. No one knows where the original inhabitants went. Downriver to Dartford and Gravesend? Far away into Essex? In their place have come Bengali shopkeepers, stone-eyed Asians in *muhjahdeen* fur hats driving mini-cabs. Like the blokes in suits, tapping at their mobiles as they head out into the dawn, they don't look as if they're settled in. Nobody seems to be permanent. Nobody – not the brown women in saris who look blank if you ask for directions or the mini-cabbers who need an A–Z to get to Lewisham – seems to know where they are. Presumably they're already waiting for the next migration, the next grey street with its blocked-up windows, the next beaten-up Rover with the radio tuned to the Gujarati station playing Bollywood film music.

At the end of the street orange light glows out of the Rashids' mini-market. It's the kind of place where they sell, separately, bags of crisps that have 'Not to be sold separately from multi-pack' printed on them. Through the wire cage that twists over the plate-glass window I can see the sari'd bulk of Mrs Rashid hunched into the tiny compartment between the till and the rows of spirit bottles. Mr Rashid will be at the back of the shop, weeding out the cartons of milk gone past their sell-by dates – or not weeding them out. It's impossible for me to look at the Rashids without thinking of Father and Mother and what they'd make of it all. Inevitably they would have been appalled at the idea of people called Rashid even keeping a shop (Mother once confessed to me that she hated the idea of leaf tea because of the brown fingers that had picked it). What I think would have shocked them even more, though, is the absence of what would now be called customer relations. I used to watch Father sometimes when anyone came into the shop. Even as the doorbell clanged

you could see the attentiveness spread into his face. Then,
as whoever it was moved into view, he'd kind of hover, not
exactly defensively, but giving the impression that the act
of purchase was a sort of holy compact in which he was
proud to play a part. And that of course was before either
of them opened their mouths. I don't say that Father *liked*
all this, but he knew that it was his duty. The Rashids, on
the other hand, just sit there. You can see their point. Why
sell civility as well as the groceries? Where's the benefit?
Father went bankrupt, whereas the Rashids, according to
local rumour, make enough to afford six weeks annual
holiday back in the Punjab.

Inside the shop a stale, sweetish smell rises off the fake
grass mats with their little pyramids of mottled bananas
and boxed dates. Further along, in defective refrigerator
tanks, the *halal* stuff sits and rots. Sure enough, Mr Rashid
is pottering away at the back of the shop. He looks up
when he sees me, checks that I'm not a criminal or a basket
case and carries on tinkering with the tube of unhooked
strip-lighting. Paying for the cigarettes and the *Standard* –
the last from the pile – something, probably the memory of
Father behind his till, the acknowledgement of some
shared heritage, prompts me to nod at Mrs Rashid. She
stares back impassively, like a piece of teak.

*

Back at the house the red eye of the answerphone is
pulsing away. As I press the 'Play' button I twist my head
round the open door of the front room. The TV is still on,
but the boy has disappeared. Upstairs, I suppose. In the
first week or two I made the mistake of going after him.
Nowadays I leave him be. The answerphone message is a
woman's voice, youngish, a sentence or two lost in static,
and a number. Actually, Lennie has already filled me in on
this one. (*Gel from the radio rang about you Ted. What you
reckon then?*) It's a mark of Lennie's out-of-touchness that
he still thinks the BBC means money. God knows what he
told her. (*I told her you was dead busy, but there was no*

harm in asking. OK?) I transfer the number onto the scribble pad before walking through into the front room and extinguishing the blare of the TV. The boy leaves no spoor. Apart from the blue exercise book there's no sign that he's been here. I pick up the book – a school-issue one with *Daniel King* traced on the front in hulking capitals – and read the opening page.

I live with my Dad in a big house near the river

Before that I lived with my mum. Not here but a long way off.

On Saturdays my Dad buys me a comic.

In the house across the road, framed in the light from the uncurtained window, a bloke and a girl are shouting at each other. I can't hear them, but I can tell from the look on the bloke's face and the way the girl is squeezing folded arms across her chest, as if it will somehow deflect the yells. Sometimes she opens her mouth and yells back. They do this for a good five minutes and then drop their arms and gaze at each other, either exhausted or abashed.

*

About comedy and fear. Thirty-two years ago I saw a film of Lenny Bruce performing in a club in Chicago. There weren't more than fifty people there – a few students who'd heard he said 'fuck' a lot and a handful of Beat survivors in sunglasses and suits. I can't remember what the final joke was about except that it went on for ten minutes and had seven or maybe eight interconnected threads. At the end when he suddenly dragged them together (the cop, the dog, the drug-store, the preacher's necktie) in a couple of sentences there was a silence, in which the audience checked it all back in their heads, and then an extraordinarily loud exhalation of collective breath, fifty people sighing out of sheer relief. After that, quite a long time after that, they started laughing.

*

Come half-past seven I go up to change. London turns dead at this time of night. The white vans and the battered Fiestas are jammed up against the pavement now, the skinny boys are all indoors eating their tea and waiting for the football to start, and the streets are silent. Like I say, I haven't lived here properly for twenty-five years, but the old rhythms creep up on you, steal into your blood. Somewhere down below a car door slams and there's a rumble of conversation. Walking down the stairs, I turn into the boy's room and find him stretched out on the bed beneath the posters of Robbie Fowler, reading a paperback called *Goosebumps*. He shifts when he sees me, draws the book into the shadow of his chest as if it's something he fears my reaction to.

'Are you OK?'

'Fine.'

Another thing I've noticed since I came back here is that whereas the girls look older than their ages, the boys look younger. With his cropped hair and his bush-baby eyes, Daniel would pass for eight.

'What did you have for tea?'

'Same as you.'

'There's sandwiches in the fridge if you get hungry.'

Hastily I shoot through the rituals of the next two hours: what to do if the phone rings (leave it) or the door-bell goes (ditto), what you can watch on TV and what you can't, what to do in an emergency (Mrs Finney in next door's basement). When I say goodbye, he surprises me by hurling himself headfirst into my stomach and clinging there with his arms wrapped round my waist.

Two minutes later, standing outside the locked door, coat flapping against my legs in the breeze, I put my hand inside the jacket pocket of my suit. The letter that came last week, the letter from Shena which I still haven't dared open, burns against my fingers.

Interview with Ted King

Did you hear the one about the man who decided to be a stand-up comic? All the sit-down jobs had gone.

When did I get the idea that I wanted to tell jokes for a living? Sometime back in the 50s, I suppose, listening to the Light Programme comedy shows on the big radiogram that my father and mother kept in the parlour, or going to watch the variety bills at the Yarmouth Regal. Variety's long dead now – it's been killed off by TV and pop music – but in the 50s it was still going strong: nearly every big town had a theatre that was on one of the touring circuits … Essentially it was just a concert with a lot of different acts that ran for a week until the performers packed up and moved on to the next place on the tour. The great thing about it was that you could actually see most of the people you heard every week on the radio – Max Miller, say, or Arthur Askey – and even the occasional film star. Sometime around 1953 – it was right at the fag-end of their career of course – I even got to see Laurel and Hardy. It was a huge disappointment, they barely knew where they were.

My parents didn't like the big-name acts. My mother thought that Max Miller was 'vulgar', which of course he was, although he talked so fast that half the time you couldn't work out what he was being dirty about … I liked the kind of acts that these days you'd call 'surreal'. Wilson, Keppel and Betty. Cardew the Cad. The Western Brothers. I don't suppose you've heard of many of them. Cardew the Cad was an immensely tall middle-aged man – I think his real name was Robinson – who dressed up in a blazer and short trousers, with a long scarf wound round his neck, and he did fantasy monologues about the public school he was supposed to be at. The Western Brothers were about the nearest that Variety ever got to satire: a couple of chaps in evening dress – one of them might even have had a monocle – who put on silly-ass voices and sang songs that in a very mild way guyed things liked the Royal Family or the Empire. My parents didn't like the Western Brothers either. My mother thought they were 'too clever by half', while my father always said he couldn't see what the joke was. But the real reason, I think, was that they were a bit shocked at the idea that anyone could find these things funny …

There's no point in pretending that I was some kind of child prodigy – you know, the kind of kid who tells jokes round the supper table and wins talent contests on the pier. They still had what were called 'concert parties' in those days – old chaps dressed up in pierrot costumes who performed at church socials – but I'd have run a mile from anything like that, and if you'd told me I'd end up spending my life on a stage I'd have laughed at you. It was simply a hobby – listening to *Hancock's Half Hour* or sitting in the back row of the Regal hearing the Western Brothers sing a number called 'Play The Game You Cads' – and I hadn't the least idea – or the desire, if it came to that – that it would ever come to anything. Certainly no one at home ever gave me the least encouragement, and I'm sure that if my father and mother had ever lived to see any of it they'd have been deeply shocked. Appalled even, I don't know …

from *Here to Entertain You: The Upward & King Story*,
BBC Radio 2 documentary, 1976

The Man In The Corner Shop

I wonder if you can imagine what it was like to be the son of a small shopkeeper on the East coast of England forty years ago?

For a start, the shop dominated your life. Theoretically opening hours were from eight in the morning to six at night, six days a week, but in practice anyone who rapped on the shutters for a couple of hours after that got served, and Father always ate his meals with one ear cocked for the jangle of the doorbell. My chief memory of him as a child is of a harassed-looking man with greying hair putting his fork down on a half-empty plate and scurrying off to sell someone a threepenny bar of chocolate or a box of matches. I don't suppose Father ever worked less than a seventy hour week. Worse, it was the kind of business where things were always happening at odd times. At least two nights a week Father used to do the accounts, which as he was 'bad at figures' meant that he rarely got to bed before midnight. I can see him now, sitting at the kitchen table with his head down over a pile of invoices and the big metal spike he used for securing bits of paper, a cup of tea going cold at his elbow, trying to work out what had happened to a stray box of Yarmouth rock, or whether it was worth laying in another half-dozen jars of Erinmore to take advantage of a 5 per cent discount the suppliers were offering. Shopkeeping life was full of these niggling little decisions. Both my parents, I noticed, referred to the shop as 'it', as if it was a living thing. Father would complain that 'it' didn't get much forrader, or that 'it' was a trial. From an early stage I think I conceived of the place as a kind of dreadful, pestilential growth which had coiled itself around them and wouldn't let go until they died.

Worse even than this – worse than the nagging customers and the gangs of children who came in trying to pilfer sugar mice and sherbet dabs – was the state of cut-throat warfare that existed with the people you saw around you. There were about a dozen shops in the square. I can't remember all of them, and the smaller ones were always changing hands, but the big ones have stayed in my head. On the far side there was Salaman's, the off-licence, followed by a tiny wool and knitting shop and a general hardware place that sold everything, from lengths of plywood to nails and twists of chicken-wire. Then came Wedderbury's, and next to it Dunstan's, the big grocer's, and then a nondescript newsagent who was always closing down, reaching an arrangement with his creditors and then starting up again. I don't remember our side of the square quite so well – probably because it wasn't directly in view from the doorway where I was always hanging about – but there was certainly a fish shop, where Mother sometimes bought dabs and half-pints of cockles, and a bakery. I used to like waking up in the mornings on baking days and smelling the scent of yeast in the air. Most of these shops weren't in direct competition with Father, but there were three or four of them who more or less openly impinged on his trade. Officially this was illegal – all the leases were owned by the Church Commissioners, and there were rules as to what you could and couldn't sell – but the big stores had ways of getting round this: selling cheap cigarettes in what were called 'economy packs', for instance, or giving bars of chocolate away as 'free gifts'.

Father's problem was that he wasn't a big enough operator to compete with the smart shops on the far side of the square. If he'd had the capital, or had been prepared to take risks, he could have undercut, taken a lease on one of the next-door shops when it came up, done half a dozen things that would have taken the weight off his back, but the money was never there. All he had was the tiny sum – I think it was about £900 – he and Mother had inherited from Grandpa Lutterworth, and no bank manager would ever have lent him a penny. Not that Father would have wanted him to. He was one of those timid, unadventurous types who regarded borrowing as a kind of sin, and the thought of paying interest on someone else's money filled him with horror. I can remember once, on a Saturday when the bank was shut and some emergency came up, him having to touch the sub-post-master next door for a loan and being so embarrassed that the money was repaid by half-past nine on the Monday morning.

What made it worse was that he had struck up a kind of friendship with Dunstan, who owned the grocer's shop and was his biggest competitor. It used to puzzle me sometimes. There was Dunstan – he was a big, barrel-chested man with popping blue eyes and a habit of swinging his arms as he walked – trying to ruin him, and yet Father scarcely seemed to notice. Two or three times a week Dunstan would stump over from across the square and the two of them would stand talking in front of the tobacco and the packets of potato crisps; or rather Dunstan would patronise Father in a rather conspicuous way about the shop, asking him why he persisted with particular lines or didn't colonise the bakery two doors down, which everyone knew was on its last legs, while Father mumbled about things being all right as they were. I can see them now – the big man in his white grocer's overalls (he called Father 'Alf' or 'old man') prosing on with his hand lying casually over the nearside counter, with Father bobbing his head in a kind of respectful way from behind the till. I once caught a glimpse of Dunstan looking at Father when his back was turned to the shelves, and it was rather like a cook eyeing up a turtle that he plans to make into soup.

All the time I was growing up Father was slowly going bankrupt, and I don't think I even noticed. The only thing I can say in my defence is that I was at the age where what happens at school or on a soccer pitch is more important than whether or not your parents are making a living, and also, curiously enough, that Father and Mother scarcely seemed to see it themselves. They'd had difficult times in the past, I think, and in some ways the evidence of the books didn't worry them as much as it ought to have done. There was a vague feeling that things would 'get better' – I can remember them cheering up when Attlee lost the 1951

General Election as Labour was supposed to be 'against' the small businessman – and that good times were just around the corner. I can't imagine what Father thought those good times would consist of – maybe he simply saw it in terms of selling half a dozen extra boxes of chocolates every week – but I'm sure this vision sustained him through the dull afternoons (there was a period between about two and four when hardly anyone came into the shop) and the late-night battles with the account books. Sometimes, in the evenings mostly, when tea was over and Mother had finished her housework, they'd talk in a kind of vague, listless way about their predicament, about how trade was bad, or that Salaman's had started a line in cut-price cigarettes. Once or twice, too, Mother would go and stand in the shop and stare reproachfully at the stock, as if she couldn't quite believe that people weren't coming in to purchase all the stuff laid out before her – the packets of Capstan Full Strength, the piles of candy bananas and so on – but I don't think I took much notice. It was merely the kind of thing your parents talked about. Don't get me wrong about this. If someone had told me at thirteen or fourteen that Father was heavily in debt, I know I'd have been seriously concerned – for a start, unlike many kids at the time, I knew what debt meant – and tried to help as best I could, but the thing was that nobody did. The situation just drifted on in a way that was very common at that time, with nobody knowing what the solution might be or how it would all end.

Meanwhile, I was growing up. At thirteen, I was already an inch or two bigger than Father, with yellowish-coloured hair and a nose bent slightly out of joint after an accident that I'd had falling downstairs as a child. I wasn't clever – although I'd scraped into Yarmouth Grammar School, which pleased Father and Mother no end – but I could play games a bit, which was all that counted at that age, and I was fairly popular. School I don't remember much of, except for a general air of chalk-dust and the eternal boiled cabbage smell that hung over the refectory, and being caned once for exploding a firework in the corridor, which was against the rules but everybody did it. It was an old-fashioned place, with a school song about happy warriors marching through the vale of life, and the boys divided up along class lines: the solicitors' and doctors' sons on one side, shopkeepers' and small tradesmen's sons on the other, and a handful of untouchables whose fathers worked on the buses or in low-grade clerical jobs. (I can remember one boy whose father was a farm labourer walking through the school playground to a huge shout of '*Tractor!*' every morning for five years – that was how seriously we took these things.)

I suppose if anyone had taken an interest in me, made me read the right books and nagged me about homework, I could have made something of school, but they never did, and in any case I was too busy pursuing the infinitely more enticing life that lay beyond the school gates: hanging around outside the local girls' school in search of a 'click' as it was called or taking the train to Carrow Road on a Saturday afternoon to watch Norwich play. I think Father and Mother were quite proud of me then. Father used to straighten up from whatever he was doing when I came into the shop wearing my grammar school blazer with my hair Brylcreemed up into a Tony Curtis quiff, and shoot me a look that was kind of shy, admiring and indulgent all at the same time. Somehow this survived all the rows we had at this time – the usual stuff about staying out late and clothes and going about 'looking like a Teddy Boy'. It's a good feeling, you know, that your parents approve of the kind of person you are, even if – as I did – you then go and let them down.

Sometimes, looking back at this from the vantage point of ten or fifteen years later – stuck in some grimy northern town on a Sunday morning in the 60s, frowsting in digs with Upward somewhere on the South Coast with the rain falling over the terraced streets – I used to wonder about Father and Mother, what exactly they got out of life, what made them tick. In the end I decided that there wasn't any great mystery about it, that they were just quiet, simple people who 'kept themselves to themselves' (Mother) and weren't ever troubled by things that went on outside their tiny orbit, not because they didn't know they were there, but because they took no interest in them.

What I'm trying to say, I suppose, is that my parents had no self-consciousness, no idea that even the life of a provincial shopkeeper in a flyblown seaside town was something you could take pleasure out of if you tried. For a start neither of them had any friends. There was an old couple called Edgell who sometimes came round to play cards on a Saturday evening, and Father was a member of the Royal Antedeluvian Order of Buffaloes – a kind of sub-masonic men's club that met every Friday night above a pub near the market square – but the idea of spending time with people to whom you weren't related, simply because you enjoyed their company was quite alien to them. Sometimes, talking to Father or picking up stray fragments of conversation, I got a hint that his life before he met Mother hadn't been quite so circumscribed, but it was all quite gone now, and impossible to recreate. As for Mother, I think a part of her was merely frightened by the occasional glimpses of the outside world that she got through the newspapers or the radio. I can remember both of them being very exercised by the Ruth Ellis case (she was a nightclub hostess who'd shot her boyfriend, and there was a furious row about whether the death penalty should apply). Father, chewing away on his bread and butter over the kitchen table, said in his mild way that it 'wasn't right' to execute a woman, whatever it was that she might have done. Mother, on the other hand, wanted her to hang.

No doubt all this makes Father and Mother seem like the worst kind of joyless drudges. In fact they were companionable enough. Curiously, evenings are the time I remember best at the square, with the radio playing *Variety Bandbox or Your Hundred Best Tunes*, Mother drowsing over the paper, me at the kitchen table doing my homework and Father poring over one of his scrapbooks or getting up to answer the shop door if a neighbour came round wanting a packet of fags. You don't get times like that now – with everybody stuck in the same place, the sense of time passing at its natural speed. Sometimes, when

I was in my middle teens and was let out in the evenings
for an hour or two, I'd come back and find everything
exactly the same as I'd left it – Mother fallen asleep in her
chair with her mouth open and her reading glasses low on
her nose, Father snipping the newsprint from around a
picture of the Duke of Kent. The half-dozen or so
photographs I've kept from those days all have this queer,
sleepy air: Mother standing outside the shop with her head
bent against the sun and the shadows running across the
street before her; Father staring vaguely from a perch in
the dunes, somewhere near Hopton, with the sea grass
sticking up around him like porcupine quills; the three of
us taken together – God knows where or by whom –
Father and Mother in mackintoshes, me in my school
blazer and grey flannel trousers. My smile is quite genuine
and unforced. The young Queen's on the throne, Winston's
in Downing Street, Germany's a dustbin of bomb-craters,
and it's all going to be all right. Christ! If only I'd known.

*

Sometimes, in odd moments long after they were dead, I
used to wonder what it was that Father and Mother believed
in. Well, I never really found out, never truly got to the
bottom of what made them the people they were. Given
their position at the very bottom of an ant-heap of local
tradesmen all strenuously trying to cut each other's throats,
you'd have thought they would have incubated the most
fantastic resentments about the social order of which they
were a part – but no, they were the most rabid conservatives
and accepted everything that got thrown at them in the
same way that they accepted the three times table. Part of it,
course, was that hidebound small shopkeeper's mentality
that Mother had had in her veins and Father had acquired
by marrying her. When I grew up and found out about
Poujade, the French tobacconist who started his own political movement, I understood immediately the kind of things
he wanted to achieve. Father and Mother would have been
Poujadists, no question. They believed in – to take only the

most obvious things – the Queen, the Royal Family, God, the House of Lords, the Conservative Party, capital punishment, gentlemen in evening dress, BBC announcers, cut-glass accents, the Empire, Eisenhower and 'a fair day's work for a fair day's wage'. Father, in particular, used almost visibly to cringe whenever anybody with what used to be called an 'educated' voice bought something in the shop.

Beyond these absolutes, though, a certain amount of equivocation stole in. Mother used sometimes to talk darkly about big business and how it was 'doing the small man down', and she had peculiar moments of irritation at the pyramids of social precedence she supported. I can remember her once gazing at a photo in the local paper – it might have been of the wife of the Lord Lieutenant of Norfolk opening a garden fête – and her expression changing suddenly from mild interest to furious disdain.

'I don't suppose she's ever darned a shirt in her life,' she remarked bitterly.

These outbursts punctuated my childhood. You never knew what was going to set them off: a tax demand; a neighbour in a too-ostentatious dress; a local boy who'd 'made good' – that is, got a superintendent's job at the Norwich Union Insurance Company and had his picture printed in the *Mercury* – any of these could incite her to fury. Of the two of them, I think Father was probably the kinder, the less liable to take offence or be cast down by circumstance. He was a very patient man, who'd go out of his way to oblige a customer, shook his head over the newspaper reports from Korea and thought it was a shame that 'these here blacks' weren't allowed to run their own affairs. Oddly the 'Empire' was one of the few things Father and Mother disagreed about: I think Mother's family had belonged to some queer ginger-group called the Empire Loyalists, and I remember her being very upset – perhaps the most upset I ever saw her – when they put a stop to Empire Day sometime in the 50s.

And all the while time was passing. 1953. 1954. 1955. The new Queen was crowned and the whole school was given the day off. My class voted to spend it at the home of the

solitary boy in the form whose parents had a TV set – thirty
of us packed into the front-room eating sandwiches out of
paper bags and cheering vaguely whenever the procession
came into view. 1953 was the flood year, when the tide
swept over the sea defences all the way along the East
Coast and dozens of people got killed. Even in Southtown
the flood water was two feet deep, and the floor of the shop
stank of salt for weeks after. In 1955 there was a General
Election and the Conservatives got in again, which cheered
Father and Mother up a bit. I turned fifteen, grew another
two inches, discovered Elvis Presley and got myself a
regular girlfriend called Marjorie Lovelace, who went to
the girls' grammar school and whose parents resided in an
altogether higher social league than Father and Mother
(she talked about 'lavatories' and 'napkins', which was a
sure sign that you were upper-middle-class). They were
good times, and even now if you asked me where I'd most
like to be it would be back on the dunes out Gorleston way
with Marjorie Lovelace on a warm evening in August, bikes
chucked in the sand below, watching the sun set out across
the sea and then bicycling home through the back lanes
with a last snog in the alleyway that ran off the side of the
square. All the while, though, I could see that things were
changing, that the shop was doing badly, and that the future
was rearing up at me in a way it hadn't done before. People
started asking me what I was going to 'do', and Father and
Mother were worrying about jobs and the School
Certificate. You know the feeling you sometimes get of
standing outside your life and watching it happen? Well,
that was me back in 1955, wanting to concentrate on
Marjorie Lovelace (who though she would have died
sooner than let me take her blouse off, didn't mind having
her breasts stroked from the outside) and 'Heartbreak
Hotel', but conscious all the time of the icebergs of work
and money and responsibility looming up before me.

   I'm not one of those people who get sentimental about
their childhood. Later on I met blokes who'd been to
private schools and didn't seem to have done a hand's turn
until they were twenty-one who used to talk about their

'lost youth' with enough conviction to make you think that a part of them really had died back on some cricket-field at the age of eighteen. I was never like that. It's what being a lower-middle-class shopkeeper's son does for you, I suppose. Come the age of sixteen you realise that childhood is childhood, and that bills have to be paid. What stockbroker's son ever thinks that? A good half of me was aching to get out of school and get some kind of job that would mean wearing a suit and earning money. When you're sixteen and live over a confectioner's shop, with your parents breathing down your neck twenty-four hours a day, that sort of thing means a lot to you. At the same time I didn't have any illusions about the kind of life I'd been leading here in the Yarmouth backstreets in a world made up of Father, Mother and the shop. In some ways it was a kind of cyst that the twentieth century had passed by, a little time-capsule full of fat men rolling out of pubs, and draggled-looking women with broods of noisy kids. The old ways ran on, like black hounds under the moon. Old people died with tumours on them the size of grapefruit because their children 'didn't want to go bothering the doctor.' When I was about fifteen there was a terrible scandal when a girl bled to death giving birth to an illegitimate baby (which also died) in a wooden hut on the marshes. Things happened then that you don't see now. I can remember Father and Mother shaking their heads over the dead girl and her baby when it made the papers. Father thought it was 'a shame' and 'a pity'. Mother, I could see, blamed the girl, although this wasn't something she could actually bring herself to say. But what really struck me was how they accepted that the whole thing was inevitable, that a schoolgirl getting herself pregnant was bound to end in some kind of dreadful tragedy.

1954. 1955. And all the while the shop was steadily losing money, and Father was looking thinner and more worried. Even by this stage I still didn't properly know what was going on. I knew that Father was 'doing badly', because it was all my parents talked about, but I don't think the enormity of the situation had really dawned on me. Things would pick up. Somebody would come in and buy half a dozen boxes of Milk Tray for raffle prizes. That was how everybody – myself included – imagined things. They didn't know that it was all too far gone to be reclaimed, that the old life of the square, of Father dusting the shutters prior to taking them down at 8 a.m., and the delivery vans parked on the forecourt, would be blown away for ever. Father spent most evenings now doing his accounts, working out if he could save on another order of tobacco, or whether a wholesaler's bill could 'stand' for another week, but even then I don't really think he knew what was hitting him. People in that state lose their ability to fix cause to effect. Gissings, the big confectionery chain, which had branches all over Norfolk, had a shop on the far side of the square now – God knows how they'd squared it with the Church Commissioners – and Dunstan's had started undercutting with cheap ice-cream and bargain boxes of five threepenny bars of chocolate for eleven-pence-halfpenny. It sounds a huge joke, I know, but it was how shopkeepers went bust fifty years ago.

To do Father justice he did make some sort of effort to save himself from the meltdown. Early in 1954, I remember, there was a minor crisis when the delivery vans stopped calling and – this was quite unprecedented – the shop ran out of cigarettes, but some kind of deal was struck and he managed to stagger on. Turner, the newsagent at the far end of the square retired, and I've an idea Father scraped together the money from somewhere to buy the goodwill, because the shop suddenly started selling newspapers, and the shelf behind the sugar mice and the fruit salad was taken down and replaced by a table full of copies of *Woman's Realm* and *Caged Birds*.

It didn't last, though – managing the paperboys and getting up at six to sort out the rounds was a bit beyond Father by this stage – and there were endless rows with customers about missed deliveries. After about six months the paper idea was given up. Then Father got involved in some swindle run by one of the potato crisp manufacturers, whereby if you put in a big enough order and were prepared to stick up display boards in your window you could have a 5 per cent discount on the stock. Plenty of people in the square sold crisps, though, and in the end they just lay in the cardboard boxes going musty. Poor Father! I can see him there now in that narrow space behind the till, with one hand smoothing his brindled hair back over his scalp and the other adding up a sum on the back of a paper bag, looking up at me in that vague, diffident way he had. God knows what he felt about it all, and how it must have been eating him up. That kind of thing marked you in those days, and for a small tradesman to end up in a bankruptcy court was the moral equivalent of leprosy – an awful public admission that your life had been a failure.

I think what hurt Father most was the realisation that one or two of the people he'd assumed were on his side were actually scheming to do him down. Dunstan didn't call at the shop so much in those days, and I remember one afternoon – it would have been in the summer of 1955 – when Father saw him coming from across the square and quite deliberately shot the bolt in the door and went off into the kitchen. I was standing in the sub-post-office doorway at the time, looking on in that half-fascinated, half-frightened way children have when they know some secret adult business is afoot. Old Dunstan tried the door a couple of times, rattled the handle for good measure, and then caught sight of me hovering between the spindles of sixpenny seed packets and plastic combs.

'Where's your dad then?' he asked, a bit suspiciously. I'd always hated Dunstan, and he knew it.

'Don't know, Mr Dunstan.'

Dunstan took a step forward into the sub-post-office's interior, cool and aquarium-like in the summer heat, as if he half-expected Father to be cowering in there, beneath the posters advertising government bonds and the Junior Saver's Club.

'Not like him to shut up at this time of day,' he said. 'Anything the matter?'

'No, Mr Dunstan.'

I watched him start back across the square and then slipped down the alleyway, through the yard, and back into the kitchen. Father was sitting glumly in one of the big armchairs reading the *Mercury*. When he saw me he divined instantly what had happened. There was silence for a minute.

Then he said: 'The bastard!'

I watched him as he did it, and there was a kind of disbelief in his face, as if even then he couldn't quite believe what everyone in the square had known for years – that Dunstan was waiting for him to sell up in much the same way that a vulture hovers over a sick antelope.

'The bloody bastard,' he said again – it was the first time I'd heard him swear.

I suppose in a way it was the closest we ever got to one another, standing there in the kitchen on a summer afternoon with the flies buzzing near the larder door and the noise of children's voices coming in across the square, until he got up and went back into the shop, and the spell was broken.

*

That early part of my life starts to fade away now, turn fragmentary and indetachable from what came afterwards. At some point Father and Mother must have explained to me what was going on, and in particular Father's periodic absences in town, but I don't remember. The School Certificate exams were looming in any case, and after two years idling at school I knew that any chance of a job afterwards depended on what I did in the next month or so. The box-room Betty used to sleep in had been empty since she left, and I worked up there sometimes, stretched out on the bed with a copy of *Hartson's Basic Geography* in front of me, or a list of French verbs I'd decided to memorise. Funnily enough, those days – they were evenings, mostly, in early summer – are peculiarly vivid to me: watching the light fade across the square and beyond the distant church spire, with the sound of Father and Mother pottering about below, and, later on, the noise of the wind getting up (I smuggled Marjorie Lovelace up there once when they were out, but nothing much happened). The rest is oddly out of focus: watching the bulldozers filling in bomb craters; the train-ride along the Acle Strait to Norwich; the figures silhouetted in Wedderbury's windows as the lights went on; foraging among the rockpools for driftwood and onions, which were washed up from the North Sea trawlers and lay across the beach in great strings; files of elm trees dragging across the bare, level plains; the noise of the sea; solitary people lost in the echoing space and silence.

*

Every Whitsun bank holiday Monday we went down into Suffolk for the Framlingham gala.

I was in Framlingham – which nobody within a ten-mile radius called anything other than 'Fram' – a few years ago, and it hadn't changed much: a sleepy kind of market square, where dogs lay and drowsed in the sun, two or three streets of shops, the church, and, dominating it all, a huge tumbledown castle overlooking a damp meadow where they held the gala (they shifted the animals out a day or so before, but anyone who didn't keep one eye firmly on the ground while inspecting the stalls and sideshows was liable to end up in a cowpat). We used to get there just after lunch, and spend an hour or so watching the livestock exhibitions, the fire brigade display and the beauty pageant prior to having tea with the Pagetts, Uncle George, Aunt Sheila and their family.

I've never been able to work out how exactly we were related to the Pagetts: I think my Mother's mother and Aunt Sheila's mother might have been cousins. Certainly there was a photograph of Grandma Lutterworth amongst the clutter on the sideboard, and Aunt Sheila and Mother sometimes used to exchange excruciating confidences of things they'd done together back in the 20s. I think Mother was a bit embarrassed by the Pagetts. They were a real old country couple – Uncle George would have been about

sixty-five, Aunt Sheila maybe a year or so younger – with
flat East Suffolk accents, who pronounced 'have' as 'hev'
and the gala, in which they took a benign and incurious
interest, as the 'gayla'. Neither of them had ever been out
of Suffolk in their lives, although Uncle George may have
made it to the Suffolk Regiment's HQ at Felixstowe
during the Great War before being turned down on
account of bad feet. Aunt Sheila's pre-marital career in
service had taken her as far as Ipswich, but that was about
the limit of their mental world. Mother, of course, God-
fearing shopkeeper's daughter that she was, was privately
horrified by the thought of having a second cousin who'd
been a parlourmaid, but she managed to grit her teeth at
the anecdotes about butlers and anchovy toast and what
the master (Aunt Sheila always referred to her ex-
employer as 'the master') had said in 1914.

For myself, I always liked Uncle George and Aunt
Sheila, and entered enthusiastically into the whole social
experience of which a couple of hours spent in their
company on a warm summer afternoon consisted. They
lived in a queer rabbit-warren of a place half a mile out of
the town itself, which was always crammed with people –
most of the children were grown up and married by now,
but the gala was one of the big social events of the year –
with a big, neatly-kept back yard where Uncle George,
who'd been a market gardener before he retired, grew peas
and radishes and delicate little James Greave apples. Inside
there'd be a throng of second and third cousins, most of
whose names I never got round to discovering, crowded
round the tea table, with Uncle George – he was a canny
old chap with a red, nut-cracker face, bent nearly double
from rheumatism – sitting in an armchair by the fire. They
had a fire even in May. Beyond the table was a monstrous
sofa piled with knitting patterns and back-numbers of
Reveille, a low-brow weekly paper full of pictures of chorus
girls' legs, which Aunt Sheila took 'for the coupons'.

When I wasn't gorging myself on Aunt Sheila's home-
made jam – which was glorious stuff, as unlike shop jam as
a bottle of Nuit St Georges is unlike Rioja – or blushing off

Uncle George's requests to know if I was 'courting', I used to amuse myself by sneaking occasional glances at Father and Mother. It was an interesting study in contrasts. Mother, it hardly needs saying, was horribly ill at ease and simply sat there on the sofa barely opening her mouth. Father, on the other hand, who was quite happy to descend to a social level considerably lower than the one he was used to, chattered amiably about football with the Pagett cousins and invariably got taken out into the garden to see how the fruit was coming on. I used to look at Mother sometimes as she sat there on the sofa, nervously guarding her Sunday dress from the hordes of tearaway children, and wonder what it was that kept her from joining in, making the kind of small talk that other women ventured about their children and their husbands' jobs. Later on I realised that it wasn't even class consciousness that did it, but a kind of fundamental aloofness and detachment from the Pagetts' world – a world of teeming children, the *Daily Mirror* and endlessly stewing cups of tea. When she did make an effort, it was always to betray what even I could see was an invincible ignorance about the sort of landscapes that Uncle George and Aunt Sheila inhabited – asking them how much they paid their window cleaner, or how the younger children were doing at school.

Those afternoons at Fram! With the noise of the brass band drifting in through the window from Gala Meadow, children running in to show their parents goldfish in water-filled plastic bags they'd won on the sideshows, and Uncle George falling asleep over the fire and waking up occasionally to drat one of the kids who'd tumbled under his feet. Forty years later it sticks in my head as a vision of red-faced women shrieking gossip at each other, children skirmishing under the table, half a dozen conversations going on at once.

COUSIN WILLIAM: Fa! Hev you bin down to Gala Meadow yit?
UNCLE GEORGE: I hev not. Was intendin' on sittin' here with a cuppatoi.

MOTHER: *Can't* seem to get those dress patterns like you used … And I must say …

AUNT SHEILA: What's that you were saying, Eunice? Bill, *tell* them children their tea's ready.

COUSIN WILLIAM (*proudly*): *I* bin. Tobied on down there an hour since. Reckoned on looking at that there dicker someone was a showing of …

MOTHER: Went into Norwich for the sales in January, but they didn't have a thing.

UNCLE GEORGE (*highly amused*): You keep a dicker! Ha! (*seeing me at the table*) That boy of yours'll be a caution, I'll be bound. All the young chaps is these days.

MOTHER: Not him. Far too much schoolwork to do, I'm very pleased to say.

AUNT SHEILA (*nostalgically*): If you'd a had my mother, you'd hev had to make your own dresses, my dear.

COUSIN WILLIAM: Them old dickers! Just scrunch up the thistles, they does, like there was no hay worth eatin'.

'Dicker', by the way, meant 'donkey', while 'Fa' was short for father.

This particular Bank Holiday, though, something was up. For some reason we got there late, long after lunch. Rain was falling over the castle turrets, and Gala Meadow, where the livestock paraded and they had the children's races, was a sea of mud. Back at the Pagetts' Uncle George sat and sulked in his chair, a pair of cousins idled at the table playing spillikins with their huge labourers' hands, and even Aunt Sheila seemed irritated about something. Father and Mother, too, looked agitated, sitting side by side on the sofa like a couple of cats who've just seen an Alsatian on the other side of the street. It was a bit before tea time, the rain was easing off now, and since I'd exhausted the possibilities of the Pagetts' front room, turned over the yellowing copies of *Reveille* and glanced at the bookcase, which was full of back-numbers of *Farming Week* and a copy of *Pilgrim's Progress* Aunt Sheila had won as a Sunday School prize, I wandered back into the town. Here the water was still coursing along the gutters

and the streets were full of people in their best clothes
coming out of doorways where they'd taken shelter, and in
the distance you could see lines of draggled bunting
hanging over the privet hedge that backed onto the
meadows. In ordinary circumstances I'd have gone and
walked round the castle ramparts, which was something I
always got a kick out of, or hunted down an ice-cream van,
but somehow I didn't feel like it. Part of this was to do with
Father and Mother and the shop, a bit more with Marjorie
Lovelace, with whom, and despite now being allowed to
put my hand inside her blouse, I was getting rather bored,
but most of it was to do with a feeling of altered circumstances looming up at me, the thought that all this – the
square, the long rows of sweet jars, even Fram in the rain –
was about to change in a way I couldn't begin to comprehend, much less do anything about. In the end I walked
into the churchyard at the far end of the winding main
street, found a half-empty packet of Gold Flake that
someone had dropped, cadged a match, and sat there
under a dripping tree smoking them until an old chap with
a shock of white hair, who was probably the churchwarden,
danced out of the porch and drove me away. Back in the
street there was a crowd of people standing outside the
Conservative Club listening to a little man in a morning
suit declaiming something or other, and I remember stopping to stare at a second man, some kind of chauffeur or
servant I think, who was standing next to him holding up
an umbrella to keep off the water from the dripping gables,
before heading back to the Pagetts with a feeling of
absolutely awful foreboding. My cousin Ernie, William's
son, was leaning against the front door when I got there,
and winked as I turned in at the gate.

'You don't want to go in there, young Ted.'

He was a big, gormless kid of about my age with one of
those vacant, rural faces.

'Why not?'

'Some kind of argyment. I dunno.' He must have caught
the cigarette smoke on my breath, because he went on:
'Got a fag, hev you?'

'No.'

The front door was half open, and you could hear the raised voices in the hall. As it turned out there were only four people in the front room – Father and Mother and Uncle George and Aunt Sheila. As I came in Aunt Sheila was halfway through a sentence, but she thought better of it, and the only noise was Mother snivelling faintly on the edge of the sofa. Father sat next to her, looking as if he'd just seen a ghost.

'Hop off out of it, young Ted,' Uncle George said, not unkindly.

For some reason, though, I didn't go – something, I suppose, to do with wanting explanations, an eternal fed-upness, which practically every teenager experienced in those days, of being kept in the dark and generally disregarded. Mother started crying a bit louder, Uncle George looked faintly embarrassed, and by degrees the tableau broke up. Aunt Sheila tossed her head – not a figure of speech, she really did toss it – and stumped off to the kitchen. Father got up from the sofa and began dusting down the sides of his trousers, which was one of his characteristic gestures when he was nervous or otherwise upset. Ten minutes later we were back in the car.

Nobody said a word on the way back to Yarmouth. There was a thunderstorm outside Lowestoft and we had to park in a layby, but even then neither of them would say anything. In the end, over the next couple of days, I wormed it out of them that Father had borrowed money off Uncle George – £100 it might have been, certainly no more than that – and not been able to pay it back. Funnily enough, I wasn't particularly shocked by this. What really shocked me was Mother's reaction to my finding out. It was clearly the most shameful thing that had ever happened to her – rather as if, I dimly understood, I'd found her in one of the big hotels along the front in the arms of some fancyman.

Two weeks later the final letter came from the bank, and Father shut up the shop for good.

Apparently the Ngongi tribe of equatorial Guinea can survive on as little as 200 millilitres of water a day. The averagely pampered Westerner needs a minimum 700 millilitres to sustain the basic processes of life, but the Ngongi, habituated to the routines of sunshine, scrub and dried-up wells, can make do with the equivalent of a large tea-cupful. I came across this fact in a newspaper account of two West African teenagers named Yaguine and Fodé who stowed away on a Sabena airbus flight from Conakry to Brussels. Eight days later, after the airbus had completed a further three round-trips between Brussels and Guinea, an airport technician found their bodies decomposing in the right-wing wheel arch. Two or three times in the past few days I've found myself wondering about Yaguine and Fodé. When did they realise the enormity of what they'd done? When did they understand, up there in the freezing night with the engines tearing above them that this was no passing chill but the hand of death? And what did they say to each other when they knew?

In a small way, the people round here have the Ngongi spirit. Not the wide-eyed prospectors' certainty that drives teenage boys to freeze to death in wheel arches, but the ability to make do with what's available, to calibrate effort to likely reward, to create an illusion of well-being that – who knows? – is as sustaining as the real thing. The other day I saw a kid in what looked like a Tommy Hilfiger sweatshirt. Close inspection revealed that it was an ordinary grey top on which somebody had carefully etched the designer's name in black marker pen. Not that you don't see plenty of genuine Hilfiger gear round here – a kind of inversion of the look-after-the-pennies-and-the-pounds-will-look-after-themselves routine, whereby the street vixens wear designer leggings, have mobiles and forty-a-day cigarette habits and still push prams whose occupants look as if they were fed exclusively on lard. For the most part, though, the commerce of the street is fantastically low-level, like the small ads in the local paper: *Girls' shoes £5, My Little Pony playset, hardly used, £7, Abba CD £4.* Who wants to buy a pair of girls' shoes for £5? The same people, presumably, who have mobile phones and underweight babies. All part of the average human being's eagerness to adapt himself to his environment and engage in its commercial rituals. No doubt My Little Pony playsets, hardly used, are the spiritual equivalent of Sotheby's (where I went once and watched Upward spend £5,000). Or the Ngongi on their 200 millilitres of water a day.

*

Not greatly to my surprise I find Lennie waiting for me outside the club: a small, uncertain figure in a sheepskin coat, tossing his car keys from hand to hand and casting anxious glances at the Cavalier parked two or three spaces up the street.

''Ow're you doing then me old china? You're looking good.'

Lennie, on the other hand, is looking very far from good. Somehow it's difficult to put a finger on Lennie's odd incompatibility with the environment in which he moves. The pat he administers on my shoulder as he falls in beside me seems painfully lightweight and insubstantial.

'I didn't know you were a Plumstead Over Sixty?' I say.

'Ah well, we're none of us as young as we was. And there's some good Jewish boys here, you know.'

Lennie's Jewishness, like the smashed veins on his cheeks and the chunky soccer manager's jewellery decked about his person, dates him irrevocably of course. He belongs somewhere in the 60s, back in a world of cross-talk comedians, *Saturday Night at the London Palladium* and George Best, whose manager, oddly enough, Lennie once was (*'E was a nice boy, Georgie, but, phew, sooner you than me*).

'How's Mrs M?'

'She's OK. She sent you a message. Said. "Tell 'im it's time we saw you on TV again." '

'Sounds more like a message for you.'

'I know. I know.' Lennie's expression as he says this is genuinely piteous, like a child denied some long promised treat on grounds which no one will explain. Nobody seems to have told him that career opportunites are somewhat restricted for seventy-year-olds whose finest moment was staffing the Bobbie Gentry Show back in 1968.

'What about the stars of tomorrow, Lennie? Where are they?'

'Ah, they're not interested are they? All want to be pop stars and footballers. I got this good boy – my great nephew actually – plays the harmonica at bar mitzvahs and that. Now, Moishe, he could be the new Danny Silverstein. I keep telling 'im. But 'e's too busy doing 'is computer course.'

It says something for Lennie's longevity that I don't remember the original Danny Silverstein. Perhaps, on the other hand, he never really existed – just a compound of the various elements floating around in Lennie's subconscious to be arbitrarily plucked forth and given a name.

Inside the community centre orange lights burn off a vestibule dominated by a portrait of the Queen Mother – its founding patron, apparently – clad in the royal fashions of the 50s. Further inside, through half-open swing doors, a few people can be seen moving about. Lennie checks his watch.

'Still ten minutes yet. Let's 'ave a drink.'

As we prowl along the empty corridor towards the bar I realise what strikes me as incongruous about Lennie. There is an odd, rivery smell coming off him, faint yet perceptible, almost as if he rose up out of the Thames half an hour ago. Watching him move towards me across the tattered carpet with a gin and tonic in each hand, I can still smell it: a mixture of fish, the river at low tide, salt air. The smell rises as he settles in his chair.

'You OK, Lennie?'

'I've been thinking, Ted. You know … I was at Lew's funeral the other day.'

'Lew?'

'Lew *Grade*,' Lennie says crossly. ''Im and me went back

a long way, y'know. So there I was – no one I knew –
thinking, funny, there's no sign of Bernie Cohen or Monty
Yadinsky. And then all of a sudden I realised they was all
dead.'

Lennie has a weakness for old showbiz troupers.
Especially Jewish ones. I doubt his acquaintance with Lord
Grade extended much beyond standing in the same room
as him at a 1973 Variety Club reception. All the same there
is something rather uncomfortable about the images
stoked into being: mourners passing this way and that over
the wet grass (I've read the newspaper reports, as it
happens), mist hanging in the air, and in the midst of it all
a seventy-year-old Jewish variety agent who smells of fish
grieving for Bernie Cohen and Monty Yadinsky.

'Anyway, I started thinking about Lew and those good
boys that were gone.'

Outside, through thick plate-glass, rain falls slowly over
the grey highway. Cars whine up the hill towards Abbey
Wood and Greenwich. Glimpsed in the glass's reflection,
Lennie looks faintly crumpled: limbs too small for the
sheepskin carapace from which they protrude. Experience
tells me that this is the prelude to a more substantial
lament: Lennie's monologue on the death of comedy.

Lennie on the death of comedy? 'I just don't understand what's 'appened. Morecambe & Wise? Now they
were funny. Benny Hill? 'E was funny. Mike and Bernie
Winters? Well, they was all right. Sort of. But this new lot.
'Alf the time you just don't get it. I once paid twenty quid
to see Newman & Baddiel at Wembley Arena. Walked out
after 'alf an hour. I saw old Abie Myerscough the other day
and do you know what 'e said? "Lennie, mate, it's all
fucked – 'scuse my French – they don't want nice Jewish
boys as can play the 'armonica and tell some jokes your
mother could listen to anymore." '

There are wider implications here. Lennie has failed to
adapt. His first wife died in 1974. Her replacement (*Nah,
she's a good woman. Devoted to me*) sits at home nagging
him about villas in Alicante. Looking at Lennie these days
I get a sense of a life becalmed, like the big hulks you see

out in the Thames at low tide, marooned in mid-stream with the current flowing round them. Perhaps that's where Lennie gets his peculiar odour.

The fish smell rises again as we move off into the hall. Here about three dozen of the Plumstead Over Sixties have distributed themselves in about twice that number of metal-backed chairs. I have a look at them while a man in a suit takes us through the preliminaries. Husbands and wives, mostly, the men in check trousers straining above cannon-ball paunches, the women in 'costumes'. These are Lennie's people, I suppose, old-stagers who know who Danny Silverstein is and remember the décor of the Crossroads Motel.

Lennie introduces me. In public his accent goes spiralling up into unknown regions of Bow Bells pastiche. No one seems to mind. He even tells a few jokes. *Wotcher girls and boys. Now tonight we've got a real treat in store. No, I'm not going to take me clothes off ... Seriously, tonight's guest needs no introduction. But I'm going to introduce 'im anyway. Look, I've even got some notes. And as Adam said to Eve in the garden of Eden, there must be another leaf somewhere ...*

They love it, of course. A little old man in the front row turns purple in the face when he hears the Adam and Eve joke and has to be slapped on the back by an equally plum-faced neighbour. This is a new Lennie, a bright, capering spirit come up from the depths to confound us all. Maybe, thinking about it, this is Lennie's tragedy: that he really wanted to be one of those Jewish boys who played the kazoo and told jokes about the rabbi's beard falling into the gefiltefish soup. Who knows? At the end he even does a little shuffle, hands splayed out on either side of his face, like an arthritic tap-dancer trying to remember the steps, and gets a round of applause all to himself.

*

I once read somewhere that Ken Dodd used to conduct a minute-by-minute analysis of every live show he ever performed. (This was before the age of video.) Each night when he came off stage he'd collect a tape from the soundman's cubbyhole, take it back to his hotel and sit there until the small hours ransacking the spools for evidence of skewed delivery, lowered applause levels, that faint background whisper which is an audience turning restless. First thing next morning he'd work on his running order in the light of this intelligence. To anyone who saw him again the following night the effect was barely perceptible – a couple of dropped one-liners, perhaps, or a longer sketch slowed down by twenty seconds or so. All this in a two-hour spectacle involving half a dozen other people and three or four changes of clothing. At the time I was cautiously admiring of this type of perfectionism. Now I think he was slightly mad.

Not that borderline sanity is a handicap, you understand. Upward, in particular, had original views on comedy that emerged from the realms of minor psychological disturbance.

'Of course,' he used to say, 'it's as well to realise that not being quite right in the head's a positive advantage sometimes. Every time I see one of them bug-eyed blokes in bowler hats lurking by the side of the stage I always think, "There's another one the doctors have let out for the day." That kind of thing has a big historical tradition. You'd be surprised.'

'Like medieval kings laughing at cripples?'

'Exactly. Look at someone like Marty Feldman or Freddie Davies. I'm not saying they're not perfectly responsible members of society, but stick them on a stage and your average audience will start laughing out of sheer bloody nervousness.'

'So what would happen if you had a comedian who was a genuine madman?'

'Naturally it'd depend. Of course, if you just foamed at the mouth I can't imagine anyone would be particularly interested, although y' could probably make a fortune doing it in the States. But I used to have an old aunt who went around picking up burnt matches off the floor and shutting them in the oven. You can take it from me, Ted, that was absolutely hilarious.'

*

Some golden rules of comedy. Doing a TV cross-talk act you look at the *vis-à-vis*. Opening an end-of-pier show in front of 1500 people you look at the space between the balcony and the back row of the stalls. Working a club, on the other hand, you look at the audience, singly and severally. You have to be careful, though. Once, somewhere up north, Upward completely blew it by playing to a woman with a gatling-gun laugh who ended up having hysterics.

There is little danger of this happening with the Plumstead Over Sixties. Actually I go down rather well. The women smile. The men look on benignly. Lennie, parked in the front row and clearly losing interest, starts turning out the pockets of his sheepskin coat. The sex on TV joke gets a huge laugh. So does a Jewish joke of a kind you couldn't tell outside a place like the Plumstead Over Sixties these days, about pound notes being green because the Jews used to pick them before they were ripe. The little old man in the front row nearly has a heart attack over that. Oddly enough, I don't get the feeling that anyone is taking much note of what I say. They like having me here, of course, they wish me well, but it's what I represent that's important: a glimpse back into that lost world of the 60s and 70s, black and white television, Wilson and Heath and Henry Cooper – all rubbish, of course, but known rubbish, connected to them in a way that the modern stuff isn't. Sensing the mood out there – Lennie, I note, has given up ransacking his pockets and is wiggling a cotton-bud in one ear – I delve into the memory archive for a joke about decimal coinage. It gets a huge laugh.

*

Curiously enough, there's another act on the bill. As soon as I've resumed my seat Lennie leaps up and announces

that after a short interval the Stan Rubinovitz Trio with
Titch Johnson on saxophone will be here to entertain us.
About half the audience decide to leave immediately.
Lennie and I followed them out into the orange-lit foyer.

'Great show, Ted. Seriously.'

'You were pretty good yourself.'

'Funny you should say that actually.' Lennie's face turns
over a bit. 'I used to do warm-ups for Frankie now and
again in the early days. But it never came to anything.'

'Frankie?'

'Frankie Howerd.'

Another good Jewish boy, of course. 'Shonks' Father
used to call them – a name I never found in any dictionary
– not out of malice but from an urgent need to classify.
'Look at that shonk,' he would say whenever a picture of
Bing Crosby or Liberace appeared in one of the illustrated
papers.

'Between you and me,' Lennie goes on confidentially, as
an elderly man in a dinner jacket – presumably one of the
Stan Rubinovitz Trio – swings past us propelling an electric
piano before him, 'that one about the Jews picking pound
notes was a mistake.'

Perhaps, after all, Lennie is adapting to his environment. Certainly he's found out about political correctness
from somewhere. Looking at the Plumstead Over Sixties
as they drift past us into the foyer, I can detect a narrowly
overcome reluctance to treat with the modern world.
There are mobiles out, dialling minicabs. One old boy is
even loading himself up in an electronic pensioner's
carriage. The whirr of the wheels, the hovercraft glide,
returns me to Yaguine and Fodé in their wheel arch. Fodé
was fourteen. Four years older than Daniel.

'Lennie,' I say. 'Did you read the stuff in the papers
about the kids who stowed away in the airbus?'

Lennie completely misconnects. 'Them asylum seekers?
You got to keep them out. There's half of bleeding Europe
queuing up at Dover from what I hear.'

Lennie's parents, it should be said, came over from
Munich shortly after the Reichstag fire. World history to

Lennie is consequently Jewish history: Whitechapel syna-
gogues, Mosley's blackshirts, punch-ups in the East End; a
bit later the Stern Gang and Menachem Begin. Oddly
enough, the Jewish conspiracy angle on world events is one
to which Lennie keenly subscribes. To him, the people who
run the globe have names like Wasserman and Berkovitz,
sit on Senate committees and own the combines who own
the mid-west grain silos. Lennie's never heard of Bill
Gates, but if he had he'd be able to tell you that his real
name is Finkelstein.

Back inside the hall the Stan Rubinovitz Trio is tuning
up. It sounds like a single instrument until you realise that
the faint scraping sound in the distance is a snare drum.
Lennie's gaze is darting back and forth down the corridor,
head rising up out of the sheepskin like an elderly tortoise
sniffing the air.

'Actually,' he says, 'I forgot to tell you. Was someone
else on the dog wanting you. Not that BBC gel. Some
geezer.'

'Did he say what he wanted?'

'Nah. 'Ad some funny name too. You know, initials and
that. D.I. Something. I give 'im your number though.'

'Thanks, Lennie.'

Lennie clearly isn't interested in the mystery caller.
Neither does it seem to strike him that 'D.I.' is short for
'Detective Inspector'. Outside in the street tiny screaming
kids run past, though it's already 8.30. Over the noise of
the Stan Rubinovitz Trio – now grown to a considerable
racket – a voice is jauntily intoning:

> *I got a girl*
> *in Kalamazoo.*
> *I liked her looks when I carried her books*
> *in Kalamazoo.*

Did you hear the one about the old lady who went for a
tramp in the woods? He got away.

*

Later a maniac in a beanie hat with a stereo pumping out
what sounds like the noise of a dysfunctional cement-mixer
minicabs me home. The house is quiet. Upstairs the boy
sleeps blamelessly beneath his coverlet, flanked by an
empty crisp packet and half a dozen copies of the *Beano*.
Michael Owen looks on above him. I stand there for a
minute or so checking his breathing. Even when they've
reached the age of ten you still do this, still assure yourself
that they're alive. Down in the hall the red eye of the
answerphone winks dutifully away. I go to sleep thinking of
Yaguine and Fodé, Lennie, Shena's letter, the Stan
Rubinovitz Trio's eerie shuffle.

Teenage Kicks

After the letter from the bank things happened very quickly.

As it happened, Father's smash-up was much worse than anyone expected. It turned out that he'd been playing off suppliers against one another, as well as stringing the bank along, and there was money owing all over the place. In the end, when the accountants had been through the books, all the creditors had been paid and the stock disposed of, there was slightly under £200 left, which wasn't much even by the standards of 1956. For a time Father and Mother talked vaguely about 'getting back on their feet' and 'starting afresh', but although Father did go after one or two shop manager's jobs in the town, I don't think their hearts were in it. Everyone in Yarmouth knew that Father had 'failed', which was the word people used for bankruptcy in those days, and that the chances of him getting another job were practically zero. Of the two it was Mother who took it to heart. Father was upset, of course – he'd run a business for twenty years and now it had collapsed round his ears – but he was still capable of functioning in a more or less normal way. Mother, on the other hand, was merely distraught. For her, the shop going was a kind of judgment on her life, and an invitation for the people she knew to mock her.

As for me, I don't remember being particularly exercised by the closed shutters and the chaps in grey suits from Larking & Gowan, the big Yarmouth accountancy firm, trying to fix a re-sale value on the boxes of pipe tobacco. Naturally I was sorry that Father and Mother were upset, but the wider implications didn't bother me. For a start I knew that one of the consequences of this knock to Father and Mother's self-esteem would be a loosening of the bonds that tied me to them. Which is selfish, if you like, but that's how you think when you're a kid of

sixteen whose horizons up until now have been bounded
by a market square, the North Sea and a pair of stuffy
middle-aged people whose chief object in life seems to be
to stop you doing the things you want. I liked my parents,
and if they were somehow to walk into the room tomorrow
I daresay I'd be happy enough to see them, but at the time
I know that I regarded them as an obstacle to my progress
through life and I couldn't wait to push them aside.

We had a month's grace in the shop while the Church
Commissioners disposed of the lease. It was an odd, unreal
kind of life. Father and Mother had nothing to do except
read the paper and conduct sniffy, dispirited conversations
with each other. I'd left school – at least it was generally
supposed that I wasn't going back in the autumn, but
nobody seemed to know what I ought to be doing.
Meanwhile there was a ghasty symbolism about the events
going on around us. Every time a van arrived to take away
some unsold stock or a chap with a ladder turned up to fix
a 'To Let' board above the window it was like a nail being
hammered into the coffin of my parents' lives. On the day
they burned off the S. LUTTERWORTH over the
shopfront Mother simply went to bed for the afternoon, so
great was her misery, and even Father looked a bit green.
Later that night they must have had some kind of confer-
ence, because when I came down to breakfast next morning
it was to find Father sitting very solemn in the big chair by
the kitchen table, with the light gleaming off his bald head,
while Mother fussed around near the sink. It was so
unusual for Father to make a speech that I can remember
what he said practically word for word. He and Mother had
been having a talk (*sniff*). They'd been thinking (*sniff, sniff*)
and what they'd decided was that they were going to stay
with Uncle Ralph for a bit – Uncle Ralph was Father's
widowed elder brother – until things 'picked up' (*sniff*) and
Father could 'see where he stood'. As for going back to
school, no one was going to stop me, but in the circumstances it might be best if I got a job (*sniff, sniff, sniff*). And
that, more or less, was that. A fortnight later the shop was
shut up, Father and Mother removed themselves to Uncle

Ralph's house at Gorleston, and I went to lodge with a family called Enright who lived near the market square and started work at the Sun Alliance office.

Do you remember those old office buildings in the 50s? With a fat commissionaire on the door, a couple of bored receptionists doing their nails in the foyer and, inside, rows of little cubicle offices stretching away down the corridor like rabbit hutches? The Sun Alliance place was exactly like that. It was the biggest insurance firm in Yarmouth, spread over three floors, with a huge panelled boardroom at the top where the directors met, and it employed about 150 people, most of them men but with a couple of dozen secretaries and typists. This being the 50s, and Yarmouth, the most exacting protocols applied. As a junior clerk you were expected to call the other junior clerks by their surnames, the senior clerks 'Mr' and anyone over the rank of department head 'sir'. The secretaries were addressed as 'Miss', or very occasionally 'Mrs' (the Sun Alliance wasn't keen on employing married women, but they were prepared to let them stay on for a few months after the wedding), and if they suspected you of 'cheeking' them they'd report you to the office manager, an old bloke named Penworthy who never seemed to do anything except fill inkwells and worry about misplaced ledgers. The clerks' room looked out over the market square, and in winter, with the paraffin heaters on and a pleasant fug rising over the long rows of stools, there were worse places to be. Sitting at my desk, with the gulls flapping outside, listening to the thick plate glass moving in the wind, I used to measure out the time with squares of chocolate, a square every fifteen minutes, looking up at five to find the bar gone, the gulls vanished out to sea, and the shop windows glowing greeny-gold in the dusk.

As for the work itself, a child of ten could have done it. The Sun Alliance might have had four or five thousand policy holders, and my job, quite simply, was to maintain the eight huge filing trays in which their addresses were kept. Other times, if things were slack, I'd be sent out on my bike with an envelope for one of the local solicitors or accountants who doubled up as our representatives, but all through that first couple of years if you'd asked me what I did I'd have answered quite truthfully 'I do addresses'. And if you think this was a humble occupation, I should say that there was a gaunt old spinster called Miss Cattermole, who'd been at the place thirty years, whose task was to assemble the change of address details *before* I filled them in on the filing cards.

And yet I didn't care about the hours spent over the filing trays, or Miss Cattermole sniffing dejectedly in the background – there was a bit of a frost between us as I gathered I'd been appointed over her head – or the derision of the older juniors who looked down on 'kids straight out of school'. I was sixteen years old, had thirty shillings a week in my pocket that were mine to keep, and within certain broadly defined limitations could do more or less what I wanted. In those days, of course, this kind of freedom was faintly unusual. People watched over their children then in a way that they don't do now – not so much because they wanted to stop them doing things they disapproved of, but because they wanted them to go on being children. I've known girls of eighteen training as typists whose fathers walked them to work every morning and collected them again at night.

What was I like at sixteen? What were you like at sixteen? I was five feet eleven by then, which was a goodish height for the 50s, and what with Mrs Enright's cooking and the stodgy lunches they served in the staff canteen I was starting to fill out a bit. Inevitably, I was completely selfish and I'd have run a mile rather than do something I didn't want to. If you'd have asked me what I believed in in those days I'd have been hard put to tell you – probably just a watered-down version of the stuff Father and Mother had dinned into me over the years. At the same time, without even thinking about it, I was pulling away from Father and Mother. I used to go over and see them at weekends, of course, but the old life we'd had together was smashed to pieces, and they knew it. All I remember of those times is Uncle Ralph's dark front room, with Mother's face peering through the bad light and Father pottering in with one of his scrapbooks, which he'd balance on his lap while he drank his tea. Neither of them liked living with Uncle Ralph, I discovered – the cottage was too small for the three of them and Uncle Ralph, who was a good ten years older than Father, rather looked on them as his house-keepers – and they were still talking about moving on as soon as Father could get himself 'placed'. Even I could see, though, that Father's chances of getting another job were slightly less than me getting a trial with Norwich City.

And all the while time was passing. It was 1956 now, 1957. Suez came, with people nearly fighting on the garage forecourts for petrol and everybody saying that 'these here Gyppos' ought to be taught a lesson. If anyone tells you that British public opinion was against Suez, then all I can say is that they never came anywhere near Yarmouth. There was a murder case down by the quayside – a woman whose husband had found her in bed with another man – and one of the senior clerks at the office had a heart attack at his desk. It was a good half-hour before anyone noticed, but what I really remember is them shifting the body onto a stretcher and the bottom of his trousers riding up to reveal long woollen combinations. I'd been at the place nearly a year then and was getting to know my way around. Curiously enough, I made a goodish impression at the Sun Alliance. By the time I was seventeen I'd been taken off 'addresses' and put onto drafting correspondence to customers, or phoning people up to check their personal details. I suppose if I'd had any sense I would have been plotting my future, putting money away and taking corre-spondence courses in business administration and that kind of thing, but I was seventeen, selfish in a way that horrifies me to think about, and as far as I was concerned the £5 a week that my wages had been raised to was there simply to pay for my principal hobbies, which were listening to radio comedy shows and chasing girls.

Girls! Looking back, I don't suppose there were many times between the ages of sixteen and eighteen when I wasn't thinking about girls, or if not directly then about something vaguely connected to them – clothes, say, or Tony Curtis hair-cuts, or the chances of getting a ticket for some youth club dance or other. This kind of mental preparation was important, because girls weren't at all easy to come by in Yarmouth in the 50s, and to find them meant putting yourself through some extraordinary social rituals. To begin with you had to haunt somewhere where girls – respectable girls, that is – went: a youth club or a church social. Then, after you'd been seen around a bit, you could ask a particular girl for a date. Usually she'd say yes, although in terms of your chances this didn't mean anything. The protocols for 'first dates' were set in stone. You went with another couple, or, worse, the girl would ask if she could bring a friend, and the three of you would traipse along the front for half an hour before ending up for an entirely speechless tea at one of the cafés in town. The second time, which always took place on a Saturday afternoon, you went on your own on something called a 'pier walk', which consisted of wandering up and down the pier half a dozen times before retreating to a tea shop again. The third time, if there was a third time, you got asked to the girl's house for Sunday tea – the most gruesome bit of all, as it meant being asked questions by her parents. Four decades on I can still remember those questions. What do you do (they'd know this already, but that didn't stop them asking it)? What does your father do? Where do you live? Do you go to church? What kind of church (you had to be careful here – everybody hated Catholics and were sniffy about most of the nonconformist sects)? One of my most enduring memories of those years is of sitting in the front room of some bandbox house, set back from the front, with a cup of watery tea in one hand as a suspicious-looking middle-aged man prosed away from the chair nearest the fire and the girl and her Mother sat uncomfortably together on the sofa. The worst thing was that you could always tell from the girl's face how it was going.

The odd thing about these relationships (they used to last about two months, by the way, until one of the parties 'met someone else' or 'didn't think it was serious') was, on the one hand, their staggering formality – no one would have dreamt of going out on a date without being dressed up to the nines – and on the other their almost complete sexlessness. Kissing a girl goodnight too adventurously or making a meal of helping her on with her coat (the trick was to turn her unexpectedly towards you so that she more or less fell into your arms) had you marked down as 'fast' or 'unreliable'. Girls talked openly about 'saving themselves' in those days and thanked God that they weren't factory women who 'made themselves cheap'. Looking back, I sometimes wonder why I went through with it – sat through those sofa-bound afternoons with girls who barely knew whether the earth went round the sun or *vice versa*, with their parents (who were like my parents only somehow staider and less individuated) conspiring over the teacups – and I suppose the answer lies in sheer loneliness.

Meanwhile the time was passing. 1957. 1958. They were building houses now, all over the outskirts of the town, and in the early mornings you could see the brickdust rising like red fog. 1958 was a hot summer, I remember, and people went lobster-coloured in the sun. A boy drowned in the the sea that year out near Scroby and there was a panic about lifeguards and scarlet flags to tell you when the water was unsafe. I'd just turned eighteen, had my wages raised another pound a week, and in the intervals of worrying about National Service was going out with a girl called Julia Betterton, who I was quite mad on – she was a small, very delicate blonde girl who never said anything but simply sat on the other side of the table staring at you for all the world like a china doll. They were good days back then – even at the time I knew they were good days – striding over the market square in the mornings with the sun flooding in over the arm of the sea, rushing out in the lunch hour to meet Julia for a sandwich and a stroll along the Marrams, but I could tell they were slipping away. At eighteen, even in a provincial town bounded by the sea and the marshes I could see that – that life wouldn't always be the same, and that it was beyond my power to change it. I'd stopped living at the Enrights' by this time and had gone into digs at a house on Marine Parade. It was a big place – three or four

storeys, with a warren of attics at the top. The old woman
who owned it lived in the basement, but apart from a knock
on the door on Friday nights to collect the rent you were
left pretty much to yourself. Now and again I used to cycle
over to Gorleston in the evenings to see Father and
Mother, but there was a sense – and I'm sure I grasped a
little of this at the time – in which they were fading away
out of my life, stuck and motionless while I was moving on.
Just hearing them talk depressed me beyond measure. They
used to sit by the fire endlessly spinning out the same
complaints about Uncle Ralph (who might have been
bedridden by this time – certainly I never saw him when I
came to the house) and people who'd 'dropped them' since
the smash. Poor Mother! It was only later, when I thought
about it, that I realised just what a comedown her life must
have been after the shop went. As for Father, he had this
dreadful trick of forgetting to put his teeth in, so that his
face always seemed slightly fallen in and withered.

Other times, when I wasn't seeing Father and Mother or
Julia Betterton, I just used to lie there in my room with my
hands clasped behind my head and think about things –
not out of fear, you understand, but with a huge
expectancy, a kind of feeling that in some way I didn't
quite understand my life was taking shape, everything
around me gathering pace and purpose. Sometimes I used
to smuggle Julia up there in the evenings – one of the
things I liked about her was that she could see the point of
spending time like this – and we would just stare at each
other. She had a way of curling up on the bed not quite
asleep while I stroked her hair – it was very pale, yellow-
gold hair, I remember – or tried to tune in to Radio
Luxembourg on the big Bakelite set. Christ! I can't begin
to describe what it felt like, lying there on a summer
evening with the sky turning blue-black out over the sea,
and the noise from the town filtering through the window,
and Julia stretching herself out lazily like a cat at my side.
God knows what we talked about – jobs, probably, and
families (her parents kept a shop too, and they were
sympathetic about Father) and pop music – the kind of

thing teenagers talked about in the 50s. And though I can't remember the words, the *atmosphere* is as vivid to me as the room I came out of ten minutes ago.

But, as I say, it was all slipping away, rushing on down the slope in front of me. The letter from the army board in Norwich was already lying on the mantelpiece at Marine Parade. I daresay that if I'd had any guts I'd have sat down and thought about it a bit, about Julia, the Sun Alliance, Father and Mother, and what I might be like, or want to do, in two years' time. But two years is an eternity when you're eighteen, quite unquantifiable, and so I just sat and waited, enjoying what I had while it lasted and not caring about what lay ahead. It was July turning into August now, and blisteringly hot. There was nothing to do at work, and I sat at my desk and idled, cheeked old Penworthy even more than usual, and went on long, leisurely 'errands' to Southtown (the greengrocer who'd bought the lease of Father's shop had already gone bust, I noticed, and been replaced by a general provisions merchant who looked as if he was about to go the same way) and once as far as Gorleston.

Four weeks. Three weeks. It was dark by half-past seven now, the military band had played its last Sunday concert on the Marrams, and the pleasure beach would close in a week. Julia and I spent the spare time going for walks across the marshes, round Cobham Island, anywhere we could be on our own and talk. All that time there was a feeling – not ever put into words – that something was going to happen between us. Thinking about it now, I can't put it into any definite shape, except that it was to do with sex or the promise of sex. I think I thought that if Julia wouldn't sleep with me – and I had this detailed but curiously unerotic vision of her lying stark naked on the bed like the odalisque in the painting – then she might at least promise that she would at some unspecified future time. That was how people lived their lives in those days, people like me anyway. To get anywhere near a girl then you had to spend months scrambling over an assault course made up of God, money, parental disapproval, what you did for a living and what your father did for a living. Anyway, I had it all planned. On a particular afternoon about ten days before I was due to leave, we were going to take the train into Norwich, have tea at the Prince of Wales Hotel, watch the early showing of a film and then get the mid-evening train back to Yarmouth. Even at that stage, when I'd kissed her hundreds of time and spent a dozen evenings lying next to her in the attic at Marine Parade, I had no real conception of what might happen, and I couldn't have written down what I wanted from the day if you'd paid me.

In the end, of course, it was a complete disaster. That morning I looked up from my desk to find old Penworthy craning over me with a face like grim death and waving me off to the superintendent's office. This in itself was enough to put the wind up me – you were never called to the superintendent's office unless it was the sack or someone had died. As soon as I got there I could tell what had happened. Oddly enough, what I remember of the next few minutes is staring out of the window beyond the superintendent's office where they were trying to put back a shop awning that had blown down in the wind. It turned out that Father had had a stroke earlier in the morning. He was expected to live, Penworthy said, but beyond that they couldn't say. By the time I got through on the phone they'd taken him off to the Northgate Hospital, which was the big local hospital, and I finally got to see him, ironically enough, at exactly the time Julia and I were supposed to be having that tea. I don't remember much else of the day except Mother sitting cheerlessly at the bedside and the look on Father's face, which wasn't pained or vacant but simply a bit dogged, as if he were wandering about underwater and couldn't quite make out what the shapes and shadows consisted of. Over the next week or so I got to see Julia a couple of times, but it was all a frost, just sitting in coffee bars and not knowing what to say. The rest of the time was spent at the hospital, listening to Mother glooming on about the future and watching Father vaguely trying to open his mouth. He never spoke again. A fortnight later I was in Catterick.

The Ngongi continue to haunt me. Yesterday I even went to the local library to see if they could supply further information. Personally I wouldn't recommend the local library to anyone seriously interested in books. Or to anyone seriously interested in anything except Bruce Willis videos and wok cookery. Still, they had some stuff about the Ngongi. Apparently the tribe pursues a classic nomadic existence. No sooner have they encamped at one watering hole, fed their oxen, sung their primordial songs, tapped out their primeval rhythms on the birchbark drum, than the urge to depart becomes uncontrollable. A week is about the longest time the Ngongi remain in any one place. All this has led to an interesting controversy in the field of professional ethnography. On the one hand some experts have proposed a theory of nomadic existence, a kind of internal rhythm of life that forces people to move. Other students think that if you give the average nomad enough pasture for his livestock he tends to stay put. Predictably no one has asked the Ngongi about this. Neither has anyone ever given them enough pasture for their livestock. Despite these deprivations they seem to be a cheerful people, content to inhabit a world of endless horizons and diminishing returns. Once again, the ability to adapt is all.

I have an inkling that the Ngongi would feel pretty much at home around here – this in spite of the British National Party stickers and the *Nigger Scum Out* slogans on the viaduct overhangs. South-east London has its own nomadic existences, its oases, its sparse clumps of pasture. Never mind Mr and Mrs Rashid and the other newcomers from Bengal and Uzbekistan, the white people are on the move too. The old East End – the great grid of identikit terraces that stretches all the way from Mile End to Upney – is breaking up, so they say. The diaspora is based on money. With money you can prospect the flatbeds of Romford and Upminster. Without money you end up

somewhere like here. The streets are full of off-white vans
unloading, families piled on street corners trying to establish their bearings with regard to pub, chippy and corner
shop. Meanwhile the older tribes are disappearing, gathering up their tents and moving on. God knows where they
go. There are other bolt-holes further down the Thames.
Dartford's not so bad, you hear people say. Lennie has
been seriously investigating a retirement complex near
Gravesend. (*Getting a bit too old for this malarky, know
what I mean*?) I know what he means. Everyone's moving
downriver, borne on the restless tide. As I say, I think the
Ngongi would feel at home.

*

There are real gulls, it turns out. At low tide the mudbanks
are a playground for oyster-catchers, terns and razor-backs.
The other morning I watched a cormorant perched on a
PLA hulk in midstream and flexing its wings in odd
origami patterns, just as if Yarmouth and Gorleston lay
across the way rather than the Beckton towerblocks.
Oddly, there was no comfort in this apparition. It was an
alien bird, out of place on the mudflats. Like the London
pigeons, the gulls look ground-down and unhappy.
Something tells them they're in the wrong place, fetched
up in this urban backwater, far away from the world they
know.

Autumn comes early here. By mid-September the dusk
is already stealing in at seven and the wind blowing off the
river has an edge to it. Standing on the shoreline in the
early evening, the view is like a sepia postcard: derelict
wharves rotting into the river, behind and beyond the
Dockland cranes. To the west familiar landmarks rise into
view. Eastwards, downriver, the mist lifts off the surface of
the water in ghostly folds and eddies. Nearer at hand there
are odd explosions of light: police launches chugging by in
mid-stream, a late tourist boat three-quarters empty and
knowing it, heading back to Greenwich Pier and
Westminster. Above, the sky fades away into dusky pinks

and blues. There's a general sense of things settling down for winter, down into the burrowing world of dark streets, pale faces seen under the arc of the lamps, the flaming lanterns outside the pubs and the minicab offices.

Like the Ngongi, I'm busily adapting myself to my environment. First thing I take the boy to the school gates and watch him track his way across the scabbed tarmac to the door. I note that I'm the oldest parent by about twenty years. The other dads are bullet-headed little thugs in their thirties. In the afternoons I go out walking. A mile or so downstream the river loops southward, the houses recede from the shore and a different landscape shifts into view: reservoirs and sewage farms set back from the bank, mean little fields. Like the gulls, what ought to remind me of Yarmouth only reinforces its absence. Not salt hanging in the air but something ranker, more decayed: dark ooze and stagnant water. Apparently on a ship bound for the west coast of Africa there comes a day when the wind has a new smell – the heavy, rotting smell that comes from centuries of mangroves decaying into the swamp.

But perhaps the parallels with the Ngongi have been stressed enough.

*

Two days ago I took the train into town and headed for the West End. Curiously enough it was Lennie's idea. (*See the sights, me old china! Look up a few mates!*) When it came to it there were precious few mates to look up. The Casbah in Gerrard Street was an escort agency; Pantalino's where Upward and I once performed in front of Princess Margaret sometime in the mid-60s seemed to have disappeared altogether. But some odd homing instinct took me to the Empyrean in Wardour Street, where I hadn't been for five years and not played for ten, a month before the crash as it happened.

Fenced in behind stout blue shutters, entry through the same dark glass door set far back in the passageway approach, the Empyrean didn't seem outwardly to have

changed. Inside there'd been a certain amount of refur-
bishment. Perhaps a dozen people were seated at the line
of tables, mostly in ones and twos: there was probably a
bigger dining area out of sight round the back. It was
uncomfortably hot. Fetched up in this austere subter-
ranean grotto, looking over a menu card in the shape of a
butterfly's wings, it was impossible not to be struck by a
dense wave of nostalgia: Upward, Paula, Ravenscroft in his
shiny dinner jacket, balloons descending fitfully to the
floor. Carried away on this, beyond the plum-coloured
decor and the silver-painted stage into a kind of dream
world full of dead but all-too-recognisable faces, I felt
massively irritated: change, decay, the past not being able
to match up to my expectations of it, all that. In the end I
ordered an omelette and a glass of wine.

There was a burly maitre d' standing by an inner
doorway, leading out into a kind of gazebo hung with vines.
I waved him across.

'Does John Ravenscroft still own this place?'

'No sir.'

'Dan Kavanagh? Tim Jenks?'

'Never heard of them sir.'

'When did all this' – I flicked a hand at the plum wall-
paper – 'get put in?'

'Couldn't say sir. All before my time.'

Only the bill brought back the Empyrean's former
glories. I paid it and wandered off towards the vestibule.
There was no one about. Fixed to the wall of the cloakroom was a panorama of old photographs. These showed
the Empyrean in various stages of its development: red-
faced men in evening suits brandishing champagne bottles,
hawkish women in long dresses, a naked girl climbing out
of the wreckage of a giant birthday cake. Three or four of
the faces – showbiz people, the odd politician – I knew, or
knew of. And then instantly, like a coin falling into the interior of a slot machine, I saw that the short, stubby man in
the tuxedo, flanked by two statuesque brunettes got up as
Edwardian parlour maids, was Upward. There was no
getting away from it. No getting away, either, from the

complete vacuum in which it existed. Some of the photos had dates. Others commemorated significant anniversaries. A riot of blue balloons in one picture looked as if they came from an election night party. Upward's portrait, on the other hand, was lost in space and time.

The maitre d', now definitely suspicious, lumbered across.

'Everything OK, sir?'

'Perfectly OK.'

Outside the clouds were moving west beyond Oxford Street. A man in an expensive suit loped past at a tremendous pace in the direction of Shaftesbury Avenue. Five yards away vapour rose off a deliquescing block of ice somebody had left out on the pavement. It was barely two o'clock. I wondered about going to see Lennie in his culvert round the back of Old Compton Street, in the small room with the Sid James posters and the box-card index that Lennie's had thirty years and keeps for sentiment's sake (I looked inside once and found Sir John Gielgud's name and address in amongst the rows of tap-dancing harmonica players). Then I decided against it. I have enough ghosts to follow.

*

Actually I get the feeling Lennie thinks my heart isn't really in it. I can tell this from the way he chides me over the phone. *You got the kid to support now and all ain't you?* He's right, of course. I have the kid to support. Not to mention the small matter of myself. Lennie's latest scheme is that I ought to write my autobiography. Even better, have my autobiography written for me by someone else. (*You could just sit there and spiel it, and 'e could take notes. It's 'ow they all do it.*) I don't like to tell Lennie that the world of showbiz memoirs has moved on a bit since he fixed up for Barbara Windsor and Ronnie Knight to tell all to the *People* back around the time of the three-day week. But every comedian is a hero to his agent. According to Lennie I'm still a 'household name'. But then so, apparently, are his tap-dancers and Captain Ludo and his performing seals, who last appeared on *Blue Peter* in 1978.

Meanwhile, I've had a couple of conversations with the BBC girl. As I might have forecast, Lennie had got it substantially wrong. Just a producer wanting eye-witnesses for one of those social history documentaries. I get the feeling that I might be seventeenth on a list of eighteen candidates, but there's talk of a budget and vague suggestion that we should have lunch. The girl, whose name is Lucy, says things like 'I look foward to working with you Mr King' and 'Graham will be delighted'. I don't think she has a clue who I am. Or was.

Little Boy Soldiers

We were sweeping for mines out near the Nicosia–Kyrenia road.

In those days, of course, sweeping for mines was a chancy business. I've seen TV documentaries about mine-clearance where everybody wears plastic visors and the equipment can turn up a dropped halfpenny at twenty paces. Back then your only protection was a flak jacket, and the metal detectors worked within a radius of a couple of feet. The trick was to do it in pairs: one of you – the NCO, usually – eyeing up the ground for scuff marks or other signs that the surface had been disturbed, the other inching forward with the sweeper, which wasn't much more than a three-foot long stick with a kind of soup-plate stuck to the end. There were various theories about how you were supposed to sweep. Some of the older men said you should imagine that you were giving the ground a coat of paint and the sweeper was the brush, but the latest idea was for a kind of criss-cross movement, on the supposition that you'd pick up anything between the interstices as you went. What made the job easier, up to a point, was that nobody really believed there were any mines. But practically every week a report would come through, sometimes from a Turkish village, more often from one on the Greek side, that men had been seen out digging by the roadside, and the unit would get a call from Brigade HQ to investigate.

I don't suppose I went on the mine detail more than half a dozen times, but for some reason – probably because I was shit-scared – it seems vivid to me in a way that the rest of that time in Cyprus doesn't. The scenery was always the same – the road stretching on past tiny villages with names like Guanyeli and Autokoi, where a few white housefronts poked up out of the scrub, and the mountains rising up in the middle distance, all framed in the relentless glare of the sun. It was only a few weeks after the Guanyeli massacre, when the Turkish villagers came across some Greek detainees – who'd been left to make their own way home having been taken in for questioning – and literally hacked them to pieces, so there was no one much about. Occasionally you'd see a peasant, usually a very old man with a beard, goading his donkey through the scrub, or a file of children on their way to school, but mostly you could wander through the foothills for hours and not see a soul. Not that you ever did wander very far. The thing I remember best about Cyprus, apart from the endless sweep of the mountains and the heat, is waiting all the time for the flat but curiously malignant thump that meant a bomb had gone off somewhere.

Generally there'd be about half a dozen of us out on the road, together with a jeep and a Bren carrier that ferried the equipment and covered us while we did the sweep. Captain Groves, who always said that he didn't believe there was a single mine in the whole of Cyprus, usually sat in the driver's seat of the jeep smoking a cigarette. Upward would be in the Bren carrier. That left two of us to do the sweep, someone else to act as lookout – which meant wandering up and down the road stopping the oncoming traffic and staring vaguely up into the hills – and a final pair of hands to shade in the area surveyed on the local OS map. As it turned out I only ended up doing the sweeping a couple of times, but it wasn't something I'd care to repeat. I used to find myself staring at a particular patch of ground, looking helplessly for odd landmarks that would convince me that I'd already swept it, while the NCO coached me forward. 'Come on Kingy, straight ahead. Just fucking move the thing for Christ's sake' etc etc. Every so often you'd come across something under the surface and there'd be a ghastly wait until someone brushed off the topsoil to reveal an old exhaust pipe or a metal plate. Once there was a terrible panic when Upward thought he heard something moving in the bushes ten yards back down the road and touched off a couple of dozen rounds from the

Bren before anyone could stop him. They left a hole in the dirt six inches deep and converted the goat that had been making the noise into a pile of blood and guts. No one blamed Upward in the least. The NCO swore a bit, but Captain Groves said it was all right, and when he saw how shaken up we were he gave us each a fag – strictly against the rules, but Captain Groves was always doing things like this – and we stood around smoking, looking at the hole in the dirt and the mangled goat, and throwing uneasy glances back down the road. That was what being in Cyprus for any stretch of time did for you.

Though I knew both of them for years after, it's from those days that I remember Groves, and in some ways even Upward most vividly – standing there under the boiling sun, with the sweat running down their faces and the mountains looming up in the distance. All down to fear, I suppose, or perhaps the sense of being involved in something collective in which we all had a part to play: Captain Groves' humorous, rubbery face under his peaked cap and his voice saying 'Cigarette, King?', Upward manhandling the Bren, the dead goat's carcass spilled out over the roadside.

*

I suppose if I'd wanted I could have got out of National Service. By this stage the plans to abolish it were pretty well known, and people were falling over themselves to fix up deferrals or inventing fake illnesses that would fool the army doctors. There were stories of blokes who'd got excused on grounds of flat feet or chronic acne. Even with Father being ill, though, I scarcely thought about it. I'd spent eighteen years in Yarmouth, watching the gulls out over the sea and never taking a breath that didn't taste of salt, and a good part of me didn't mind the idea of two years on the other side of England, or even abroad. Even leaving Julia – who unsurprisingly stopped writing to me after a month or two – somehow paled beside the thought of this new life lived out in a tent or in a barracks some-where in Europe. That was how people thought, forty years ago. Because they'd never been anywhere, they believed all the stuff about joining the army and seeing the world, just as they believed anything they were told about the people they'd find there.

Anyway, I was posted to Catterick for basic training, which wasn't too bad. What irritated me, I suppose, was that apart from the seven hours or so you spent asleep there was hardly any time you could call your own. Reveille was at 5.30, breakfast at six, and by eight you'd be on the drill square under the eye of a vicious little corporal called Slater. What with lectures and route marches you were glad enough to spend the hour or so of free time you were some-times allowed at the end of the afternoon just lying on your bed staring at the ceiling. Predictably, it was the constant activity that some of the recruits – they were thin, pale boys of about my own age, with a handful of older blokes who'd done three years' university – couldn't take. There was a Jehovah's Witness named Warner who used simply to fall on his knees every morning and pray while, around him, twenty other men washed, dressed and defecated with one eye on the door in case Slater was prowling around to catch people smoking. Curiously, no one taunted the Jehovah's Witness. 'There's that fucking Warner saying his prayers,' they used to say, or 'Put a word in for me, will you mate?'. But at bottom I think they were secretly impressed. As for me, I soon got used to living cheek-by-jowl with twenty other recruits, none of whom I'd ever set eyes on before, and the endless feeling of there never being enough time to do things. I won't say I thrived, but I'm the kind of bloke who *can* always survive in situations like that – laugh at people's jokes and generally keep out of harm's way. At least four of the blokes in our platoon didn't last beyond the first three months. One was a mental case, who'd been sent there as the result of an administrative mix-up, two cracked up under the strain, and the fourth, a Welshman named Williams who used to talk to himself after lights out, blew his trigger finger off with a Lee Enfield out on the range.

But if, like me, you came from a family that knew some-thing about the army (Father had done time in the

Norfolks during the war) or even if you'd listened to the forces sketches on the radio, then there was an odd kind of familiarity about Catterick. The most obvious way in which it conformed to the ideas I'd picked up in advance was the air of complete confusion that seemed to hang over every decision concerning your personal destiny. When I arrived I signed up for the Education Corps – I rather liked the idea of loafing around at a desk all day reading books – but it turned out that the university boys had already got wind of this, and all the places were taken. Then there was a scheme for me to join the Royal Armoured Corps, but for some reason that didn't work out either and in the end I fetched up in the Oxford and Bucks. This had its downside – half the regiment was already out in Cyprus, and the other half was set to follow – but there were advantages, too, one of which was the recruits, who were mostly country boys from the farms around Oxford and didn't think it funny that you came from a place like Yarmouth. The other way in which everything seemed like a scene from *Privates On Parade* was the names you got given. Anyone called White was immediately referred to as 'Chalky', anyone sent on the radio course was 'Sparks', and even at half an inch under six foot I was tall enough to be called 'Lofty', which carried the extra disadvantage of being picked as wheelman during drill. I suppose in the end that's what sticks about the army – the sense of reading from a script which nobody had changed since Passchendaele. That, and the dreadful feeling of futility – spending hours blancoing the webbing on your uniform on the off-chance of an inspection, or making sure the done-up laces on your boots were exactly the same length. None of which had the effect of making people disciplined and methodical – as sergeants would sometimes claim, if asked – but simply left them angry at having wasted their time.

I hadn't been at Catterick more than a fortnight before I met Upward.

Even at a distance of forty years I've a precise recollection of that afternoon – it would have been in October sometime – and the mist drifting in across the moors, the formations of khaki figures moving slowly across the parade ground and the files of recruits sweeping up the fallen leaves. Upward was in my platoon but not in my hut, so although I'd seen him around the place – he was a short, stocky bloke with bright red hair and a set of gappy teeth that looked as if they'd been pegged on with Araldite – we hadn't yet spoken to each other. Some errand or other had sent me to one of the lecture rooms, but the lecturer I was supposed to be delivering a message to wasn't there and I walked back along the corridor poking my head vaguely into doorways and rather enjoying the break in routine, with a cast-iron excuse if anyone wanted to know what I was doing. There was no one much about and most of the rooms were empty, but in one of them I discovered Upward. He was standing by the big rectangular blackboard with his back towards me, not saying anything apart from a grunt or two, but moving sinuously from side to side. Every so often he'd bang the point of his index finger against the blackboard and make a little hissing sound, flip the piece of chalk held in his fist over his head and catch it with the other hand. It took me about half a minute to work out that he was imitating a sergeant called Barnes who lectured us on Field Studies, but when I did the effect was so overwhelming that I burst out laughing. Upward heard the disturbance and turned round. I couldn't tell if he was pleased or not.

'This one's Satterthwaite.'

Satterthwaite was the mess corporal. Again, Upward didn't say anything – I think once he'd nodded to me he was hardly conscious I was there – he simply minced up and down a few times, stuck his bottom in the air and produced a flawless pastiche of a man plonking down a tray of plates on a table covered with breakable objects. I laughed again, at which Upward grinned, whipped his cap out of his shoulderflap, jammed it on his head, bared his teeth – he looked a bit like the boy in the MAD comic – and saluted.

'The management would laik to state that they will not – ai repeat *not* – be extending Mr Upward's engagement.'

Then he winked and marched out, colliding with a

tough parachutist called Sergeant-Major Hardwood who
wanted to know what a couple of Other Ranks were doing
in a lecture room.

Every platoon had its resident wag, of course. Usually
they were oily little blokes who called the sergeant 'Sarge'
and crawled to the junior NCOs, but even by the standards
of Catterick Upward was something special. There was a
story that he'd once held up a formal parade by imitating
the noise of the staff captain's car failing to start. I got
another glimpse of him in action a week later when about
three dozen of us were having an unarmed combat session
with a corporal called Faraday. After we'd been through
the usual routines of treading on our opponents' insteps
and pretending to gouge out each other's eyes, Faraday
called us together and announced that he was going to
teach us all about 'falling'.

'Now, falling, thass a difficult thing to do, see? Any one
of you was to fall straight over on the square here, straight
down on your side, you'd break your collar-bone, no question about it. Doesn't matter how careful you do it, unless
you know how to roll your shoulder you're talking a fortnight in plaster. Now, watch me.'

We watched as Faraday flung himself dramatically
down onto the tarmac. He landed on the point of his
shoulder, tried to say something and then fell back into a
dead faint. Somebody sent for a stretcher to take him
away, and another corporal was summoned to take charge.

'Now,' he said. 'No point in thinking you can skive off
just because the instructor's indisposed. Where did you get
to with Corporal Faraday?'

There was a silence. Then Upward piped up: 'Please
corporal, we'd just got to the part where you break your
collar-bone.'

A couple of nights after that I got to talk to Upward in
the NAAFI. He was on his own – for some reason wags
were never very popular with the rest of the hut – and a bit
wary. I think he thought I saw him as a kind of free show
you could come up and laugh at. I say 'talk', but you didn't
talk to Upward, you just listened. Essentially, being in the

same room as him cast you in the role of spectator to an extraordinary monologue that could go on for an hour, provided there wasn't a parade to attend or the mess bell went. I say 'spectator' because it was a visual thing as well, with Upward acting out parts or illustrating points with weird and curiously voluptuous gestures. Once, when I had a pen and notebook handy, I tried writing one of them down afterwards. It went something like this:

'We are all of us lying in the gutter, but some of us are looking at the stars. A man called Oscar Wilde said that … Wilde by name, wild by nature (*pause*) … Obviously never been to Catterick … Reminds me of the carpenter whose cabinets were all crooked. He was banned for possessing an unnatural vice (*pause, nodding to someone leaving the table*) … Whalemeat again, as the eskimo said to his wife …'

Inevitably, this doesn't do justice to Upward's delivery, or the look on his face, which was complete deadpan. If I say that he was the kind of bloke who raises a laugh simply by walking into a room, then perhaps you'll understand what I mean. And yet the really curious thing was that half the time you never knew whether he thought he was being funny. I can remember another time when they were short-staffed at the NAAFI and Upward ended up serving behind the bar. For some reason an officer turned up – there might have been an all-ranks football match going on outside – rubbed his hands together (it was a freezing night in November) advanced on the wooden counter and announced that he wanted a pint of brandy. In fact, as everyone including the officer knew, they didn't serve brandy in the NAAFI, but Upward merely gave a little bob of his head and enquired: 'Martel, sir?'

There was another time, out on a training exercise, when a container in the process of being winched across a stream unexpectedly snapped back and knocked Upward – an interested spectator on the bank – into six inches of water. Seeing him motionless, the NCO – Sergeant-Major Hardwood, as it happened – jumped anxiously into the stream beside him. Upward opened his eyes.

'Kiss me, Hardwood,' he said.

Again, Upward denied he was being frivolous, claiming that he thought himself gravely injured (in fact he sustained mild bruising) and thought these the right words to utter. The sense he gave off, even when doing something outrageously funny, of being a bit of a dark horse, extended over the whole area of his private life, what he'd done before the army, all aspects of him not covered by khaki, so to speak. Publicly, he gave out that he'd been an engineering clerk in Preston – he had a flat kind of Lancashire accent. At the same time he was capable of showing unexpected flashes of expertise. Once, during a lecture about living off the land, a NAAFI sergeant produced a shrivelled, pink-grey carcase on a tray and announced that he was going to explain the best way of boning a rabbit. Upward, who happened to be at the front of the throng of heads, sniffed slightly and remarked:

'That's cat. Count the ribs.'

It was cat, too. Nobody quite knew how Upward had come by the ability to make this judgment. There were plenty of dark horses in the platoon: Plimworthy, whom everyone suspected of being a failed officer candidate, or Stubbs who had a picture of Khrushchev in his wallet and sat on his bed at night reading Communist pamphlets. None of them were as dark as Upward.

Among other things, Upward had a pronounced, and deeply melancholy, philosophical side. Once when we were cleaning equipment in an otherwise deserted drillroom, he suddenly demanded, with extraordinary force:

'D'you believe there's a God?'

It was difficult to know what to say. The way Upward had brought out the question showed that he felt strongly about it. Support or denial could be equally upsetting to him.

'I suppose so.'

Upward put down the part of the Bren gun he was polishing with a piece of lint and turned towards me.

'Of course there is.'

'You think so?'

'Stands to reason.'

'It does?'

There was a tenseness about Upward as this dialogue unrolled that I can't begin to describe. He was sweating, I noticed, and his fingers shook against the lint.

'Bound to be. If there wasn't a God, how could anyone ever be punished?'

'Is that important?'

'Of course it is. Think of all the wicked things people would do if they thought they weren't going to be punished for them. Think of what you and I'd do.'

'What?'

'I don't know. Something awful, I daresay. But the important thing is, *we need to be stopped.*'

Again, I never worked out if Upward meant this to be taken seriously, as a joke, or as a combination of the two. At any rate he never showed the faintest interest in the religious facilities on offer at Catterick. But the conversation about God was somehow symptomatic of his whole approach to other people, his inability to fit himself into normal channels of communication, and the confusions and resentments that this sometimes provoked.

At the same time this melancholic, unpredictable side went hand in hand with a quite startling jauntiness. Public jauntiness, at any rate. In the context of army routine Upward led an extraordinary charmed life. Countless NCOs 'had it in' for Upward: somehow he always survived, dodged the charge, emerged from the orderly room with the mildest of rebukes. I liked Upward from the first, mostly I think because he was completely unlike me: jaunty, devious, calculating, always one step ahead of the game. There was also, although this is difficult to put into words, an odd sense of familiarity. Something about Upward's gestures, the red shining face, teeth, made me think that in however marginal a way, somewhere deep in time, our paths had already crossed.

It was December 1958 by this time, and snow lay piled up on the moors overlooking the camp. In the evenings even a trip to the NAAFI seemed too exhausting to be borne. I used to lie on my bed reading old copies of *Film*

Fun or dog-eared paperbacks with titles like *Hard-hearted Sal* that went round the place, while the wind tore in against the side of the hut and the lightbulbs danced under the ceiling. Often I wrote home – not because I thought Father and Mother would be interested in the kind of life I was leading, but because I badly wanted to connect myself to something that existed beyond the world of regimental brasses and saluting anything that looked like an officer on sight. Mother's letters weren't very communicative. Father was 'better' but he couldn't do more than sit in a chair and stare at whoever was bringing him his tea, and I got the impression, reading between the lines of Mother's pale, watery handwriting that faded away into the Basildon Bond notepaper on which she wrote, that they didn't really have enough to live on. I know I didn't worry about this as much as I should have done. I was too wrapped up in being on my own, and Upward, and the thought that in a month or so I'd probably be in Cyprus. There was, too, the feeling that, whatever happened, in the end something would be sorted out. This wasn't the 30s – and I'd heard enough about the 30s in my time. At any rate Father and Mother wouldn't starve. Somehow the kind of life they were habituated to would go on: sitting in a tiny house a mile or so inland, listening to the wind smashing against the eaves, while Father mumbled over his scrapbook and Uncle Ralph rapped on the floor upstairs with his stick for another cup of tea.

Meanwhile, there was Christmas to be got through at Catterick, which meant concert-parties, carol services and a piss-up of such epic proportions that one of the corporals ended up in hospital with alcohol poisoning. It was the oddest time, Christmas in an army camp. Not only was there a sense that normal rules didn't apply – at tea on Christmas Day, for instance, served up with sticks of celery, we simply stood up at the tables and chucked them back at the cooks – but the place was full of people allowing themselves a kind of psychological holiday. Sergeants you hadn't seen smile since you stepped off the train would suddenly consent to strip down to their underclothes and perform ritual dances,

or sing maudlin regimental songs going back to the days of
the Sudan campaign. This air of temporary licence wasn't
altogether pleasant. On the one hand you had no idea what
might happen next. On the other there was a feeling that the
old rules would mysteriously snap back without anyone
telling you, and that laughing at the sergeant's combinations
as he performed the Elephant Dance would suddenly get
you put on a charge.

On Boxing Day afternoon they had a concert in one of
the lecture halls. It was the usual kind of thing – a couple of
song and dance routines, an aspiring tenor singing 'The Sun
Was Declining', a skit on Cinderella transferred to the
sergeants' mess – but all the while there was a ripple of
excitement going through the audience over whether
Upward would appear. Finally, at the very end, somebody
announced that they were going to conclude the proceedings with a really class act: a *prima ballerina* was going to
perform the Dance of the Sugar-Plum Fairy. No one quite
knew what to expect, but someone put a gramophone
record on and in a moment or two a figure in a kind of
improvised ballerina's costume marched out onto the stage
and began to leap about. It took me at least a minute to
work out that it was Upward, not only because the figure
was heavily made up, like one of the Ugly Sisters in a
pantomime, but because whoever it was could obviously
dance. It went on for about five minutes – Upward pirouet-
ting on his toes, gambolling unrestrainedly around the stage,
taking giant leaps from one vantage point to another,
executing high kicks, but always managing to find his
balance. At the end, in a pre-arranged gesture, somebody
threw a single rose onto the stage. Upward contrived to
catch the stem between his teeth. Opinion was divided as to
whether Upward had made a success of this routine. One or
two people present complained that they'd thought 'that
bugger Upward was supposed to be funny'. There was a
certain amount of confusion over whether he had been
attempting to pastiche a *prima ballerina* or merely imitating
her. Upward reported that he'd later been summoned
before the company commander and congratulated for his

part in the proceedings. This, according to Upward, gave rise
to the funniest conversation in which he'd ever taken part.

It's not exaggerating to say that this was the moment
when I saw the point of Upward, got the hang of him, knew
somehow of the extraordinary impact he was going to have
on my life, there in the draughty lecture hall, with the wind
whistling in from across the moors, the cigarette smoke
hanging in the air, Upward's face scarlet under the dancing
lightbulbs.

A month later we were in Cyprus.

*

It was on the plane out over the Mediterranean that I
worked out where I'd seen Upward before. Not, as it
turned out, at the Sun Alliance (for a time I wondered
whether he'd been an agent for one of the northern
branches that I'd come across in the office) but on the
stage of the Yarmouth Regal. Two, or maybe three years
back, I'd seen a variety bill containing an act called Eight
Lancashire Lads. In fact, as I subsequently found out, the
Lancashire Lads were a famous variety institution. The
original line-up went back at least to the 30s – Father had
seen them before the war and reckoned that one or two of
them looked a bit long in the tooth even then. The
Lancashire Lads were a clog-dancing act. The show began
with the curtain raised a couple of feet above a blacked-
out screen, with the boys in front of it dancing in black
stockings and gold-painted clogs, so the audience got an
illusion of weirdly detached feet. In normal circumstances
I probably wouldn't have remembered them, but by this
stage they'd started introducing patter into the proceedings. Upward, I soon established, had been the young
red-haired feed, butt of various jokes about 'courting' and
keeping pigeons in his loft.

A bit surprisingly, given the veil of concealment that
hung over the rest of his career, Upward happily owned up
to being a Lancashire Lad.

'Oh aye. Did that for a year. Biggest bloody disaster I

ever knew. There had to be eight of you, because there always had been – the lead bloke in them days was the grandson of the chap who'd founded them – but that meant there was never any money. Plus there was only about two of them actually came from Lancashire by that time, so you had to be careful if ever you played up north.'

'When did you leave?'

'Just after Suez. You won't believe this. We were on at the Scarborough Hippodrome. One of my clogs came off halfway through the first number. Of course there was a row about it afterwards, but I'd had enough of it by then so I just slung my hook.'

Upward's professional stories were always worth listening to. He had a particularly good one about Morecambe & Wise being received in silence at the Glasgow Kelvin Hall and the doorkeeper saying 'They're beginning to like you lads,' as they came off. Then there were the Pilkington Sisters, who according to Upward actually consisted of a mother and her two daughters. Again, it was impossible to work out whether Upward had enjoyed his time on the variety circuit, whether it was something he put up with on the grounds of gaining experience or actively disliked.

In any case, all these revelations – if they were revelations – lay in the future. At the time I didn't recognise their significance and certainly had no idea of their implications for me. There were other things to think about. The last letter from Mother, which I remember reading on the flight and in a roundabout way probably brought me to Upward, the memory of the Eight Lancashire Lads crashing their way across the stage of the Yarmouth Regal, the blue of the Mediterranean beneath: all this mysteriously fused in my head as the plane touched down and stayed there, so that even now I can remember the particular things Mother was complaining of – Uncle Ralph's sulks and the hospital speech therapist that Father 'didn't take to' – effortlessly combining with the rows of pinetrees set back from the airstrip and the blue-white mountaintops rising in the distance.

*

The week before we went to Cyprus, a staff lecturer filled us in on the political situation we could expect to find there. Basically it went like this. The island – I had a vague notion, misremembered from school geography lessons, that it was a bigger version of Gibraltar – was still a Crown Colony under a British Governor, and the idea was that we were preparing the place for independence as a self-governing part of the Commonwealth. The Greek three-quarters of the population wanted *enosis* or union with Greece, while the Turkish minority wanted *taksim*, in other words secession from the rest of the island in their own enclave, which would then be united with Turkey. The Greek nationalists were split up into factions: EOKA, who were right-wing, EDEK, who were left-wing, and EAXEC, who were out-and-out communists; and when they weren't massacring the Turks or shooting us, they weren't above having a crack at each other. Among other things, this caused endless confusion whenever anything serious happened – a bomb going off at a petrol station could mean that any one of about five things was going to happen, ranging from a pact between the socialists and the communists to a Turkish uprising. Sitting in the middle, of course, with orders to keep the factions apart while somebody tried to patch up a constitution, we were fair game for everyone.

By the time we got there the really serious stuff was over, but that didn't mean you could relax. Most of the time was spent manning roadblocks, hanging around in villages waiting for political leaders to arrive or depart, or simply standing in the road trying to search passers-by. Every now and then there'd be a flap – a trooper out on patrol wouldn't come back, or there'd be reports of an explosion at a village five miles away – and the temperature would go up a few degrees, but mostly it was a case of sitting around waiting for something to happen. Oddly enough, though I must have been there six months, I don't

remember anything much about Cyprus, certainly nothing
about the people. Everyone hated the Cypriots, who they
said were simply peasants, and there were stories of
Grivas, the EOKA leader, arranging ceasefires and then
leaving booby traps when he knew British soldiers would
be going in to attend to casualties. As for the work, one
roadblock is pretty much like another. If I've any recollection of those six months, it's of small things: roadside
shrines, which I suppose dated from the war, with a few
flowers rotting in an old glass above a picture of some
teenager sweating under the weight of a bandolier, orange
groves glistening in the sun, queer processions of livestock
– a couple of goats, a chicken and pig, say – being herded
through the scrub by an old woman. That, and squatting
outside the tent first thing in the morning trying to prise
open a can of foul-tasting muck called 'self-heating soup'
while the sky changed from deep violet into the purest
imaginable blue and the dew dried under your feet.

But there were other reasons why I don't remember
much about Cyprus. Upward was part of it, of course –
Upward legend, Upward lore, Upward's imitation of rico-
cheting bullets, which could get a roadblock detail looking
uneasily over their shoulders from twenty yards away. But
the main reason, I think, was the effect that service life had
on me as a person. Being in the army – even there in a
Crown Colony at the fag-end of the 50s – did strange
things to you. Less than a year before I'd been a clerk in an
office a mile from the North Sea whose main concern was
whether the girl I was seeing that night would turn up on
time, and now I was a crop-haired bloke in khaki who got
up at five every morning, could get water to boil over a
candle, and was uneasily conscious that the next figure
who appeared over the horizon could easily be out to kill
me. As for 'teaching you skills', which was something the
army newspapers went on about, I once itemised the
various things I'd picked up in uniform and they included
being able to mix up the kind of polish that would enable
you to see your reflection in the toe-caps of your boots,
fitting thirty pounds of equipment in a pack meant for

twenty, and cooking breakfast for six people in a single saucepan. But that was what the army did to you in a way, got you to expend vast amounts of mental labour on solving problems that anyone with any sense would have made sure weren't there to be solved in the first place. The base at Nicosia was full of people running around trying to find new ways of making butter keep or getting ground-sheets to dry in the sun without going discoloured.

Captain Groves' theory was that people needed these distractions to stop them going mad.

'Standard army practice since Waterloo,' he explained. 'Why do you think Wellington never let his men have enough food? Gave them something to do, of course. Tell a man he's got to find himself something to eat and that if he doesn't no one else will find it for him, and he won't have time to wonder what he's doing in the army in the first place, and whether the cause is actually worth fighting for. Plus you give him a feeling of resourcefulness. God knows, I've never seen soldiers so happy as when you tell them to pitch a tent at the bottom of a drainage ditch or halfway up the side of a mountain where there's no purchase for the tent-pegs.'

I suppose I first properly came across Captain Groves – the Honourable Jacinth Mountstuart Elphinstone Groves, to give him his full title – about two months into the Cyprus tour. It was a bright, sharp morning in February with the mist clearing a bit towards the mountains, and we'd been sent out to a Turkish village in the hills to clear up after an EOKA attack. When we got there we found that the damage wasn't as bad as we'd been told – two of the houses had been blown apart with grenades, and there were a couple of casualties – so once we'd dealt with the bodies (one of them I remember was an enormously fat chap, probably the village headman, whose belly literally fell down to his knees) and looked around the approach roads for signs of a repeat performance, there wasn't a great deal to do and the NCO decided we could take a breather. By this time it was nearly midday and Upward and I wandered down to the end of the main street where somebody had said you could buy dates and goats' cheese.

We'd got the cheese, tried and failed to get the old woman on duty to sell us some of the local wine, when Upward stopped and said:

'Let's go in here a bit.'

There was a biggish house, set back a little from the road, with a kind of trellis-work gate that was mostly in fragments and hung off the stanchions, with bits of debris lying about on the grass. Beyond this was a second gate, set in a high fence and half-open. In the distance two or three voices – English voices – were borne back on the breeze.

'Probably nicking something,' Upward deduced. 'Let's go and take a look.'

Stepping through the inner gate, we came across a sight that even now, four decades later, is extraordinarily vivid in my mind. On the far side of a ragged, overgrown belt of laurels various people – Captain Groves, two or three other officers – were sprawled over a square of bright emerald grass. Behind them a copse of spruce trees led down to the road. As I looked on, Captain Groves' batman emerged from one end of the hedge carrying a couple of bottles of wine, one of them with the neck smashed off, which he set down on a camping stool next to some loaves of bread and bowls of olives.

'Private party,' Upward murmured out of the corner of his mouth, and then, slightly louder, 'Sorry sir, we'll be on our way.'

For some reason, though, neither of us stirred. Captain Groves, who was propped up on one elbow smoking a cheroot while another private offered various bits of food for his inspection, nodded affably. One of the other officers laughed a bit. I saw that, unwittingly, we'd stumbled on one of the escapades for which Captain Groves was famous. His exploits, occasionally recounted by admiring NCOs, included training a corporal to act as croupier in late-night baccarat sessions and – somewhere in Kenya, where normal rules didn't apply – running a company brothel.

'That's all right,' Groves said. 'It's Upward, isn't it? And King. All cleared up in the village? Why not sit down and have a glass with us?'

I daresay you'll think there was nothing very amazing about a couple of squaddies being invited to drink wine with their company captain on a hillside in Cyprus, but let me tell you that by the standards of the British Army it was more or less unprecedented – like being offered a cigarette by your headmaster or being asked to lunch in the senior staff dining room at the Sun Alliance. The wine was extraordinary, too – God knows where they'd stolen it – like crisp-tasting nectar. The odd thing was that Groves didn't seem at all embarrassed at having us there, simply talked about the morning's operation and the football results back home. From below we could hear the noise of lorries reversing in the village, but it was all somehow irrelevant, too remote and far away to be worth bothering about.

Anyway, this went on for about twenty minutes, and we'd eaten a plate of bread and olives apiece, when suddenly Captain Groves clapped his hands together and said to his batman: 'All we need now is some entertainment.'

The batman was a Liverpudlian conscript called Murphy, and famously slow on the uptake.

'Entertainment, sir?' he wondered.

'That's right, entertainment. Upward, I've seen you in Christmas concerts. Go on, sing us a song.'

Upward sniffed a bit at this, while not looking as if he thought this request the least bit surprising in the circumstances. 'A song, sir?'

'That's right. A song. As filthy as you like. I shan't mind. Go on.'

Upward stood up and looked rather thoughtfully down towards the trees. One of the other officers sniggered.

'I won't sing you a song sir. But me and Kingy here, we'll do you a turn if you like. Look, this is the sergeant's mess at 11.30 on a Saturday night, see?'

All of a sudden he was off on an extraordinary monologue about Sergeant-Major Hardwood losing his paybook and someone else complaining about watered beer. I could see it was coming and, sure enough, after a minute or two he threw me a line – something about Hardwood's boots, which he was supposed to spend every Sunday afternoon polishing. Somehow I managed to chuck it back, and Upward went off again, doing an impression of another NCO being chased by a bee. I don't remember much else about it, except for Groves and the others guffawing and Murphy stopping clearing up the lunch things with his mouth hanging open in surprise.

After about five minutes we stopped and just stood there looking embarrassed but also faintly pleased with ourselves. There was a silence, then a round of scattered applause, Captain Groves starting to say something, but the whole thing was instantly blown apart by an immensely loud explosion, or rather series of explosions, from the village. In the distance, down the hill, I could hear people shouting. There was smoke rising over the trees.

'That was the Bren if I'm not much mistaken,' Captain Groves declared, pulling on his tunic. 'For Christ's sake, Murphy, clear that mess up and let's get out of here.'

And so we sped off back to the village, scared stiff that we'd find a terrorist attack in progress, only to discover that some idiot subaltern had been trying to correct the elevation of the Bren with the barrel pointed towards him and the safety-catch off and succeeded in putting half-a-dozen bullets through his chest. He didn't die, apparently, but his face as they dragged him away on the stretcher was the colour of rice-paper. What else is there to say? A fortnight later I got word from Yarmouth that Father had died in his sleep, and went home for the funeral. When I got back, a week after that, it was to find that Upward, for some reason, had been transferred to another unit. And yet this didn't worry me. I knew, you see, that I'd find him again, that it was the start of something, not the finish, that somehow, out there under the blue Mediterranean sky, with Captain Groves leaning back on his elbows as he lit another cheroot, I'd been given a glimpse of the way my life was going to take shape.

This afternoon, back from the Empyrean, I opted to fetch the boy from school. The rain which fell half an hour ago has a bad effect on the crowd assembled at the gate. Fine weather has them all parked alongside the railings, even straying into the first few feet of the asphalt. Now they're massed under umbrellas on the other side of the road, waiting behind the wheels of boxed-in cars. Reading a book about Sid Field the other day – the kind of showbiz biography Lennie likes, where friends of the subject are routinely introduced as *Mr Comedy himself* or *that big-hearted star of stage and screen* – I discovered that Sid was so loath to tear himself away from the amphitheatres of his professional life that he'd frequently beguile the time spent waiting outside his children's primary school by staging impromptu performances for the other parents. Often by the time his own offspring emerged from their classrooms it was to find their father – still wearing his trademark coat and hat, apparently – halfway through one of his monologues, with a dozen or so fellow-parents egging him on.

Even today these performances are fondly remembered by those who witnessed them.

Hemmed in by the tough girls with their prams, the little bald blokes with hangdog expressions, the big men who come stalking up out of the sidestreets with a couple of mastiffs on a choke-chain, I haven't the faintest inclination to follow his example. I can see Daniel by this time, wandering out of the main door, head down, deep in conversation with a pair of bullet-headed acquaintances. What do they talk about? The price of Mars Bars? Michael Owen? I honestly don't know. Catching sight of me at the gate, he slips forward a yard or two and nods gravely.

'I was going to walk back with Justin and Jamal.'

Six weeks here and already he's slipping into the local argot. 'Walk' is coming out as *wawk*, 'with' as *wiv*, while

'Jamal' – apparently the name of the big-eyed black boy a couple of paces behind him – is definitely tri-syllabic.

'Don't worry about it. You'll see them tomorrow.'

'OK.'

As he falls in behind me I flick the top of his head with the flat of my hand in the way you see soccer managers on the TV mark their approval of promising trainees. He raises his eyes in mock disgust. *That poor old bastard*, I imagine him saying to Justin and Jamal, *what does he think he's like?*

'Good day?'

'It was all right.'

There is a mark just above his eye I haven't noticed before, a reddish abrasion the colour of the pink candy shrimps Father used to sell in the shop.

'Somebody hit you?'

'Just some kid.'

'Anyone I know?'

'No.'

At these times I steel myself for confidences, but they never come. My whole information base on Daniel's school is dangerously short on data. Apparently they have football on Tuesdays and Fridays, and there's a Miss Cox who everybody likes and a Mr Rees who everybody hates. Last week somebody threw up in a corridor and you can't bring mobile phones in though lots of kids do. As for his mates, Jamal lives in some Afro-Caribbean family colony on the estate looked after by his three aunties; Justin's dad works on the ferry at Woolwich.

Beyond the school gate and the rows of stalled cars, he keeps behind me and slightly to the left. If you saw us you'd wonder at the exact nature of our relationship. Grandfather and grandson? Middle-aged man tailed by pre-teen stalker? From time to time other children rush past or come loitering by on the other side of the street. He doesn't look up. Psychologists – I boned up on this – say that the ten-year-old is the most self-effacing of all children. Their aim, apparently, is inconspicuousness. Krieger records the case of an eleven-year-old entered by mistake at the wrong school who spent three weeks happily attending classes on whose lists he didn't appear before anyone found out. Invisibility is all.

'Got much homework tonight?'

'A bit.'

'How's Miss Cox?'

'All right.' Something in the way he says this makes me glance back. 'Actually she had a row with her boyfriend.'

'That's bad.'

'It's all right, though, because she was getting tired of him anyway.'

'Good.'

*

After a can of Coke from the fridge and a canter through the children's programmes on TV he falls asleep on the sofa. He does this perhaps two or three afternoons a week. At first I worried that it was an early symptom of some ghastly children's disease – leukaemia, maybe, or rheumatoid arthritis. But it turns out – Krieger is very persuasive on this point – that ten-year-olds are prone to nervous exhaustion, particularly when placed in an unfamiliar environment.

He sleeps with one arm thrown back over his head, the other pressed tightly against his chest. An hour now since the last shower, there are shafts of sunlight creeping into the room. His face is quite expressionless at these times, no clue as to what goes on underneath. Every so often the hand thrown back over his head twitches slightly and he adjusts his position, burrowing further into the sofa, curling his legs beneath him. The TV, which I haven't yet turned off, switches from kids' programmes to the early evening soaps: fat Australians glumly reproaching each other; the other one about the depraved Yorkshire village. While he sleeps I take the opportunity to riffle through his schoolbooks: brightly-coloured plastic ring-binders with PROJECT stamped on the outside; tiny blue exercise books of the kind Mother used for her household accounts.

The promise of their covers is not matched by what lies within. Miss Cox, who I take to be the impresario of these exercises, sets essays on 'Who is your favourite footballer?' and 'Write about being at the seaside'. At their foot she provides cheerful encouragement: *Excellent Daniel. This was really exciting*. She seems easily pleased. On one page, under the heading 'Write about a journey you made recently', Daniel has written:

My Dad and me went on a train. We went from the place I used to live to the place I live now with my Dad. All our things fitted on the luggage rack, except a parcel which my Dad carried. I had a comic and some food my auntie made. When we got to London we took a taxi. It cost £34. When we got to the house I went exploring round it. My Dad didn't, because he'd lived there before.

Beneath it Miss Cox, she of the turbulent love-life, has written: *This sounds like a really interesting trip, Daniel*.

Later I go down to the kitchen. Some time later Daniel appears in the doorway, eyes puffed with sleep.

'Would you like your tea upstairs?'

'OK.'

His appetite is what Mother would have called 'fancy': a minutely itemised catalogue of likes, dislikes, certainties and not sures. Even with the things he likes you can never tell. In some Persian caliphate, Dan the caliph, myself the venturesome chef, I'd have been a candidate for the bowstring long ago. In the end I cook him sausage, beans, tomatoes and oven chips.

Outside dusk is settling over the street. Back upstairs car headlights bounce off the windowpanes. Downriver ships' hooters are calling to each other in mid-stream. Daniel lacks my absorption in the cityscape. The questions he asks are all deeply particular. Where's the cinema? Is there a bigger park than the one we go to? The sprawl of London, whose outer fringes we inhabit, is of no interest to him. Or maybe he just needs a sense of perspective. Krieger says that ten-year-olds are like lions in this respect

– staking out chunks of territory with remorseless zeal but blind to what goes on beyond their boundaries.

Bedtime is a notional nine. Even this makes Daniel a source of derision to his mates: Jamal who lolls up through the small hours listening to his aunties chat, Justin combing through the satellite channels on the portable his dad lets him have.

'What would you like to do now?'

'Watch my tapes.'

There are half a dozen of these: thick three-hour reels of old *Match of the Day* and satellite games that somebody did for him back home. Most of the kids round here support West Ham or Charlton. Dan, for some reason, is a Liverpool fan. I know the names now. Fowler. Owen. Carragher. Pale-faced, adenoidal boys who lope around the pitch as if they're a bit depressed by the weight of expectation that rests on their shoulders. Later, while Robbie, Michael and the others are still darting over the green baize surface, he goes to sleep again. I carry him upstairs in my arms, a bit shocked once more by the slightness of him, the ridges of his back ribs pressing against my hands. Krieger says that this anxiety, this paralysing terror about your children, is common in the older parent. Krieger, I note from the jacket of his book, doesn't have any children himself. How can he know about it? Or anyone?

*

Several messages from DI Stevens. He tends to call in the afternoon when I'm out prowling the shoreline or doing errands. DI Stevens is a policeman. Curiously, he hasn't openly said as much, but the respectful, dogged and slightly bored-sounding Estuary monotone gives it away. That and the buzzing of routine officialdom in the background. No indication of what DI Stevens wants, or any thought of urgency. Perhaps there will be a time when, mysteriously, our paths converge and whatever the business is will suddenly be contracted. London is full of these missed connections, messages left in limbo, accidental comings together and fallings apart. Lennie is always claiming to have been desperately trying to get in touch with me, leaving instructions that I never picked up. (*Was this BBC thing you'd have been a natural for.*) I don't believe him, but it amuses me to see the sincerity with which he keeps it up. Perhaps DI Stevens is one of those people who simply delight in leaving messages, for whom actual contact is a step backwards rather than a problem solved. Or maybe he simply has faith in our ability to find each other. Apparently this is a characteristic of the Ngongi's journeys across the desert. Two fragments of the tribe, setting off from bases hundreds of miles apart, navigating only by the stars, have the ability to achieve a rendezvous almost at will. Perhaps we are really only desert travellers marching on through the freezing African night.

*

The envelopes from Shena – there are three of them now – sit on the mantelpiece. Sometimes I take them down and look at them. Other times I make futile attempts to conceal their existence – push news-papers in front of them or hide them behind the clock. But I never open them. I never get near to opening them.

*

The day I went back to the Empyrean I woke up with a queer feeling of having passed a milestone, inched beyond some memorial post on the mountainside where a bygone traveller had halted. It took me until the end of the evening, long after Daniel had gone to sleep, to work out what it was, but it was the day I'd outlived Father. Naturally, this set me thinking about him and comparing the two of us, though to be honest there wasn't a great deal you could compare. Father was five feet six and would have weighed under nine stone when he died. Me, I'm one of those tallish blokes with broad shoulders and a red face, the kind of person you'd think twice about pushing into in a pub. All the same, he was a better man than me. Seriously. He had something I don't possess, or only have when it suits me – a kind of decency, a fear of imposing himself, that you don't often come across these days. The easy thing to say was that Father was just scared, but I think it ran deeper than this. I think he genuinely did live his life on the do-as-you-would-be-done-by principle and believed until his dying day that if you do people a good turn then they'll do you one back. The difference between us, I suppose, is that he looked for the best in people and was disappointed when he didn't find it, whereas I expect the worst and am pleasantly surprised on the occasions when it turns out the other way. The other difference is that he died in near-pauperdom, whereas I sit here, if not in affluence, then in a house that's my own and with enough money to get by. I've no idea what Father thought about his life, and whether he reached the standards he must have set for himself, but I'm pretty sure he thought he was a failure. As for me, I'm not at all sure what I think about my life, but I wouldn't put money on its being judged a success.

Talking to a Friend About Girls

UPWARD:	So when did you first ... you know?
KING:	When did I first what?
UPWARD:	You know ... when did you?
KING:	When did I what?
UPWARD:	You know ... *that*.
KING:	Oh ... *that*.
UPWARD:	Yes, that ... I mean, when did you?
KING:	It was a long time ago.
UPWARD:	I can see that.
KING:	It was that Eunice Braithwaite. Her from Market Street. Big girl, she was.
UPWARD:	They all were.
KING:	What? You mean there was more than one of them?
UPWARD:	So what happened?
KING:	Well, I felt a right ha'porth.
UPWARD:	I've never heard them called that before.
KING:	No, seriously. My mother warned me. She said, 'You mind what you're up to, Teddy' – she used to call me Teddy in them days – 'We've never had no perspicuity in our family.'
UPWARD:	You mean promiscuity.
KING:	Nor that neither..
UPWARD:	But what happened?
KING:	Well naturally I had my best suit on. You know, for a special occasion and that. But it all went wrong when we got on the floor.
UPWARD:	On the floor, eh? You didn't hang about.
KING:	Oh no. You got points deducted if you didn't get on with it ... and then we kept bumping into the other couples.
UPWARD:	(*admiringly*) *Other couples!* Pair of swingers

you must have been!

KING: Oh no. This was a foxtrot.

UPWARD: Yes, but afterwards. You know. Did you?

KING: Oh … that. I should say so.

UPWARD: You did?

KING: Oh yes. Me mother had told me. She said, 'Make sure you behave like a gentleman should.'

UPWARD: So you did it?

KING: Oh yes.

UPWARD: What? All the way?

KING: Nearly all.

UPWARD: Well, how far did you get then?

KING: How far?

UPWARD: Yes. How far?

KING: Well, I only had one and three, so we had to get off at the Town Hall. She let me hold her hand at the bus stop, though.

UPWARD: What, all of it?

KING: Well, nearly all of it.

1965

Love Song

South of Yarmouth, down from the marshes and the salt-water creeks, the farming country began: acre upon acre of wheat and flaring barley, criss-crossed by tiny dirt-track roads and here and there a farmstead slanting down in the dip between two fields, or a hamlet of farm-workers' cottages grouped round a pub. In those days mechanisation was still coming in, and even the smaller farms would employ half a dozen labourers. Ask me what the difference is between then and now and I'd say it was movement. Modern farms are soulless places. You can climb over a hill-top looking down over a sea of wheat and not see a human being for fifty weeks of the year. Forty years ago the countryside had life in it: old men with faces that looked as if they'd been carved out of teak cycling through the early mists; loitering families come to picnic in the ditches; beet lorries lumbering off into the distance over the flat horizon. That's the other thing I remember, of course, the extraordinary flatness, just the fields going on endlessly beneath the wide sky, with perhaps a file of elm trees every so often as cover from the wind. At Parmenter's I remember once stopping to count the church spires, and there must have been a dozen of them stretching across the flat as far as Acle.

God knows what I was doing at Parmenter's that fort-night in August. It was summer 1960, I'd been out of the army a couple of months, and I literally had no one to spend time with. Father was dead. Mother wouldn't be shifted from Uncle Ralph's. The people I'd known before at the Sun Alliance were friendly enough, but two years had gone by since I'd left Yarmouth and that's a long time when you're twenty. All that summer I'd floated round the place like a ghost, noting the things that had happened since I'd been away, the shops that had changed hands, the people who'd died – and even then it was a weird feeling coming back to a place you thought you knew everything about and then finding it ever so slightly different, like an oil painting the artist has had second thoughts about and retouched. I'd been anticipating a summer in the office. Mysteriously, though, it turned out that there was a couple of weeks holiday owing, and as I didn't fancy going off on my own somewhere I signed up for a couple of weeks at Parmenter's farm.

It was one of those tiny, family farms that have practically disappeared now – swallowed by the big combines and the agribusinesses, I suppose – about a hundred acres of arable and pasture with a herd of dairy cows that looked as if they'd wandered out of the Ark. As it turned out, the harvest wasn't due to start for another week or so, but there were five or six fields of blackcurrant bushes coming into bloom, so I signed up for a fortnight's fruit-picking. Blackcurrants are a sod to pick at the best of times – they're fiddly things, and you can't help taking a handful of leaves with you as you twist off the bunches – but I didn't care. It was enough to be standing in the sun and not hearing somebody shouting at me to pick up a rifle or read a map reference. That, and having people around you whom you could take or leave as you felt. Most days there would be two or three dozen of us in the rows: farm labourers' wives, mostly, who picked like the wind and knew exactly how much green stuff you could leave in the bucket and not get pulled up for it; families of gypsies making their way up through Norfolk to Lincolnshire for the potato harvest. Theoretically you picked until the light got too bad to see, but even in mid-August it was sometimes nine before the twilight set in. Officially I was cycling back and forwards from town, but it was easier some nights just to roll up in a blanket by the side of the rows. You'd wake up at dawn, just as the mist started rising off the hedges likes strands of greying cotton-wool, wash your face in a stream that ran behind the back of the orchard, and then stride off through the dew to the meadow where

the gypsies parked their caravans to see if you could
scrounge a box of matches to start the fire.

The merest chance drove me to the Parmenters, so
slight that for years afterwards I used to wonder whether it
was chance. On a farm the size of that you couldn't help
walking into the farmer two or three times a day, and by
the end of the second week I was on nodding terms with
Mr Parmenter – he was a short, grey-haired character in
his fifties – and even come across his wife once or twice
cleaning out the coops or turning over windfalls in the
orchard. The labourers' wives said there was an old grandmother, too, living in the farmhouse, but nobody I knew
had ever laid eyes on her. Usually this would have been as
far as it went – in those days a farmer would have died
rather than be seen fraternising with his casual labourers –
but for some reason on the Saturday I was due my wages
the Parmenters' overseer had disappeared somewhere and
word had been left for me to go up to the house. It was a
scorching afternoon towards the end of August and there
was no one about. Normally if you so much as set foot
inside a farmyard a couple of dogs would come and see
what you were up to, but the flagged stone square outside
the farmhouse was quite empty. It was about half-past five,
I suppose, and inside the house there were odd sounds of
tea things clinking together and a radio playing softly in
the background. All this is very vivid to me: the slow tread
across the yard, the noise my boots made on the raised
concrete doorstep, the sound of the bolts being drawn back
as someone opened the big oak door, Mrs Parmenter, who
eventually fetched up on the far side of it.

'Keep the front door locked, we do,' she said – she
pronouncd it *du*, in a way that even then was a bit old-
fashioned. 'Parmenter's in the top field, so perhaps you'll
sit and wait.'

She was a big, untidy-looking woman in a print dress
and apron, with her hair coming down at the back, a bit
suspicious at first but not unfriendly once she'd established
that I wasn't about to cheek her or steal anything – no
middle-aged Norfolk woman in those days would give the

time of day to a man under twenty-five. Presently I was in a high, brick-walled kitchen, dominated by an enormous deal table covered with blue and white china (as I'd suspected, they were about to have tea) with a round sepia portrait of George VI – the one in which he looks like an exceptionally frightened rabbit – hanging above the fireplace, being introduced to a gaping old woman in an invalid chair (Mr Parmenter's mother, it turned out) and a loafing boy of sixteen or so. Oddly, I don't even recall that Mary was there for the first few minutes – I think she may have been fetching something from an upstairs room – and when I try to recast the scene it contains only Mrs Parmenter, the old grandmother and the boy, with Mr Parmenter coming in a shade later and hovering a bit uncertainly between the table and the fireplace – they had a trick of arranging themselves in a room that emphasised the family likeness, and even now I try to recreate it it's in terms of those high, curiously remote faces, the eyes deeply set back in the head.

Looking back at the Parmenters I haven't the first idea how to describe them. Even now, forty years later – and it's a subject that haunted me deep into the 60s and 70s – I couldn't tell you what went on in old Parmenter's head or what made him and his wife regard the world in the way they did. They were extraordinary people, and the extraordinariness was so much a part of them that it took a certain amount of time to establish just what set them apart from the rest of humanity. Once you'd done it, though, spent an afternoon in old Parmenter's kitchen, say, or helped his wife wash up after lunch, the strangeness of it all rattled in your ears like thunder. For a start, the Parmenters' detachment from what might be called the ordinary world – the world of newspapers, sport, entertainment – was absolute. None of them, for example, had ever opened a bank account, taken a holiday, even travelled over the county boundary as far I could make out. Mrs Parmenter used to talk about Norwich, which I think she'd visited three or four times, with a kind of sacramental awe. As a phenomenon this wasn't unusual. Norfolk in those days was full of old folk who barely knew the Second World War had taken place, or who thought that Churchill was still Prime Minister. The Parmenters, though, were very far from senile. They were simply middle-aged people who'd lived through great stretches of recent time which they now claimed to have no memory of. It used to puzzle me sometimes. There they sat in their farmhouse, employing maybe a dozen people, paying tax, presumably going along with a whole mass of government regulations, and somehow about 95 per cent of modern life had passed them by. Once, when I'd got to know him a bit better, I tried asking old Parmenter about the war, and what came out was an extraordinary patchwork. He'd heard about Hitler, and I think he was just about aware of the atom bomb, but the rest of it – Stalingrad, Italy, the Normandy beaches – was completely beyond him. I got the impression that the Parmenters had spent the war years alone in their farmhouse with the radio turned off, closing their ears to the sound of the bombs and pretending that the whole thing wasn't happening.

Predictably, the landscapes they'd created around them faithfully reflected this outlook. Lounging in their parlour at the back of the house, with its photographs of Mr Parmenter's grandfather in a billy hat and sprouting sidewhiskers fondly regarding a prize sow, ancient farm implements, old Staffordshire china from the last century, you sometimes got the feeling that you were sitting in a room where time had stopped in about 1913. The most modern book in the house was a copy of *The Lion, The Witch and the Wardrobe* which Mary had been given as a Sunday School prize. Everything else on the shelf went back deep into the 30s. In the two years I was in and out of the place I never saw a newspaper. The women's magazines Mrs Parmenter occasionally drowsed over on a Sunday afternoon came from a huge, endlessly recycled pile kept by the backdoor and otherwise used as wrapping paper. Some of them were as much as thirty years old.

It might be wondered, given these circumstances, and that they were rather garrulous people, what it was that the

Parmenters talked about. You'd have thought it impossible perhaps to get through an afternoon's conversation without mentioning something as up to date as the Cup Final or the Prime Minister, but somehow the Parmenters managed it. Stuck in the parlour with old man Parmenter one afternoon, I once scribbled down a list of the topics that came up, so fascinated was I by his ability to operate entirely beyond what seemed to me the normal parameters of life. It went as follows:

Varieties of apples and their relative size
His grandfather's funeral
The distance between Cromer and Sea Palling
Next week's weather prospects
An argument Mr Parmenter had had with a local landowner,
*   date unspecified, but apparently some time in the 40s.*

All this probably makes it sound as if I disliked the Parmenters, was simply amused by them or thought them simple curiosities, but this wasn't the case. They were friendly people, and I liked them, even the old, mad grandmother who I gathered had last stepped out of the house in 1947, or the teenage boy Horace, who'd rebelled against the family worldview sufficiently to buy a motorbike on the hire-purchase, which worried Mr and Mrs Parmenter no end. More to the point, perhaps, they liked me. Even now I don't really know why, after I'd collected my money and drunk my tea that first Saturday afternoon, Mrs Parmenter diffidently suggested, amid a tremendous rustling of the copy of *Woman and Home* she held across her knee, that if I happened to be cycling round that way some future Sunday afternoon there was a fair chance I'd find them at home. At bottom I think it was that even the Parmenters had begun to realise something of the sequestration in which they held their children, and saw me as a kind of vague and unthreatening remedy. I'd been in the army, too, which was something Mrs Parmenter had just about heard of and was more or less a point in your favour in those days, and I imagine, when it came down to it, that they were simply entertained by me – a talkative young chap who worked in an office but wasn't above picking fruit as a holiday job.

In the same way, I can't begin to explain the force that drove me out on my bike through the backroads a Sunday or two later to see if the Parmenters were as good as their word. I'd been back in Yarmouth for three months, and everything had changed. Worse, I'd changed too, and I knew it. The time in Cyprus had taken me out of myself in a way that scared me a bit. Half of me wanted to be off with Upward somewhere, swapping jokes or planning out comedy routines – I had a stack of them upstairs in an old army file by now, that I'd written in the past six months – the other half lingered way back in a past I knew it was beyond me to reclaim, back with Father and Mother in the square, sitting over tea in the half-light, with Father springing up from his plate to fawn over a customer who wanted a threepenny cigar. Meanwhile, I drifted through the days at the Sun Alliance, and spent the evenings mooching along the front or lying in bed in my digs listening to the radio. I suppose if I'd have thought about it I could have found ways of getting round this feeling of not belonging, joined some club or signed up to run the local Boys Brigade, which was the kind of thing people did in those days. But I was twenty, going on twenty-one, and I'd seen a bit of life beyond Yarmouth by this stage and I knew the place for what it was – a kind of sink that no one in their right minds would think twice about leaving. And at the same time, short of going to some high-up at the office and asking for a job as a travelling representative, I hadn't the least idea of how I could do it.

Anyway, there I was, on a Sunday afternoon in mid-September pushing my bike along the dirt-track that led to the Parmenters' steading, halting occasionally to light a fag or stop the huge sprays of cow parsley that pushed across the path from jamming in the spokes, and generally nosing around the place in a way that wouldn't have occurred to me while I was picking the Parmenters' blackcurrants. In the fortnight I'd worked there I hadn't registered much more than the acreage and the boundaries, but now it struck me that it was the oddest place – overgrown and wild in a way that you rarely found in Norfolk. Even here on the approach road the cow parsley had been allowed to grow eight or nine feet high, and there were great banks of lavender spreading away towards the wheatfields that clearly no one had done anything about for years. There were toads out on the path – great fat things the size of small cabbages – and I watched them for a bit, while the cow parsley jammed into the wheels again and the bees lofted backwards and forwards over my head towards the lavender. The house was a quarter of a mile away, almost lost behind a clump of rhododendrons, and seeing it gave me the oddest feeling, exactly the sensation I'd had in the Parmenters' front room, of time somehow having stopped, the whole twentieth century – Lenin and Hitler and Winston Churchill – only let in on sufferance, and the people wandering around in it simply ghosts whose real lives had stopped a quarter of a century back.

Curiously enough, when I tapped on the back window – I knew enough by this time not to go round to the front – it was to find that most of the family was out: gone on the bus to see some cousins at Stalham, Mary said, who opened the door after I'd hung about for a minute or two. She didn't seem in the least surprised to see me. Though it must have been seventy in the shade there was a fire going in the kitchen, with the invalid chair pushed up close to it, and I could see the old woman lying fast asleep with her head twisted awkwardly to one side. There was a silence for a bit, and then Mary tapped the basket she had dangling on one arm.

'I've to feed the hens.'

It was more of a statement than an invitation, I suppose, but I tagged on behind as she went off across the yard to the coops and stood there while she plunged her hands into the straw and dislodged a dozen or so pale brown eggs. Later on, when I've tried to think about her, it's always that picture that rises up: a thin, brown-skinned girl with a lot of thick, blondish hair in a cotton dress that looked as if it had belonged to her mother. She would have been about nineteen then, but she had a way of looking at you – gravely, with her eyes wide open – that made her seem a lot younger. When she'd finished with the hens, she said:

'There's a cup of tea if you'd like.'

'Thanks.'

'I'm sorry you'll have to wait for Mother and Dad.'

'It's all right.'

In the event we hadn't been more than ten minutes over tea before the Parmenters were back, dressed in their Sunday best, with the boy Horace even wearing a straw hat, and sweating like troopers from their walk up from the road. Like Mary they weren't in the least surprised to find me in their parlour. Neither were they at all exercised by the thought that their daughter had spent the last half-hour entertaining me in their absence, which most self-respecting parents of the time would have agonised over. They were kind, simple people, I decided.

I was wild about her from the start, of course. I can't explain it. I don't suppose you could. Part of it was the queerness of it all, coming upon this place smack in the middle of nowhere, full of people who probably thought Neville Chamberlain was still Prime Minister, and a strange, silent girl sitting by the fire like a princess in a fairy tale. A bit more of it was simple curiosity, the feeling of walking into a world whose dimensions and rules you could only guess at. The Yarmouth people looked down their noses at 'farmer folk'. Father and Mother would have been scandalised if they'd known I was making eyes at a farmer's daughter – they were shopkeepers, you see, and farms meant pigswill, blood and dirt. But by far the largest part of it was Mary herself. Obviously I wasn't a complete starter with girls – there'd been Marjorie and Julia, and a girl who worked in the NAAFI at Catterick – but this was the first time I'd been really rocked back on my heels. You know that feeling you get when you're about twenty and you realise for the first time that the whole business is horribly serious and dramatic and at the same time completely unavoidable? I suppose the thing that struck me about Mary – apart from her looks – was how completely unlike any other woman I'd ever met she was. That's an obvious thing to say, I know, but it was true. Fat, thin, blonde or brunette – all the girls I'd known at school or at the Sun Alliance had been more or less the same: chatty, super-refined and horribly stupid. And now here was this quiet, curiously *demure* girl, who didn't speak unless you spoke to her first, but was always unobtrusively present in your consciousness – laying down tea things neatly on a table, standing seriously next to her Mother to receive a pail of scraps that had to be taken out to the yard.

When I eventually got to talk to her alone they were the sketchiest conversations, full of strange little inferences and implications that I couldn't begin to explain. And that was when you could find anything to talk about. Films, actors, pop music – all the safe young person's topics of the time were out because she seemed never to have heard of them. Most of our early times together were simply spent in silence, and if I've a memory of those first few Sundays it's of her head down over a piece of embroidery while I mooned around by the fire – they kept the fire stoked even at Midsummer and the atmosphere inside the house was like a furnace – or listened to old man Parmenter prosing on about the beet harvest.

After a while, of course, I found out a bit more about the Parmenters – not enough to satisfy my curiosity, but sufficient to understand a very little of the kind of people they were. Oddly enough, they weren't really locals – old Parmenter's family originally came from Cambridgeshire – and every so often one of them would use a dialect phrase that you'd strain yourself to comprehend. There were hulking family secrets, too, that you had to be on your toes to spot, as the Parmenters had a habit of closing ranks whenever one of them looked as if it might be let out of the bag. It took me nearly a year, for instance, to establish that the boy Horace, occasionally stigmatised by Mr Parmenter in moments of extreme exasperation as 'backward', was very nearly simple. I used to watch him sometimes

puzzling over a paper that I'd left on a chair, or staring at
the letters that occasionally came from Mrs Parmenter's
cousin in Canada ('Canady' they called it) and it would
have broken your heart to see his face – kind of baffled,
resigned and yet hopeful at the same time, as if he
somehow thought that in the end, if he stared hard enough,
the meaning would miraculously jump into place before
his eyes. The Parmenters, I discovered, were deeply
ashamed of Horace, kept him out of the way and according
to Mary had practically given up on getting him educated
from the age of eight. At the time I don't think I found
anything shocking about this. It was simply how people
behaved forty years ago. Old folk whose faculties had gone
could spend years vegetating in some mental home with
their relatives cheerfully pretending that they didn't exist,
and families would move heaven and earth to stop a
doctor writing 'died insane' on the death certificate.

In any case, not one of the great Parmenter family
secrets that I eventually stumbled upon – the fact that old
man Parmenter was working some kind of tax fiddle with
his dairy herd, or that they'd lied about Horace's age to
keep the school inspectors off his scent – bothered me in
the slightest. It was all somehow incidental, barely visible
below the surface of the real pursuit. What the Parmenters
made of this fixation with Mary, which would have been
evident to a child of five, was anyone's guess. I could see
from the look on Mr Parmenter's face whenever I turned
up that he knew pretty well what I was about, but all the
while there was a polite fiction maintained that I was a
friend of the family who just happened to be passing. In
these circumstances, and what with Horace, who had the
characteristic half-wit's ability to turn up when you least
wanted him, it was a wonder we contrived to spend any
time together, but somehow we managed it. We used to go
off on long, dawdling walks on the pretext of inspecting the
fences – something old man Parmenter was obsessed with
– or checking that none of the cows had got out into the
road. In this way I was able to build up a fairly accurate
picture of the kind of life that went on here on a farm that

was only six miles from Yarmouth but might as well have been on the moon for all the resemblance it bore to the adolescent lives I'd previously encountered.

Until Mary had been about fifteen, I gathered, things had been relatively normal. After all, even the Parmenters couldn't stop her attending school, and I think that at one point she'd even been allowed to join the Girl Guides in the village, but after that the life of the farm, old man Parmenter, the idiot boy, had simply swallowed her up. I asked her once if she'd ever wanted a job, or at any rate to do something that took her away from her parents, and she gave me a kind of puzzled look, as if she couldn't quite fathom that there were existences other than the one she led. It was as if the idea that most girls of nineteen didn't spend their time collecting eggs or sweeping up the scraps of Mrs Parmenter's darning wool had simply never occurred to her. Once, I remember – I'd told her about my job by this time – she asked me about the Sun Alliance.

'Those girls who work there? What do they *do*?'

'Oh, clerical work. In the canteens, some of them. Or secretaries.'

'What does a secretary do?'

I explained what a secretary did, and she thought about it for a while, and then nodded as if some deep, nagging doubt far within her had been answered. There were other conversations like this: about Marilyn Monroe and Hugh Gaitskell, Little Richard and Donald Soper. Years later Upward and I wrote a sketch that grew out of these exchanges, in which Upward played a middle-aged woman who had to have everything – even how you opened a crisp packet – explained to her. I was never happy doing it, for it seemed to mock something that wasn't stupidity but genuine incomprehension. There's another echo of her, perhaps, in a routine called 'An Anthropologist Calls' – the one where a chap with bifocals and a tape-recorder turns up at a house on Tyneside and proceeds to study the occupants as if they're a tribe of South Sea Islanders. ('And this, would I be right in saying, is a piece of *stotty cake*?') All this, though, was in the future. The present was really just a

series of endless walks: southwards over the ploughed
fields, with the flints gleaming up out of the freshly turned
soil and the gulls milling overhead, to tiny villages sleeping
in the autumn mists, through the grounds of decaying
country houses – empty since the war – where the grass
grew up six feet high against the windows and there were
pheasants nesting in the smashed conservatories. Norfolk
was full of these places – great ruined barracks which no
one could afford to keep up any more, where the agent
might call twice a year. Once, I remember, we broke into
one through a tumbledown side-door and stood in what
would have been the hallway. The floorboards were green
with mould and there were wild mushrooms growing up
the staircase. The kitchen was piled with ancient rubbish,
and children's toys and old sardine cans lay under the
mouse-droppings.

One of Upward's favourite maxims, often dished out in
BBC rehearsal rooms, once at least in the tense moment
while we lurked behind the stage-curtain, was that no one
ever bides their time. Later, thinking about the Parmenters
– something I used to do long after the last traces of reality
had been stripped from my memory of them – I realised
that the time I'd spent with them was a proof of this, that
what I'd imagined to be a kind of treading water was actually a deliberate paddling towards the shore. To have no
plans, after all, isn't necessarily to be excluded from plans. I
suppose if I'd had any sense I'd have suspected that I was
using the Parmenters to compensate myself for something
I didn't have, but I was twenty years old, and the implications of what I was doing scarcely occurred to me. It was
1960 now, 1961. Kennedy was in the White House and the
papers were full of the H Bomb and CND, news of which
had even percolated to Yarmouth (Mother thought they
were 'a dirty lot of students', I remember, who could do
with a wash) but I hardly noticed. I'd slipped out of life, I
suppose, left the real world of the Sun Alliance and wattle-
necked dignitaries proceeding to the senior staff luncheon
room, for an alternative universe made up of the
Parmenters' kitchen, rain falling over the cornfields, rooks

soaring through the dead air and old Parmenter mumbling over his seed catalogues by the fire. And in an odd way it was a kind of comfort to know that all this existed, that you could fill the newspapers with dire warnings about Russia and the Bomb and still have people like the Parmenters (I tried Mr Parmenter once on CND and got the usual blank look) who simply refused to take any notice of them. In fact there was something breathtaking about the Parmenters' detachment. You got the feeling that had the news bulletins suddenly announced that there were Soviet warships off Gorleston and a row of nuclear warheads trained on East Anglia, Mr Parmenter would merely have pulled down the blinds, shovelled more coal on the fire and pretended that it wasn't happening. At the time I think I rather admired them for this. Even now a bit of me still sympathises with old Parmenter. After all, how many people who've lived through the last forty years wouldn't admit that it was all so much rubbish? But the problem was that none of these things – rain coming in on the wind, Mary's face in the fire-light, Horace pretending to write his name on a piece of paper and then slyly pushing the pen away – were detachable from the others. And of course I never knew. But, then, how could I?

*

And all this time, of course, I was thinking about Upward. When he'd been transferred to the other unit back in Cyprus, we'd agreed that we'd try and stay in touch. Even at this stage there'd been a vague plan that we should start writing sketches with a view to sending them in to the radio – the Variety halls were dying on their feet by this stage and everybody knew it was the BBC that counted. But then when we were back in England he got posted somewhere on the south coast, and by the time I was out of the army he'd disappeared somewhere and the letters started coming back 'Not known'. I suppose if I'd had any guts I'd have tracked him down, written to the army authorities and asked them to forward letters, but

somehow I didn't. It was just a fire that I kept quietly
stoked up – the hillside in Cyprus, Captain Groves and the
smoke rolling up from the village. The same was true of all
the other things that went on outside the Parmenters' front
room. Yarmouth, the Sun Alliance, family – it was all still
boiling away, just as it always had done, but somehow
distant and second-hand, as if whatever happened took
place behind a pane of glass, and the words were spoken by
voices I could barely hear. Counting National Service I'd
been at the Sun Alliance office nearly five years, had my
salary raised to ten pounds a week and got promoted to
something called assistant supervisor, which basically
meant stopping the clerks from flicking paper darts at each
other. I can just about remember the person I was at
twenty-one – tallish, not bad-looking – the butter-coloured
hair I'd had when I was a kid had gone sandy by now –
dressed up to the nines in a light-grey suit with the tie
gathered up in what was called a Windsor knot, spending my
time phoning up people who wanted to cash in their life
insurance, nodding respectfully while old Penworthy went
on about his pet scheme to update the commission agents'
address file. That was the sort of thing you talked about in
insurance companies in 1961. I think, though I don't know,
and I never asked, that Mother was proud of me. I used to
go and see her sometimes on Saturday afternoons – they
still made you work on Saturday mornings in those days –
and it was never any good. Poor Mother! Somehow in the
years since the shop had gone and Father had died she'd
grown smaller and less solid – not diminished in the way
that people in books are said to 'fade away', but kind of
worn-down and querulous. I used to look at her sometimes
as she fussed around Uncle Ralph's lounge, scooping up
books – she'd taken to reading those ghastly novelettes
with titles like *All She'd Dreamed* – or hunting for tea cups
with feeble, little old lady movements, and marvel at what
time had done to her.

Still, even in her dog days, Mother wasn't quite without
resource. In particular, she'd got to know an old woman
called Mrs Moss who lived a couple of doors away, and the

two of them spent long hours frowsting in each other's front rooms or going in to Yarmouth on the bus and turning over the stuff in the shilling arcades. Mrs Moss – she was a tall, gaunt old girl with steel-rimmed spectacles – was a member of some odd religious sect, it might have been the Jehovah's Witnesses or even the Plymouth Brethren, and she was always trying to steer the conversation round to whether Mother was 'saved'. I sat through one or two of these sessions – endless debauches of weak tea and sugary biscuits – and came away with the most terrible feeling of depression: I can remember Mrs Moss, who was perhaps about ten years older than Mother, sitting up to administer the tea, and she looked exactly like a deathshead. I suppose if I'd have been less self-centred I'd have done something about Mother, fixed up to take lodgings together, say, or taken her out to places, but of course I didn't. Even now I can still kick myself for what I know I felt about Mother when I was twenty-one or thereabouts, that she was just a dreadful kind of encumbrance who as soon as she saw me would start sniffing about Uncle Ralph or the pittance they gave her as a widow's pension. But she was lost to me, you see, in the way that most of that early life of Father and Betty in the back room of the shop was lost. Once around this time, I remember, I had to cycle through Southtown one Saturday and for some reason I stopped to look at the shop. It sold woollen baby clothes or something by this stage, and there was a draggled, middle-aged woman standing in the doorway next to the sub-post office chewing her underlip with the kind of look on her face that you knew meant they hadn't had a customer all day. Well, there was the place where I'd been born, spent my childhood, sat poring over the *Eagle* and *Look and Learn*, while Father quietly went bankrupt in the next room, and it meant nothing to me. Or hardly anything. I was much more concerned with the afternoon I was going to spend at the Parmenters' and the walk I knew I was going to take with Mary.

By this stage the Parmenter thing had been going on six or seven months. Probably you won't believe me if I say

that I don't have any concrete memories of it. The back-
drop is all there in my mind – to this day I could tell you
the titles of half a dozen books on the Parmenters' solitary
bookshelf – but what was said and done has disappeared
somewhere. What I remember most, of course, is Mary –
coming up the track to the house once on a misty afternoon in the early spring, with the cows clustered up close
to the fence and fog hanging over the edge of the fields,
and seeing her from a long way off doing something in the
yard; another time watching her hanging out clothes to dry
on the line, and the wide sweep of her hair dragging away
from her forehead. Even by then we hardly said anything
to each other. And if anyone had asked me why I felt the
way I did about her I couldn't have told them. Just something to do with her quietness, mildness, the idea that you
could say whatever you wanted and she'd just smile back,
a kind of tremulous, subdued excitement I always felt
whenever I was with her. The Parmenters, true to form,
were completely matter of fact about it all. In fact there
were times when I suspected them of encouraging the
affair: ostentatiously clearing out of the house on Sunday
afternoons on fanciful-sounding errands, or commissioning
us to take Horace for a walk in the fields.

Once, at one of these times, she said: 'You're boiling up
on account of me, aren't you?'

'I suppose I am.'

'Dad said you were. Said he could tell.'

I took her in my arms then. She didn't resist, just kind of
sagged forward with her head against my shoulders while
I kissed the side of her face and watched out for Horace,
who could be heard thrashing about in the undergrowth
fifty yards away. If I'd had any sense I'd have said goodbye
to the Parmenters there and then, gone back to Yarmouth
on my bike and never returned, but of course I didn't. I just
assumed that because I'd set my heart on something, it
would work out. From the point of view of the world I'd
been brought up in, this was quite par for the course.
People fell over themselves to 'settle down' in those days.
A girl who wasn't engaged by the time she was twenty-one

lived in terror of being thought on the shelf, and the Sun Alliance was full of earnest nineteen-year-olds saving up for their weddings.

Anyway, I don't recall the preliminaries. I just remember deciding one day – in the way that you decide you need a new suit or your car needs servicing – that it had to happen. The curious thing was that I knew somehow I hadn't really made a decision at all, that I was caught up in something that was impossible to get out of. I remember reading a book once about a hotel cashier itching to leave home and start a new life with his mistress, who suddenly finds that somebody has left the hotel safe open. After what seems like an age, he decides not to take the money, only to discover that somehow the safe is shut and the money lying in his hand. That was how I felt about Mary. I think that in an odd way she knew it too. Certainly that's the only explanation I can find for what happened next. It was sometime in April, one of those bitterly cold days in Norfolk when the wind scrapes against your face like steel wool, with rain coming in from the sea. All that morning I'd been mooching about in my digs, listening to the comedy shows on the light programme or trying to read the *Sunday Express*, but mostly just brooding about Mary. By the queerest coincidence the previous day had brought a letter from Upward – the first I'd had in months – from an address somewhere in the Midlands. It didn't say much – Upward's letters never did – just things about sketches he was writing, and I remember sticking the envelope in my shirt pocket as I lugged the bike down the steps of my digs with the idea of reading it properly later. In the end I don't know if I ever did.

I got to the Parmenters about half-past two, confidently expecting to find the lot of them in a coma in front of the fire, but no, there was no one much about, just the old lady asleep as usual in her chair, and Mary folding up newly-starched sheets from a pile on the kitchen table, so I had a cup of tea from a pot that might have brewed an hour ago and sat and watched her. After a bit she had to put the sheets away in the airing cupboard, and for some reason, not really knowing what I was doing, I trailed after her. And that's about it, really. When we did finally go to bed about an hour later I don't remember much about it, just a curious look on her face at one point, and then waking from what seemed like a day-long sleep, but was actually about five minutes, and lying there in complete silence except for the sound of the pigeons in the eaves, with the light fading in the distance and the wind rushing at the big, square window.

I don't know if Mary actually went and told her mother what we'd done, but from that day onwards there was never any doubt that we were going to get married. The thought of *not* getting married barely occurred to me. To find myself at twenty-one, married to a girl of twenty and living in a two-bedroom terrace somewhere in Northtown seemed a perfectly reasonable destiny. Even at that age, despite the army and Upward, I didn't have the wit to look beyond the Yarmouth backstreets, the sea and the dunes. It was how people were in those days. If you'd have asked any of the clerks at the Sun Alliance what they wanted out of life, nine times out of ten it would have been some moon-faced grocer's daughter from Gorleston, two kids and a semi-detached. I was just the same. About 20 per cent of me still pined for the days I'd spent with Upward and the promise they'd seemed to hold, but by far the larger part of me wanted to marry Mary, live in a house that was my own, wake up next to her in bed in the morning. I suppose that seems a fairly humble ambition. All I can say is that it didn't then. Birth. Childhood. Work. Marriage. Death. People didn't kid themselves they were going to live for ever in those days.

The next six months I can't begin to piece together, mostly because nothing very much happened. Any self-respecting Yarmouth family whose daughter had announced she was getting married would have been falling over itself in excitement by this time, but I knew enough about the Parmenters by now to realise that this wasn't their style. In fact I sometimes wonder whether old Parmenter didn't view the thought of acquiring a son in law as about on a par with buying a pig. As for Mary, I never did find out what she thought about it. All I can remember is the silences. We used to sit there in the evenings by the fire, while the Parmenters regarded us in a kind of bovine, matter of fact but I think approving way. Oddly enough, the only person who showed the least animation at the prospect of my getting married was Mother. Somehow, probably through Mrs Moss, who had a county-wide intelligence network of this sort, she'd 'found out' about the Parmenters – who they were, where they lived, who they were related to – enough at any rate to be completely horrified. It puzzled me a bit to think that Mother, who'd greeted any piece of news I'd brought her in the past five years with paralysing indifference, should have been so upset by the thought of me marrying Mary. In the end, though, I realised that she regarded it as a kind of personal insult. I can remember her standing in Uncle Ralph's kitchen – somehow the memory is much more vivid to me than anything connected to Mary – telling me that I was 'throwing myself away' (she actually used those words) and then crumpling up in a way that I hadn't seen since the FOR SALE boards went up in the square. At the time I can remember being mostly indifferent to this – I'd had an idea that Mother was going to be 'difficult'. Now I think that in its way this kind of disapproval was faintly impressive. It showed that for all the horrors of the past five years – and from Mother's point of view they were horrors – she'd managed to keep her dignity. All the same, I know that I didn't take the slightest notice. Maybe if Father had been alive the two of them could have talked me out of it, but Mother was fighting a losing battle and she knew it.

In the end we got married almost a year to the day since I'd first turned up at the Parmenters to pick blackcurrants. It was the very end of the summer, with the beech leaves already turning gold above the Parmenters' yard, and I remember standing outside the church – it was a tiny affair in the middle of a field a couple of miles from the farm – watching the people stream down the hill from the road

while the breeze from the sea ripped over the wheat and
Horace, who'd been pressed into service as Best Man,
shambled around in the vestibule sucking boiled sweets
out of a paper bag. Getting married is an odd business. It's
as if the whole thing was designed to terrify you, or at any
rate to leave you with a feeling of huge unease, as if all the
people staring at you back in the body of the church were
thinking 'It's your turn now you bastard, yes, you, you
bastard, and now see how you like it!' Most of the guests I
didn't know from Adam – I think they were mostly relatives of the Parmenters – but Uncle George and Aunt
Sheila had come up from Fram for the day and there were
one or two of the people from work. Mother and Mrs Moss
sat at the very back of the church like a couple of ghouls
and declined to attend the reception. I remember being
exhilarated and cast down by turns, one moment thinking
about the two week honeymoon we were having at
Sheringham and the £20 the Sun Alliance had given us, the
next feeling a bit annoyed that Upward hadn't bothered to
reply to the invite I'd sent him. And all the while the thing
simply surging on around us – the rows of stolid Norfolk
faces in their pews, Horace quietly shoving another sweet
in his mouth when he thought no one was looking, Mary's
face under the veil, Mother crying in the background. Oh,
it was a proper Norfolk wedding all right, even down to the
pony and trap to take us back to the reception, and the set
of bells I later discovered – we were staying the first night
at the Parmenters' – that some wag had tied to the bed.

*

From time to time in the 70s, sparked by a feature in the
TV Times or a newspaper interview, we used to get letters
from people who'd known us earlier on. Occasionally the
connections they claimed went back as much as fifteen
years. Scriptwriters knocked into in BBC canteens wrote
from obscure towns in the north of England to criticise
recent appearances and offer 'fresh material'; novelty acts
with whom Upward might have exchanged half a dozen

words backstage in 1965 re-emerged to claim guest-spots
on forthcoming shows. Nearly always well disposed, sometimes a bit less so, these letters had one common factor – a
kind of telescoping of past time that pushed their writers
into areas of our lives where we knew they'd never been.
Taken together, the vision they offered was unsettling – a
sort of alternative life full of stages never trodden, cues
eternally missed, and yet so plausible as to cast endless
doubt on your own memories. To put it another way, in a
world of vague reminiscence, anything seemed possible. At
the same time, I had to admit that my own memories of
Upward fell into the same unreliable pattern. Looked at
from the point of view of strict chronology, he instantly
dissolved away to nothing, popped up again in the most
unlikely places. It was only by trying exceptionally hard to
recreate these dead landscapes that I could prove he
hadn't been there. Somehow the early 60s is one of these
grey areas, a time when Upward is there in memory but
not in fact. Upward, Brenda and the Minerva – all of them
somehow belong to this period, run in and out of my
memories of Yarmouth, Mary and the Parmenters, for all
that some part of me knows they were never there.
Perhaps this is just a classic showbusiness delusion – *the*
classic showbusiness delusion – assuming that whatever
touches the centre of your life will always touch the rest.
On the other hand, Upward himself was fond of saying –
although these mightn't have been his exact words – that
glamour would always crowd out the non-glamorous.
Whatever the truth, when I think of those days it's always
in terms of continuity, things moving forward, worlds in
view, not the dreadful kind of half-life I know it to have
been.

*

We started off living in a two-bedroomed terrace in
Kenilworth Road in the Northtown, plausibly represented
by Mother – who had probably never ventured down it in
her life – as the worst street in Yarmouth. Do you

remember those old back-to-back terraced houses? Ours cost £200 a year, and the first thing we had to do on the day we arrived was to burn sulphur to drive out the bugs. Kenilworth Road! It's odd that you can live for two years in a place and yet have no idea of what it was like. But I remember the downstairs lay-out, which was simply a front door opening into the main room, followed by a kind of back-parlour, with a tiny kitchen behind. The Parmenters had given us pieces of furniture as a wedding present – huge mahogany sideboards and tables that were too big for the rooms and lay around the place taking up space, as if the Queen of Brobdingnag had dropped them there by mistake. The lavatory was outside in the yard. There was a whole row of them running down the back of the street, and early in the mornings the smell hit you in the face like camphor. We hadn't been there more than a week before the bugs returned, of course, and one of my strongest memories is of cooking something on the rickety gas-stove and watching one fall splash! into a pan of milk.

Later on I tried very hard to recreate that time at Kenilworth Road and work out exactly where it had all gone wrong, but I never quite managed it. It was all too mixed up with other things, from later and before: Mother's face, the view out to sea from my office stool, the Parmenters' kitchen. At first it wasn't too bad. We were only a couple of months married in those days, and I can remember coming back early in the evening with a pint of shrimps or a couple of crabs from the fish-market, and having them for tea in the parlour, with the late sun coming in over the rooftops and the lines of washing. The idea was that Mary would look for work, in a shop perhaps or one of the local dairies, and we'd use the extra money to move somewhere better. Beyond that I don't think I envisaged anything other than that we'd be together, and that eventually there'd be children. That was how people thought in those days. Ask them what they thought they'd be doing at thirty and they'd have laughed in your face, because they knew that, more or less, it would be exactly the same: same job, same faces around you, the *Yarmouth*

Mercury on the tea-table, the crab-boats hauled up on the shale, Cromer, Sheringham and the seaside towns marching on up the coast.

What did we talk about on those evenings in the back-parlour in Kenilworth Road, with the light fading away across the yard and the noise from the street growing fainter and the bugs marching two-by-two across the ceiling? God knows. Quite often we'd just sit there until it was practically dark, not saying anything, until, getting up to fetch the tea or switch on the radio, I'd find she'd fallen asleep in her chair. Other times she used to talk about her family – not informatively, but in a kind of solicitous, anxious way. Were they all right? Was Horace all right? She was particularly exercised about Horace, I recall, worried that the Parmenters wouldn't know how to cope with him now she was gone. I remember once asking her about this, a dreadful conversation full of desperate euphemisms and wool-pullings, but crucial in that it revealed to me all kinds of things about her childhood, and the Parmenters, and the odd enclosed life of the farm.

'I mean, when did you, did anyone, realise that Horace was, well, *different*?'

'When he was five or six. I remember once, they sent a letter saying he should go to a special school.'

'What happened about that?'

'I don't know. Nothing, I suppose. Dad used to say there was no harm in a person being slow.'

'But didn't anyone …?'

'You don't *know* about Horace,' she said. 'Not like me. I used to try and help him do his sums. When he was at school. Easy ones, they were. A hundred take away ninety. Seven times seven. And he just couldn't do them. Just couldn't. And won't ever. Do you *understand*?'

Needless to say, once we'd moved in, Horace was a regular caller. He used to turn up after tea sometimes on his motorbike, in that silly, moon-faced way he had, and lounge around the place eating enormous meals or listening uncomprehendingly to the radio. Now and again I'd take him to a football match or the speedway and he'd stand there on the terrace with his mouth half open, never quite able to work out what was going on. At weekends, of course, we spent whole days with the Parmenters – endless tracts of time lost in boozing tea by the kitchen fire or helping old Parmenter with jobs around the farm. Oddly enough, I didn't mind about this. I could cope with the Parmenters, the old mad grandmother drooling over her chair – she'd last made a sensible remark about the time we got engaged – old Parmenter standing in the doorway with his jackhammer swinging in one hand and eyeing me up for an afternoon of fence-mending, the scorching fires and the endless tea, because I knew what to expect. What I couldn't cope with was the life of Kenilworth Road, the silence that hung over it and the tremendous sense of gloom that seemed to infect every activity that took place within its walls. I used to watch Mary sometimes moving around the house – clearing tea-things away from a table, say, or ironing – all the things I'd watched her doing in her mother's kitchen and marvelled at – and she did it with a dreadful, self-conscious gloom, as if I was an ogre whose castle she'd strayed into and no amount of pleading would ever let her out again. It was the same with sex. She was willing enough, I suppose, but she'd lie there with a sort of pained, absorbed look, as if what we were about to do was simple torture. I've a dreadful memory – not always brought out, but there all the same – of simply rutting away at her, slamming down on top of her so hard that she practically bounced up and down beneath me, and then going downstairs and smoking half a dozen cigarettes in front of the fire while I waited for the explosion of noise that, mysteriously, never came.

I was furious, of course, furious and puzzled, and also a bit ashamed, of myself, her and the situation we'd fetched up in, but there was nothing I could do about it. Whatever lines of communication had existed between us had simply closed down, and that was that. Occasionally, in the midst of all this, I'd embark on conversations with her, rambling affairs that invariably ground to a halt in monosyllables.

'Are you happy living here?'

'Yes.'

'Is there anything you don't have that you want?'

'No.'

'Do you love me?'

'Yes.'

Once, after one of these interrogations, I lost my temper and hit her. We were in the front room, I remember, around tea-time, with the bicycles flying past in the road outside and children's voices mingling with the noise of the gulls. I can't even recall what she said, or didn't say, only leaning over and slapping her on the side of the head, not hard, but hard enough to make her topple over onto the sofa. It sticks in my mind as one of those terrible, odd moments when everything suddenly fades away into dense, far-off surfaces and colours: the blue of the light outside, a man's figure passing not ten feet away on the other side of the window, bits of furniture turned into standing stones.

And all the while, of course, there were other things going on. For a start I was making serious attempts to find Upward. I'd sent a registered letter to the last address I'd had and even written to one or two of the other blokes in the section on the off-chance they might know where he was. It was no good though: he'd vanished off the face of the earth. At the same time I'd finally plucked up enough courage to go and see one of the high-ups at the office and tell him that I wanted a change. Officially this kind of self-promotion was frowned upon at the Sun Alliance, but curiously enough I ended up being offered a job as what was known as a 'regional agent'. This meant travelling round the area and interviewing prospective life-insurance clients, and I jumped at it – not merely because of the extra two quid a week on the table, but because the idea of getting out of the office, being my own man up to a point, rather appealed to me. Norfolk's a big county. You can travel seventy miles along the coast from Yarmouth and still not be in sight of the Lincolnshire border. And that's more or less how I spent the next year – crawling along backroads near Swaffham or Holt to talk to some shop-keeper who wanted £500-worth of life cover. Long

Stratton, Garboldisham. Mundesley. Fakenham. Thurton. Brooke. How many of those places have you heard of, I wonder? I hadn't heard of half of them myself until I went out on the road in what would have been the spring of 1962 – Godforsaken villages huddled in the mist, each with its church and its pub and half a dozen shops, and most of the adult population straining to leave for the big towns. Oddly enough, I quite enjoyed the work. It paid commission, too, which was worth having on a biggish policy – or would have been if it hadn't been for the frost that waited for me every night in Kenilworth Road.

I found out about the letters quite by accident, one night when I came home early and discovered some sheets of notepaper lying on the kitchen table. They were headed 'Dear Mother and Dad' and furnished a carefully itemised account of everything she'd done that day, right down to the grocery bill and the conversation she'd had with the man who'd come to read the gas meter, all filed away with love from your affectionate daughter Mary Parmenter. Years later – God forgive me – I wrote a sketch for Upward based on this idea: the newly-married wife writing home to her mother – the decisive shift being that Upward set it up north and delivered it with a Lancashire accent: *Dear Mam. How are you and how is little Ernie and the budgerigar? Has our Dad come home this week? Married life is very strange, but I am not letting anything get on top of me. Mrs Ackroyd from opposite says it's up to a husband to take his wife's part, and I said, yes, mine does that all the time …* Towards the end it all got a bit edgy – Upward used to speed his voice up in a relentless monotone: *It is 10.15 now and no one has been down the street for a whole minute. No actually, Mam, that's not true because I just saw a cat. Which reminds me, how is Mrs Arkwright from next door?* Upward always liked the sketch, which he said was exactly like the way a particular kind of northern woman behaved. The real letters weren't funny, or tense, just boring, quite devoid of personality or even interest. If she'd spent the time abusing me I could have understood it, but she didn't. It was all shopping lists and what we'd had for breakfast – that kind of thing.

All the same, the letters were much too big a thing to be ignored. Once I said to her:

'What do you write about?'

'What do you mean, what do I write about?'

'When you write home, what do you write about?'

'Oh, just things.'

'What kind of things?'

'Things.'

She didn't seem to mind that I knew. I used to wonder how these despatches from life at Kenilworth Road were received at the farm, whether they piled up unread in the kitchen, or whether the family sat round discussing them. I had a vision of Horace poring over them in secret, tongue hanging out of his mouth with the effort of decoding these weird signals from an alien world.

It was summer 1962 now, and we'd been married nearly a year. One night I came home from work and found her gone. I've never forgotten the stillness of that house, the light pouring in across the step of the open back door – there was a cat sunning itself, I remember, which jumped away when it saw me – the crockery piled up by the sink. I knew where she'd gone, of course, and after I'd had some tea I got back in the car and drove over to the Parmenters to collect her. They weren't in the least put out – not even by the fact that she'd apparently walked the whole way from Yarmouth – just looked at me in that dull, incurious way they had. Everything there was exactly the same – playing cards all over the table, the old woman asleep in her chair, Mrs Parmenter drowsing over a copy of *Woman and Home*.

And yet I knew that somehow I'd changed my mind about the Parmenters – that whereas in the past I'd found them nice, simple people, now I thought them simply ludicrous. I can't really explain this. I just know that by the time I got back into the car with Mary – she came willingly enough – that I never wanted to see any of them again. Later on, of course, I tried asking her what it was that had made her go, but it was no good, and I don't know that we ever had a proper conversation again. I can remember fragments of those last days, but nothing like the whole. She used to move restlessly around the place turning out drawers and looking for things she could never find, or stand in the front doorway staring vaguely down the street. And then, a week or so later, she was gone again. For some reason this time I didn't immediately shoot off to fetch her. I just sat in the house and waited. I suppose if I'd thought about it I'd have gone over there and tried to reason with her, but at the same time I knew that the Parmenters weren't people you could talk to, not in that way. You could have turned up in their yard and driven a tank through the house and they'd have squared it somehow with the world they knew, gone on playing cards or stirring the fire, and never said anything. In the end, though, about a week after she'd vanished, old Parmenter came to Kenilworth Road – a little red-faced man, dressed in the suit he'd worn to the wedding and looking faintly embarrassed. I gathered Mrs Parmenter had practically ordered him to come. As to what was said, I couldn't begin to recreate it, so hedged about was it with silences and imputations. At the end, though, something seemed to strike him and he rummaged around in the pocket of his suit.

'Got this for you,' he said, handing me a large brown envelope.

I waited until he'd gone before I opened it, though I could see the writing on the front wasn't Mary's, and shook the contents over the carpet. Five-pound notes, forty of them.

And that's the story of my married life.

*

It's not quite true to say that's the last I saw of the Parmenters. Ten years later, coming down the steps of the Blackpool Winter Gardens where we were doing a summer show, I ran smack into a tall, pasty-faced character wearing a cellophane mackintosh – the temperature was in the 80s, I remember – and carrying a thermos under his arm. It was Horace, who must have been about twenty-seven. I was in a tearing hurry, and, worse, I had a reporter from the local paper in tow to whom I was supposed to be feeding some story about the TV series, but something made me stop and say hello. He was just the same, of course – manifestly not all there, but in a way you couldn't quite put your finger on – and we talked a bit about his parents (who he maintained were 'poorly') and the farm, which was apparently just about functioning. I think he knew who I was, but when I asked about Mary he clammed up altogether and gaped at me. A bit after that he started shuffling off. There didn't seem to be anybody with him, so I never found out what he was doing outside the Winter Gardens on a July afternoon in 1972. I can remember watching him sway off down the parade, with one or two of the passers-by giving him a glance, and thinking that I ought to follow him – who knows? He might have had the rest of the family with him – but somehow I knew it wouldn't be any good.

'Who was that?' the reporter asked, not particularly interested.

'Oh,' I said. 'Just somebody I used to know.'

Yesterday I made a new friend. At least I think I did.

It's quarter to four on an iron-grey afternoon in November and I'm outside the school gates with the usual crowd of parental flotsam: the tough girls with their prams and their stabbing cigarettes; bonehead dads in their scarlet Charlton Athletic tops. A pit-bull or two on a choke-lead twists nervously. It might rain, which means that every eye intermittently rises skywards. Londoners *hate* the rain, I notice. The mildest drizzle sends them fleeing into shop doorways or to the sanctuary of the bus shelters. Daniel, soon glimpsed in the first or second knot of children, looks flustered, scuttling across the tarmac as if trying to avoid something. Or someone. A slightly older kid – not one of the usual ones – is a yard or two behind. He doesn't really hit him, more a flap of fingers on the side of the head, but what do you do? Daniel looks pale and also outraged, as if he can't quite believe anyone could do this to him. By this time I'm between the two of them, one hand on Daniel's shoulder, the other gesturing to the kid – I don't remember saying anything – what the consequences will be if he repeats the action. At this point one of the bonehead dads detaches himself from the silent throng by the gate and comes lurching across.

''Ere you, that's my fucking kid you're talking to.' Impossible to reproduce what he actually says. *Ereyou, thass my fuckenkid yer torkintew.*

About five foot seven. White T-shirt, jeans and trainers. Shaven head merging into genuine hair loss. There are hundreds of them in this part of London. It's a kind of uniform. 'Who took your purse lady?' 'Oh he was bald and wearing a white T-shirt, jeans and trainers, officer.' I look at him for a bit – there are other parents taking an interest by this stage – and then, curiously enough, remember a line that Upward once threw out in a sketch.

'That's a pity. Couldn't you part-exchange him for something?'

Bonehead takes a step forward and then stops. Even at fifty-seven I'm not the kind of bloke you take unnecessary liberties with. In the end he thinks twice about it, blinks at his kid, by now a hugely interested spectator, gives him what I take to be a playful cuff but actually sends him staggering over his heaped Umbro bag, and says in a tone of absolute ground-down weariness:

'Leave it out will yer, Neil?' Another glance at me. 'Fuckin' kids eh?'

'That's right.'

Bonehead has his cigarette packet out now, the non-professional's calling card.

'I seen you around,' he says, sweeping his hand across the vista of the school gates, as if this somehow explains our little stand-off. 'Have a fag?'

I have a fag. Daniel and Neil, meanwhile, are looking sheepishly at the tarmac, initial interest in what their dads might be about to do to one another replaced by gargantuan embarrassment.

Bonehead ('the name's Kev') turns out to be a bit of a talker. Also concerned to disseminate information about himself. Apparently he lives on one of the big estates down by the river, ('Full of fuckin' kids running around pissed out of their heads of course.') and used to work in the freight over in Silvertown until the jobs went east to the Isle of Grain. There are several other Neils and a couple of girls ('gels'), the latter back in the flat under the care of a friendly neighbour. Kev's wife works in Woolwich. Kev supports Charlton, only they're fucking hopeless this season. All the time we talk, or rather Kev talks and I nod or grunt in agreement, I notice him shooting inquisitive little glances at me. Finally at the street corner fifty yards from the school gates, where the road forks and bends round to the river, he says what six or maybe seven people a year say to me:

'Seen you before ent I?'

We bid each other farewell with a great shower of shouts and salutations – 'See yer mate!', 'Take care!' – the

way the boneheads do outside pubs. A bit later I say to
Daniel:

'Why was Neil trying to hit you?'

'Don't know.'

'Did he do it before?'

Pause. 'A bit.'

'Did you tell the teacher? Did you tell …?'

'No,' Daniel says seriously. 'That'd be grassing.'

I'll be perfectly honest. I hate all this: ten-year-olds
talking like gangster films, vicious little bastards in white T-
shirts. All the other stuff, too – the sorrowings over
wretched princesses, the football nonsense. If I had the
money I'd send Daniel to some fearful place full of boys
with names like Piers and Jonjo with regulation haircuts
and proper accents, and have him taught Latin and Greek
rather than leave Miss Cox to tell him about her boyfriend.
Only you don't, do you? Only you can't, can you? You
accommodate yourself to what's there and you make the
best of it. Like the Ngongi, arriving at the solitary oasis
with its flyblown pond half-full of stagnant water, you
thank God that there is a pond rather than simply the
parched and treeless desert.

*

The headscarves the old women wear, not changed in forty
years, eyes down over the grey pavements, the bags
balanced in either hand, down from the river, the lie of the
land set back, away from the warehouses and the pock-
marked mud.

*

Several calls from Lennie. Apparently my evening at the
Plumstead Over Sixties went down a storm. 'A knockout' is
Lennie's exact description. There's a return engagement
waiting if I want it. Plus several other similar outfits are
interested. I tell Lennie I'll let him know. Lennie's also very
keen on the BBC thing (*Nice girl. Really genned up on you*

and that), which he thinks could lead to something. Lennie's optimism is incurable. I wonder if his other clients, those Jewish harmonica players in Bethnal Green and bands of red-jacketed close-harmony singers, are subjected to the same paralysing blasts of misplaced confidence.

Actually I've already been surprisingly proactive – to use a word that's even begun to turn up in Lennie's vocabulary – over the BBC thing, to the extent of having lunch with one of the production people. Lucy, the assistant producer, looked to be about thirty-five. Over the lunch, which took place in a subdued winebar round the back of Langham Place, she filled me in on the series. As ever, Lennie had got it substantially wrong. A series called *The People In History*, full of pre-millennial cud-chewing, with a final programme featuring us in the guise of *The Comedy Men*, put together by way of old tapes and eye-witness voiceovers.

'Who's going to be talking about us?'

'Oh, I daresay you could write the list yourself. Bruce Forsyth. The Ronnies. You could probably give me some ideas.'

There was a slight edge to Lucy's voice as she said 'ideas', which made me wonder if certain aspects of *The Comedy Men* weren't altogether to her taste. Actually, meeting people like Lucy is pretty much a new experience for me. She belongs, in fact, to a social category that I've barely come across: polite, interested, slightly disdainful. Whatever she says – and she uses upper-class little-girlisms like 'gosh' and 'frightful' (as in 'frightfully expensive' and 'frightfully sweet') – has, you feel, a permanent sub-text, something like: *I may have to work at the BBC, times being what they are, but I went to Oxford and I know my way round a gallery or two and whatever cultural topics we may stray into the probability is that I know more about them than you.*

'Will there be any money in this?' I asked at the end of the pitch.

'There'll be a bit,' she said briskly. 'Not very much, though. After all, this is the BBC, darling.'

I was a bit reassured by the 'darling', which clearly came

in quotation marks, a conversational flounce she'd
borrowed from somewhere and wasn't overly happy with.
Looking at her as she ate her salad and drank sparingly
from a glass of mineral water, I wondered if I hadn't got
her slightly wrong, mistaken reserve for bitterness.

Lucy turned out to be unexpectedly knowledgeable
about Upward & King.

'I ordered some of your tapes up from the library. The
last TV series. One or two live performances someone had
filmed.'

'What did you think?'

'I thought one or two of the studio things were a bit
before their time. The one about Mrs Thatcher in the shop
I mean ... But some of the live material was, well, rather
old-fashioned.'

'Old-fashioned?'

'A bit dated.'

She meant 'offensive to women', of course. The sexism
thing hit comedy like a tidal wave in the early 80s, alongside and sometimes in association with the alternatives – a
whole new set of rules that most people in the business
could barely grasp. They threw Benny Hill off the
networks for sexism. I can remember in about 1982 doing
a student charity gig with an old bloke called Eric Hopkins,
whom we rather liked, who'd spent twenty years working
the northern club circuit. Eric, who was a great one for
flowered suits in the Max Miller style, bounced on stage,
took a look at the audience and began 'People say you are
what you eat ... Well, I'm a cunt.' I think he lasted a minute
before they booed him off.

'I'll be perfectly honest,' Lucy said, giving her lips a delicate little pat with a napkin. 'I was quite impressed. I mean,
my *father* used to like you. He said you were like
Morecambe & Wise. But when I looked I thought he was
completely wrong, that the personalities were quite
different. Kind of sad in a way.'

Kind of sad. Outside there were leaves bowling down
Mortimer Street, and a policeman on a horse was trying to
negotiate a row of bollards that someone had placed in the

road. The horse came juddering to a halt on the far pavement. In profile, leaning across the table with one hand on the Perrier bottle, caught suddenly in the early-afternoon shadow, Lucy's face looked less intent, less of today. She had little tendrils of hair that fell away from her blonde, page-boy cut, down over her ears.

'Sorry. You must get terribly fed up with people talking about you like that.'

'You get used to it.'

Whether Lucy took this as a rebuke I don't know, but she became noticeably less brisk. Even so, whatever signals she was giving off I found difficult to decode. One thing was unmissable, though. Rather like Kev from the school gates, she was a great volunteerer of information: time in job (six years, before that something in publishing), domicile, career path.

'Where do you live?'

'South-east. Plumstead. Abbey Wood way.'

'Gracious. That's a long way out. We live in Putney, but my boyfriend says he needs to be nearer to work.'

'What does your boyfriend do?'

'He's a management consultant.'

I don't know if I was supposed to be impressed by this, or indeed whether Lucy is impressed herself. Afterwards we ended up walking back together towards Oxford Circus, her departure point for a trip to interview an ex-Home Secretary ('Honestly, I think he'll be hopeless, but Graham says he once appeared on the Morecambe & Wise Christmas Show.') Ten, perhaps eleven inches shorter than me, she bobbed along at my side like a cork. She agreed to get back to me with a preliminary treatment within a week.

'Should I send it to … Lennie, is it? Or straight to you?'

'I should keep Lennie out of this.'

'I saw the other tape, you know,' she said soberly. 'The one where he …'

The one where he … I let that pass, walked off along Oxford Street, past the rows of Queen Mum calendars, hot-dog vans and leaflet purveyors. Looking back I could see her poised on the lip of the stairs and delving into her

bag, the wind whipping her hair up into a kind of helmet.
She talks extraordinarily, by the way. The way I imagine
Virginia Woolf talking. Or George Eliot.

*

As I suspected, DI Stevens turns out to be a policeman. I find
him on the pavement one morning as I come back from a
stroll by the river, one arm sprawled over the roof of a red
Mondeo, the other scanning the upstairs windows. Fiftyish, I
suppose, with grey-black hair made comic by a pair of much
darker eyebrows. As I swing into the doorway – I can see he's
waiting for me, but don't feel like making the first move – he
flaps his ID card in the air a yard away from my face.

'Ron Stevens. Fraud squad. Mind if I come in?'

'*Fraud squad?*'

''Sall right,' he says matily. 'Not about your tax return.
Just a few questions, OK?'

Apparently policemen still have those working-class
Londoner names: Ron, Dennis, Harold. Back in the 70s
Upward and I did a parody of one of the current cop
serials, in which everyone was called Dennis and talked in
what we imagined to be police argot: 'Dennis, did you lean
on Harris like I asked?' 'That's right, Dennis, I fingered his
collar good and proper.' 'But did he sing, Dennis, that's
what I want to know?' 'Sung like a bleeding canary,
Dennis. Proper nark' etc etc. Once inside, Stevens slips up
to the first floor with surprising eagerness and starts
looking at the pictures, the Water-Rat charity night and the
Palladium ensembles.

'You know,' he says delightedly. 'I used to watch you on
the TV. Friday nights. You'd come on in a coat and he'd be
sitting there by the lamp-post, and you'd say "Me and him,
we're here to entertain you."'

'And did we?'

'What? Entertain us? More often than not. You should
have stayed in the business,' he says, dropping his voice a
tone. 'I don't like these young blokes. Too chippy.'

I make us tea and he trips round the room a bit more

turning over Daniel's schoolbooks, takes a squint at the pile of videos stacked above the television.

'Still,' he says. 'It's not easy on your own, is it? Like Ernie without Eric. Ah well. You ever come across a character called Martin Cartwright?'

'The MP?'

'Was.' Stevens picks up one of Daniel's ping pong balls, flicks it in the air and catches it in the palm of his hand. The effect is surprisingly disconcerting. 'Lord Cartwright of East Mersey he calls himself now. Labour peer. Ever met him?'

'Now and again.'

'And when would that have been, sir?' Given the previous affability, the 'sir' snaps in the air like a cap pistol.

'I don't know. 1975. 1976.'

'It's all a long time ago, isn't it?' Stevens says helpfully. '1976. Do you know I was a bobby on the beat back then? Twenty-five I would have been. Would that have been about the time you knew Gavin Newsome?'

'I suppose so. Yes.'

'It's all right sir. It's amazing what they have in the files these days. Even the showbiz gossip.' He improvises gamely: ' "TV comedians Upward & King were on hand to entertain guests at Gavin Newsome's lavish charity ball. Arthur Upward remarked, 'I told the ones down the front that if they didn't feel like clapping they could rattle their jewellery.' " Remember that?'

'A bit. It was a long time ago.'

'I'm with you there. Think about it. You were a TV comedian and I was a bobby on the beat. But some people have long memories. You'd be surprised. Did you see the stuff in the papers last week?' Without waiting for me to nod, he goes on: 'Newsome's an old man now. Must be seventy at least. Most of the money's gone, too. But somebody's blown the whistle.'

Outside there are low grey clouds hanging over the approach to the river, gleaming white light beyond. Perhaps one of Turner's ships is out there instead of the tourist boats and the PLA barges. Nothing would surprise me about London now.

'What about?'

'Newsome and Cartwright. Backhanders. *Money*. Where did it all come from? Where did it all go? That charity do in 1976. The 25th of June 1976 to be exact. Who was there?'

'You tell me.'

'Gladly. Half of London. If I looked out the *Who's Who* entries we'd be here till teatime. It's all right sir. Nobody thinks you had anything to do with it. Nobody even thinks you knew what was going on. But, well, we'd like to know.'

'About what?'

'Who you saw. Who you talked to. Where you went. I know, it was twenty years ago and you were the cabaret. Or whatever. But let me tell you sir, there's old blokes in their sixties shitting themselves just now about what's coming out of the woodwork. Old women too.'

Stevens loves all this, of course. Who wouldn't? The Ngongi have a series of elemental rituals designed to enliven cold nights around the desert campfire: The Bringer Of Bad Tidings; The Teller Of Tales: He Who Saves The Scattered Flocks. From the age of three, according to the ethnologists, Ngongi children have a reasonable understanding of mimesis.

'Anyway,' he says. 'I'll come back, if I may. Give you time to think. A period of quiet reflection. If anyone rings you up – anyone out of the ordinary, that is – you'll make a note of it, won't you?'

Back on the pavement, mist is slowly descending. Stevens peers at it, steadying himself. He has terrible skin, full of smashed veins and odd runways of flesh.

'Do you know the sketch of yours I most liked?' he says, by way of a farewell. 'The one where you talked about women. You know, he'd be bragging about what he'd done the other night and you'd just say something quiet like to bring him down, and the look he'd give you would be sheer poison.'

I watch him drive off. There is, of course, no such thing as a lost world.

Talking About Boys

KING (Greta), in blonde wig and tank-top, sits in cafe.
UPWARD (Shirl), hair cascading round his shoulders, in
polka-dot dress, joins him.

KING: (*gives appraising look*) Purple suits you, you
know.

UPWARD: Aye. You can either wear it or you can't, and
I'm one of the ones that can.

They look at each other.

UPWARD: Give us a fag.

KING: Honest Shirl, I'm down to me last forty.

UPWARD: Y'tight cow … so who was it last night then?
Him as works in the abbatoir up McElligot
Street?

KING: Him? No … him as works in the funeral
parlour on Inkerman Terrace.

UPWARD: (*impressed*) Oh yeah? Where'd he take you
then?

KING: Oh, you know. The usual.

UPWARD: What? I thought the chip shop shut Thursdays?
Or was it round the bus shelter in Slug Street?

KING: As if any self-respecting girl'd let herself be
taken there! The idea! I read that Mrs
Whitehouse as writes in the papers, you know.
I know what they're after.

UPWARD: What's wrong with the bus shelter in Slug
Street? I've had some very happy moments in
the bus shelter in Slug Street.

KING: Actually he took us to the Frog and Toadstool.

UPWARD: (*gives little squeak*) Ooh! *Posh*. I suppose you'll
be telling me you were drinking Babycham
next?

KING: And anyway Shirl, you'll never believe what he said … Thing is, Shirl … Well, we're *engaged*.

(*both rise from their seats, punch the air in triumph, then sit down again*)

UPWARD: How many times have you been engaged now, Gret?

KING: Six … seven. But the thing is I've got a kind of *feeling* about this lad.

UPWARD: What's his name?

KING: Trevor. Trevor Ramsbotham.

UPWARD: What kind of a feeling?

KING: You know, a land of dreams, the two of us … doing things … together. You know. Like unblocking that drain under me mam's sink. Or putting out the rat poison last thing.

UPWARD: I'm happy for you love, I really am … have you told your mam?

KING: Actually Shirl, we haven't seen mam for a couple of nights, and – (*her gaze strays out of the window*) – oh my God! Shirl!

UPWARD: What's the matter, pet?

KING: It's him. Trevor. With his arm round some floozie. Look.

They look

UPWARD: (*dispassionately*) Aye, you're right. A real painted harlot. You're well out of that, love.

KING: I suppose I am.

UPWARD: And it's no way a classy job. I mean, fiddling around with a lot of, well, dead people.

KING: Convenient, though.

UPWARD: What?

KING: If anyone dies, that is.

UPWARD: I suppose so. So what are you doing tonight?

KING: We could go down the bus shelter in Slug Street.

The voices fade

1972

Light Goes Green

Did you hear about the disturbance at the butcher's? The butcher sat on the bacon slicer, and all the customers got a little behind with their orders.

Life, Upward used to say, was pretty much like the experience of telling jokes in front of a crowd of 300 people. I always thought there was something in this. The hasty arrival on stage, the pleased or at any rate tolerant faces of the audience, high expectations, the confidence with which you spoke the opening lines, leading to a period of uncertainty, the audience wondering if its money mightn't have been laid out better, the comedian worrying about his choice of material, wondering if there weren't time to change tack, finally either triumph or collapse, graceful withdrawal – showered with praise – or death.

'Think about it,' Upward used to say. 'The stand-up's a kind of metaphor for how most people live their lives, only more compressed. You're out there. Everybody's watching you. You want to stop, think a bit about what you're saying, work out if they like you or not, but there's no time, you just have to press on regardless, and in the end they'll either start clapping or chuck things at you.'

Like most of Upward's opinions about life, or Upward's opinions about comedy, it was hard to know how seriously he meant you to take this. Newspaper articles about 'the secret of laughter' always annoyed him: they struck at the uncertainty which I suppose was his own definition of its mystery.

'Just imagine,' he would say, gloomily, 'how bloody awful it would be if there really was a secret. Suppose Arthur Haynes' (a comedian Upward disliked) 'really did know the trick of telling a joke that made you laugh, every time, bang on the button. Think how tedious it would be.

Like asking some absolutely unattainable girl for a shag and knowing all the time that she was going to say "yes".'

For some reason I've always connected these remarks to the atmosphere of Temple Chambers – part of a compound made up of red buses in the Strand, endless marble corridors and the scent of coffee beans. In fact they date from a slightly later period, and in the case of Upward's theories of comedy come from as much as two or three years farther on. Perhaps this is just an example of Upward's ability to impose himself on things, to dominate situations or stretches of time in which he was only fleetingly present. I don't know. At any rate, it was impossible to separate him from Truefitt & Hislop's duck-egg green carpets, high ceilings and the clogged, blue-grey Embankment skies.

What was I doing in London? For a couple of months after Mary had walked out I hung around in Yarmouth wondering what to do with myself – I had this vague feeling that if I bided my time she'd miraculously turn up on the doorstep again – but in the end I could see it was no good. Even more than that, though, I was tired of Yarmouth and the life I'd been living there all those years. It wasn't dislike – after all, I'd been born there and most of the important things that had happened to me had done so in the couple of square miles between St Nicholas's Church and Southtown – just boredom with the gulls and the sight of the Pleasure Beach Ferris wheel looming over the horizon and the eternal smell of salt. God knows there are worse things to smell outside your front door first thing in the morning than salt hanging in the air, but at the time I didn't see it. Maybe if Mother had wanted me to stay I'd have done it, but the truth was that she didn't seem particularly interested. I can remember going over to Uncle Ralph's one night to break the news that I was off, and her staring vaguely at me – Mrs Moss was prowling around in the kitchen as we talked – not really seeming to take it in.

Looking back I'm a bit shocked at how easily this severance was effected. In a way it's proof of how little there was to keep me. For a while I worried what to do about Kenilworth Road, which was still full of stuff the

Parmenters had given us. In the end, though, I just sold the furniture off to a second-hand dealer and sent the money to the farm. I can remember standing in the front room after they'd come to take it away with an odd sensation of something lost and irretrievable that I could never call back. A day or so later I went to London, took digs in Hammersmith – they were kept by a dusty old woman who said she'd once been ladies' maid to a duchess – and got the job at Truefitt & Hislop.

Even now I don't quite know why I was so set on the place, wanted to live there or thought it would give me what I wanted. The papers hadn't yet come up with the notion of the 'Swinging Sixties' but already there was an idea that this was the place where smartly dressed blokes were pulling in the big money. I'd absorbed plenty of this kind of propaganda in the back rows of cinemas throughout my teens. Apart from the obvious things, though, I hadn't the faintest idea of what I'd find when I got there. I can remember the first Sunday morning taking a bus into the centre with the aim of finding Chelsea, and getting hopelessly lost somewhere in Kensington, which seemed to be all dingy little squares mouldering in the rain and the shriek of kids playing in the fenced-off gardens.

Once in a blue moon Mother wrote. It was mostly stuff about people in Yarmouth and Uncle Ralph – all the old talk that I'd listened to for years, since before Father died. But at the same time I could tell that something had happened to Mother, that beneath the usual complaints about money and her relatives, she was excited about something in a way that I hadn't ever seen before. It turned out that Mrs Moss's husband had died and she'd proposed that the two of them should set up house together, and Mother, who was heartily sick of cooking Uncle Ralph's meals, was itching to accept. At the same time, Mrs Moss had some harebrained scheme for buying the lease of a cheap shop somewhere in Cromer or Sheringham and setting up as second-hand dealers. They'd even, I later found out, opened a joint bank account in anticipation. Naturally, all this was just nuts to Mother – I think she saw

it as a chance to get back within sight of the old life she'd
had – but it shocked me in a way. It wasn't just the surprise
of Mother being galvanised out of her awful little world of
slaving for Uncle Ralph, or the thought of its probable
consequences – I had this dreadful vision of Mrs Moss,
grinning her deathshead grin, guarding the till of an empty
shop crammed with flyblown lumber – as the realisation
that nothing was certain any more, that all the fixed points
were gone.

*

Truefitt & Hislop were coffee brokers, with offices in one
of those big, labyrinthine buildings between Fleet Street
and the river. The *News of the World* was fifty yards away
in Bouverie Street and people said that the file of expen-
sively dressed but slightly unreal looking women you could
sometimes see disappearing through its revolving doors
were call-girls come to sell their stories. I got the job by
replying to a newspaper ad, using a reference that I'd taken
the precaution of getting from old Penworthy before I left
Yarmouth. Before I arrived I had the idea that the place
would simply be an outsize warehouse, but in fact most of
the real business got transacted in the London and
Commercial salerooms in Mincing Lane where I sometimes got sent on errands. This was an enormous hall where
you could buy and sell anything from coffee, cocoa, hemp
and jute to exotic stuff like shellac or soya beans. Temple
Chambers was where the administrative side went on, and
the only clue as to what the firm dealt with was the tray of
samples inside the front door.

  Even by the standards of the 60s, Truefitt & Hislop was
an old-fashioned concern. The senior partner appeared in
a morning suit, and I once saw the office manager – an
extraordinary old character named Huckerby – telling off
a secretary he'd spotted eating an ice-cream in the street.
But I liked the atmosphere in the great silent chambers –
and they always were silent, even when a dozen men and

women were busily at work – and the people I met there. They were quiet, youngish blokes, mostly, with their sights set on jobs as commodity brokers, who thought this would be a good place to learn the trade. But what really struck me about Truefitt & Hislop was its complete detachment from anything resembling modern life. The Sun Alliance might have been a provincial insurance office with business practices that would have disgraced Mr Gradgrind, but at least the people who worked there knew which decade they lived in, knew, too, of the effort that would be needed to maintain themselves into the next. At Truefitt & Hislop, despite occasional panics over bad harvests in Brazil, the sense of detachment was absolute. I remember seeing one of the junior partners pick up a newspaper a day or so after the 1964 General Election. The City had been in a flap about a Labour victory for nearly a fortnight, there was talk of a run on the pound and money leaving the country, rumours of this agitation had even penetrated as far as Temple Chambers, but no, this young exquisite simply registered the picture of Harold Wilson standing on the steps of Number 10, sniffed slightly and then flipped the paper over to the sports page. Wilson, you see, was just some dreary little man who'd bamboozled the public into electing him Prime Minister, not someone you could take seriously.

As for the clerical duties required of you at Truefitt & Hislop, these were slightly less arduous than the upkeep of old Penworthy's boxes of address cards. Essentially, as a clerk your job was to file orders as they came in and liaise with the warehouses – these were mostly down by the docks – to make sure that they got filled on time. There was the occasional flap about getting letters ready in time for the early evening post, but by and large you were left to yourself and provided that you got on with your work nobody took the slightest interest in you. Oddly enough I didn't mind the sense of anonymity that working in a place like Truefitt & Hislop gave you. After what had happened in the last couple of years I was happy enough to be left alone. From a window in the big staff room at the back of

the building, which doubled up as a kitchen, there was a
view out over the Thames and I used to stand there sometimes in the autumn afternoons as the dusk stole up over
Temple Gardens and the lights began to go on along the
Embankment, watching the distant passage of the boats.
Other times I used to sit on a bench outside the Howard
hotel watching the taxis thunder up towards the Strand,
interested in the throng of aquarium faces behind their
glass. It seems to me that I was perfectly happy. And yet all
the time I knew I was waiting for something – I had no idea
what it was, simply that it was there – that would swoop
down and alter my life for ever.

It was a dull, grey morning in November – not much of
a day, I remember – with fine rain falling over the roof of
Temple church and its dingy gardens. In the distance a
church clock – not Temple, but another one, further away
towards Fleet Street – was striking eleven. Time hung
heavy at this hour. With the first post sorted and dealt with,
there was usually nothing to do until after lunch, sometimes not even then. I used to go and stand in a kind of
communal office, halfway between the partners' rooms
and the main area where most of the clerks worked, where
there was a noticeboard and an old jellygraph machine for
copying circulars that was always breaking down. I was
hanging about here smoking a cigarette and reading an
announcement about the firm's Christmas dinner – which
sounded a melancholy affair – when another of the clerks,
a bloke called Benson, wandered diffidently into view.

'There's a chap wanting you in reception.'

'Someone from London and Commercial?'

An occasional visitor from the sale room was about the
limit of my dealings with the outside world at Truefitt &
Hislop.

'Don't think so. Never seen him before. Funny little
bloke in a Trilby hat.'

This was unprecedented. I went off in pursuit. To the left
of the reception area, always manned by the same grim
receptionist, there was a small room where messengers
from the warehouses and the other city firms that Truefitt

& Hislop 'corresponded' with were sometimes put to wait. Here, behind panelled glass windows, head down over the *Daily Mirror*, a short, squat man with red hair sat smoking a cigarette. It was Upward. Seeing me, he dropped the cigarette into a cup of coffee that rested on the arm of his chair and folded the paper under his arm.

'You took some finding.'

'So did you.'

'I wrote to your mam,' Upward said, a touch accusingly. 'Took near on a year to get a reply.'

'Never mind.'

At twenty-five – which was the age I reckoned him to be – Upward seemed to be hurtling towards middle age. He was fatter than I remembered, and the set of his face was more pronounced that it had been in the Catterick days. He looked – and I'm conscious of thinking this at the time – like a number of things: a prosperous northern businessman in London on a day-trip, a 'likely lad', an extra from an Ealing comedy. All these images were somehow enhanced by the suit he'd got on: a weird, three-piece affair in a dazzling red check. Upward caught me looking at the suit.

'Nice cloth, isn't it? Apparently the Household Cavalry use it for making up hunting caps.'

'It looks like a carpet.'

'I'm thinking of wearing it on stage,' Upward said easily. 'Like Maxie. Look, this is a line of old women in a bus queue, see?'

He went into a kind of crouch and made a few movements that for some reason were extraordinarily like that of someone elderly holding a heavy bag and becoming steadily more irritated by the non-arrival of a bus. I laughed out loud.

'Got to see someone in Aldwych. What time d'you get off for lunch?'

'Half-past twelve. Quarter to one.'

'I'll come back then then. All right?'

'All right.'

We said goodbye at the lift, and I walked back to the room with the noticeboard and the jellygraph machine, where a secretary was copying a circular that had something to do with sugar futures – an area in which Truefitt & Hislop took a subsidiary interest: '*beetroot first running 88 per cent analysis f.o.b. Continental parts … 96 per cent c.i.f. London/Liverpool.*' I stayed there for over an hour, aware of my surroundings, but mentally detached from everything except the spectacle of Upward standing by the lift shaft in his scarlet suit.

He was waiting in the street when I went downstairs at 12.30. In the interval the wind had caught his hair, lifting it off his head to show the beginnings of a small bald patch beneath.

'You're going bald.'

'Am I?' Upward fingered the crown of his scalp without much interest. The intervening hour seemed to have depressed him a bit, somehow taken the bloom off our reunion. The scarlet suit, I noticed, badly needed brushing.

'See your bloke in Aldwych?'

'Wasn't a bloke.'

Being encouraged to admit that he'd spent the last hour with a woman, however innocuous the meeting might have been, had a galvanising effect on Upward's spirits. His eyes sparkled. He aimed a small, delicate punch at my shoulder.

'Anyway. 'Ow've you been?'

As we walked up the hill towards Fleet Street, past the *News of the World*, where print lorries jockeyed for position and fat men in raincoats clustered on the steps, I started to tell him something about why I'd left Yarmouth, Mary, London, the years that had passed. At intervals Upward nodded or made some barely relevant comment, but I could see that his mind was far off, wrapped up in its own affairs. This, it now seems to me, was completely typical of him. When he sought people out it was because he had something he wanted to say to them, needed an audience. Even now, striding up a London backstreet with someone he hadn't seen for four years, he was completely self-absorbed, listened out of politeness, waited for the moment when he could unload all the serious business collected in his own head.

There was a pub halfway along Fleet Street, round the corner from the *Daily Telegraph*, called the Cross Keys. It was one of those places – there were dozens of them in the 60s – supposed to have an 'atmosphere', which in this case meant that bands of journalists hung around drinking brandy and treading their cigarette ends into the dun-coloured carpet. Upward claimed to have eaten an early lunch. I realised this was simply his way of making sure that the conversation proceeded on his lines. Sure enough, while I ate a sandwich, he started on one of the long, disconnected monologues that I remembered from army days, a kind of recapitulation of Upward's life to date in which fantasy, prejudice and fact came uncomfortably mingled together. Even now, over thirty years later, I can remember whole sentences of this harangue, so mesmerising was the way Upward delivered it.

'Had two years of it now, I mean doing it *professional-like*. Up north, mostly. You ever been up north, Ted? Well, y'should. Might teach you a thing or two. I mean, they're still livin' in the Dark Ages compared to, compared to …' He stopped and looked round for some point of comparison between northen doughtiness and southern softness, but found only journalists, brandy glasses and cigarette smoke. 'Was stopped on a train near Sheffield, and just to amuse myself I started counting the factory chimneys. Well, I got to thirty-seven before the train went on … Staying in the bed and breakfasts, too, boy. That'll show you a bit of life. Chamber pots under the bed, toast like bleeding paving stones … You know the one about the black man that walked into a pub in Hartlepool with a parrot on his shoulder? Talking parrot that ordered a pint and asked for a game of cribbage. And so the landlord says, interested-like, "Where did y'get that then?" And the parrot looks down at the black man and says, "There's bleeding hundreds of them in the jungle in Africa …"'

There was a lot more of this. Listening to it, I remembered another of Upward's characteristics, his trick of picking up conversations as if they had only just been interrupted, no matter how many hours, or in this case

years, lay between them. In the end I lost interest and just
stared out of the window, where leaves were blowing along
the street and couples with umbrellas picked their way in
and out of the traffic, back again at the now deserted bar.

'Sorry if I'm boring you,' Upward said, without irony.
'You know how y'mind runs on when you've not had
anybody to talk to. What time is it?'

It was twenty past two.

'I must be getting back.'

'Must you? All right. Well, it's been nice seeing you,'
Upward said vaguely.

We picked up our coats and stood for a moment around
the bar – horribly bleak and cheerless, it now seemed to me
– which contained only the barman polishing glasses,
barely visible behind a blanket of smoke. Almost as an
afterthought, Upward said:

'Doin' anything tonight?'

'No.' It was the truth, too.

'Well, come here then.' He fished in his pocket and
produced a small rectangle of pasteboard. It read: *Minerva
Club. London's finest niterie. Eight till late. Members only*.

'What happens at the Minerva Club?'

Upward smiled, a smile I remembered from the platoon
details at Catterick – half pleasurable anticipation (things
might get better), half gloomy foreboding (things will
probably get worse).

'I do, you daft bugger. Arthur Upward entertains. Songs,
sketches, jokes old and new. Come about nine.'

'All right.'

Outside in Fleet Street the afternoon was already
turning grey. Upward swivelled on his heels, made a mock
salute with two fingers against the side of his head, and
then plunged off in the direction of the Strand. I waited
until he was lost to view before turning back down
Bouverie Street to Temple Chambers, where the afternoon
post had come in and there was a pile of telephone
messages over the desk together with a note from one of
the partners asking me to go round to Weingott's in High
Holborn to pick up a cigar humidor. For a time I tried to

deal with these calls to duty, but it was no good. Something had wound down inside, ground to a halt, that could never be restarted. At the same time, something else had begun to march forward. Whether it was the memory of Upward haranguing me in the filthy pub in Fleet Street or the glimpse of something else beyond it that prompted this, I don't know, but I knew – knew beyond all shadow of a doubt – that my life would never be the same again.

*

Over the next few months, through a mixture of dropped hints and direct questioning, I managed to work out what Upward had been up to in the four years since we'd last met. Much of it, as he'd maintained, had been spent in the north of England, but not all of it – by no means all – as a professional comedian. So far as I could make out, there'd been one or two precarious periods ('dodgy times', Upward called them) when he'd been reduced to taking clerking jobs, at one point even selling things door-to-door. According to Upward, he had worked successively as a bookie's runner, a bakery assistant, an apprentice barman, a petrol pump attendant, a cinema usher and, finally, as a vacuum cleaner salesman.

For some reason Upward liked talking about his brief career selling vacuum cleaners.

'That was when I realised I had to do something – lugging the things round the backstreets, trying to flog 'em to housewives on the never-never.'

'But I thought you said all you needed to sell things door-to-door was patter. Surely you could do that?'

'Aye, but it's *technical* patter ent it? How much dirt it could pick up and how you could poke it under chair covers. There was a bloke in our office who got fascinated by them. You know, so that if ever some woman wanted a demonstration he'd lay all the parts out on the carpet and show how they worked. Got dozens of orders, he did.'

There was a bitterness about Upward as he said this.

Failure, even in the comparatively unexalted trade of vacuum cleaner selling, rankled with him.

'I thought being a door-to-door salesman was a good way of picking up women?'

'You thought wrong.'

In the end, however, chance had supervened. Somewhere up north in the course of his travels – Preston? Bolton? Skelmersdale? – Upward had fallen in with an old connection from the Eight Lancashire Lads, who now worked as a booking agent. This man had got him an engagement at a working men's club somewhere else in the north – Accrington? Leeds? Lancaster? – where someone from the northern branch of the BBC light programme had happened to hear him. This had led to two or three radio broadcasts, not too badly received, after which Upward had decided to chance his arm in London. By the time we met at Temple Chambers, he'd been there a couple of months.

Three years on the road in the north, whether selling vacuum cleaners or doing stand-up in working men's clubs, had made Upward even tougher, if that was possible, even more self-contained. In the army I'd had the feeling that though he kept himself away from people he was uncertain about them, and that the faintest overture of friendliness would have been returned with interest. All that had gone. In its place came a complete confidence in his abilities, mixed with an eerie singlemindedness over putting those abilities to work. Professionally, too, he'd moved off into different territory, talked about 'reveals' and 'snaps' (a routine where you use a small joke as a stepping stone to the crescendo), and 'holding' an audience. It was from Upward, for instance, that I first got hold of the idea that certain jokes couldn't be used because they were 'too funny'. I don't mind admitting that all this rather frightened me, that whereas in the past I'd been simply admiring of Upward's expertise, now I was rather awed by it, wondering whether it hadn't been achieved at too great a cost, whether the Upward I'd known in the army hadn't been pushed aside by this new, tough-minded intruder. All this, though, lay in the future.

*

The Minerva turned out to be in Frith Street, stuck
between a strip club and a derelict Chinese restaurant.
Armed with Upward's card, on which he had scribbled
Please Admit Bearer – A. Upward, there was no trouble
about getting in. Inside the path lay downward and ever
downward, along sharply descending passages and flights
of stairs, through doorways where burly men in dinner
jackets lurked vigilantly, to a kind of cavern far under-
ground containing a dancefloor, a raised stage and a small
bar. Twenty feet above, around three sides of the room, a
gallery stretched away into darkness. Here at the lower
level about thirty people sat at rickety tables grouped
round the edge of the dancefloor listening to a florid man
in a tuxedo singing a medley of Beatles songs. I had been
there less than a minute when Upward came shambling
out of a side door by the corner of the stage and veered
over the dancefloor towards me, nearly colliding with a
waitress dressed in fishnet stockings and a halter top who
was approaching from the other side.

'I should leave the champagne,' Upward said, breathing
heavily from the dash across the dancefloor. 'It costs two
quid a glass. That's all right darlin',' (to the waitress), 'we'll
have a couple of beers.'

We had a couple of beers. Upward drank his in tiny,
fastidious sips. Dressed in an evening suit – something I'd
never seen him in before – he looked pale, hugely ill at
ease.

'Are you all right?'

'Course I'm all right,' Upward said belligerently. He
looked around the room once or twice, getting nods from
the bar staff and a stout man who stood by the stage. 'Not
many here tonight.'

'How many do you usually get?'

'Depends. Fridays and Saturdays are the big nights.
That's when you get people down for the weekend. And
foreigners. Weekends, like I say, it depends. But it's quality

that counts, not quantity. Y'see that bloke over there?' – he motioned up to the gallery, where a grave-looking man in spectacles was reading the *Evening Standard* – 'that's a Labour MP, that is. And them two there,' (two crop-haired middle-aged men in raincoats by the bar) 'who d'y' think they are?'

'Peers of the realm?'

'Plain clothes policemen, more like. Always coming in to see if we're breaking the by-laws.'

'Do you break the by-laws?'

Upward laughed nervously. It was difficult to know what to make of him in this new environment. Above our heads the gallery was filling up.

'Got to go,' he said, after a minute or so of silence. 'On in twenty minutes. You just stay here. Anything you want, ask the waitress.'

I watched him move off across the dancefloor, glance up for a moment at the man in the tuxedo, then disappear.

It was about half-past nine. The man in the tuxedo stopped singing abruptly, lit a cigarette and went over to talk to somebody in the small orchestra at the side of the stage. There was a faint ripple of applause. After a minute or two the orchestra struck up again and a line of chorus girls wearing sequinned skirts and elaborate headdresses – rather like the Variety performers I'd seen in Yarmouth ten years before – emerged stealthily from behind a curtain, and danced up and down while the man in the tuxedo shimmied unconvincingly in their midst. The buzz of conversation, which had lessened a bit while the girls came on, rose again. In the end the girls tramped away. One by one the stage lights were switched off until all that remained was a single spotlight trained on a microphone stand.

From the wings a voice said – slightly resentfully, as if this was a new arrangement, only just introduced to the club – 'Ladies and gentlemen, Arthur Upward!'

Nothing happened. The orchestra launched into a syncopated introduction, kept it up for half a dozen bars and then stopped. Somebody dropped a cymbal. Still nothing happened. Finally there was a kind of scuffle in the darkness to the right of the stage which ended with Upward flinging himself – rather than simply moving very fast – at the microphone. I looked at him carefully. Even paler than before, cigarette sticking out of his mouth, dishevelled despite the evening suit, he looked as if he were about to faint.

'She was only an Admiral's daughter,' Upward bellowed in a voice so loud that the microphone hummed with static, 'but she had discharged seamen in her naval base.'

There was silence, then a roar of laughter, which Upward quelled immediately by twisting the microphone off the stand and waving it in front of his face.

'Discharged … seamen … naval … base … It's not supposed to be funny you know.'

He was on for about half an hour. It was extraordinarily filthy, far worse than anything you heard then on the radio or the Variety hall stage, delivered with such relentless, machine-gun attack that the effect was simultaneously exhilarating and a bit exhausting. Watching Upward at the microphone stand, you wanted him to slow down, stand back, let other people in on the mystery of his private demons. The audience, I noticed, hardly knew what to make of him. They laughed at the obscenities, but you could see they found the wider spectacle – Upward's white face, jerky movements, hectoring voice – deeply unsettling.

Eventually, at the end of a complicated routine about a lodger and a vegetable marrow, Upward stopped, bowed perfunctorily and left the stage. At the time I wondered whether this was just another element in the air of mystique Upward wanted to drape over his performance. Questioned a day or two later, he put it down to simple boredom and fatigue.

'No, I just got fed up. Had to get off the stage. Happens to you sometimes.'

A bit later, when the man in the tuxedo had returned to the dais to sing 'That'll Be The Day', he re-emerged from another door at right-angles to the stage and came slowly over to the table. Arrived there, he stood with his hands pressed together over the back of a chair, moving his feet up and down like an athlete limbering up.

'Why don't you sit down?'

'I can't. It's my nerves.'

Upward's face as he said this was deadly pale. He looked as if he was going to fall over. In the end he managed to lever himself downward onto the chair. A waitress brought more drinks. Upward drank half his off in a gulp.

'What did y'think then?'

'You didn't look as if you enjoyed it very much.'

'No? I suppose not. D'you think the people enjoyed it?'

'A bit. I think they were a bit scared as well.'

'You think so?'

The whole tone of Upward's questioning suddenly changed. Before he'd just been polite. Now, leaning across the table, cuffs of his white evening shirt dropping into the ashtrays, his face was creased with curiosity.

'Well, they're a rotten audience. Rotten. They don't come here to see me.'

'No?'

'Course not. The blokes come here to see if they can pick up the waitresses, or see if one of the chorus'll get her tits out. The women come cos they've been told to. Or to play cards in the back. I'm supposed to keep them *amused*.'

We sat there for a few minutes more as balloons – let slip from a restraining net beneath the rafters – cascaded through the air and collected in droves under the table. Looking back, I'm surprised to find how characteristic the evening was of Upward and the way he behaved. Annoyance, absorption in his audience, interest in technique – all of the things that later became obsessions with him were there in embryo. After a while he pushed his empty beer glass decisively towards the centre of the table.

'Come round the back,' he said. 'There's someone you ought to meet.'

At the outer doorway, where the passage wound on towards the street, there was a kind of cubby hole, staffed by an immensely tall negro in a dinner jacket. Behind, harsh lighting showed another staircase rising steeply into darkness. Nodding to the negro, Upward took me up to a small landing, around which three or four tiny offices were grouped. In one of these, empty except for a couple of tables and chairs and some crates of beer, a youngish, red-faced man was making calculations in a pocket-book. Hearing the noise of our footsteps, he looked up.

'Seen you before, haven't I?'

'Sir.'

Oddly enough, I wasn't in the least surprised to find Captain Groves sitting in a back room at the Minerva Club. It was all part of the net Upward had thrown over the evening, turning it into a sort of alternative world where nothing could take you unawares. Out of uniform – he was wearing a smoking jacket and a bow tie – he looked younger, a bit fatter too.

'A lot different from when we last met?'

'That's right.'

'Enjoy the show?'

I gave a watered-down version of what I'd told Upward. Captain Groves looked interested.

'Always thinking that myself, you know. Try not to bludgeon your audience. Let them breathe. But Arthur's doing very well. I've the highest hopes for him.'

I took a look at Upward while these compliments were being pronounced. He was standing rigidly to attention, eyes staring blankly at the far wall, thumbs neatly positioned alongside the creases in his trousers. Even here, in the midst of a Soho November evening, it wasn't hard to remember the Catterick parade ground.

Without warning a buzzer on the desk exploded into life. Captain Groves stood up sharply.

'Trouble downstairs. You'll have to excuse me.'

Odd noises sounded in the near distance: a surge of footsteps, what sounded like breaking glass. Upward looked on unconcernedly as Captain Groves disappeared down the staircase.

'What kind of trouble?'

'There's always trouble. I got a bottle chucked at me last week. If you want to run a club in the West End you've got to pay for it.'

'Does Captain Groves own this place?'

'Up to a point. There's a bloke called Cooper hangs about too.'

By this stage we were back in the main body of the club. Here several things were going on simultaneously. Two or three men were scampering across the stage. Another man – the big negro I'd seen on the way up to Groves's office – was sitting next to one of the tables with his head in his hands. Smashed glass lay across the floor. Most of the people had disappeared.

'Let's get out of here,' said Upward matter-of-factly.

He led the way behind the bar to a kind of broom cupboard. Stepping through the door at its rear we found ourselves in the street.

'Does this sort of thing happen quite often?'

'First time in a fortnight,' Upward said.

He didn't seem particularly put out. This, too, I thought was a throwback to his army manner. Somebody would sort something out. The unit Upward had attached himself to would regroup, find a new position. Fresh orders would be issued. It was about ten o'clock, and Frith Street had turned bitterly cold. Beside us, taxis cruised silently past the heaps of piled refuse bags. From the club doorways an occasional tout edged forward, saw the look on Upward's face and edged back again. Twenty yards down the street, Upward stopped suddenly.

'I'm staying just round the corner. You want to come and have a drink?'

By this stage I was aware of feeling incredibly tired. There were a dozen questions that I wanted to ask. A few paces further down the pavement, Upward darted into a tiny alleyway full of entrances encrusted with doorbells. In one of these a steep flight of steps led up to a white-painted door.

'Been here a fortnight,' Upward said, jabbing a key into the lock. 'Best digs I've had in ages.'

Half into the hallway he stopped, overcome by the deluge of flaring light: strip-lights overhead, half a dozen table lamps and wall brackets.

'For God's sake, Brenda,' Upward said irritably. 'Turn some of these things off can't you?'

Upward's digs consisted of the largeish main room in which we stood, with a kitchenette in the corner, and a couple of other rooms beyond. In the doorway of one of these a tall girl with untidy blonde hair, wearing a short purple dressing gown, stood over an ironing board.

'Brenda,' Upward said, either introducing her or simply calling her to attention. 'This here's Ted King. That army chap I was telling you about.'

Brenda stared remorselessly back.

'The one you broke into the NAAFI with at Catterick?'

'No, not that one.'

'The one you said owed you two hundred quid?'

'Nor that one neither.'

Upward looked a bit embarrassed at this, probably because it represented a side of his life that I knew nothing about.

'Look,' he said firmly. 'I've got to talk to Ted here. This place looks like a knocking shop. Why don't you go out for a bit? I'll give you some money. Why don't you go to the Tin Tack or somewhere?'

'The Tin Tack doesn't open till eleven.'

'The Coal Hole then,' Upward said, losing his patience. 'Here's twenty quid. Go to the Coal Hole, there's a duck, and come back in an hour.'

Brenda put her head on one side.

'Will *he* still be here?'

'I shouldn't wonder.'

In the end she accepted the four blue five-pound notes that Upward produced from his wallet and went into the bedroom, where – oblivious to the open door – she started to put on some clothes that were lying over the bed. Upward fished out some beer bottles that lay cooling in the sink. A bit later the door slammed.

'Nice girl, Brenda,' Upward said, pouring the beer into tumblers. 'Nowt up top, though. Nowt at all.'

'Do you and she …?'

'Oh yes,' Upward said. 'Abso-bloody-lutely.'

I looked at him as he said this. There wasn't a flicker of irony. I realised that this, simply, was the world Upward had moved into, a place where blonde girls in dressing gowns stood over late-night ironings, while their boyfriends told jokes in nightclubs.

'Where did you meet?'

'She works in a club in Meard Street,' Upward said. Obviously Brenda, or at any rate the practical detail of Brenda's life, was of no interest to him. I tried one or two other conversational openings of this sort, but it wasn't any good. Upward wanted to talk about his performance. What did I think of the hurling himself on stage routine? Of the unexpected departure? What about the jokes? Were they too blue? Not blue enough? There was a peculiar intensity about the way he asked these questions. Finally he said:

'Look at these.'

There was a bundle of papers piled on the lip of the ramshackle sofa. Upward picked it up and dropped it into my lap. They were comedy sketches, quite funny ones. I browsed through them for a minute or two.

'Notice anything?'

'They're written for two people.'

'That's right. I need a feed.'

For a second I forgot what the word meant. 'A what?'

'A stooge. Someone to feed the lines. What about you?'

'I couldn't do it.'

'Yes you could.'

'No.'

We looked at each other for a bit.

Upward said: 'At least think about it. You could rehearse. No one'd let you on stage until you were sure of yourself. What have you got to lose?'

'I've got a job.'

'Give it up.'

By then I think each of us knew that though I'd eventually be worn down, it wasn't likely to happen on the spot. Upward looked at his watch.

'Sleep on it,' he said. 'Me, I'm going to bed.'

It was a quarter to midnight, too late to be sure of getting the last tube to Hammersmith. After some discussion Upward made up a bed for me on the sofa. Some time in the small hours Brenda came back and blundered about for a bit in the darkness. I listened to the sound of Upward and her scuffling for a while and then fell asleep.

What's a Greek urn? About seventy-five pounds a week.

Fifty-three years ago this summer, in a café on the front at Blackpool, George Hattersley stood Max Miller a plate of cheese sandwiches. I know this because George has told me. Several times.

'I'm just sitting there, the way you do, and this bloke standing by the till catches my eye and I see it's Maxie. Joke is, 'e's left 'is wallet at the hotel. So of course I say "Anything you like Mr Miller. Be my guest." And Maxie says, "I only came in for a snack. Not a bleeding banquet, you know." Must 'ave stayed talking for 'alf an hour.'

Over the years this tale has grown in the telling, starting off as a hastily-borrowed half crown, returned to George that night at his own hotel in a manila envelope, blossoming into a kind of tableau – the famous comedian, publicly embarrassed, the willing acquaintance – ending up as a dramatically outlined double act, the two professionals putting on an impromptu show for the café's startled customers. Curiously, I don't mind these embellishments. The more George tries to evoke this far-off scene, the happier I am.

'But what did he look like? Describe him to me.'

'Maxie? Well, he looked like … You must have seen the pictures of him? Jewish, of course. Funny thing was, he only wore them clothes of his on stage. Time I met him he was just wearing a check suit and a Trilby hat. Though come to think of it, 'e had them trousers that roll up to the knee with long socks underneath, what d'you call 'em, plus-fours?'

We're sitting in the main room of George's flat in the sheltered housing complex George inhabits in Walthamstow. Outside the road winds through neatly scalloped grass verges and identikit low-rise bungalows, out of which occasional old folk emerge. On the mantelpiece are framed souvenirs of George's professional career: dinner-jacketed and fancy-tied, taking a bow at the Bristol

Hippodrome in 1947, the fourth element in a close harmony quartet swooping over a BBC microphone sometime in the 50s. I've an idea that, forty years ago, probably at the Yarmouth Regal alongside Father and Mother, I even saw George perform myself. George is keen to abet this fancy.

'Every chance you did. Every chance. Used to do the eastern circuit. Yarmouth. Norwich. Cromer. Lynn. Three times a year. You *must* have seen me. Must have done.'

It was Lennie who shoved me in George's direction. (*This old bloke, amazing really. Used to know Max Miller and that. Before my time of course. But 'e remembers them all.*) I suppose George must be touching ninety. At any rate he remembers the day the First World War ended, seeing Queen Mary's coach once in Windsor, watching Winston Churchill turn up for the second house at the Holborn Empire in 1941. All this has impressed him in its way. You can tell that he feels it's been quite a romance, his career, that somehow these nine decades or so of English life wouldn't have been quite the same without him in it. He was *there*.

'Shall I get you a cup of tea, George?'

No reply. George has gone to sleep. He does this quite often, chin slumped down on the point of his breast bone, hands gripping the arm-rests of his chair. Knees sticking up towards his shoulders, he looks like an exceptionally frail grasshopper. I stand up to stretch my legs, smelling the room's distinctive smells: camphor, mint humbugs, old blankets, piss. George's wife died in 1978. His children packed him off here a good ten years ago. The idea of George standing in Windsor High Street watching Queen Mary's coach makes me think of Lucy from the BBC. George, undoubtedly, is a person in history. Accounts clerk in the dead 1930s. Turned pro in 1936 ('First night I was due on they closed the theatres on account of the old king dying'), ENSA concerts on Luneberg Heath. But I think Lucy wants something a little more up to date. The questions weren't bad. *Do you believe England is a better place now than when you were a child? What do you believe are the most significant changes to have taken place in English*

*society in your lifetime? Who do you consider to be the
politician who has most lived up to his or her promises in
the past fifty years?* Plus a neat little note on rose-strewn
writing paper conveying the writer's enjoyment of our
lunch and looking forward to 'seeing you again'.

I was so amused by the questions – the idea that this
kind of thing was even answerable – that I tried them out
on Lennie. His answers, for what they're worth, were
'Don't make me laugh', 'The bleeding immigration' and,
well, perhaps you can guess the last one. Lennie gave up on
politics years ago. The last time he cried, he says, was
watching the TV news report on Mrs Thatcher's resig-
nation speech.

Lennie has been following the newspapers this last
week. (*Would you believe it? All them blokes with their
'ands in the till?*) DI Stevens was right. Someone – nobody
quite knows who – has been singing. The songsheet takes
in all manner of familiar names, not heard of in twenty
years. The Bank of Bristol. Mayflower. The pyramid selling
scam. No one charged as yet, apparently, but then these are
old men, ill men, famous men. There was a picture of Sir
Gavin Newsome in the *Guardian* the other day: white-
haired and stick-tethered at the end of his Surrey drive,
shooing away reporters. Cartwright's gone to ground
somewhere in Essex. The real interest, as far as I can make
out, takes in the plans to buy up a chain of defunct theatres
and relaunch them as casinos – fruitless in the end, but
leaving mementoes in half a dozen south-coast council
chambers. Backhanders for planning permission;
committee chairmen on the payroll; councillors moon-
lighting as 'design consultants' – that kind of thing. There
was another picture in the *Guardian*, too, next to the one
of Sir Gavin (donations to the Conservative Party usefully
listed alongside) of a balding man in thick spectacles,
remnants of greasy black hair swept back over his head.
Cooper, described as an 'entertainment magnate with
property interests', didn't look to have changed much.
There was some eye-catching stuff about his early 70s run-
ins with the Obscene Publications Squad.

Lennie was particularly excited at the thought of Cooper's involvement.

'Dennis Cooper? Used to book acts for 'is clubs. Thirty years ago.'

'What kinds of acts, Lennie?'

'Singers. Dancers. What other kinds are there?' When I read him the bit in the paper about 'exotic floorshows' he sniffed a bit. 'You don't want to believe everything you read in the papers, Ted, mate.'

Oddly enough, for a theatrical agent Lennie maintains quite a high moral tone. (*Nah, I don't hold with it, all them girls showing off their tits.*) His idea of smut is Barbara Windsor in the *Carry On* films.

Outside the rain falls. A big Jaguar is nosing slowly through the tiny streets of this old persons' toytown, sending water spraying over the verges. George's eyes open and he blinks once or twice, startled by everything – gas-fire glowing by his knees, family photos, silent visitor.

'I didn't think you were coming today,' he says.

'You were telling me about Maxie.'

'Maxie?'

'Max Miller.'

The Ngongi have a tradition of extending respect to their elders: the toothless jaws gibbering in the firelight; the line of dutiful faces. If this were equatorial Guinea George would be telling me about the lion hunts of his youth. As it is he is telling me about Max Miller. Twenty minutes later I leave him hunched over a cup of tea, face wreathed in steam, like an old wizard inspecting the latest draught from his protégé's cauldron.

*

'I like your house,' Lucy says.

Seated in the front room, workbag drawn up on her knees, Lucy has the inquisitive look women assume when they come to survey single men's houses. I can remember Paula putting it on a quarter of a century ago: the urge to throw open cupboards, alter the alignment of curtains.

'It hasn't been lived in a great deal recently.'

'You could do a lot with it,' she says.

Here on a visit, the space between us has lessened a bit. In particular, the fantastic unfamiliarity I'd diagnosed on our first meeting had cracked into more recognisable shapes. Among other things, it turns out that Lucy comes originally from Norfolk – Holt, on the other side of the county. Sitting on the sofa, turning over the copy of *Nintendo Warrior* bought as a present for Daniel, she looks less like a BBC ice-maiden and more elfin – the kind of girl who wouldn't have seemed out of place on the end of the TV dance troupes twenty years ago.

'Anyway,' she says. 'You can see from the running order which clips we're using. Still no sign of anything from Mrs Upward?'

'She was never the greatest correspondent. I'll try again if you like.'

'Only Graham' – Graham is the producer – 'is keen that we try all the angles, get as big a context as possible.'

Even now, the stuff about angles and contexts bothers me a bit. Lucy, I can see, has run through the tapes of the *Upward & King Show* and the radio programmes from thirty years ago and found something symbolic. Or if not symbolic then connected to time in a way that I can't see. Upward, for instance, always maintained that he hadn't any particular grudge against Harold Wilson, was even prepared to vote for him, simply found him funny.

'When do you want to do the interview?'

'Next week sometime?'

Lucy, on her own admission, is thirty-seven. There has been a lot less recently about the boyfriend and the house in Putney. Presumably even girls of thirty-seven feel their age, see the conveyor-belt of their future stretching out ahead. Once or twice, I notice, she gives me a look of what can only be shyness, a vulnerability drawn from an older world that she no longer inhabits.

'Where's Daniel? I must give him his magazine.'

'He's upstairs somewhere.'

Standing in the hall I shout up the stairs a couple of

times. There is no response: Daniel takes fright at visitors.

'Never mind. You can give it to him for me.'

What sort of life does Lucy live? What does she do in the house in Putney? Always with women, even with professional helpmeets like Lucy, I've made phantoms I could later chase – images of things, known and unknown, tracked back across their lives. Lucy must have been to college. What did she do there? How have the intervening fifteen years in London passed? For some reason I badly want to know. Thinking about it, its secrets and mysteries, its dawns and departures, makes me unexpectedly miserable.

'I'd better go,' Lucy says. 'Stuff to do back at the office. I'll ring with a progress report in a day or so.'

Suddenly, not quite knowing where the impetus comes from, I find myself suggesting we have lunch again. Unexpectedly, Lucy assents. From the window I watch her moving away along the street, oddly purposeful and determined. On cue, Daniel appears in the doorway.

'Who was that?'

'Just someone to do with work. Look, she brought you a present.'

Daniel stares at the magazine. 'Why did she give me that when she's never met me?'

'I don't know. Perhaps she's just interested.'

The year Lucy was born was the year I met Mary. When she was at primary school I was doing cabaret in Soho. I think about these things as I cook Daniel's tea: sausages, chips and beans. Krieger, whom I have consulted, says that a growing ten-year-old needs all the carbohydrates you can throw into him.

… As for what makes Upward & King *funny*, the answer is as indefinable as in any other comic medium. Part of it is their grounding in the old atmosphere of the Variety halls, the way in which, as they advance to the front of the stage, at least half of their gaze seems to be concentrated on ghostly rows of faces above and beyond the studio audience. A great deal more lies in the rich vein of near-surrealist whimsy tapped in every third or fourth sketch: Upward fancying himself pursued by a giant bee; King filing outlandish expenses claims ('Six elephant's foot wastepaper baskets') matter-of-factly on his tax return; the two of them embarked on a kind of endless, absurdist dialogue between a shop proprietor and his customer, where the exceptionally alert viewer might just discern that the matter in hand had something to do with money for the Christmas Club. They did a marvellous sketch set at a doctors' surgery, another one featuring Harold Wilson as a seedy prep school master trying vainly to quell the irruptions of his class ('Now, just be quiet young Benn, d'y' hear?' etc.). Inevitably, physical and vocal dissimilarities give these exchanges their bite: Upward short, burly, pugnacious; King tall, saturnine, pacific; the one urgent and loquacious, the other restrained and reticent. If I had to find a single word capable of supplying the essence of their performance, that word would be *tension*, the tension that exists between two people who, broadly speaking, like each other, each of whom is sometimes exasperated beyond measure by the other's behaviour. King's interventions in Upward's by now trademarked monologues about girls are a pattern example of this: barely disguised resentment that altogether fails to conceal ruefulness at his own lack of success, while contriving, with lavish subtlety, to puncture each revelation as it looms up before him …

Kenneth Tynan, *Observer*, 1973

Frith Street

Waking at half-past five, even in the depths of winter, the first thing you became aware of was the shouts from the street, near at hand but strangely subdued – like drowning men summoning their last energies before disappearing beneath the waves. These came from the drunks stumbling home from the drinking clubs. Before this came the noise of the refuse carts, which I was never awake to hear. From six to half-past it was more or less quiet, apart from the whirr of an occasional milk float, but by seven the street would be alive with the sound of footsteps, tradesmen taking down shutters, lorries reversing into the narrow alleyways. Upward – not the only one – resented the twenty-four hour quality the place seemed to possess. Up half the night, rarely in bed before three, he used to spend most of his afternoons asleep, sometimes in bed, more often than not simply collapsing on the sofa in the corner of the rehearsal room.

It's odd how you can turn nostalgic over somewhere as battered and tuppence-coloured as Soho. I can't have lived there for more than eighteen months, but for some reason the place is as vivid to me as the front room in Southtown, or Yarmouth harbour, and if you put me down blindfolded at the end of Old Compton Street I could probably find my way to the French Pub or the Colony Room or half a dozen other places where I used to spend my time. Dean Street! Berwick Street market! I don't suppose they mean much to you, but for about a year and a half they marked the boundaries of the world I lived in. There was a run-down café where I used to have breakfast – Café Continental, I think it was called – at the top end of Frith Street, and I can remember the inside even now: the squares of mirror stuck on odd places over the walls, the steaming urns and old Walenski, who owned the place, sitting at the back reading a copy of *Polska!*

It was a strange time to be around in Frith Street, Brewer Street and the square mile or so of back-alleys and tumbledown mews where I spent most of my time. In theory Soho was still 'respectable'. There were strange old shops which looked as if they'd been there for a hundred years; the streets were full of tiny family firms who made violins or bound books; but everyone knew that the rents were rising and the crooks were moving in. People used to talk about the old villains of the 50s – Melvin and Muller, Jack Spot and Billy Hill – with a sort of nostalgia, merely because they weren't the sort to throw paraffin heaters through shopkeepers' windows, which was the favourite trick of the Maltese gangs (whom everyone called 'Maltesers') from Wardour Street. Not that this meant very much to me, of course. The closest I got to a gang fight was having Reggie Kray pointed out to me once in a club in Greek Street.

It took only a couple of days hanging around with Upward to establish that the Minerva was not exactly a brothel – there was hardly such a place in Soho – but a well-known resort of prostitutes. The 'girls' – there were about a dozen of them, ranging in age from seventeen to an extraordinary old crone who claimed to remember Armistice Night – all had rooms in the nearby streets, which meant that Captain Groves couldn't be charged with running a disorderly house. I think his percentage was 70 per cent, and he wasn't above sending stooges along to make sure he wasn't getting short-changed. Apparently, just before my arrival there'd been some police trouble, but Captain Groves had smoothed it over somehow – being called Captain Groves helped, of course – and before very long he started expanding. There were a couple of drinking clubs he owned in Meard Street (which informed judges maintained was the worst street in Soho) and a restaurant up near the Square. I suppose in retrospect I'm a bit shocked to have been wandering around on

the fringes of all this, but at the time I don't think the
morality of it bothered me very much. I'd found something
I wanted to do, and the fact that it took place in a hole in
the ground in Frith Street where people went to pick up
women was the price you paid for being a beginner. There
was also the fact that, outwardly at any rate, it was difficult
to see what all the fuss was about. I'd been brought up in
Great Yarmouth, where the watch committee would have
a fit if anyone had tried to stage what was then known as
'indecent dancing'. Here I was in what Father and Mother
would have marked down unhesitatingly as a den of vice,
and yet apart from the fact that some of the girls weren't
wearing very much it was all horribly ordinary: men in
evening suits with those frilly collars, 'hostesses' sipping
Coca-Cola at a guinea a glass (whatever they left of it was
poured straight back into the bottle), Frank the barman's
head bobbing up from behind the soda siphons to keep an
eye on the drunks. Later, of course, I found out about some
of the things that went on beneath the surface, but by that
time I was getting ready to leave the place and it could all
be washed away, rather like the glitter powder some of the
hostesses dusted into their hair, which got everywhere in
the club and stuck to your hands at all times.

*

I suppose if I'd been the carefree spirit Upward hoped I
was I'd have chucked in my job on the spot. As it was I
spent another three weeks at Truefitt & Hislop working
out my notice. Upward, though he accepted this, was
contemptuous of the attitudes he thought it reflected.

'The trouble with you,' he used to say, 'is that you're too
bloody middle class. Seeing out your time for a bunch of
shit-stabbers who couldn't care less whether you stay or
go. The idea!'

He was right, of course. God knows what Father and
Mother would have thought if they knew I'd thrown over
a job without abiding by the statutory conditions. Those
last three weeks were the time I enjoyed most – watching

the light fade across the Thames, or dodging the buses in Fleet Street. In the pub on the last afternoon I let on that I'd got another clerking job somewhere in the City. Three days later, with a suitcase in each hand and £200 in my wallet – my entire savings – I was walking up Frith Street towards Upward's flat.

Queerly enough, quite a lot survives from that period – I mean actual sketches that eventually resurfaced on radio or TV. The one about the two men on the life-raft was written maybe a week or two after I'd turned up. And there's a piece about a bloke taking his dog to the vet that later went through endless re-writes and re-stagings but probably has its origins back there. All this time, of course, Upward was still doing his one-man show at the Minerva, but in the afternoons we used to rehearse in an old, high-ceilinged room on the top floor of a house in Lexington Street. Some of my sharpest memories of Upward are from that time – seeing him in the doorway, red-faced and furious, rubbing his hands against the cold, or bent over one of the old packing cases with which the room was littered with a cigarette in his mouth striking out a line of dialogue in the script. At the outset I'd been worried that it would collapse around my ears, that having found me again Upward would throw me aside the instant he discovered I wasn't up to his own lightning pace. Gratifyingly, this didn't happen. All the same I don't think I ever quite worked Upward out, established what it was he wanted from me, how he thought I might provide it. He had fixed routines – lumbering round the room for an hour or more in silence until his mind got going, vanishing on odd errands I was never party to. 'Got to go out', 'Got to see a man', 'Something to pick up'. Sometimes Brenda would come and collect him – a subdued-looking Brenda in slacks and a pastel-coloured raincoat – and they'd disappear somewhere, leaving me in the empty room with its view out over the rooftops towards Regent Street, and the single-bar electric heater.

It was the same at the flat, where I spent a week kipping on the sofa before Captain Groves fixed me up with a room in Carlisle Street. In the army I'd had a fair sight of Upward's temperament, but it wasn't until I lived with him that I cottoned on to his utter gloominess, an awful depression of spirit that caught up everyone around him and eventually had them playing bit parts in a kind of tragic drama of which Upward was the undisputed star. In the mornings, while Brenda bustled round the flat in her dressing-gown making vague efforts to 'tidy the place up' and I read the paper, he'd sprawl in one of the armchairs with his hands behind his back, not saying a word.

What puzzled me about these fits of gloom was their complete lack of connection to the patterns of Upward's life. I'd known melancholics before – Yarmouth had been full of grim little men fretting themselves behind shop counters or office desks – but in each case there'd been some explanation to hand, some basis on which this dissatisfaction with environment could be teased out. Upward's dejection, it seemed to me, was much more deep-set, in fact practically cosmic, never alleviated by conventional prods to the ego – money, comfort, a good audience – occasionally terrifying in its intensity. Even odder, perhaps, was Upward's habit of being cheered up by things going wrong. A heckler booing one of his jokes, a row with Brenda – these happened about once a week – a financial crisis: all these turned him unexpectedly gleeful. I was halfway up the stairs to the flat one afternoon when there was a loud crash, followed by the spectacle of Brenda, wild-haired and with a coat flung over her shoulder, in flight towards the street door. Inside I found Upward kneeling on the hearthrug sweeping glass – quite a lot of glass – into a dustpan.

'Christ!' he said savagely. 'D'y' know what that mad bitch has just done?'

'No.'

'Chucked a fucking table lamp at me, that's all.'

There was no mistaking the note of exaltation in his voice. It had been there at Catterick when the PE sergeant had broken his collar-bone. There was no doubt about it. Upward liked having table lamps thrown at him, liked noise, upset, passionate arguments, bitter reconciliations. The smashed glass lay in a heap on the carpet for a fortnight.

As for Brenda, there was no getting away from Upward's original judgment. She was quite the stupidest girl I'd met in my life. At first, confronted with Brenda's ignorance over who was Chancellor of the Exchequer or how to send a telegram, I'd marked her down as residing in the same category as the Parmenters, but this, I soon saw, was a mistake. The Parmenters, not counting Horace, were merely badly informed, and if a piece of information looked as if it might be useful to them they remembered it. Brenda, on the other hand, was simply stupendously, invincibly ignorant. It used to puzzle me how a woman could exist in the second half of the twentieth century on the mental resources Brenda had at her disposal, but she managed it somehow. She could just about read, but arithmetic, geography – any kind of calculation – was more or less beyond her. Upward, who had a sadistic streak where Brenda was concerned, wasn't above exploiting these weaknesses by way of ghastly, unsparing question and answer sessions.

'Now Brenda, lass, here's a question for y'. What's the capital of France?'

'Don't know.'

'If you wanted to go to America, how would you get there?'

'Ask you and you'd take me.'

I used to look at Brenda's face sometimes during these interrogations, but it was devoid of feeling. You could see that at periods in her life, various people – parents, schoolteachers perhaps – had tried to engage her in these strange rituals, and she'd decided that this was the only way of keeping her dignity.

'You oughtn't to talk to her like that,' I told Upward one time.

'Why not?'

'It's humiliating for her.'

'No it isn't. You'd be surprised how much she likes it. Likes me talking to her, that is.'

There was something in this. When not throwing table-lamps at him, Brenda was devoted to Upward. She spent long hours in the shops in Carnaby Street buying him presents. Upward, I noticed, never knew how to respond to these gifts, usually ostentatious bits of clothing that showed no understanding of the things he liked to wear.

'Christ,' he would say later, staring at some magenta waistcoat or a pair of yellow wash-leather gloves. 'What am I supposed to do with this? Hang it on a bleeding flag-pole?'

At the same time he was genuinely glad to receive them. I've an idea that in sketching Upward's relations with Brenda through dialogue, I'm in danger of misrepresenting them, conveying only the patronage at the expense of other currents running deep beneath the surface. Probably that was how Upward wanted it. For her part, Brenda was capable of the most fantastic projections of their life together. There was one extraordinary conversation along these lines that took place about a month after I arrived in Frith Street.

'Do you think Arthur's going to make a success of this comedy thing?'

'I shouldn't wonder.'

Brenda had a trick of shooting out more or less unanswerable questions at random: 'Do you think it will rain on Sunday?' 'Why do Chelsea play in blue?'

'You'd be surprised how serious he takes it. All day in that rehearsal room.'

It was about six o'clock on a January evening – mid-morning, Soho-time – and we were alone in the flat. Upward had disappeared on one of his errands. Outside snow was falling gently over the tops of the surrounding houses. Abruptly Brenda changed tack.

'Snow always makes me feel sad,' she volunteered.

'Does it?'

'That's right. It makes me remember when I was a little girl.'

Somehow there was no way of entering into this, of working out what Brenda might have been like as a little girl. She got up from her chair, picked up a pile of clothes that lay on the sofa, rearranged them to her satisfaction, and sat down again.

'Do you know what we're going to do when Arthur's made his money?'

'No idea.'

'Open a hotel.'

'A what?'

'Open a hotel. Up north. Manchester maybe, or Leeds. Not commercial travellers or anything. You know, a *posh* place.'

Of all the things Brenda had said to me in the month or so that I'd known her – and she was a confidential girl – this was by some way the most bizarre, so outlandish as to be practically unreal. I hadn't any idea what to say.

'A posh hotel?'

'That's right. We've often talked about it. Two dozen beds, say. Arthur'd work out front, I'd be in charge of the kitchen and that.'

For some reason I assumed this was one of Brenda's momentary whims. These were quite common – to be snuffed out by a word from Upward or a second thought. In this case, nothing could have been further from the truth. For the next ten minutes, while the snow fell over the rooftops and car-horns sounded in the street below, Brenda talked about the hotel. She did this with utter seriousness. There could be no doubt she believed it would happen:

'Not too grand to begin with, of course … a *French* restaurant, that's what people like these days isn't it? … Cotton sheets, not those nylon things … Dancing on Saturday nights … None of them unmarried couples coming in with fake wedding rings …'

Eventually Brenda stopped.

'When it's finished,' she said, 'when it's all done, Arthur and me'd take it kindly if you'd come and stay with us.'

'Thank you.'

'There wouldn't be a charge, of course.'

'No.'

Upward came back at eight, frowning, with the faintest
suspicion of a bruise above his left temple. Later on
Brenda and I went to see him at the Minerva. Nothing
more was ever said about the hotel.

*

So you can see, it was an odd kind of life I was leading here
in the mid-60s in Frith Street: mornings spent frowsting in
my room in Carlisle Street (it was above a butcher's shop
and in summer the stink from the bins filled the house);
afternoons rehearsing with Upward; evenings at the flat
with Brenda or at the club. Small things and big things
came mixed together. Churchill died, and even the dirty
bookshops closed down for a couple of hours and Captain
Groves shut the Minerva for the day as a mark of respect.
Apparently he and Churchill had been to the same school.
The £200 I'd brought with me from Hammersmith was
dwindling away now, but after a bit Captain Groves gave
me a job helping out behind the bar, which basically meant
making sure the hostesses were ordering enough drinks,
and bringing up crates of brown ale from the cellar. A
while later I was promoted to what was known as 'liaison
man' (Captain Groves ran the place on military lines),
which consisted of ferrying messages from the bouncers
out on the door to the main office, keeping an eye on the
people in the main body of the club and lending a hand
when things got nasty. Once or twice I've tried to imagine
the person I was in those days, tried to work out what I was
like and what went on in my head, but I never got very far.
A photo or two survives from that time – on the steps of
the Minerva, with a ferocious crew-cut (long hair hadn't
quite come in by then) and a Crombie coat, alongside
Upward in a pavement café somewhere – but they don't
amount to much. I turned twenty-five that year, which
back in Yarmouth would have had people muttering about
what you were 'doing with your life', but that didn't worry
me in the least. I was gripped by the oddest feeling of
exhilaration, of doing something I liked, and not worrying

about what Father or Mother or anyone else thought, and not caring a damn about the future. It used to astonish me sometimes. Two years before I'd been glooming away at Kenilworth Road, and now here I was in a dinner jacket with my hair smarmed up in little wrinkles on the top of my head telling fruity-voiced old blokes and women with a thousand pounds worth of jewellery round their necks where they could leave their coats. There were women, too, half a dozen of them at least: cashiers, receptionists, dancers – the kind of girls Soho was full of in those days. I can remember taking the first of them, a blonde girl whose name I can't even recall, back to the room in Carlisle Street, getting her clothes off and then falling on her in a kind of frenzy, I was so desperate. As for the others, all that remains is a jumble of fragments: a girl called Alice who worked in a club in Brewer Street standing stark naked over a chest of drawers searching for a packet of cigarettes; black sheets on a bed belonging to a woman called Selina who was probably a tart, though I didn't enquire at the time; rain falling on a window somewhere near Soho Square. I'm not proud of this, and I don't recall there being very much pleasure in it, but I remember having a kind of feeling that it was something I had to do, a way of getting rid of Mary and all the other ghosts from long ago.

In any case, all this was much less important to me than the real business of Upward and the rehearsal room. I don't think I could ever quite convey the excitement of those winter afternoons in 1965, with the electric fire gleaming through the murk and footsteps clanging on the wooden stairs outside. At first I'd just assumed that Upward wanted me for the role of straight man, the stooge who offers lines to the comic and gets annihilated in return. It turned out, though, that he had something more ambitious in mind. Comedy double acts in those days operated on a rigid formula: the 'lead', usually small and bumptious, and the stooge, usually taller, or at any rate physically differentiated in some way. The stooge's job was simply to volunteer lines of varying degrees of innocuousness, and give the lead a chance to score off him. At its

most basic level – the kind of thing you saw at the
Yarmouth Regal – this would find the stooge saying, in a
faintly lugubrious way, 'Turned out nice again today', so
that the lead could immediately turn it into a put-down:
'Pity you couldn't turn out nice again to match it.' This
always got a laugh. At the same time it encouraged the
audience to side with the lead, the 'smart man' who was
running rings round his lead-booted adversary. Upward's
idea was that the stooge, if not actually undermining the
lead's jokes, should be nearer to his fighting weight,
certainly capable of challenging his pretensions, sometimes
overthrowing them altogether. There was a whole range of
sketches, loosely titled 'Talking about girls', that followed
this blueprint – Upward blustering, contemptuous and
superior, gradually being brought down to earth.

UPWARD: Saw you with that Alice Hackthorpe the other
    night.
KING (*shyly*): She's my girlfriend.
UPWARD: Oh yes! Does she know?
KING: (*slow on the uptake*): Does she know what?
UPWARD: That she's your girlfriend.
KING (*hurt*): Of course she knows … She knows more than
    you think … I bet she knows more than you know.
UPWARD (*outraged*): Knows more than I know? Let me tell
    you, there's not many people know as much as I know
    … For instance, did you know that the capital of
    Ecuador is Quito? There's professors of Geography at
    Oxford University don't know that.
KING (*obligingly*): There's people living in Ecuador don't
    know that.
UPWARD: What?
KING: Hundred and thousands of them. Never done geog-
    raphy. Sad, isn't it?

The ending was typical of the way Upward worked. In his
solo show at the Minerva, whenever the audience turned
restive or a gag looked as if it was about to fail, he'd shout
out something like, 'Look at that pink rat over by the fire

escape', or pick some woman near the front and yell: 'It's
all right love, there's just the two of us. Give me a moment
to put my trousers on and I'll be with you.' This might not
raise a laugh, but it always got people's attention. For all
these attempts to subvert the usual patterns of cross-talk, I
knew that once we got on stage it was Upward who would
carry us. Permanently aggrieved, put-upon, bouncing with
conceit, a bit like Hancock but angrier, tougher, he was the
kind of comedian people laugh at on sight, who then
makes himself funnier by seeming to hate himself for
raising the initial laugh. An early sketch that we didn't
perform much – it needed too many props and assistants –
always seemed to symbolise this talent for comic exasperation. It took place in a police station where a detective
(Upward) was preparing to interview a suspect (me).
Leading the suspect into the interview room, Upward
discovers that the electric light has failed. They find a
second room. After ten seconds the second light fails and
plunges the room into darkness. In a third, the table at
which the suspect sits suddenly collapses. The sketch ends
with Upward calling for a toolbox and making repairs
while continuing to ask questions: 'So where were you on
the night of the 13th?' (*bang*) 'Just look in that box and see
if there's a nail, will you?' etc. No one watching it could
doubt that Upward really was cross, or that the properties
of a comedy sketch hadn't ignited some wider anger – a
universal dissatisfaction, practically, deep inside him. There
was a sense of relief when it was all over. You felt – something Captain Groves once said, watching from the wings –
that it was all a bit much, faintly exhausting. Oddly I
remember much more about Upward in the act of
performing than off-stage – standing there pale-faced
under the arc-light with the sweat pouring off his forehead,
tossing the microphone anxiously from one hand to the
other. Given what happened later, perhaps that's not such
a bad thing.

*

Mother died in the spring of 1965. I hadn't even known she'd been ill. There was a mix-up in forwarding letters from the old address – I'd moved out of Carlisle Street by this stage – and I didn't find out until a week later. By the time I got through to Uncle Ralph's on the phone they were already clearing up after the funeral. I wonder if you can imagine how I felt about that? Mother dead, and me not even there to stand over her grave? But it was all par for the course for our family. No one at Uncle Ralph's would have had the first idea of how to go about getting in touch with me in London, and I suppose it was my fault for not keeping better contact.

It turned out that she'd died of heart failure. I don't mind telling you that Mother's death cut me up. I hadn't seen her for a bit, but every so often there'd be a letter, usually about the shop and Mrs Moss and how the council wouldn't let them display the bigger stuff out on the pavement, and I'd kind of gathered, reading between the lines, that Mother was having the time of her life. Yarmouth, when I got there a day or so after the funeral, seemed a bit smaller than I remembered, and even more flyblown, and I recall walking around the streets in a new suit I rather fancied myself in – it had very slight bell-bottoms, which were all the rage just then – hoping to meet someone I knew but not finding anyone, and noticing the changes since I'd last been there. The square was much the same, except that Wedderbury's had sold out to one of the big outfitting chains, and Father's shop was a kind of ice-cream parlour. I remember standing there for a long time under one of the beech trees – they'd grown to an enormous size and badly needed pruning – smoking cigarettes, admiring the bell-bottoms of my trousers, but somehow seeing Father's face like a ghost in what had been the shop window as he bent over the till or weighed out sweets into a paper bag, and thinking, of all things, of the day – it would have been thirteen years before, now – that Betty disappeared.

After a bit I cheered up slightly and went round to Uncle Ralph's. He'd gone out somewhere, but one of his

daughters, Aunt Hilda, who I hadn't seen for six or seven
years, was there hoovering the front room carpet in a
vague kind of way. She was a gaunt, stringy woman with
her hair perpetually done up in curlers whom I don't
suppose I'd ever really exchanged a word with, but she
seemed happy enough to see me, launched into a detailed
account of Mother's last days and eventually took me
upstairs with the idea of going through Mother's things.
There wasn't a great deal to see. All the clothes I told Aunt
Hilda she could keep or chuck out as she wanted to.
Mother's secret vice was revealed in the pile of paperback
novels wth titles like *Hawaiian Romance* hidden under the
bed. The other things – odd bits of jewellery, an old diary
or two and a photograph album – barely filled a carrier
bag. I stuffed this under my arm and went off into the
centre of Gorleston with a definite idea of having a talk
with Mrs Moss, but somehow I couldn't face it. I got as far
as the shop – it was a bit more superior than Mother had
let on, and there was a sign advertising 'Teas and light
refreshments' – and then stopped. I could see Mrs Moss by
the till talking to someone and looking more than ever like
a deathshead, and I've an idea that she even glimpsed me
through the window, but in the end my courage simply
failed me. Somehow the thought of standing there amid
the dirt and the mothballs talking about Mother with old
Moss while people came in and haggled over dirty
mattresses was more than I could bear, and I slunk off to
the cemetery, where it was raining and the entranceway
was blocked by half a dozen black Daimlers carrying the
mourning party of some Yarmouth councillor who'd died
that week (I'd read about this in the *Mercury* at Uncle
Ralph's). They'd buried Mother alongside Father, and
someone had added 'Eunice Mary, loving wife of the
above' and her dates further down his headstone. It was
raining pretty hard by now, but I stood there for half an
hour or so while Alderman Bumstead's interment went on
ten yards away and some workmen came and started on
another grave in the next row, listening to the noise of the
sea booming in the distance and somehow seeing Mother's

face there amidst the newly cut flowers, the bright grass
and the dripping trees.

Later in the train I turned the contents of the carrier
bag out onto the spare seat beside me piece by piece. There
wasn't much, and what there was was the kind of stuff you
wondered about. Why had Mother wanted to keep a
brown envelope containing a packet of beads and a Union
Jack button? The photo album I remembered from childhood, and it didn't seem to have been added to since then,
although there was an odd, grainy picture of Father and
Mother from quite late on in the murk of Uncle Ralph's
front room, with Father looking kind of dreary and faded
behind the *Mercury*. In the past they'd sometimes talked
about letters that Father had sent home during the war.
There was no sign of these. The diaries were standard
Letts' 'commercials' from the early 50s, stamped with the
name of Smith Brothers, who were the big wholesale
grocers in town, and whose boss Father might just have
known at the Buffaloes. They weren't much more than
three inches square, with four or five lines available for
each day, but beneath the reminders of *Annunciation of
BVM* and *Maundy Thursday*, and *Dividends due* Mother
had scratched in a telegraphic account of her life in the
back parlour at Southtown. It took me a minute or two to
penetrate the particular shorthand she used for this task –
Father was 'F', for instance, I was 'T', while the shop was 'S'
or simply 'it'. A typical entry might go: *Van came at 8.
Boxes all over street: Mr H not pleased* ('Mr H' would have
been Mr Hargraves, the sub-post-master.) *F worried about
it. Fixing up to see bank again. T in new uniform. Back late
from school.* Or: *Picnic on dunes. T upset about something.
F up late doing books. Nice day.* Christ! I remembered that
day – the trek to the beach with our lunch done up in paper
bags, the endless search for a spot 'out of the wind',
Father's pale face as he champed his sandwiches and the
breeze flattening the coarse grass. God knows what I was
upset about, but reading this brought it all back. The effect
was unexpectedly shocking – not just to have bits of your
life set out before you, but the fact that Mother had done

it at all. In all the years I'd known her I'd never twigged she'd kept a diary, and it wouldn't have surprised me if Father hadn't either. The last volume dated from 1956. Inevitably it was all about the shop, the bank, the wholesalers stopping deliveries and 'F' being 'very worried'. *Letter this morning. Don't know what we shall do. T to school to do exam. Geography, he said.* I remembered that morning, too: half the shop's stock piled up in the middle of the floor, Mother in tears and an atmosphere you could have cut with a breadknife.

The train rattled through Ipswich and the Suffolk market towns, over the Stour and the huge expanse of black marsh with curlews picking at the water's edge, on into Essex, but I kept on reading. It was like a drug: Father, Mother and the old days, with the rain falling over the square and the lights going on in Wedderbury's, and the boys coming round delivering the evening paper, and Mother's voice in the yard and the smell from the bakery. Heaven knows I wasn't sentimental about it, but it made me think about Father and Mother in a way I hadn't done for years. I don't believe I reached any startling conclusions about them – except that Mother's urge to set things down on paper revealed a side to her that I'd never known about – I just felt a bit guilty about all that misery burning itself out in the parlour behind the shop while I went around chasing girls and nagging Father and Mother for extra pocket-money. It's what children do, of course, but it doesn't help to have it explained to you. But there it was, Mother was dead – her last few months hadn't been too bad from the sound of it – and Father too, there was nothing to be done, nobody could ever come into Lutterworth's again in search of a packet of Player's Navy Cut, and the whole thing was over. The carriage was starting to fill up by now – it was late afternoon on a Friday with people heading up to town – and in the end I put the things back in the bag and started thinking about the weekend, when Upward and I were actually going on stage together for the first time, and praying that it would be all right. I knew, you see, that these were old ghosts, and that though they'd come to haunt me from time to time the old world – Father, Mother, Yarmouth, even Mary and the Parmenters – was gone forever.

Curiously enough, though I hadn't told anyone the time of the train, Upward and Brenda were there to meet me at the station. I remember it as a typical Upward moment, typical of the way he did things, the impression he wanted to create, the eventual sacrifice of everything to his own egotism: the handshake in the dusk of Liverpool Street, the pat on the back—

'You all right?'

'Yes.'

'It go OK?'

'More or less.'

It's all mixed up in my mind with the trip back across London in the Friday night crowds, Brenda loitering behind us to look at the ads on the tube, Frith Street, and posters stuck to one side of the Minerva's battered door announcing the first public performance of 'Upward & King'.

My dreams are keeping me awake. Father and Mother back in the shop with the blinds drawn down and yellow light winking off the surfaces. Flat, even fields with distant sea. Waking up at these times – 3 or 4 a.m. – in silence except for the far-off traffic noise, the room seems too small, airless, fenced in. Members of the Ngongi, fetched up in cities or dragooned into the medical centres, will often be found at night straining at the walls that surround them. They think they're slowly moving forward to crush them, apparently.

Daniel sleeps uneasily too. Whatever he dreams rolls up to the surface and pulls him awake. Sometimes he drifts into my room and stands there by the bed, a quarter conscious. He has this curious, fresh, little boy smell – warm and somehow nourishing. Once, at one of these times, he said:

'Am I going back to live with Aunty Shena soon?'

'Soon.'

'After Christmas?'

'Probably.'

This is not a lie. Not necessarily. Who knows what will happen? Another letter came yesterday, on whose top left-hand corner someone had gone to the trouble of writing URGENT PLEASE OPEN THIS. I didn't open it. Urgency, as Upward often used to say, means different things to different people.

*

Kev and I are mates now. Big mates. We shout 'how do?' and 'all right?' matily to each other across the asphalt, have matey halves of lager in the pub down the road from the school before it's time to pick up Daniel and Neil. Unprompted, Kev has worked out where he first saw me: on television when he was fifteen or so. All this has a curious, two-way effect on Kev's attitude towards me. On the one hand, Kev is definitely admiring of the TV connection, with its attendant claims to expertise, power and money. On the other, Kev's a little bit puzzled – no, a lot puzzled – that I'm sitting with him in a pub in south-east London when I could be schmoozing with the chatshow hosts. Kev likes having me around, I deduce, but the fact of having me around is a kind of confirmation that I've failed. If I had power, money and expertise I wouldn't be talking to Kev.

What do I think about Kev? What interests me is his ability to switch between temperamental styles at the drop of a hat: apoplectic in the pub over some TV football match (*Kill the cunt! Go on, stamp on 'is 'ead!*) one minute, amiably nodding at his son the next. Professionally, I'd say Kev's life was governed by the roles he creates for himself: bloke, parent, jack-the-lad, consumer (like everyone else Kev is a mobile phone/cable TV/playstation obsessive). Demanding roles, too. Half the time when I see him Kev looks resentfully exhausted by the stresses of having to fix that stare, make that call (all Kev's mobile calls are, of course, completely unnecessary – calls to the football chat lines and the astrologers), yell amicably *Neil will you stop fucking about and get over 'ere* across the street. And yet I *like* Kev. I don't quite know how to put this into words. You could do worse than Kev, with his clueless observations about sport and the things he reads in the papers, and his bristled bald scalp, a whole lot worse.

Kev's outside the school gates now as I arrive to collect Daniel, Neil in tow, and smiling with edgy excitement. It doesn't take long to establish that something is up here in the asphalt playground and the polished corridor. There's a police car drawn up by the gate and a little cluster of anxious faces round the main door. Kev waves a hand up when he sees me, flicks a finger at the throng.

'What's up, Kev?'

'I dunno. Some bloke comes in and goes after one of the teachers or something.'

'Did they get him?'

'Nah,' Kev says. ''E's holed up in one of the offices or something, saying 'e's going to kill 'imself and that.'

Or something. And that. Kev's speech is peppered with these redundancies. He can't let a sentence out of his mouth without larding it with something that will nullify its meaning. Worried about Dan, I start off across the playground, stop as I see him loping towards me out of one of the side doors. He looks wide-eyed rather than frightened, mildly amused. It turns out that Miss Cox's boyfriend, recently evicted from her flat, arrived on the premises half an hour ago to plead his case. He did this in front of a class of thirty ten-year-olds. Frostily received, he opted to cut his losses by chasing Miss Cox out into the corridor while trying to throw a chair at her.

'What happened then?'

'It was OK, Dad. Jamal had his mobile so he called the police. And Justin went off to get Mr Crisp.'

Mr Crisp is the PE teacher, a six-foot-three-inch hooligan popularly supposed to have been a commando in the SAS. Nothing will please him more, I suspect, than the chance of incapacitating Miss Cox's boyfriend. What kind of children are we bringing up here, I wonder? For a moment a part of me is enraged at the thought of a brushed-off moron picking up the pieces of his self-esteem by chasing a girl round a classroom while some ten-year-old kids cower behind their desks.

There's a minor commotion going on over by the main doorway. The crowd parts and a couple of policemen – one older and bald, the other young and self-important – appear, propelling a handcuffed figure between them. Miss Cox's boyfriend is impossibly weedy, with one of those ridiculous paintbrush goatee beards. He looks as if he writes poems, or whatever the modern equivalent of writing poems is. No wonder Miss Cox told him to go.

As they reach the gate and the waiting police car the silence is unexpectedly broken.

'All right my son,' Kev yells delightedly. 'Give her one for me, eh?'

One or two people laugh. The younger of the two policemen grins. Miss Cox's boyfriend looks, if anything, even more doom-laden and ground-down. Far off, in the grey, clouded distance, I can see the gulls massing over the river.

*

Several phone calls from Lucy. I have an idea, reading between the lines, that the boyfriend is, or will shortly become, an ex-boyfriend. No explanation is forthcoming. I don't ask for one. She seems particularly keen to know if I can glean any more Upward material. I tell her I'll write another letter to Audrey. 'How's Daniel?' she asks, several times. I get an odd sensation of something running beneath the surface, a kind of willed complicity I can't quite put my finger on moving across the wires between us.

*

The red Mondeo is parked outside the house when we get back and DI Stevens is leaning negligently against the door. How long has he been here? Twenty minutes? Half an hour? When he sees us he skips down the steps and waits for us to pass. A brown paper parcel containing something flat and oblong sticks out from under his arm.

'Thought this might be a good time to call,' Stevens says. 'Mind if I come in?'

'Be my guest.'

Inside there is post lying on the doormat – circulars, electricity bills, another buff rectangle with PLEASE OPEN! inked on the corner. The answerphone light pulses. Daniel moves off into the front room and switches on the TV, not in the least interested in Stevens, or me. Stevens picks up the envelope and looks at it knowingly.

'Someone here's pretty keen to get in touch with you by all accounts.'

'I shouldn't wonder.'

'Don't mind me pointing it out, do you? Only it's the kind of thing that tells you about people.'

'What does it tell you?'

Stevens pirouettes on his heels with surprising grace for

a short man of fifty running to fat. 'Well, in your case it says that you don't like opening post, doesn't it?'

We go down into the kitchen where I make tea while Stevens prowls nervously round cupboards and sinks, pulls out a recipe book and looks at it, slots it back. Seen for a second time, he looks much more extraordinary than before: hair rising off his scalp like spun sugar, the dark eyebrows half comic, half sinister. In the end he says:

'You'll have seen the stuff in the papers?'

'Some of it.'

'Amazing isn't it, the memories people have? Twenty years, a quarter of a century ago, and it's just like yesterday isn't it? Secretaries. Commissionaires. All lining up to dish the dirt. I interviewed Lord Cartwright the other day. Interviewed! Pretends he's gaga half the time. But I know better. Ever come across him, sir?'

'Once or twice. He was at Sir Gavin Newsome's place once when I stayed there.'

'Was that when they talked about bringing in the army? Doesn't seem possible, does it, these days? But I can tell you, there were others used to talk about it. Coppers too. Now, your pal Upward. He knew Cartwright well, didn't he?'

I try to remember what Upward had said about Cartwright.

'He used to talk about him now and again.'

'Lots of hospitality, too,' Stevens says. He recites in a curious, high-pitched voice. 'I've a note of a luncheon at the Gay Hussar, March 1984, attended by among others Mr Arthur Upward and his wife Paula.'

'His wife was called Audrey. My wife – my ex-wife – was called Paula.'

'Sorry, sir. My mistake. And your friend never said anything about that occasion? These occasions?'

'Nothing. Besides, we weren't working together by then.'

'No, of course you weren't, were you? But you saw him, didn't you? You and your ex-wife? Remind me what Mrs King's name is again.'

'Was. Paula.'

'I'm sorry, sir.'

Upstairs I can hear the low rumble of the TV. Outside the window the light fades over low, cheerless rooftops. Three weeks to Christmas. Stevens blinks seriously up at the crockery shelves, hefts the brown paper parcel under his armpit, squints at his watch.

'Tell me sir, what did you think about that lot when you knew them? Newsome and Cartwright and the others. Cooper. When you used to see them. When you used to tell them jokes. What did you think of them?'

What did I think of them? I ponder this for a while as Stevens takes the packet out from under his arm and swaps it back from hand to hand.

'I don't know. It was part of the world I was caught up in, I suppose. You never knew who you were going to meet. What they were going to say.'

'And now you don't meet them and that's that?' Stevens says. 'Do you know what I think, sir? I don't think it'll come to court. All too long ago. Or rather not the kind of thing we want to remember. After all, it's a brave new world now isn't it, and we're all working for the same things?'

'Are we?'

'Oh yes, sir. Not the shadow of a doubt. Now, before I go would you do me a favour?'

Unravelled and laid out on the kitchen table, the parcel turns out to contain a copy of Upward's autobiography. I pick it up and leaf through it for a moment, marvelling at the cheek of some of the pictures, the one side by side with Sammy Davis the result simply of Upward's happening to leave a restaurant at the same time.

'What do you want me to write?'

'Oh, I don't know. Something like "from the other half". That should do it.'

I do this. Stevens pores over the inscription for a bit, smiling slightly.

'Thank you, sir,' he says. 'Much appreciated. I'll try not to bother you again. Leave you to yourself and your responsibilities, if you take my meaning.'

We wander upstairs to the hallway. I can see Daniel's

silhouette framed by the light in front of the TV. Stevens stoops down and picks up the envelope marked PLEASE OPEN!

'Do you know what I'd do if I were you, sir?' he says. 'I'd open it.'

*

Twenty minutes later Daniel comes into the kitchen to raid the biscuit tin. He looks round once or twice as if expecting Stevens to rematerialise.

'That bloke. Was he a copper?'

'Yes. What do you know about coppers?'

'I know a bit.'

I look at him as he says this, striving to find something that will connect him to the ten-year-old I was, Father and Mother in the shop, Southtown and the rest. I suppose it shouldn't surprise me that there isn't anything. Does he wonder about it? Or does the past simply not exist to a ten-year-old boy? The children of the Ngongi have a kind of folk memory, apparently: drought, rains, emigration, the red ants in the dunes. Real events blend effortlessly into symbolic high points. A wedding is always 'the wedding', a death always 'the death'. I gather him up in a half-embrace, head bent against my shoulder, which he accepts for a while before twisting away. Searching for something that will keep him here, keep his face in front of me, I say:

'Do you like living here?'

He thinks about this. I can sense him meditating likely answers, weighing the relative advantages of truth and not giving offence.

'If you wanted we could live somewhere else.'

'Where?' He looks less interested now, as if he knows I began the conversation without any definite end in view.

'Dan,' I say. 'When that man came into the classroom after Miss Cox, were you scared?'

'A bit. Neil said he was a wuss though.'

He stacks the biscuits up in the palm of one hand, half a dozen of them at least, claps the other hand over the top and wanders out.

*

Later, when Daniel is eating his tea, I go out round the corner for a packet of fags. Early in December the place undergoes small but significant changes. The off-licences break out in a rash of artificial snow and special offers. Orange peel accumulates in the gutter. Even the Rashids' shop isn't immune to these ghostly twitches on the seasonal thread. Approaching the window through the early evening shadow I can see what might just be an approximation of a yule log propped up on a bed of artificial grass and a stencilled sign that says 'A MERRY XMAS TO ALL OUR CUSTOMERS'. Inside vegetables rot under the sickly strip-lighting. Mrs Rashid sits stark and motionless at the till, as if in a trance. Her husband is at the back of the shop arranging the little bags of crisps marked 'Not to be sold separately from multi-pack' on a shelf. Something in the way he bends over the cardboard box at his feet stirs a memory of someone else, a long way off. I pay for the cigarettes in a silence broken only by the jangle of the till, the rustle of the crisp packets and Mrs Rashid's ponderous breathing, walk out into the road again. Invisible here, a quarter of a mile away beyond the house-fronts and the backs of warehouses, the river declares itself by its smell, that odd reek of stagnant water and burnt oil. On the instant I realise that Mr Rashid, head down over the wholesaler's boxes, reminds me of Father: the same pious absorption in the task, a punctiliousness not at all excluding a sense of pride. One of my sharpest memories of Father, oddly enough, is of coming into the shop to find him standing by the door, arms folded across his chest, raptly surveying the rows of chocolate boxes and the jars of pipe tobacco, a little monarch all alone in the world he'd created.

Suddenly I feel an irrepressible urge to go back there, back to the square, to Father and Mother's ghosts and the old world, to see what's become of it, what shapes and colours it's taken on. It's thirty-four years since I went to

Yarmouth but it can't all have changed, surely? Railway station, churches, familiar landmarks – surely they'd still be there? Or at least there'd be something remaining that you could fasten on to, keep for yourself? If it comes to that, Father's shop will still be a shop. Or even if it isn't, there'll still be enough to remind you of what had been: beech trees in the square, say, or Wedderbury's big high windows gleaming in the twilight. Walking back down the empty street, past the lines of cars, watching the helicopter lights moving through the violet sky, I start making plans. Even allowing for the change at Norwich, Yarmouth isn't more than three hours away by train. With someone to look after Daniel, I could manage half a day there and still get back in the evening. Half a day would be enough for the kind of thing I have in mind: Father and Mother, the beech trees and Wedderbury's windows.

Back at the house, Daniel is perched in front of the TV, hands cupped beneath his chin. Down in the kitchen I sit listening to the bump and judder of a train moving in the distance towards Plumstead, trying to remember what Yarmouth station looks like. Try as I may, I can't manage it. The incidentals – the approach, the wide hall beyond the ticket barrier, the curved street outside – are all there. For some reason, though, the thing itself, the point of it all, utterly escapes me.

*

Later in the evening Lucy phones. She seems a bit subdued, but interested in the Yarmouth trip.

'Who's going to look after Daniel? Will he be OK on his own?'

'There's a kids' party he can go to that afternoon. And then I can collect him later in the evening. It's not a problem.'

The children's party, which I'd forgotten about until reminded by the strip of fluorescent cardboard on the mantelpiece, is Neil's eleventh, courtesy of Kev at the flat.

'So what will you do when you get there?'

'Walk around. Take a look at the sea. How's the programme?'

'All the things I told you about have been fixed. They should finish cutting it together in a week.'

'That's good then. Makes me feel like a radio celebrity again.'

There's a pause.

'How's the boyfriend?'

'Actually,' Lucy says, 'we've split up. At least he's not here at the moment.'

'I'm sorry.'

'There's no need to be,' Lucy says. 'I'm glad I found out about the things I found out about when I did. Look,' she goes on, 'there are one or two things I need to go through. Little details for the voice-over. Can I come over some time next week?'

Once again I get the sense of something stirring through the distance between us, something that Lucy knows about and I don't.

'Come next Thursday,' I tell her. 'The day after I get back. And then I can tell you all about it.'

'Yes,' Lucy says. 'That would be nice.'

TV Times

INTERVIEWER: How would you describe yourself as comedians?

UPWARD: Us? We're funny comedians. That kind.
Seriously, we're the sort you could take your
wife to see. Even leave her there, if you
wanted to.

INTERVIEWER: What would you say your influences were?

KING: Gordon's. Teacher's. We're not fussy.

INTERVIEWER: Seriously. Is there anyone you've
consciously modelled yourselves on?

UPWARD: Harold Wilson, now he's funny. But he needs
management. And too much of it's
unscripted.

INTERVIEWER: Do you differentiate yourselves? Would
either of you say you were the straight man?

UPWARD: I do the talking. He's the quiet one.

KING: …

INTERVIEWER: I beg your pardon?

UPWARD: He says he's the quiet one.

INTERVIEWER: You've been together a long time?

UPWARD: Like my fiancée's knees.

KING: You shouldn't talk about his fiancée. It's a
sore point.

UPWARD: I'll say it is.

INTERVIEWER: What do you hope to do in television
comedy?

KING: Stay in it. Seriously folks, we've seen the
competition. Morecambe & Wise. Mike and
Bernie. *Songs Of Praise*. We're just happy to
be here.

UPWARD: *You* might be.

KING: But you haven't got my sunny disposition,
have you?

UPWARD:	Never touched it.
INTERVIEWER:	Is there a life after comedy?
UPWARD:	Is there a life after what?
KING:	You're not taking us seriously.
UPWARD:	But we don't take ourselves seriously.
KING:	We're professional comedians. I don't think you could get much more serious than that.

1973

What It Was Like

So what was it like being on stage? People were always asking you that. Women, sometimes, but mostly men. You'd be walking down Oxford Street, say, on your way to the BBC, coming out of a pub round the back of Langham Place, sauntering into some hotel foyer somewhere (Blackpool, Bournemouth, Morecambe) and there they'd be, edging surreptitiously across the road, the pavement or the carpet to nod – they always nodded – paw at your elbow – they always did that, too – and ask, shyly but as if they really wanted to know, *'What's it like being on stage then?'* Thinking about it, it was mostly blokes. Fat ones. Thin ones. Prosperous-looking ones. Down-at-heel ones. And always the nod – as if in some long ago schoolyard you'd swapped cigarette cards together – always the tug at your elbow – as if they wanted to reassure themselves that you weren't made of ectoplasm – and the urgency. *'What's it like being on stage then?'* As if the answer would get you a better life, a better wife, a better job, a better car. And you'd say 'Sorry' or 'Pardon' or 'In a hurry', or stop and scratch your signature on a piece of paper, or a fag-packet or a calling-card, which was usually enough for all but the most persistent ones (who were capable of following you down the street, to the door of your car, to the door of your house, at which point you said 'Bugger off' or 'Calling the police', which finally sent them away). But you didn't stop thinking about the question, which was an interesting one and had exercised your mind ever since you first did it.

So what was it like being on stage then? Funnily enough, being on stage was a lot like *not* being on stage. Apart from the lights, that is. And the smoke. And the faces. Which is to say that there were two of you talking to each other, to all intents and purposes having a normal conversation, except for the pauses, the gaps in this world you were creating, where the laughter flowed in. Laughter, you found out pretty soon, had a life of its own. You could say something, wait for the laugh, feel it start to fade, open your mouth again, and suddenly another wave would roll in from somewhere, somewhere you couldn't see, and nearly drown you in its intensity. Laughter also had – and you found this out even sooner – a death of its own as well. You could build the waves up, have them crashing round your head as you clung onto the microphone stand for support, stretch out for that last paroxysm of delight, and suddenly, without warning, there'd be utter silence. And you'd smile – you always did that – stare back at the faces – you always did that, too – while you worked out just what trick you'd failed to master, just exactly where you'd gone wrong.

The worst thing was the faces. It's not true that comedians don't see the people they're performing to. What else are you supposed to look at? You saw them all: animated, impassive, grim, eager, loving it, hating it, missing it. Sometimes they were tiny rows of pin-heads back in the far distance. Other times they were great balloons with the features sketched on in charcoal. You could never tell, just as you could never tell how you wanted them to react. You didn't want them to turn away, because that meant they'd lost interest, but you didn't want them staring at you full-on, because that meant you couldn't get away from them. All the time you looked at them you were in danger of coming apart from the person you were working with. It was a double act, so you wanted the faces on your side against him, but you knew you could never take the faces for granted, because if you gave them an inch they'd be back on the other side. You loved them, but you hated them, you wanted them to go away, but you also knew that if they did that you'd want them to come back again.

The next worst thing about being on stage was Upward. Upward was like the faces only not quite so bad. You wanted Upward to like the way things were going – you always wanted that – but you knew that the worse things went, the greater the chance of Upward making some face-saving intervention – and you wanted that, too. You wanted to come in on cue, and you wanted not to as well. You wanted to be certain what was going on in Upward's head – and you never could be certain – and you wanted, mentally, to be all over the place because you knew that made for better comedy. You wanted what you were doing to coast zestfully through gag after gag, which meant, of course, that there was a danger of you being predictably unexpected, or unexpectedly predictable, depending on what the audience wanted from you. When you were on the stage you wanted to be off it, but when you *were* off it, back in the dressing room, say, under the bright lights with Captain Groves fisting you a champagne flute, emerging light-headedly into the stone-cold, small-hour air, you wanted to be back on it. You were always planning some of the act, and you were always stopping yourself planning it because you knew that, if you did, what you said would probably be funnier. And then, at the end, when you stood side by side on the shiny, slippery stage with the sweat sizzling off your wrists, wide-eyed in the smoke, while the audience clapped or whistled, or did whatever they did – and somehow you were always too tired to notice – you were always vaguely disappointed, annoyed that you'd spent a second too long coming back at the line Upward had dropped without warning into the middle of the last-but-one routine, or ridden the laugh instead of driving it off elsewhere.

And what was it like being on stage with Upward? People were always asking you that, too. Men sometimes, but mostly women. You'd be cruising down the front at some blighted holiday resort, pondering your prawn cock-tail in a restaurant window, tripping up the steps of some suburban theatre somewhere (Croydon, Wimbledon, Romford) and there they'd be, edging nervously across the esplanade, the doorway, the coconut matting, to blink – they always blinked – come to rest a foot from your shoulder – they always did that, too – and ask, anxiously,

but as if they really wanted to know, '*What's it like being
on stage with Upward?*' Thinking about it, it was mostly
women. Young ones. Old ones. Unassuming ones. Brazen
ones. And always the blink – as if in some long ago dance-
hall you'd held hands together in the corner – always the
coming to rest a foot from your shoulder – as if you had a
force-field around you that couldn't be breached – and
the urgency – '*What's it like being on stage with Upward?*'
As if knowing the answer would get you a better life, a
better husband, better sex, a better figure. And you'd say
'Fine' or 'Cheers' or 'Meeting someone', or stop and
scrawl your signature on a table napkin or a menu card or
an envelope, which was usually enough for all but the
most persistent ones (who were capable of turning up in
your hotel corridor, in your room, in the back of your car,
at which point you said 'I'm married', whether you were
or not, or 'Calling the police', which finally shooed them
away). But you didn't stop thinking about the question,
which was an interesting one, and had exercised your
mind ever since you first did it.

So what was it like being on stage with Upward then?
Funnily enough, being on stage with Upward was a lot like
not being on stage with Upward. Upward, you found out
pretty soon, had a life of his own. You could say something,
something scripted, something you'd gone through a dozen
times that week in the rehearsal room, and suddenly
Upward would be off somewhere, somewhere you couldn't
follow, leaving you stranded on the beach while the real
action was half a mile off in the billowing surf. Upward also
had – and you found this out even sooner – a death of his
own as well. You could build the routine up, have the gags
snap into place like a row of suspender clips, almost unable
to believe your luck, stretch out to offer Upward that final
line – proudly yet humbly, because it would bring your
final humiliation – and suddenly, without warning, there'd
be utter silence. And you'd smile – you always did that –
stare back at Upward's red, perspiring face – you always
did that, too – while you wondered just what trick you'd
failed to master, just exactly where you'd gone wrong.

*

Upward always liked to say that we'd never done the same
show twice. Strictly speaking, this was only half-true.
Upward had certainly never done the same show twice in
his life. On the other hand, I had. About two or three
hundred times, in fact.

Upward had original views on why an audience came to
see us, even more original views on what an audience was.
He used to say:

'Let's say a hundred people turn up. Twenty might be
there because they genuinely want to see you. You know,
what you do strikes them as funny. Another ten might be
there because they've got it into their heads that they
might like to see you. Another thirty don't care either way
– they're just the kind of people who turn up to things.
Another twenty will be people who've come along with
other people. Another five will be there by mistake.
Seriously. That's your first problem, right? That everybody's come to see you for different reasons.'

'Or for no reason.'

'Exactly. There might be people there who're actively
hostile. I once did a show up north where the place had
been in trouble with the watch committee over smutty
jokes, and the front row was full of Salvation Army lasses.
But you've got another problem, and that's the range of
your audience. Let's say sixty of them are men and forty of
them are women. Ten of them might be fairly intelligent.
Eighty of them will be varying degrees of average. Another
ten of them might be imbecilic. What do you do? How do
you get the bottom ninety to laugh at something the top
ten are interested in?'

'Aren't there supposed to be universal absolutes? You
know, a man who slips on a banana skin is just funny,
whether you're an Oxford don or a dustman?'

'It doesn't work like that.'

'Laughter the unifying force?'

'No.'

Upward's theory of comedy – why people came to see us, why they laughed – was frankly elitist. He believed that the members of an average audience, at any rate the sort of audience you got at the Minerva, didn't really know how to respond to what they saw. They might want to laugh, but there wasn't any guarantee that they would laugh. Nothing could be taken for granted. Worse, Upward thought, the audience was in the grip of a collective neurosis, wanting to laugh but worrying that other people would despise them if they laughed at the wrong things.

'So what do you do?'

'What do you do? You go for the top man, of course.'

According to Upward, every audience had two, or at most three, controlling intelligences – people who knew what was funny, were prepared to respond to what was going on on stage and, most important of all, could influence the other spectators. The problem, according to Upward, was that such people weren't easily swayed. If they weren't impressed, their silence could damp down the enthusiasm of other people by a kind of telepathy. This meant they needed careful handling: reassurance, discreet asides, catchphrases. As Upward described it, there were actually two performances going on – one in which you fished for, and flattered, a handful of sophisticates, another in which you encouraged them to take their discovery of how funny you were to the masses.

Watching Upward as he rocketed around stage at the start of a show, quickly throwing out feelers into the audience, working out where the laughter lay, I used to understand something of the difference between us. Whereas I was part of a picture made up of the faces, the smoke, the stage light and Upward himself, Upward lived in a world of his own. But there was more to it than this, I realised. I repeated my lines; Upward wove patterns. Sometimes at the start of a routine he'd pick up a phrase and play with it, throw it out to the audience and catch it back, and then store it for later use – bringing it out again, say, halfway through the next sketch. At these times whatever we were doing teetered like a juggernaut in mid-lane.

There was no knowing which way it would turn. There was nothing you could do. You merely had to wait until Upward had finished, hoping that the stopping-off point bore some resemblance to the original running order.

So what was it like being on stage with Upward? Being on stage with Upward was a lot like *not* being on stage with Upward. Except that everything had moved up a gear, got brighter, louder, more extreme. Sometimes in mid-sketch, especially when Upward had gone off into one of his closed, private whirls, you'd shoot him a mute, imploring look – an access-requested look, an exclusion-zone look – and watch it break on the shoreline of his stare. Or you'd miss something – some catchphrase you didn't know about, some gesture that hadn't been rehearsed – and spend the rest of the half-hour wondering what would happen afterwards. We used to have fights in those days. Most double acts end up fighting, of course. But these were proper punch-ups. Back in the dressing room, grim and furious after ten seconds or so of weak applause, Upward would suddenly put down the cigarette, the bottle or the towel he was holding and wing a fat hand into my face. I might respond by picking up the chair that lay between us and throwing it at him. In reply, Upward might launch his head meatily but unhurriedly in the region of my shoulder. Eventually, after a minute or so, as if at some pre-arranged signal, we'd stop, light cigarettes, negligently rearrange the furniture, give each other playful little cuffs and slaps, sink down into chairs. A bit later Captain Groves, whose office lay along the corridor, might put his head round the door and say unconcernedly, 'Everything all right boys?' And you'd say 'Fine', or in Upward's case 'Champion', or 'With you in a minute.' Once, by some fluke of anticipation, Captain Groves arrived in mid-scuffle. He stood in the doorway for a minute or two, with the ash collecting on the end of his cigar, and a slightly puzzled look on his face, watching the sailing chairs and the savage head-butts. Then we heard him marching back along the corridor.

*

There are patterns now, figures visible in the mist. For some reason this time has a kind of clarity that's absent from earlier parts of my life. Later parts, too. Where did it come from, that heightened sense of awareness? What produced it? It's difficult to tell. But the late 60s are very vivid to me in a way that other times are not. Not simply in the things that happened around me, but in the contours of my own life. Brighton seafront in 1968, a girl whose name I can't remember sitting in a hotel bedroom a year or so later, Upward's face in the rehearsal room – all this is much more real to me than vast tracts of recent life. Loafing with Upward once in a seaside café in the rain one Sunday morning at some resort where we were doing summer season, a train ride north one November through the South Yorkshire slag-heaps where you waited for a daylight that never came, horses seen in a field somewhere in the West Country – grey horses, they were, with long steelwire manes – lolloping away through the mist. There was a feeling of well-being, too, that I can't quite put into words, the sensation of having left certain things behind – Father and Mother, Mary and the gulls – and not being worried about what might take their place. It's not true to say that I forgot Yarmouth at this time – how could I? It was there every time I smoked a cigarette, or went past a corner shop, or saw one of those maps of southern England that makes it look like an angel taking wing, and the east coast is the angel's head. But there was a way in which it was all somehow filed and docketed, ready for me to take up again when I wanted it, not when it wanted me.

We left Soho early in 1966: 'not before time' according to Upward. The official line was that the BBC wouldn't give airtime to a double act that played three nights a week at places like the Minerva, but at bottom I think it was simple restlessness on Upward's part, that he was tired of the flat, the grey Soho dawns and performing to fat men in tuxedos. Brenda disappeared somewhere. Counting up what we'd put away in the past six months we found it came to £500. The plan was to go on the road, log up experience, get our names known outside Soho and then come back to London for a proper go at the BBC, which in those days was the Holy Grail of anyone who took themselves at all seriously. Sometimes we'd be in a pub in the West End and some fat little middle-aged man would march in with the *Daily Mail* under his arm and a couple of sidekicks trailing in his wake, and Upward would go rigid with suppressed emotion. There was never any need to ask him who it was.

We had an agent by this time – an old white-haired bloke who claimed to have represented Tommy Handley – and there was talk of a 'sound test', which was the name they gave to radio auditions, but in the end it all fell through and we went off on the road.

So what was it like going out on the road? Funnily enough, nobody ever asked you this. All that's left now is a jumble of impressions – the colour of the fried egg yolk at breakfast in the boarding houses, which wasn't so much pale yellow as a kind of light green, spending the night once in a bed-and-breakfast somewhere up north where they didn't even have beds, just a couple of mattresses spread out on the floor, waking up one morning in some godforsaken room in Liverpool and seeing a rat perched on the chest-of-drawers feeding off a packet of sandwiches that Upward had left there the night before. Out of interest I totted up the number of different beds I slept in that first year, and it came to 129.

In those days there were recognised routes around the country for comedy acts. The south coast was one: Ramsgate, Brighton, Bournemouth. Another was what was known as the 'east run', from Skegness up through Grimsby and Hull to Harrogate. Variety was long gone by this time, but in its wake lay a chain of concert halls and theatres that managers were still trying desperately to fill. This meant that you ended up in some weird line-ups – fifth on the bill, say, behind a beat group, a male-voice choir, an impressionist and a gang of plate-spinners. A bit later we moved up to the northern club circuit, where the money was better but you had to keep an eye on your material. Upward had warned me about the working men's clubs:

'Two hundred piss-heads out of the pit or the foundry on a Friday night with their wives dressed up like parrots, and if it isn't about mothers-in-law or niggers you might as well go home.'

He was right, too. When we went on stage the first time – it might have been in Worksop or Chesterfield – doing the set we'd used on the south coast, not a soul clapped. I remember looking out into the crowd – they used to sit five or six to a table with a forest of beer bottles piled up in the middle – and no one was even looking at us. They weren't hostile, they'd just marked us down for what we were: 'smart', know-all southern comedians. Even then there were huge differences in what the audiences wanted out of comedy. Southern audiences liked you to score off your opposite number; northern crowds preferred you to tell jokes against yourself. We played a few dates in Scotland around this time, and it was even worse – if you told jokes about religion people would walk out. On the other hand they'd scream with laughter if you mentioned death, which was something you couldn't touch south of the border. In the end Upward wrote some stuff which was nearer to the old northern variety routines – sketches where we played Lancashire housewives at the bus stop or mill girls out courting, and implied, without stating it in so many words, that we both came from somewhere west of the Pennines.

As for the life you were living off stage, it was scarcely worth the name. On average each engagement lasted three nights, which meant that you'd barely settled yourself in before it was time to pack your bags and head off to the next place, which might take as little as an hour or as much as a day. Upward was in charge of the bookings. One of my chief memories of him in those days is on the phone, in coin boxes near railway stations, in hotel foyers, in lodging house back rooms with the landlady grimly reckoning up the cost behind the door. Usually he managed to stick to some kind of pattern, but there were dreadful days when we ended up trekking halfway across the north of England on buses and rattletrap trains. Once, I remember, owing to some mistake in the arrangements, we played a night in

Leeds, upped sticks for a couple of days in Carlisle and then rushed back to Leeds again to perform in front of a dozen elderly domino players in what looked like somebody's front room.

Worse than this, perhaps, was the sheer unreality of the places we fetched up in. I'd never been in the North before, and it took me at least a month to get used to it: huge sprawling cities where every surface was black with dirt, and the bricks looked as if they'd been dipped in creosote; the endless rows of back-to-back houses with front doors opening into the street, which people like Father and Mother would have died rather than inhabit; and beyond the towns the rolling countryside, with hills rather than flat fields, the stone walls running across them like piping over a dress, and in the distance, drawn up beneath smoke clouds, the next clump of houses and billowing factories. Upward, I noticed, was completely matter-of-fact about all this. I watched him once on a train journey from Leeds to Sheffield – the filthiest landscape you ever saw in your life, with pools of stagnant water gleaming at the edges with chemicals, where even the grass had a brownish sheen – and his face was quite impassive. I couldn't look at it without thinking of the line in 'Jerusalem', which we'd sung at school, about 'dark, Satanic mills', but to him it was simply the train ride from Leeds to Sheffield. Curiously, this feeling of being in another time followed me everywhere we went. Even in the lodging houses – these tended to be run by people with some connection to 'the business' as they put it – you were suddenly back in a world that was thirty years out of date, with pictures of old Variety stars on the wall and 'father' proudly admitting to have appeared on stage with Will Hay in 1933. It was just the same out in the streets. The 60s – long hair, mini-skirts and the rest – really only happened in London. North of the Trent the towns were still full of women in granny coats, bee-hives and drain-piped Teddy boys.

What Upward made of all this – grey streets, the working men's clubs, even the 60s themselves – was anyone's guess. It wouldn't be true, for example, to say

that he was 'at home' in the north of England. Set down in
some northern city – Leeds, Sheffield, Newcastle – he had
a trick of emphasising sides of his personality that were
slightly at odds with local tastes in speech, dress and diet.
These transformations were all the more unexpected in
that they represented a complete reversal of his London
get-up. Seeing him in Frith Street – hearing him order a
drink, or clapping a friend on the back – it was impossible
to believe that he had been born anywhere south of
Lancashire. Fetched up west of the Pennines, on the other
hand, he could suddenly turn back into a Londoner.
Perhaps this is too sharp a distinction to explain the series
of carefully engineered cultural collisions that Upward
enjoyed provoking. Watching him in a restaurant in the
north-east, carefully asking a waiter to explain the
meaning of 'hot pot' or 'barm cake', it was difficult to
know what game he was playing, or if a game was being
played at all.

In the end I decided that there were bits of his professional life that he simply couldn't bear to give up, the fake
Upward walking off stage into the real world, but even this
somehow begged more questions than it answered.
Irritable, nervy, self-conscious, Upward was capable of
lightning shifts of gear, guaranteed to wrongfoot anyone
not familiar with the way he operated. Once, a bit after this
period, I watched him being interviewed by a journalist for
a Manchester evening paper. The interview began with the
two greeting each other virtually as long-lost brothers.
Upward may even have called the interviewer 'wack'.
Within the first few minutes he used half-a-dozen dialect
expressions unknown to me. There were references to 'up
here' and 'us Northern folk'. Then, without warning, the
atmosphere started to change. After a bit I realised that
Upward was having to have explained to him the existence
of the Manchester Ship Canal. Shortly after that he
claimed not to know that there were two local football
teams. It was all much too flagrant to be ignored.
Afterwards I asked him:

'What did you think you were doing?'

'What d'y' mean?'

'Pretending not to know about the Roses Match. Or Len Hutton?'

'There's too many of them bloody northern mascots,' Upward said with surprising bitterness. 'Ken Dodd. Cilla bloody Black.' He broke into mimicry. ' "My dad worked in t'pit, and we allus went to Morecambe for us holidays." They're not getting me on that lark.'

It was impossible to work out what he meant by this. Nobody, outwardly, could have been more 'Northern' than Upward. At the same time, nobody could have hated more the kind of things northernness was supposed to consist of. In the end I decided that it was simply Upward using one highly significant part of himself – where he came from – as a weapon, an infinitely adaptable weapon, too, as it could be turned on friend and foe alike. And yet knowing this didn't at all solve the problem of Upward, what he wanted, what he was after, where he was going to stop. I remember once asking him, not in any deliberate sense but simply to keep the ball rolling, what he 'wanted'. Upward put down the newspaper he was reading and gave me his full attention.

'What do I want? I'd like to shag every girl in Lancashire, eat off gold plates and have Bobby Charlton ask me for my autograph. And then I'd like to sit down and think about it.'

Some of this I noticed and thought about at the time. A bit more I simply absorbed and filed away for future reference. I was twenty-seven then, twenty-eight, and for all the claustrophobia of the lodging house bedrooms and the cheap rehearsal gaffs, I had things to think about apart from Upward. I was seeing places, too, in a way I'd never done before, not since the old army days. The names ran on in my head in clusters – Bristol, Exeter and Penzance; Broadstairs, Deal and Ramsgate; Clacton, Southend and Felixstowe. Dead English towns, for the most part, sleeping in the summer sun or the winter fogs, but I'd never seen them before. I don't remember much about them – a recreation ground near Margate, once, where I sat and smoked cigarettes for a whole summer afternoon, watching the children swarm over the slides, a boating lake somewhere on the Essex coast which had iced up in the frost, with bird tracks pittering over its surface – just the pleasure of being there, taking things in. I was growing up. It was five years since I'd last seen Mary or worked at the Sun Alliance. Somehow it seemed a lot longer – all tied up with Father and Mother and my teens rather than the immediate past. From time to time on my travels I'd send postcards back to the people I remembered from those days – Uncle Ralph, Uncle George and Aunt Sheila. I don't know if they ever received them, much less what they thought if they did.

Meanwhile, in a small way, I'd begun to enjoy myself. For a start we were seeing glimpses of a life beyond the boarding houses and the seedy theatres. Late in 1967, just as Upward had promised, we started getting radio work. Nothing very much, usually just guest spots on other people's shows, but it meant that the bookers and the club managers treated you with respect. A bit later we did warm-ups for Frankie Howerd at Blackpool. We even – God knows how Upward fixed this – had bit-parts in *Magical Mystery Tour*. If you look very carefully in the coach tour scenes, where Ringo's aunt is telling him not to be so 'historical', you can see a couple of characters sprawled over the back seat. The one in the straw hat and the carmine and blue boating blazer is Upward. The other one is me. We started doing private dates as well: a hundred businessmen in a country hotel, say, wanting jokes about Harold Wilson and devaluing the pound. There was a weird afternoon once in the very early days, when we were fixed up to play at a private party in the East End, and no one would tell us who we were performing to. We went there by cab, down the Mile End Road, then off into a warren of sidestreets. All the time I could see Upward getting more and more nervy.

'Who do you reckon it is?' he kept asking. 'Bloody Krays or someone?'

Eventually we pulled into a square where forty or fifty

people – middle-aged men in overcoats, mostly, wearing
war medals – were standing in rows outside a pub.
Suddenly a Daimler swung into the square from the far
side and there was a forest of salutes. Nazi salutes.
Dumped on the pavement by the pub door, I looked on
while the men – there were a few teenagers with short hair
and Crombie coats – filed past and Upward skulked inside
to make enquiries. He came back looking white and
furious.

'Mosley,' he said bitterly.

'What?'

'Like I said. Sir Oswald bloody Mosley.'

Without even stopping to discuss it we headed back
across the square, past the empty Daimler, towards the
nearest sidestreet. Reaching the car, something struck
Upward.

'Hang on a sec,' he said.

Simultaneously a volley of cheering erupted inside the
pub. Shouting voices, feet drumming on floorboards, the
boom of the smashed glass as Upward hurled the half-
brick through the Daimler's windscreen, the stillness that
mysteriously returned to the square twenty seconds later –
all this has stuck in my head.

In the 60s people began to tie up their own experiences
with history. Where were you when Kennedy died? When
England won the World Cup? When the slag-heap tipped
over onto Aberfan? When the other Kennedy died? When
Armstrong and Aldrin walked on the moon? It says something for the kind of life Upward and I were living all this
time that I scarcely noticed. I remember watching the
World Cup final in a hotel bedroom somewhere in the
Midlands, while Upward (who hated sport of any description) worked on a script. The Aberfan disaster made a bit
more of an impression, if only because we were in Wales at
the time and there were collecting boxes outside every
shop. Bobby Kennedy I remember reading about in the
Daily Mirror one morning while Upward sacked our agent
over the phone. As for the moon landing, who knows where
we were, what we were doing back in July 1969 a fortnight

or so before my twenty-ninth birthday. Needless to say I
can't recall that either. Like Mosley's face, the joke John
Lennon told me in 1967 and the colour of the south coast
buses, the whole thing has simply disappeared. Upward,
who had the better memory, would have remembered.

*

From the street the bare wooden steps went up sharply
and apparently indefinitely – the effect was a bit like the
Minerva in reverse – through the building. Just at the point
where you thought you could go no further, where the
view downwards became a dizzying prospect of jutting
bannisters, they reached a summit: a wide landing with a
single door set in the farthermost wall. Inside, two long,
high-ceilinged rooms – there was a kitchen and bathroom
on the floor below – looked out over the seafront: rows of
shops on the further side giving way to a rickety esplanade,
nondescript boats drawn up on the shale, beyond that the
sea itself. Of all the places we stayed in, it was by far the
most memorable: detached, deserted, eerie. Climbing the
stairs at night – there was a push-button light switch that
gave out on the second flight – you were lost in absolute
darkness. Whether the other flats were inhabited or not –
and in a fortnight's residence I never set eyes on another
lodger – no light ever burned behind their doors. Upward
used to say that it was the kind of place where you could
expect to find a corpse lying on the stairs, its throat neatly
cut, as you went down for the post. This may have had
something to do with the principal event of our stay there;
perhaps not. However sinister, its influence always seemed
to be out of all proportion to the time we spent there. It
was here, for instance, that I first heard Gavin Newsome's
name, found out some things about Upward that had
previously been hidden, other bits of information.

'Of course,' Upward used to say, 'it's not as if we do a
proper job or anything.'

This was true. All the same what we did do – both on the
stage and off – could be uncomfortably hard work. It was

hardest of all when Upward was in one of his moods. These
– they descended without warning and often went on for
three or four days – were completely disabling. Struck
down by one of them, Upward was quite capable of not
speaking for several hours, occasionally not even moving.
Marooned in a chair – and the effect was oddly like
someone left on a tiny desert island – he simply stared in
front of him until for some unknown reason, something
Upward claimed to have no control over, the spell broke.
It was always hard to know what to do when this
happened. Talking could be worse than useless (Upward
always said that at these periods the sound of a human
voice was reduced to a kind of droning). On the other hand
there were things that had to be said – stuff about that
night's performance, travel arrangements and so on. In the
end I usually adopted a policy of carrying on as usual –
something which Upward always said irritated him beyond
measure, but sometimes produced dramatic improvements
in his condition.

Reaching the top of the stairs that Sunday morning, pint
of milk in one hand, a couple of newspapers wedged under
the other arm, I knew by a kind of sixth sense that in the
twenty minutes I'd been gone Upward had been gathered
up by another of his moods. It was the last week of
September, and bright sunshine was streaming through the
skylight directly above the stairhead. The door of the flat
was half-open, but the radio left playing pop music had
been turned off. Upward sat, still in his dressing gown, at
the far end of the battered sofa. Unshaven, strands of red
hair plastered low over his forehead, he looked utterly
woebegone, even tragic. From the end of the room steam
was rising dramatically from an electric kettle: I switched it
off. Everything else – the uncleared table, Upward's
current stage costume (purple three-piece suit with a
bright yellow check) hung over a chair, a jumble of odds
and ends over the floor – seemed much as I'd left it.

'Do you want a cup of tea?'

Upward was silent. I sat down on a chair by the window
and, allowing for the incongruity of the figure in front of

me, tried to read the *News of the World*, wondering at the same time what had brought this particular crisis on. Upward's moods weren't entirely arbitrary. A hostile audience or a professional snub – the 'star' two rungs up the bill who pretended not to notice him – was usually enough to plunge him into gloom. However, nothing like this had happened for weeks. In fact the day before had brought a letter from the BBC offering us two or three slots in a series of comedy half-hours. Professionally, things were looking up. On the other hand, Upward's subconscious had an uncanny ability to sniff out trouble in advance. The cancelled date, the TV comedian not wanting to shake hands – frequently Upward's moods ran in advance of these slights rather than reacting to them. It could be that something unpleasant was going to happen that only Upward, or rather some secret part of Upward, knew about.

'Do you want to know what's in the papers?'

Again, Upward said nothing. At these times I usually found myself talking to him as if he were a deaf, elderly hospital patient whose mental state couldn't be relied on. Many years later Upward told me how much he hated this. Somehow, though, no other tone seemed suitable. I rolled out the *News of the World* on my knees, looking for something that might interest him.

'It says here that Val Doonican's just bought a new Bentley.' Nothing stirred. I went on: 'Seated at the wheel of his impressive new purchase, the popular singing star said: "*I haven't shown it to my mother yet, but she'll be glad the old pushbike's going into retirement.*" '

This kind of thing always annoyed Upward. As a general rule he hated any kind of showbiz success story, however deserving the personality involved. I read on for several minutes: starlets holidaying in the Barbadian surf, gnarled veterans of the wide screen and their teenage companions.

'Oh, and Mike and Bernie Winters have just landed a six-part series with ITV.'

'Give me that.'

Upward's face as he said this was almost deathly white. I handed the paper over and he stared balefully at it for a bit. Outside the wind whipped against the high windows. Not more than ten yards away there were gulls hovering on the current, wings raised awkwardly above their bodies.

'Not a good idea?'

'You said it.'

'It could be worse.'

'I suppose so.'

Having spoken, and thereby broken the spell, Upward cheered up a bit. At any rate he consented to be made a cup of tea and look over the picture of Mike and Bernie, while re-stating one of his most deeply held theories about comedy: that talent existed in inverse proportion to the exposure granted to the comedian.

'I mean, why don't they put an ad in the paper. "Are you talentless? Are all your jokes thirty years out of date? Well, ring a TV producer and he'll give you something really special. Oh, and lots of girls will be waiting backstage for a quick knee-trembler after the show." '

Eventually the animus burned itself out. Upward drank two cups of tea in quick succession. Then he said in a curiously humble way:

'D'y' think it went OK last evening?'

'Absolutely.'

'You think they got the end of "Talking about girls"?'

'Seemed to.'

Upward paused, lost in some remote world of laughter and acclamation.

'What about me?' he demanded sharply. 'Was I funny?'

Oddly, there wasn't any vanity about Upward as he said this. He simply wanted to know.

'You were funny.'

There was no guarantee that Upward would be pleased by this. In fact he was quite likely to start criticising you for your own shortcomings ('We can't just rely on one of us getting a laugh' etc.). But now the compliment seemed to satisfy him. He rolled off the sofa, clutched the flapping folds of the dressing gown to his chest (this was a deliberate gag – we had a routine about a woman surprised by a Peeping Tom) and lit a cigarette.

'You open any of that post?'

'Not yet.'

There was a pile of letters lying on a table inside the door, sent on by the London agent. Upward picked them up and took them into the bedroom. From within I could hear him pulling his clothes on, interspersed with the sound of tearing paper, occasional gusts of laughter.

'What's so funny?'

'There's some grand stuff here.' Upward's head appeared for a moment, half in and half out of the door. 'Listen to this. "*Dear Arthur Upward. My husband and I enjoyed your show at the Lewes Civic Theatre last week, especially the sketch about Harold Wilson, who my husband cannot stand, and I agree. My husband is often away on business, and it gets very lonely in the evenings. I was wondering if …*" D'you think it's genuine?'

'Bound to be.'

There were about a dozen letters: cheques, an unpaid bill or two, the agent's account, some fan-mail. The fan letters were always for Upward. Once or twice Upward came out into the room, half dressed, to confer on particular points.

'There's an invite here to the Kent Federation of Master Builders' Christmas ball. Think we should do it?'

'Can't do any harm.'

'Bloody bore, though, jacking down to Whitstable two days before Christmas. What about this one? Private dinner at the house of Gavin Newsome. Morrie's dead keen.'

'Who's Gavin Newsome?'

'Bloke that has his picture in the paper advertising commission selling. The Bank of Bristol. *You* know. Tried to stand as a Labour MP last time around, but they wouldn't have him.'

At this stage in my life I knew nothing about Gavin Newsome short of his name. The commission selling scheme; the Bank of Bristol; his ambition to become a

Labour MP – all this lay in the future. At the same time I wasn't at all surprised to find that Upward knew all about them. Uninterested in newspapers, bored to distraction by TV news programmes, he had a trick of picking up information about the personalities of the day by a kind of osmosis. A footballer sacked by his club, a bankrupt pop star, a disgraced politician: somehow Upward dredged them up from the choppy, late-60s sea into which they'd tumbled.

'How did Gavin Newsome find out about us?'

'Morrie says he heard us on the radio. Deeply impressed. Just the ticket for his mates at dinner.'

By now Upward had finished dressing. He came out of the bedroom for the final time, hooking the door to behind him with the toe of his shoe.

'What d'you think? Every popsy's dream?'

The question had to do with the suit – a slighly quieter version of his stage get-up, topped with a pink shirt and a bright red tie – but it was difficult not to take a wider view. At thirty, Upward looked older than most forty-year-olds: hair definitely going now, skin oddly red and abraded, as if the hair colour was working its way downward by way of compensation. Outwardly nobody could have looked more ordinary than Upward, more of a face in the crowd. At the same time there was a way in which everything about him was faintly exaggerated, larger than life. Looked at for a minute or two he suddenly seemed monstrous, extraordinary. In the beginning the fan letters Upward got – at first no more than a trickle, now five or six a week, always from women – used to puzzle me. Now I accepted them as an inevitable part of the person Upward was. It seemed perfectly logical that women who saw Upward on stage should want to write to him. The wonder was that more of them didn't do so.

'I'm off out,' Upward said. 'Down the pub. You coming?'

'Not now. Later, perhaps.'

'Suit yourself.'

There were good reasons for not going into pubs with

Upward. The version of himself that he carried into this kind of social life was basically a projection of the character he touted around on stage: loud, cocky, assertive, occasionally tragic. Put down in a bar with Upward, there was no guarantee that he wouldn't start eyeing up women who were quite obviously with someone else, argue with the landlord, or challenge someone to a bout of arm-wrestling.

I heard rather than saw him go out: a colossal slam of the door followed by the noise of feet moving regularly down the endless stairs, another slam – muffled but still fairly loud – of the street door as he stepped outside. It was about half-past twelve. Beyond the window, traffic moved sluggishly along the seafront. In the far distance, almost at the point where the sea met the sky, there were yachts tracking back and forth. Nearer to hand I could see Upward's squat, powerful figure moving purposefully through the knots of people, the pale girls still in summer dresses, arms clasped elbow to elbow against the breeze, boys in parka jackets wheeling mopeds along the pavement. If I had a plan for Upward's absence – and the odds were that he'd be gone for at least an hour or two – it was to phone a girl I'd met the week before in Folkestone, maybe even arrange some kind of meeting. Life on the road was full of these hasty assignations: phone numbers scrawled on the back of cigarette packets, afternoon trips to towns a dozen miles away heavy with the knowledge that you were never going to see the girl again, the whole thing dominated by Upward's shadow. Curiously, nearly all the girls, even the biddable ones, wanted to talk about Upward. I was once actually in bed with a girl who asked me whether he was married. As it was, the phone call was never made.

Three quarters of an hour went by. Then, quite distinctly, I heard the sound of the street door – not usually kept locked during the day – slam shut. Somebody was coming up the stairs. My first thought was that it was Upward, unexpectedly depressed by the atmosphere of the pub, or even, as had happened in the past, thrown out. But the footsteps didn't sound like Upward's heavy tread.

Interested, I went and stood on the landing. Twenty or thirty feet below a figure – a woman's figure judging from the glimpses of pink skin beneath a skirt – was moving slowly nearer. After what seemed like several minutes, several pauses for breath and at least one fruitless knocking on a door two floors below, the figure turned laboriously into the last stair-flight. Standing to one side of the stair-head, view obscured by the sun streaming in from the skylight, it took me a second or two to make out the shock of blonde hair and the scissor legs. It was Brenda. Seeing me, she stopped a step or two up the final incline and plumped the heavy canvas bag she was carrying down on the step.

'Didn't expect to see me, did you?'

'Not really.'

'Well, I've come anyway,' Brenda said ambiguously.

I came down the steps to pick up the bag. Brenda seemed to approve of this gesture, as she gave me a tiny pat on the arm.

'Nice manners you had,' she said. 'I always said.'

'Are you all right?'

Brenda looked very far from being all right. Never at all fresh complexioned, her face was horribly pale. For someone who I remembered – it was one of Father and Mother's phrases – as 'a strapping girl', she seemed a whole lot thinner. For some reason the clothes she was wearing – a shortish skirt with a kind of smock over her upper half – exaggerated both her pallor and her skimpiness. This was the great age of skinny models, of course – Twiggy and Jean Shrimpton. Brenda looked worse than that, ill rather than fashionably slim. Without answering, she went through the open door of the flat and started looking despondently around her.

'Is *he* here?'

'Gone out to the pub, I think.'

'Figures,' Brenda said. She sat down heavily in the armchair, so heavily that little flurries of dust rose up on either side of her forearms. 'It's nice to see you again, Ted.'

'And you.'

In fact I didn't know whether I was glad to see Brenda at all. Not just because she fell into the category of business concluded, even though that business was someone else's, but because she belonged to a part of my life that I'd assumed to be over. It was as if – to choose someone else whose appearance would have made me deeply uneasy – Mr Parmenter had suddenly turned up on the doorstep, or Horace been discovered parking his motorbike out in the street.

'I don't suppose you expected to see me?' Brenda said again. 'Did you?'

'Not really. No.'

Brenda wagged her head at this. Settled in the armchair, lighting a cigarette from a packet Upward had left on the table on the butt of one she had in her mouth, she looked even more unhappy. There was a restlessness about her, too, that I didn't remember from the Frith Street days. Once or twice a noise from the street caught her ear and she jerked round to the door.

'Do you suppose that's him coming back?'

'It doesn't sound like it.'

I don't mind admitting that I had no idea how to deal with Brenda. The old Brenda, who talked placidly of her future in the hotel trade, I could handle: the trick was simply to listen and make encouraging comments. The new Brenda – a shrunken, faintly hopeless version who chain-smoked and chewed her fingers – was beyond me. By rights, I suppose, I should have asked what she was doing here, a good sixty miles from London – what was the matter with her, why she wanted to see Upward. Somehow this wasn't something I could bring myself to do. Neither, oddly enough, did Brenda seem to expect it. However pleased she might be to see me, I was a factotum, the welcoming party that would eventually make way for the master of the house, when whatever business lay between them could be transacted.

Brenda smoked another cigarette. 'Make us a cup of tea will you, Ted?' she asked.

I was standing over the boiling kettle when the noise of

the street door slamming resounded beneath. It was
Upward this time: no question. Distracted by something
she had taken out of her bag, Brenda seemed not to hear
it. Muttering something, I ran out of the door. Upward,
halfway up the second flight, stopped when he saw me.

'It's Brenda.'

'Here?'

'In the flesh.'

'Christ!' Upward's face ·sank dramatically. 'Christ!
That's all I bloody needed.' He was genuinely shocked.
'Look, hang about a minute will you?'

'Hang about where?'

'Anywhere. Christ!' Upward said again.

I watched him disappear above me, taking the last few
steps at a run. The door slammed behind him. There was a
sound of raised voices, then silence.

It was nearly two o'clock. There was no telling how long
this would go on. In the end I left the building and walked
along the front to a makeshift pier where teenagers stood
jamming sixpences into slot machines and there was a kind
of pram park of sunburned mothers and their children.
There were long grey clouds coming in from the west – 'rain-
heads' Yarmouth people used to call them – and the sky
threatened thunder. Sure enough, after twenty minutes or
so, a storm blew up, sending the teenagers scuttling into
coffee bars further along the front. The promenading
mothers gathered up their belongings and disappeared. I
took shelter under the pier's metal stanchions, wondering
how long I could decently give it before going back, what I'd
find when I got there, why Brenda had come, other things.

Coming back at four, I found the street door half open
and the wind blowing leaves into the hallway. There was no
one about. Upward sat on his own in one of the armchairs
reading the *News of the World*. He looked sober, cautious,
not especially put out.

'Brenda gone then?'

'As far as I know.'

'She seemed a bit upset.'

'Suppose she did.'

Somehow with Upward the questions you wanted to ask never got asked. What was Brenda doing here? What trouble was she in? Why should this involve Upward? There was silence for a minute or two. The scent Brenda had been wearing – it was cheap and overwhelmingly pungent – still hung in the air. I walked through into the bedroom. There, for some reason, the smell was even worse. Upward, still sitting in the armchair, was gearing himself up to say something.

'I gave her fifty quid, y'know.'

'Fifty quid?'

'Said she was having a bad patch,' Upward said, a bit defensively. 'It was all I had.'

'That was good of you.'

Upward looked as if he might be going to say something else. Then he stopped. His eye fell on the letters.

'Let's have a cup of tea,' he said. 'Something I want to talk to you about.'

I made the tea. Outside fine rain was streaking the surface of the window. Settling himself back in his chair, Upward talked for nearly half an hour with huge, unselfconscious seriousness about changes he wanted to make to several of the sketches. '… Reckon we might take out that line in the Wilson sketch … Never gets much of a laugh … Important that you look at the audience while you say that stuff about his mother … Tell the joke *with* them, not *at* them.'

The room began to go dark. Upward had forgotten all about Brenda, I realised. It was as if she had never been there.

For some reason the month or so after that afternoon is very clear in my mind. A week later we went back to London to start work on the BBC shows and perform at Gavin Newsome's private dinner. Upward had his picture printed in the *Radio Times*. Not quite knowing why I did it, I put twenty five-pound notes in an envelope and sent them by registered post to Brenda's last address. There was no acknowledgement. Not so very long after that I met Paula.

What I Remember Most

What I remember most is the journey back from York. With the boy on the other side of the table reading a comic, but looking up every so often – shyly? Hopefully? Who can tell? And the train taking a while to get going, struggling a bit to leave the city and the wooded country beyond the outskirts. Eating biscuits out of a Tupperware box Shena had packed for us, and thinking Shena disapproved. The boy not wanting the biscuits or the Coke I fetched him from the buffet. Saying: 'Aunty Shena doesn't like me drinking Coke.' And me answering, 'I'm not Aunty Shena', and then regretting it. Speeding south, finally, over the plain and the sun rising suddenly from nowhere – the day overcast till then – pulsing over the grass. And me and the boy having to shade our faces from the glare. Trying to talk to him and not getting anywhere. About school, and the house, and football, that kind of thing. The boy nodding. The odd question. Computer games? Staying up late? And me agreeing to it all, all these things I haven't thought about, all these things I don't know. What does a ten-year-old boy eat? What time should he get up in the morning? How much pocket money should he have? And the boy sensing this, the uncertainty, and quietening down again, back in his seat, watching the sun speed across the fields, the other people in the carriage, me.

Not a long journey, two hours perhaps, King's Cross, the tube to Charing Cross. The boy tired but looking interestedly at the escalator ads, wanting to put the pound coins in the ticket machine. And then the taxi, the afternoon sun less intense now, burning over the water and the blackened wharves down by the river. Bermondsey, Rotherhithe and Greenwich. London names. The boy nearly asleep now, waking up near the station, sloughing through the hot *streets. The house, silent as the grave, gaping with disuse. Me opening windows, switching on electricity, while the boy explores, padding wide-eyed from room to room, looking at the photographs on the wall, the framed posters. The telephone ringing, and Shena's voice charged with tension, the boy talking to her while I hover in the background, half not caring, half wanting Shena's approval. Ransacking the cupboard for old tins – sausages, beans, tomatoes. The boy saying: 'This is two years past its sell-by.' 'It doesn't matter. Tinned stuff always keeps.' 'How long? Forever?' 'Well, nearly forever.' Eating tinned custard, cold, with dessert spoons, as the cars go past in the street.*

And before that, a month before, being in the room with Paula, with more sunshine pouring in through the open window. And Paula hunched up in her bed-jacket, hands pressed together on the coverlet, looking thinner than you could believe a person could ever look, not talking but just looking at each other. The boy away somewhere, at school, out with his friends, I don't know. And me – a terrible admission – trying to remember how old she is. Forty-five maybe? Forty-six? But no age to look like a bundle of sticks tied up in a sheet. Shena in the next room showing her dislike with sharp, heavy clumps. And me thinking of Father before he died, face the colour of oatmeal, hair all gone. And going out into the kitchen, closing the door, and Shena saying 'Three weeks', like that, no tone or feeling in the words. Hearing a noise from Paula's room, going back to find she'd dropped a library book, reached down and not been able to raise herself, propping her up again and seeing the bone of her arm, a dreadful thing, no flesh on it, the jars of pills on the shelf beside the headboard, and saying 'Can I get you anything?' and her shaking her head.

Then later, talking about Daniel, how old he is, things she sees in him, attitudes. 'Like you.' 'How?' 'I don't know. Just like you.' About Shena, the house, the doctor. 'He's a strange one, that Dr Mackay.' 'Why?' 'I don't know. Nothing you could pin down. Nothing I could pin down.' And me thinking how long I'd known her, and coming up with a quarter of a century near enough. And forty-five,

*forty-six no age to die at, no age at all. Younger than me,
younger than Father and Mother, younger than all of us.
And all the things that should have been said not said, just
lying there between us, because there was plenty of time,
always plenty of time, until the last time of all, when
suddenly there was no time, her arms on the coverlet like
spindles, nothing there at all, except the things not said,
Shena moving in the corridor, the sun cascading in over the
empty bed.*

White Stag Hunting

Did you hear about the Irishman who applied for a job at ICI? They asked him what nitrate was, and he said 'Time and a half'.

What Upward used to call 'it' – he meant success, fame and money – lasted about seven years, perhaps a bit longer. From 1972, say, to around 1980. After that, after the final TV series and the last Variety Performance, we could see things were winding down, that we were back where we'd been before, a rung or three from the top of the ladder, with younger people – 'kids' Upward used to call them dismissively – hurtling past and nothing in the world you could do to stop them. The odd thing about this ascent was how quickly it happened. One moment we'd been going backwards and forwards to dates in the train, the next we were being driven to them in a limo. Sandwiches in pubs suddenly became four-course meals in places that a year before we wouldn't have dared to set foot in. That's how it seemed at the time, though I suppose there was actually a period of about a year when you could see things moving into gear, taxi-ing forward and taking flight. I can remember a bank statement arriving some time in 1972 or 1973 telling me that I had £2,000 in my current account, and feeling hugely elated and at the same time faintly guilt-ridden on account of Father and what the money would have meant to him. I don't suppose there was a time in the whole of Father's life when his total assets amounted to more than £500.

The first TV series went out in 1972: eight half-hour episodes on Wednesday nights, just after *Coronation Street*. There was another one a year later, then a film – one of the last of the *Carry On*s, as it happened – with Upward as a randy, wench-fancying highwayman and me as his dim assistant. It was a disaster, of course, but by the time it came out this didn't matter for we'd moved up another notch. We were in panto that year in Croydon with Rod Hull and Emu, then out on the theatre circuit. By 1975 we were filling the Manchester Palace, the biggest theatre in the north in those days, for a week at a time. Oddly enough, I don't remember a great deal of it. The early years with Upward are full of sharp, vivid little memories, even down to the look on Upward's face when a line went across, but what came later isn't much more than a blur, a kind of whirl of expensive restaurants, the faces in the big theatres going back what seemed like hundreds of yards, the TV gantry lights burning down on your face. What remains, predictably enough, are one or two incidentals – cruising back in the small hours from some date up north, with Upward asleep with his head on the leather arm-rest and the Midlands towns going by in a sprawl of lights gleaming out of the darkness; ghastly dawns somewhere at the southern end of the M1, with the early lorries zipping past on the northbound carriageway, sky the colour of a fish's underbelly, and the bulk of London gathered up in the mist below.

As you'll have gathered by now, perhaps, none of this appealed to me in the way that five or six years before I'd assumed it would. I used to drift through rooms – the high, cream-coloured rooms where Upward sat surrounded by the people who appealed to him – wondering what I was doing there, when I could decently get away. The faces came and went – I shook hands with the Queen once, back-stage after a Royal Variety Performance, met Harold Wilson and talked football with Bobby Charlton – but they were never real, somehow, in the way that the old world had been. The Queen was simply a smile, Wilson a tetchy little man smoking a foul pipe, Bobby Charlton a bald thirty-five-year-old wondering what to do with the rest of his life. I wonder if you'll believe me when I say that I used to keep a list of the famous people I met? Lulu, Sir Gerald Nabarro, Rodney Marsh, Alvin Stardust, Little Jimmy Osmond, John Stonehouse, Len Murray, Malcom

McDowell. Not many of them cut much ice these days, I daresay, but that was the kind of world I wandered through, made of up charity lunches and receptions, celebrity parties and trading back-chat with the showbiz columnists. What was worse, perhaps, was that I'd gone into it thinking I could preserve a sense of detachment, keep a bit of me at one remove from it all. And yet somehow the life you were living sucked you into it. However much you tried, you could never get away. I used to disappear sometimes for the odd weekend in between tours or recordings, decamp to a hotel somewhere off the beaten track or even take a furnished room in a town miles away from anywhere, and it was always the same – stacks of phone messages, telegrams, Upward appearing out of nowhere to spirit me away. Somebody – Upward, some understrapper from the agency, even the local police force once – could always find you. Other people, too. Occasionally the old life that I hadn't given a thought to for a decade jumped up again to scare me. Once Uncle George and Aunt Sheila turned up backstage after a show we'd done at the Ipswich Gaumont and I took them out for a meal, but we just sat and stared at each other. The past, which I'd thought I could summon back on my own terms, walk into at will, turned out to have a wall round it. Worse, all through the meal, I could see that Uncle George was intent on touching me for fifty quid. He got it, too.

Upward, on the other hand, enjoyed himself tremendously.

I remember once, right at the beginning of the tornado years, perhaps even when we were signing some contract or other, asking him what he wanted from all this. Upward hardly paused to consider.

'The White Stag,' he said. He then quoted a piece of poetry he'd picked up somewhere which contained the line 'It's the white stag, fame, we're hunting'.

This admission, which Upward made quite matter-of-factly, seemed to me to reveal a huge amount about Upward. I could even visualise it physically: the stag, elusive, practically mythical, constantly disappearing

among the highest rocks and pathways; Upward, grim-
faced, determined to bring it down, convinced – and this
was the most important thing – that he knew exactly what
he'd find when, finally, the beast lay dead on the mountain
path in front of him. In a sense I suppose this was what I
envied most about him. Upward – and there was no getting
away from this – knew exactly what he wanted success to
consist of: the smiling hostess, the welcoming *maitre d'*, the
vacant table. For some reason these demands were nearly
always met. All the same, Upward had to be treated on his
own terms. This valuation could sometimes be rather high.
Not everybody shared it. Once, I remember, the *Observer*
sent quite a well-known novelist – Kingsley Amis, it might
have been, or Anthony Burgess – along to interview him.
Even now bits of what got printed still float around in my
head: 'an undeniable panache and intelligence, compromised by innate and somehow gratuitous vulgarity', 'brash,
over-confident, assertive … an apocalyptic door-to-door
salesman metamorphosed into a comic titan.' Upward
claimed he'd simply taken the man out to lunch and talked
unrevealingly to him for an hour or so. Clearly, though, it
had gone deeper than that. Somehow, without meaning to,
Upward had given huge and lasting offence.

   All this, though, was typical of the post-60s Upward, a
character I found just as mystifying as the grim clown of
the Catterick fatigue parties. The fixation with newspaper
interviews, in particular, showed a side to him that I never
got to the bottom of. Though he hated giving away details
of his personal life, Upward was simultaneously ravished
by the idea of journalists bringing accounts of him back to
the paying public. Upward's favourite football team
(Manchester City), Upward's political preferences
(Labour, but with occasional dizzying lurches rightwards),
what Upward smoked, thought about female beauty, the
Archbishop of Canterbury and the European Economic
Community – these were all subjects with which a certain
kind of newspaper reader in the mid-70s would have
known all about. All this gave Upward a kind of notoriety,
liable to break out in TV impersonations of him by other

comedians, jokes in *Private Eye*, which I don't think he much minded. It was all part of the package. The truth was – and this is something I don't think I grasped until much later on – that Upward felt at home in this new world (shaking hands with the Duke of Kent, pictured with Mike Yarwood, boozing with Sid James) in a way that I didn't, could adapt himself to the people he came across (Lord Longford, Danny La Rue, Geoff Boycott) in a way I couldn't, showed effortless brilliance in matching what he had to offer (cheek, 'Northern commonsense') to whatever was needed.

Our trail stretched all over the 70s. Look for our tracks anywhere in that odd, dead landscape of unrest and false dawns and pious hopes, decaying pasts and shiny futures, and you'll find them – on TV carol services with Angela Rippon and the cast of *Dad's Army*, umpiring the annual cricket match between the Lords and Commons, doing warm-ups for the Miss World Contest (Upward in a scarlet wig and sequins as 'Miss Galapagos Islands' claiming that his hobbies were looking after tortoises and world peace), guesting on the *Generation Game* as a couple of fantastically inept plate spinners. Such an odd, unlikely, alarming world, but with its own walkways and purlieus, its neighbourhoods and backyards: the Thames studios at Teddington Lock early in the morning with the cigarette smoke already gathering under the ceiling; Leicester Square; the Ivy, where Upward would often eat lunch *and* dinner, sometimes not even bothering to leave the restaurant between the two; the cover of the *TV Times*. I've kept some of these pictures, which used to puzzle me. Upward, you see, looked like Upward, whereas I looked like someone paid to impersonate me, to keep the show rolling in my absence.

All the same, I wouldn't want you to think I was unhappy. There was money coming in. Even then, ten years in the trade, I still got a terrific kick out of the patterns that Upward and I wove on stage. And despite the dawns and departures, the expensive cars nosing out of the Midlands dusk, I liked the feeling that I was in control of my life in a

way that I've not been before or since. It's difficult to
explain this, hard to pin it down, but back in the days with
Father and Mother, in the army, even under Upward's wing
in Frith Street, I never had a sense of being able to act on
my own. Now all that had changed. In hotels sometimes I
used to dial room service late at night simply for the kick
of having someone run around on my behalf. Quite often
I'd take holidays abroad – sometimes with Paula, more
often on my own – just for the pleasure of seeing new
places at my own speed. All this is very clear in my mind:
Bordeaux, once, in a week in June, with the villages asleep
behind hedgerows of loosestrife; Venice, another time, on a
day in November, with the water lashing over the flag-
stones. All pretty small beer, I suppose, but I liked it, liked
the unhurriedness, the foreign voices, the slow pace of
unknown lives. Ask me what's left of those days and there
it is: Upward swallowing oysters at Wheeler's; Cartwright
and Newsome round the big table; Tracy Jacks peering out
into the December twilight; Paula's face caught in the
frame of door and jambe. All gone, of course, and long
dead, but vivid for a while, and part of me.

*

At this height – two or three hundred feet – the view was
disconcerting. Gathered up in the jumble of brick and
concrete, buildings and landmarks that you knew turned
unfamiliar. Only unmistakeable objects – the Post Office
tower to the east, Green Park unfolding in the distance to
the south – persuaded you of the reality of what you saw.
The wind, thudding in against heavy plate glass windows,
made this feeling worse. Looking out at various points in
the proceedings I used to lose my bearings completely, get
confused by the lowering sky and the alien rooftops, until
a voice or a slammed door dragged me back.

  Outside it was already getting dark. The green
recording light, which had been turned off ten minutes
before, flickered unexpectedly into life again and then
went dead.

'I should really like to wrap this up in the next half an hour,' Tracy Jacks said brightly. 'Say three-quarters of an hour. How does that sound?'

There was a silence. The two technicians who had come into the main studio from the smaller ante-room fenced off with glass nodded meekly. A third man – the assistant producer, who might have been called Jacobson – scribbled something in the margin of his clip-top pad. In the distance, beyond the glass, girls' heads could be seen bobbing up and down under the light.

'What's the hurry?' Upward said.

Shirt-sleeved, with an unlit cigarette in his mouth, seated alone at the circular table, he looked pretty irritated, but still more or less friendly. Upward liked Tracy Jacks, hesitated before complaining about or to him, but he was still capable of losing his temper.

'The power's going off again at four apparently,' Tracy Jacks said. 'Not in here, of course, but it makes things difficult.'

'I can see that.'

'There's another couple of pages to get through. We can deal with the other stuff later.'

'We could deal with the other couple of pages later,' Upward said. 'I don't care about bloody power cuts.'

Tracy Jacks and I swapped glances. He was a tallish, blond, heavy-featured character of about twenty-five, whose deference to Upward occasionally reached fantastic heights. On one occasion he'd been seen to stop whatever he was doing at the desk, descend through several levels in the lift and trek through half a mile of corridor to fetch Upward a bottle of stout from the staff canteen. Another time, waiting unseen in the doorway, I'd watched him scoop up some crumbs from the chair where he knew Upward would sit into a paper handkerchief.

'Arthur …' Tracy Jacks began.

For him to use Upward's Christian name meant that a kind of pleading had begun. Upward knew this, and appreciated it. Bored by this routine, which had been enacted countless times both here and at Teddington, I walked out

into the ante-room where there was a coffee machine and
a stack of newspapers and somebody had left the radio on.

> *'Dance on moonbeams, slide down rainbows*
> *In furs or bluejeans, you know what I mean*
> *Do the Strand …'*

It was the week before Christmas, a fortnight into the
power workers' go-slow. There would be an election soon:
everybody knew. The Prime Minister's face stared out of
that morning's *Daily Mail*, lying on the newspaper rack:
wooden, unresponsive. Upward had tried and failed to
produce an imitation of Mr Heath, succeeded only in
taking off the odd, champagne-bottle set of his shoulders.
He was on much firmer ground with Wilson (all to do with
the availability of props, Upward claimed, instancing the
pipe). I looked back through the window where Upward,
the unlit cigarette still clamped in his mouth, was listening
to Tracy Jacks in much the same way that Father had
listened to reps from the sweet companies that he didn't
want to deal with: civil but unimpressed. Fatter now than
he had been a year or two ago, Upward looked tired, but
still extraordinarily energetic. He was only waiting for the
right cue, you thought, to get up and whirl round the room,
take Tracy Jacks in his arms, start doing high kicks. I
decided to go back into the studio.

'Plenty of time for a drink,' Upward was saying. 'Then
nip back here and bugger the power workers.'

For all his air of barely suppressed energy, Upward
liked to work at a leisurely pace. We had been here for a
couple of hours. Upward's plan was that we ought to go to
the BBC Club round the corner from Langham Place, and
then wind the recording up later in the afternoon.

'Arthur …' Tracy Jacks said again. 'Arthur. In another
hour or so there won't be any lights down there. I rang up
to check.'

Arguments between Upward and Tracy Jacks weren't
unusual. There was no telling how long this one might go
on. The technicians had disappeared, I noticed. In a bit,

unless he could be got to see reason, Upward would turn petulant.

'Well, let's see what Ted says about it,' Tracy Jacks went on, not very hopefully. 'What do you think, Ted?'

'If there's only another couple of pages to get through, we ought to do them now. Then you can go off down the club.'

Upward looked suspicious. He hated the idea that Tracy Jacks and I were, as he sometimes put it, 'ganging up on him'.

'*I want a drink,*' he said suddenly. 'It's not much to bloody ask for, is it? *I want a drink.*'

'Have a drink then,' Tracy Jacks said encouragingly. 'Have it here. I'll send someone to go and fetch it.'

'I don't want it here. I want it downstairs.'

It was a quarter to three. Paula would be expecting me soon. A slow fuse, which had been burning for the last ten minutes or so, finally reached the powder store.

'Why don't you get off your arse you fat cunt and do what Tracy says for a change? Go on, just do it for once.'

'Ted!' Tracy Jacks looked genuinely horrified, as if he scarcely believed anyone would be capable of talking to Upward like this. Upward, on the other hand, shifted uneasily in his chair, sat bolt upright, pulled out a box of matches and lit the cigarette.

'All right,' he said, not sounding very put out. 'Have it your own way.'

Arguments with Upward often ended like this. In fact Upward sometimes admitted that he only started them as a means of staving off boredom. While he smoked the cigarette, Tracy Jacks recalled the technician and spoke to the girls in the ante-room before finally settling himself at the sound board.

'Anyway,' Upward said, waiting until he was out of the room. 'It's a bloody awful script.'

'We should have done it ourselves.'

'It's only radio.'

Upward's annoyance about the missed drink now had a context. He was bored by the BBC, Tracy Jacks, dog-eared scripts with the producer's comments written on them in green biro, had moved on into a world of TV studios, restaurants and showbiz columnists. A world, too, in which Upward's word, if not exactly law, counted for more than it had done three years before. Upward liked imposing himself on situations: changing his mind about food; sending a waiter off into the night for a packet of cigarettes; telling drivers to make unexpected detours. Sometimes this ended up as outright bullying, usually with people whose position in life left them with no obvious means of defence. Humiliated doormen, floor managers vaguely aware they were being 'got at' – Upward's path through this period of his life was littered with casualties. To do him justice, I don't think he ever realised what a nuisance he made of himself, or why such violent offence was sometimes taken. I once saw a barman whom Upward had not exactly insulted but verbally sparred with for a minute or two pick up a soda siphon and squirt it over his head. Upward was genuinely shocked.

'Why would he want to do that for?' he asked, as they sponged him down afterwards. 'Why on earth should he want to do that for?'

It was as if one of Marie-Antoinette's gardeners had suddenly jabbed her in the eye with a pruning fork.

'All right then,' Tracy Jacks said keenly. 'Page seventeen. Let's take it from the top, shall we? Green light coming up in five seconds and *away* we go.'

It was the last instalment of an old series, begun way before the TV contracts and the newspaper profiles, in which Upward played the owner of a lacklustre travel agency, with me as his faithful but none too intelligent sidekick. Two years ago it had been quite funny. As Tracy Jacks had promised, the rest of the session took about three quarters of an hour. Upward read his lines without emphasis. By twenty to four we were finished. Outside the sky was turning blue-black.

'Are you coming down the club?' Upward asked, tossing his copy of the script pointedly into a wastepaper basket near the door.

'Not today.'

'Tarts,' said Upward theatrically, to no one in particular. 'Can't keep away from them. Well, give her my love.'

Safely behind the studio door, looking back through the square of glass, I watched Tracy Jacks heave into sight with an ashtray, already keen to catch the inch or so of ash that hung from Upward's cigarette. Then I went out into the corridor, past the photographs of Arthur Askey and Michael Bentine, Roy Castle and Eric Sykes, to the lift, thinking, as I so often did those days, restlessly and a bit uneasily, about Paula.

*

I met Paula in 1973, at a hotel somewhere in Croydon which the cast of a revue we'd been headlining at the Fairfield Hall had colonised after the show. At that point she'd have been about twenty-one – a thin, dark-haired girl who undulated about in the front row of something called the Marsha Flett Dance Troupe. Don't laugh. That's the kind of thing the second- and third-tier acts were called in those days – the Mike Sands Singers, the Butterfly Chorus, the Harry Grayson Quartet. The Marsha Flett Dance Troupe – Marsha Flett was a tough old witch in her fifties who looked on keenly from the side of the stage – consisted of a dozen girls in their teens and early twenties with names like Samantha and Patch – again, that's the kind of thing chorus girls were called in those days – whose job was to open and close the show and possibly transact a bit of business with the comedians midway through the second half. Upward, in particular, wasn't above routines which involved him walking up and down a line of female dancers inspecting the generously framed *décolletage*. Presumably I'd seen Paula before – had to have done, if it came to that, as there was a sketch in which the dancers doubled up as night-club hostesses – but it wasn't until afterwards that I properly became aware of her. I have a particular memory of her, head in profile, with a cluster of other girls, laughing at a joke that someone – probably Upward – was telling,

having supper a bit later with her and another girl called
Antonella who Upward claimed had allowed herself to be
'done' earlier that evening on one of the hotel's snooker
tables.

Paula! My God, what can I tell you about Paula? What
could you tell me about someone you were married to for
twenty years? What I remember about her now is coloured
by what came afterwards, of course, but I know the things
I felt about her at the time were more or less genuine. I can
remember a Sunday afternoon two or three weeks after
we'd met, wandering around one of the London parks for
hours on end, trying to work it all out, and then going to a
phone box to call her number and being furious when she
wasn't there. A couple of days later I even went to a
theatrical agency in Wardour Street and got them to look
up the Marsha Flett Dance Troupe in the files on the
offchance there'd be a picture – that was how I felt about
Paula back in the days of the oil crisis and the three-day
week.

Paula (her surname was Marriot)! The Marsha Flett
Dance Troupe! The Fairfield Hall, Croydon! It's another
part of time, of course, a big old amphitheatre with space
for two thousand, packed with people who'd brought their
kids to gawp at faces they knew from the television, no
smut, incidental entertainment provided by Ali Bongo and
his Mysteries of the Orient and a couple of all-in wrestlers.
Oddly enough, when I think of Paula – which is something
I've never stoppped doing – it's always that world she
seems to inhabit: girls in leotards glimpsed through half-
open dressing room doorways taping their breasts up with
sticking plaster, microphones whining feedback at you
whenever you approached, Upward's face through the
smoke, Marsha Flett working out her percentages on the
back of an envelope in the cubby hole beyond the safety
curtain. The later days, in Surrey or at the big house
looking out over the Stour, might just as well not be there.

What did Paula look like ten years later? I can barely
remember. But I can tell you what she looked like in 1973.
I don't think it's patronising her to say that she had a 70s

face. People grow out of the landscapes you place them in. Marjorie Lovelace looked like a 50s schoolgirl, which is what she was. Mary looked like the daughter of a Norfolk farmer who'd led an exceptionally sheltered life – an exclusive category, maybe, but one that would have meant something to the people she knocked up against, and certainly meant something to me. I'm not saying that Paula looked like Susan Hampshire or Felicity Kendal, but her face belonged to that kind of world: trusting, friendly, a bit uncertain, willing to make the best of a bad job. At the same time this hint of vulnerability was deceptive, as it came combined with a huge amount of professional *nous*. The Marriots, it turned out, were a real showbiz family. Paula's father had been some kind of agent back in the 50s, and old Mrs Marriot was an ex-Variety girl who looked as if she could have shown Marsha Flett a thing or two. I went round their house once or twice – they lived in Penge or Sydenham – and it was a kind of museum, full of signed photographs of Variety stars and Mrs Marriot executing the Can-Can in 1948. Naturally enough, what I did cut no ice with them at all. I can remember Paula once starting to talk about some TV show we were doing and old Marriot not even bothering to listen. To him TV was just an abomination that had killed off proper entertainment.

But the Marriots were friendly enough in their way, if a bit worried about Paula and the kind of situations she might be getting herself into. I used to go down there sometimes on a Sunday night for supper, and doze in front of the TV while Mr Marriot criticised sitcom actors and his wife nagged Paula about not eating enough. Shena, Paula's older sister, worked in a bank but I don't suppose I met her more than two or three times at this point. And though it wasn't in the least like the old days at Southtown I'm sure that the kind of routine with which the Marriots invested their lives deeply appealed to me. There's a lot to be said for knowing that your dinner's going to be on the table at 7 p.m. sharp and that it'll either be shepherd's pie or baked cod.

Mother would have looked Paula appraisingly over in a

vague sort of way and pronounced that she was a 'nice
girl'. This wasn't necessarily a compliment. It simply meant
that from the limited materials available for scrutiny
Mother couldn't find anything openly antagonistic to her
own interests. As for the Marriots and the terraced house
in Penge, I can't imagine what she would have said – it was
all so beyond her experience as to render all previous
social judgments useless. None of this, perhaps, has much
of a bearing on Paula, the kind of life we lived together,
what was said. On the other hand, you couldn't get away
from these connections. At least I couldn't. Entering Paula
(something I accomplished on the fourth or fifth time we
met, with every encouragement) I knew I was entering a
world, that however much the Marriots, Penge, family
ancestry, kept to the back of the stage they were still there,
so to speak, liable to be brought up to the spotlight or
otherwise involved at the drop of a hat. What I liked about
Paula, I suppose, was her eagerness to please, and to be
pleased. I don't mean in relation to myself, but in a whole
mass of tiny details and sensations. An hour of sunshine
when the forecast said rain, a lost five-pound note run to
earth in the bottom of her handbag – these brought out an
enthusiasm that was faintly childish.

'Gosh, that was fun,' she said when we'd been to bed
that first time – I can remember her sitting up against the
pillow with her fine hair falling down over her face – and it
was quite genuine.

Later I used to wonder what she really thought of me at
this time, but I never found anything to change the original
estimate, or alter the conviction that it was all my fault.

*

Standing in the doorway of Broadcasting House after an
hour or so in Tracy Jacks's lofted studio, you got an odd
feeling of having returned to a different world. Waved on
by the smiling commissionaire, the door held open by a
Radio One DJ on his way into the building, it took a
moment to recover. Outside it was nearly dusk. In the

distance a line of buses had come to a halt in Regent Street. Not far away, on the steps of All Souls' Church, a Salvation Army choir was singing Christmas carols. I started to thread my way north-east through the warren of streets that separated Langham Place and the Euston Road.

Paula lived in a basement flat in Nottingham Place, next door to a launderette and a students' hostel. Oddly enough, Upward had had a flat around this way a year or two back. Just now he was living in Fulham, with whom nobody quite knew. What Upward got up to remained completely his own business, ever since the day Brenda had turned up at the south-coast lodging house. Quite often he'd produce girls at social events, usually bottle-blondes of incredible gormlessness, but there was no way of knowing how they fitted into the scheme of things. More than once, recently, Upward had talked about getting married.

There was a light on in the basement: the rest of the house was dark. In the area rotting leaves and old newspapers crackled underfoot. As I rang the bell the door opened and Paula's face appeared behind it.

'Hurry up. The power goes off in a minute.'

'Have you just got up?'

She was wearing a dressing gown, with a towel wound round her head like a turban.

'I was having a bath, silly.'

Paula kept odd hours. It was quite likely that she had only woken up half an hour or so ago. I followed her into the flat's main room, where there was a children's programme flickering on the TV and a kettle boiling in the corner.

'What do we do when the lights go?'

'Candles,' Paula said. 'Look.' She pointed to a row of jam jars ranged along the window sill. 'And a couple of torches. We can hang them from the curtain rail or something.'

'Wouldn't it be simpler to go to bed?'

'Don't be naughty. Anyway, there are some blankets.'

I watched her as she skipped round the room making tiny re-arrangements and adjustments to the scheme, completely absorbed and delighted. Without Paula, it had to be said, the flat would have been hugely uninviting. It was basically a single, not very large, room with bedroom, kitchen and bathroom running off at the sides. Most of Paula's clothes lay between paper tissue on the sofa, owing to the damp, whose reek was at this point overlaid rather than disguised by the smell of burnt toast. Every available wall surface was covered by pictures of Paula: Paula aged seven in a line of infant tap-dancers; Paula at ten in a pierrot's outfit; teenage Paula in ballet gear; in an amateur version of *Oklahoma*. For some reason the effect wasn't at all self-advertising. You simply got a sense of effort, hard work, awareness of the distance yet to climb.

A church clock somewhere nearby began to strike the hour. On cue the electric light, the TV and the kettle went off simultaneously. I fished a box of matches out of my pocket and started lighting the candles. Paula dropped down on the sofa amid the piles of evening dresses and spangled stage costumes. Now that darkness had fallen, the bounce seemed to have gone out of her.

'I hate this,' she said. 'They ought not to let it happen.'

'I don't suppose the government wants it to happen any more than you do.'

Paula quite often said things like this. It was her one connection with Mother: the idea that 'they' – a mysterious organisation, never exactly defined but probably taking in all forms of civil administration – spent their time conspiring to ruin the lives of ordinary people.

'That reminds me,' Paula said. 'Upward rang with a message, just before you came. Something he'd forgotten to tell you.'

'I didn't know he had your number.'

'Well, he rang anyway. Said not to forget the Mayflower meeting in the morning.'

'Thanks. I hadn't.'

I was struck by the fact that Upward knew – had managed to get hold of, as I certainly hadn't told him –

Paula's phone number. Normally Upward showed no interest in the girls I knew.

'No offence or anything pal,' he'd once said. 'But they're all just *women*, aren't they?'

At the same time he liked keeping tabs on people. Abroad once or twice on solitary holidays, I'd been slightly startled to come back to the hotel and find telegrams from him lying on the reception desk. This habit of Upward's had produced a TV sketch, in which a husband desperate to get away from his wife relocates to ever more far-flung destinations – the Faroe Islands, Greenland, Krakatoa – only for the silence to be broken by the tap on the door, the phone call, the whirr of the carrier pigeon and so on.

'Is that another of those advertising agency things?'

'Sort of. The meeting's in the City. London Wall somewhere.'

Paula cheered up a bit. 'I thought we were going off somewhere tomorrow.'

'We can go away at the weekend if you like.'

'Can't. We're doing the Winter Dance Spectacular at Kensington Town Hall. Marsha would go up the wall if I wasn't there. What's Mayflower, anyway?'

What was Mayflower? It's true to say that at this point in my life I barely knew. There were ads for it in all the newspapers – I'd seen one only that lunchtime, waiting in Tracy Jacks's ante-room. Essentially Mayflower was the latest scheme dreamed up by Gavin Newsome – Sir Gavin Newsome as he now was – with the aim of encouraging the 'small entrepreneur'. The goods involved were mostly cosmetics. The idea was that interested parties put up a small sum – I think it was a thousand pounds – to start a small business to sell the stuff on commission. There were inducements for persuading other people – 'go-ahead friends and neighbours' as the ads put it – to join in. As the scheme was aimed at the less well-off, there were intermediaries at hand to fix up capital loans. I had an idea that the Bank of Bristol – this was a co-operative bank in which Newsome had an interest – was involved somewhere. So far Upward and I had done two quite funny TV ads in which I featured as a doubtful housewife and Upward as a glib neighbour who contrives to sell her a bottle of toilet water. I explained some of this to Paula. Outside, Nottingham Place looked even eerier than usual, the darkness of the buildings relieved only by occasional glows and pinpricks of light. Paula discovered that the water in the kettle was still reasonably hot and made two cups of lukewarm tea.

'He's a bit *grand*, isn't he, Sir Gavin Newsome? I've seen him on TV.'

I thought about this. It depended what Paula meant by 'grand'. Smartly dressed? Upper class? Well spoken? Gavin Newsome was all of these things, but I'd have hesitated to call him grand. Dukes and duchesses, members of the House of Lords were grand. What Paula meant was a faintly distinguished-looking character in a three-piece suit who talked with what Mother would have called a 'half-crown voice'. Paula having heard of Gavin Newsome – she was bored by news programmes – was a tribute to his impact on popular life. He wrote articles in Sunday newspapers about the 'commercial spirit'. There'd even been talk at one point about co-opting him into the cabinet.

'Anyway, he's Upward's friend, not mine.'

It was Upward's old trick of knowing people. Pop singers. Cabinet ministers. Tycoons. Whoever they were, Upward somehow managed to get talking to them, draw them out, draw them in. Now I remembered, he'd even managed to spend a weekend at Newsome's country estate in Sussex.

'It was all right,' Upward had reported back. 'Good grub. Drinks trays when you wanted them. Isla – Lady Newsome – she's all right. Doesn't give herself airs like some of them. You ought to come next time.'

This being Upward, quite a lot of cake had been had and eaten too. I later found out that, amid much grand company, he'd made a point of sitting down to Sunday lunch in his shirtsleeves, loudly demanded a bottle of stout instead of whatever vintage was offered, and called the Tory MP placed next to him 'old cock'.

The room was getting cold. Paula's cat – a ginger tom called Tigger – stalked through the kitchen doorway, looked at us unconcernedly and went away again.

'When does the power go on again?'

'Not for ages. Seven or eight.'

'Where are those blankets you were talking about?'

Using the blankets and a couple of sleeping bags Paula pulled out of a cupboard, we made up a kind of nest on the floor beyond the sofa and climbed into it. Lit only by the row of candles, wavering in the draughts of air that blew through the front door, the photographs of Paula in her ballet gear, as the lead in *Oklahoma*, looked a bit grotesque.

'It's cold,' Paula said. 'You'll have to warm me up.'

The usual things happened. Afterwards, while Paula slept – she did this rather like a baby, both hands gripping an imaginary parallel bar just above her head – I smoked a cigarette, watched the reflections that the lights of the passing cars made on the walls of the buildings opposite, and thought about it all: Paula, Upward, the Mayflower meeting. Nothing particularly out of the ordinary had happened that afternoon, unless you counted the power cut. Tracy Jacks. Upward in the studio. Paula's flat. I'd been there before. I'd be there again. Somehow, though, I could feel myself reaching decisions about things that I could barely put into words.

A bit later Paula woke up. Shortly after that the lights came on again.

*

We got married – eventually, and with various delays and rows – in the summer of 1975 at a church not far from the Marriots' place in Penge. Paula's face beneath the veil. Upward standing ostentatiously to one side with the ring case. A patch of grass outside the church where three or four bridesmaids – they were distant cousins of Paula's, I think – played ring-a-ring-a-roses after the service. It's all utterly distinct and real in my mind, an endless procession

of smiling faces and expensive suits. Terry Wogan was
there, Benny Hill and Michael Crawford. Morecambe &
Wise sent a telegram. On the wedding photos Paula and I
look a bit swamped, pressed into the dead centre of the
throng of faces, familiar and unfamiliar, and a bit diminished by them. After the service old Marriot, who'd now
decided I was a good thing, confided in me that he thought
his daughter had more talent than anyone had ever
suspected and the important thing was to get her into films.
Upward got drunker than I'd ever seen him and the
wedding cake was carried into the room on the shoulders
of the Marsha Flett Dance Troupe. It was a proper showbiz
wedding.

And afterwards, what happened then? I'd like to say
that we went back to the big house in Weybridge I'd
bought with the proceeds of the first three TV series and
lived happily ever after, but of course it wasn't like that. I
was thirty-five then, and if I try to remember the person I
was in those days for some reason it's much more difficult
to get to grips with than the boy in the square in
Southtown. The odd thing – something I'd never had to
deal with before – was that I had time on my hands.
Upward & King had been three years in the limelight now,
and the pattern of what we did was pretty much established. A TV series a year, usually in the spring or autumn.
Six or eight weeks in summer season at Blackpool,
Bournemouth or Margate. A Christmas pantomime
maybe, if the money was good. Odd club dates around the
country and bits of advertising work. Beyond that, though,
time hung heavy. Occasionally I saw Upward and we'd sift
through ideas for sketches, but that was a morning's work.
Newspapers used to make out sometimes that we lived in
each other's pockets – the TV series, of course, was based
on the idea that we lived in the same house – but that was
all rubbish. When we weren't working I never saw him
more than once a week. It was odd when you thought
about it. For five or six years we'd barely been apart for
more than a few hours, and now he was simply someone I
made time for in my diary now and again, like a business

partner or an accountant. He used to come for Sunday lunch sometimes, or we'd play golf – that was the trendy celebrity sport in those days, you were always having your picture taken playing golf – but it never really worked. He nearly always came on his own, which meant Paula and I had to sit there staring at him, or else he brought some more or less unsuitable girl whom you were glad to see the back of. As ever, Upward's private life – his whole life outside comedy – remained a complete mystery. He had a big house down in Kent somewhere, where we went a couple of times, but I don't think he lived there often. In any case I had other things to think about. A year after we got married, Paula miscarried. I can remember her standing in the bathroom with the blood running down her legs and a look of absolute horror on her face such as I'd never seen before in anyone. There was another a year after that, then another six months later. Sometimes we used to talk about what we wanted to do with the rest of our lives – Paula's ideas were always abstract suggestions like 'go to America' or, even vaguer, 'see the world'. Nothing ever came of them. There wasn't anything wrong between us, I don't think, simply that she was faintly dissatisfied with the situation she'd ended up in: stuck in the big house at Weybridge – the neighbours, of course, barely acknowledged our existence – childless, with a husband who sat upstairs reading. I'd discovered books, you see, by then. I used to order them up in great parcels from Foyles and Hatchards and go through them like a child in a sweetshop. In fact that's how I remember the whole of the late 70s – sitting upstairs in the study at Weybridge, with the view out over the lawn to the fields and the Surrey hills in the distance, Paula in the kitchen, only the occasional ring of the phone to bring us back to the world beyond, above all the feeling that you were happy, reasonably happy, with what you had but knew – feared – suspected – that it couldn't last. Like so much of life, I suppose.

The Wednesday morning arrangements worked out fine. By 8.15 I had Daniel packed off to school and was waiting for one of the commuter trains to Charing Cross. A quarter-circuit of the Circle Line got me to Liverpool Street with ten minutes to spare before the 9.30 to Norwich. I slept for half an hour, woke to find the train already running through Chelmsford, with its strew of soccer pitches and genteel factories, on over the Essex flats. All the time as we went east I found myself searching for familiar things. They weren't hard to find. The view out over the Stour beyond Manningtree looked exactly as I'd left it seven years ago. Ipswich was a jumble of sidings and smoke-blackened bridges. The Suffolk market towns didn't seem to have changed since I was a kid: the lines of faces drawn back beyond the safety line; the dopey porters staring out of the door of the waiting room; the rows of cars in the station forecourt. Almost before I knew it I was in Norwich, where the buildings around the football ground had been torn away to create a wasteland of car-parks and road-schemes, but the station was pretty much the same. I bought a cup of coffee in a styrofoam cup and a copy of the *Eastern Daily Press* and took them along to one of the outer platforms where a three-coach sprinter was waiting to take me the last twenty miles to Yarmouth. There was no one much about: a few old women with shopping bags and a couple of chaps in suits who talked about insurance. Needless to say, I didn't drink the coffee or read the paper. I spent the time staring out of the window, watching the landscape change and then settle down, from the spongy green meadows that marked the edge of the Broads to the flat, level plain of the Acle Strait.

And then suddenly there we were. Inevitably it was all a bit inconsequential and out of focus: a couple of slate-grey platforms, ticket office with crowing advertisements, taxis in the street beyond. It was one of those sharp, clear days that you only get on the east coast in winter – bitterly cold, with every gull in the North Sea coming inland for food – and I pottered about for a while on the forecourt getting my bearings before I headed off into the town. Before I did this I took a look at myself in a shop window, and I didn't look too bad – decent coat, most of my hair still there, not that far removed from young Ted King who'd come here a dozen times a year back in the 60s. All the same I didn't kid myself that anyone was going to know who I was. I wasn't sure I even wanted them to. I just wanted to stalk around the place for an hour or two, see how things had changed or hadn't changed and then come back, not intrude on anything. And so I set off, stopping every so often to look in windows or stare at the skyline, along the approach roads that led into the centre. Do you know, it was the oddest sensation? Like looking for the body of a human being or an animal and finding only the bones. Most of the things I remembered were still there, but they'd been changed in such a way that you had to stop to think twice or even three times about the original. The churches were still the same, and the market square, but the Sun Alliance building where I'd stared out of the window all those afternoons had been swallowed up into a huge wall of marble and glass, and fantastic things had been done to some of the shops. There was a bloke standing on the edge of the market stalls selling copies of the *Big Issue* and I went over and bought one. Lo and behold if he didn't turn round and say 'Thanks, pal,' in an accent straight out of *Brigadoon*. Surely there didn't used to be Scottish people in Yarmouth? Of course there did, but they used to come to work on the herring catch sixty years ago.

It was lunchtime now, and the town centre was a bit crowded: young blokes in suits stepping out of the big offices, crowds of girls in coats. Most of the big businesses I remembered from forty years ago were still there, but they'd been joined by a whole roster of newcomers. I headed on towards the sea, intending to take a look at the bowling greens (presumably they were still there) and the

Pleasure Beach, whose ferris wheel I'd been able to see out of the corner of my eye for the past five minutes, and there it all was, Yarmouth front in all its glory. It was out of season, of course, and most of the fish and chip restaurants and the amusement arcades were boarded up, but the whole thing cheered me up beyond measure – it was all so horribly vulgar and basic, the kind of thing you had to be practically half-witted to enjoy, run by canny Norfolk businessmen who'd swindle you out of your last fifty pence if you'd let them. I had half a mind to go into one of the arcades and blue five pounds on the machines, but I knew it would be a waste of time, and besides there were more important things to do. It was even colder down here in sight of the sea, and I crossed the road to the wider pavement on the far side, next to some raked-over flowerbeds and a display board advertising the marina. Eastwards the sea was grey-white, and there were a couple of tankers sliding by along the horizon, on their way from Harwich to the Hook I supposed. I went on a bit further and then pulled up sharp. Where the road bent round towards the Pleasure Beach and a municipal car-park there was a barrier across the pavement made up of a metal bar stretched lengthways across some packing cases. Ten yards away a police car was idling at the verge with a bored-looking constable leaning against the bonnet eating a Mars Bar. Seeing me staring at the barrier he stumped across and gave me a look.

'Sorry sir, road's closed.'

'What's the trouble?'

He was a huge, beefy lad with a corrugated face and an accent that could almost have been Fram. A bit puzzled that I needed any kind of explanation, he gestured in the direction of the car-park.

'It's the travellers, sir. Parked up by the Pleasure Beach. We've closed the road off.' He poked at the *Eastern Daily Press* under my arm. 'There's been enough about it in the papers.'

A furious little old man with iron-grey hair and spectacles balanced on the bridge of his nose – the kind of little old man who'd stood in the shop talking to Father half a century ago – came cruising across the road just in time to hear the last half sentence or so.

'That's right. Bloody gyppos parked up on council property and too idle to use the toilets. There's human excrement piled up on that beach, and what are your lot bloody doing about it, eh? You ought to run them and their fancy cars off the site and back to Ireland.'

'It's a point of view,' the policeman said.

He looked embarrassed by the intervention, but not unsympathetic. Possibly he had ideas of his own on the subject. I walked back the way I'd come, not altogether surprised but wondering what Father and Mother would have thought if they'd lived to be told that you couldn't use a municipal car-park in their town because a gang of travellers had taken up residence in it. Even Father – mild-mannered Father, wincing as he broke the rabbit's neck – would have had something to say about that. Thinking about Father and Mother, which oddly enough I hadn't been doing while I was drifting past the shopfronts and along the esplanade, made me remember what I was doing here. It was just after one o'clock. I set off towards the quayside in the direction of Southtown.

For a while – down by the quays and across the bridge – I knew exactly where I was. Even the river was the same – a greeny-grey, like washing-up water with odd shapes and protrusions visible way below the surface. But then, going down one of the approach roads to what I thought was the square, I got into trouble. Doubling back towards the river I tried again, only to resurface in a sort of cobbled courtyard packed with expensive-looking cars. There was no one about or I would have asked somebody. As it was I kept on through the yard – the buildings on either side were all smartish business premises – until at the end it opened out into a tarmac plaza with tropical plants growing in tubs and lumps of artistically arranged concrete roped off with chains. I was just about to turn back again when something in the set of the windows made me stop. On the instant I realised – and it hit me with an actual pain

– that I was standing on the west side of what had been the square. I looked around once or twice wondering if I'd mistaken things, but there was no getting away from it. After I'd stood there for a bit and taken another look at the buildings on the far side I managed to work it out. All the shops had gone, except for what had been Wedderbury's – it was the long, gleaming windows that had given me the clue – which was now an up-market marine suppliers. In their place was a row of what looked like municipal offices – three-storey affairs with green-and-white signs plastered over the frontage. The main part of the square, where the fenced-off garden and the row of beech trees had been, had disappeared altogether.

On the east side were more offices and a property developer's showroom. Dodging a few people in suits moving in the direction of the courtyard, I went over to take a look. That was it all right, where Father's shop had been, and the sub-post-office and the bakery, or rather it wasn't, because you couldn't tell where the original buildings were. I daresay if I'd have had a map of the place from the 50s I could have worked it out. As it was, all I could do was the vaguest kind of superimposing. In the end I walked up to the spot I thought most narrowly approximated to the site of Father's shop, which turned out to be some sort of employment clinic, and hung about for a while. Curiously, I wasn't as shocked as I'd thought I'd be. The past is never there when you want it, or how you want it. All the same, it shook me to see the place where I'd watched Father going bankrupt, smashed up the kitchen with Betty and chased after Marjorie Lovelace, turned into an office-block. For a second or two I wondered about going inside, inventing some excuse that would let me sit down in a chair for a moment, but in the end I thought better of it. All I could think of was Father and Mother and how the fact that the place they'd lived in had disappeared had somehow diminished them and taken them further out of my grasp.

There was a taxi creeping along the far corner of the asphalt, and I flagged it down. Pretty soon we were bowling along a B-road south of the town in the direction of the farming country. The cabbie was about my age, with an accent that wouldn't have been out of place in the square forty years ago, but he shook his head over the various names I tried him with. He remembered the shops in the square, though, and volunteered the information that most of them had kept going in one form or another until the early 80s when the council had redeveloped the site. All the time I was staring out of the window for landmarks, thinking that there used to be cows in a particular field or that surely beyond that hedge was where the houses began. The cabbie looked on with interest.

'Where exactly are we going, guv?'

It was a good question. 'It used to be called Parmenter's Farm. Ever heard of it?'

He hadn't, of course, so I sent him through the village and up the hill on the farther side. As far as I recalled in the old days the track – it wasn't much more than that – had wound off the road about half a mile out. We cruised along, past fresh-painted new houses set in the clearings (surely they hadn't been there before?) and spruce little meadows – all the raggedness I remembered from forty years back had gone – without seeing anything except a sign or two advertising what looked a fairly plush hotel. Another half-mile and I knew we were past the turn where the track had been, so I made the cabbie retrace our steps. Sure enough, there was the sign again, set back from the road to the right of a broad concrete drive.

WAVENEY HOTEL MICHELIN LISTED

Afternoon teas   Full dinner menu

Again, just as it had done when I stood in the square, something clicked. The Parmenters had gone, died or sold up, and this was the result.

'Just drive up here a bit, will you?'

In the old days it had been a rutted track, where the cow parsley grew eight feet high and you could see the banks of rhododendrons leading away to the house. Now it was a kind of small highway going through neatly-kept hedges with passing-places and little chained-off arbours with gravel floors. The cow parsley had gone, along with the rhododendrons. In the distance, up the hill, I could see the outlines of the house. There were several cars parked about, and what looked like the first hole of a golf course. For a second or two again I hesitated, even wondered about seeing whether they did lunches for non-residents. Then in the middle distance I saw a couple of figures coming down the hill towards me. They were men, a bit older than me, in their sixties perhaps, done up in the standard retired persons' golf gear – Pringle sweaters, checked caps and trousers and huge golfing brogues – each of them trundling a little golf trolley behind them like an outsize shopping bag. The cab slowed to let them by and I caught a glimpse of the lined, expensive faces – not particularly smug or pleased with themselves but relaxed and confident, as if there was no better destiny than to be strolling down a hill in Norfolk in your sixties with a golf club under your arm. After that I knew it was no good, that I simply couldn't face the sight of whatever they'd done to the Parmenters' farm, and the people who'd be hanging round it. It wasn't that I disliked it, or them, merely that I knew what it would be like – the menu done up in French and little brass table lamps stuck in the alcoves where Mrs Parmenter – my mother-in-law if it came to that – had left her knitting patterns, all this come to disturb the ghosts of people I'd known and lived with. In the end I made the cabbie reverse back down the drive – there wasn't enough room to turn round – past the golfers, who were smoking cigars under a tree, and back onto the road.

'Anywhere else, guv?' the cabbie wondered, sounding a bit puzzled. You could see his point.

'The church. Another mile down the road.'

It was impossible for anyone to muck that about, surely? We went on following the bend in the road – there were more new houses dotted about – passed another tiny hamlet with a pub done up in mock-Tudor, which I just

about remembered, and there it was, set back on the hill
behind the trees, the church where I'd got married back in
1961, with Mother scowling in the back row, old
Parmenter resplendent in his best suit and Mrs Parmenter
sniffing into a cotton handkerchief. I left the cab at the
foot of the hill and walked slowly up, past the trees,
through the lych-gate, on towards the porch. For some
reason everything looked very small. There were a couple
of benches and a notice or two about flower-arrange-
ments. They didn't even have their own vicar, just a rota
with half a dozen other parishes. I wondered how many
people came here now on a Sunday? Twenty? Thirty?
There'd have been a couple of hundred crammed in for
Harvest Festival in the 50s. Inside the church itself there
was flaking plaster all over the floor and a huge hole in
the roof of the belfry, where the bells had been taken
down. I prowled about for a bit, took a look at the Bible
lying on the big eagle's head lectern – it was a massive
King James with the 's's all 'f's, open at the Book of
Ecclesiastes – and then walked out into the churchyard.
Most of the gravestones were green with moss, but there
were a handful of new ones over by the far side, and I
wandered up and down the line for a while, certain that if
I looked long enough I'd find what I wanted. And sure
enough, there it was, an outsize marble slab commemo-
rating the passing of George Ernest Parmenter, born
1901, and his wife May Elizabeth, born 1903.

Oddly enough, the Parmenters hadn't died that long
ago. The old man, it turned out, had gone on well into his
seventies and Mrs Parmenters hadn't followed him until
as late as 1985. It seemed queer to think of Mrs
Parmenter alive in the world of Mrs Thatcher, Princess
Diana and *glasnost*. I was so intrigued by this that I nearly
missed the last line of the inscription, which read simply:
'And Mary Margaret, daughter of the above, born 16 May
1942, died 22 June 1988'. I stood looking at this for a
moment or two, quite unable to take it in. June 1988.
About the time Upward and I did the comeback show.
There was nothing else to see and I walked back down

the hill, not really knowing what to think, wondering of all things what had happened to Horace, the last of the Parmenters. Still alive, presumably, frowsting in some defectives' home or being 'looked after' somewhere. But what about Mary? What kind of life had she had in the quarter century after we'd split up? Stayed at the farm watching her parents grow old? Got married again? It seemed unlikely. For a moment or two I tried to plot the life she might have led alongside the one I'd had, but it was no good, there was no connection, no juxtaposition worth the name.

'Turning colder,' the cabbie said as I got back into the car.

It was, too. High above us flocks of birds were wheeling low over the ploughed fields. We drove back to Yarmouth with the sky turning blue-grey, wind coming in off the sea.

'My dad was a fisherman,' the cabbie volunteered. 'Wouldn't fancy being out there now.'

'No.'

'Sure you've seen all you want?'

'Quite sure.'

Well, that was true. In fact, I'd seen rather more than I wanted, a whole lot more. I got the cabbie to drop me in the town centre ('Nice talking to you guv. See you again') where the clocks said 2.30. There was a train back just after three, but in the meantime there was something else I wanted to do. When I was a kid, half a century ago, there was one duty that every holidaymaker in Yarmouth was expected to perform: send a kipper home. There were even shops that existed simply to sell the things to trippers, smoked and in special packages so they didn't perish *en route*. Did they still have kipper shops in Yarmouth? Striding back towards the station with a sausage roll in one hand – I hadn't eaten since breakfast time – I came across an up-market fish shop. Inside two teenage boys with red, well-scrubbed faces, dressed in pinstripe blue overalls and gumboots, were swabbing the floor with mops and buckets. I pretended to inspect the display trays for a bit – they were full of lobsters and shellfish which I suspected didn't come from anywhere near Yarmouth – and then swung round on them.

'I wonder if you can help me. I want to send a kipper.'

They just gawped at me, of course. A middle-aged man walking into a fish shop and asking if he could send a kipper home. You could just see them telling their mates about it in the pub that night. I tried explaining about the West Midlands holidaymakers sending fish back to their next-door neighbours in Digbeth and Dudley, but it was no good. I tried one or two other places and got exactly the same response. Oddly enough, it was this that upset me more than anything – more than the square, more than the Parmenters' farm, more than Mary – the discovery that you couldn't send a kipper home any more. It felt – I don't know – like some eighteenth-century aristocrat coming home from the Grand Tour to his country estate, stepping out into his walled garden, moving daintily towards the peacock lawn, only to find that some hooligan had pinched the sundial. In the end I simply bought a kipper from a stall on the market, took it into a stationery shop, up-ended it into a padded bag, stuck some stamps on it and wrote Lucy's name and address on the front and shoved it in the postbox on the corner by the station.

So there it was. That was what had happened to the old life, to the Parmenters, to Father's shop, to the room at the farm where I'd woken up to find Mary asleep beside me and the pigeons clacking in the eaves – all blown to smithereens, only this time by sane, sensible Norfolk people rather than the German bomb-aimers who'd done for the town my parents knew. And the truly awful thing was that I'd known it would be like this, known somehow about the square and Mary dying, known everything. I hadn't wanted it back, but at the same time I hadn't wanted it to change.

Apparently the Ngongi recognise the nondescript watering holes where they fetch up through smell. Put them down next to a dried-up pond and a few scrubby trees, and even if they haven't passed that way for years and the sand dunes have shifted to form an entirely new horizon, they'll know where they are. Well, I'd been back to the place where I'd been born for four hours or so and I couldn't smell a thing. Only the salt hanging in the clear, dead air.

On Parkinson

PARKINSON: J.B. Priestley – another northern sage, like ourselves – says somewhere …

KING: I'm not a northern sage. I come from Norfolk.

UPWARD: Ee! You've offended him there. He's very sensitive about his roots.

PARKINSON: His roots?

UPWARD: That's right. Didn't you see the bottle of lotion he keeps in the dressing room? (*turns to audience*) Carries it everywhere, you know.

PARKINSON: Sorry about that. J.B. Priestley says somewhere that comedy is society protecting itself with a smile. Do you have any comment on that?

KING: Is he a comedian?

UPWARD: Come on Ted, he's from Bradford. No, no comment there.

PARKINSON: I suspect that what I'm trying to ask you is, do you ever think about the nature of what you do?

KING: Absolutely.

UPWARD: Oh aye. But it's more fun thinking about the things you don't do.

PARKINSON: Let me try again – that sounds like the beginning of a song, doesn't it? Somebody else once said that the best kind of comedy encourages people to laugh *with* themselves rather than at other people. Communal, not discriminatory. Now, a lot of your jokes have victims, don't they?

KING: We never try to hurt people. It's just that certain things – certain situations – are simply funny.

UPWARD: It depends on what you mean by victims. Now, a government minister, some celebrity that's shot his mouth off in the press, they're fair game. That's what comedy's about – getting back at people like that. I mean, how else are you supposed to get back at them, eh? But then if you laugh at someone tripping on a banana skin does that make that person a victim? It depends who they are. It depends what's happened in the minute before they slip.

PARKINSON: So you're saying that humour has a moral dimension? That the comedian – excuse me if I get all highbrow here – is an ethical policeman?

KING: Everything's got a moral dimension.

UPWARD: We're not interested in people's morals. The Archbishop of Canterbury can look out for them. We just want to have a laugh.

PARKINSON: You've said many times that your background lies in the old Variety halls, and several critics have noted the enthusiasm with which you've reinvented some of the old routines. What do you think about, let's call it the new style of humour of the last few years?

UPWARD: Harold Wilson? He's a little belter.

KING: Monty Python? That kind of thing?

UPWARD: College kids, isn't it?

PARKINSON: College kids?

UPWARD: That's right. Read a few books and want to show off about it. No mass appeal is there, jokes about Sartre? I mean, it's telling the people who've not heard of him to piss off. (*pause*) Am I allowed to say that? The animations aren't bad, though.

KING: Not original either. People talk about surrealism. Well, you should have heard Tommy Handley.

UPWARD: And what about us? We do surrealism, we do.
             Avant garde we are, up there with the best of
             them. René Magritte. Margaret Thatcher.
             Seriously, though, Mike – is it all right if I call
             you Mike? – we're a cross-talk act. A music
             hall act. I'm short and fat. He's tall and
             gloomy. I take the piss out of him, he takes
             the piss out of me, and sometimes it doesn't
             work, sometimes it does. And then – I'm not
             saying it happens all the time, mind – people
             laugh.

KING: (*seriously*) And I'm from *Norfolk*.

1976

1979

'Christ,' Upward said peevishly.

'What is it?'

'Left my fags back at the house.'

'Go and get them then. It'll only take you five minutes.'

'I've only just bloody got here,' Upward said. He looked a bit put out, much more upset than a packet of mislaid cigarettes would normally have warranted.

'In any case,' Audrey said, with surprising firmness, 'it'll do you good not to have another one. Stay where you are, that's what I say.'

For some reason Upward looked even more upset. He stared first at me, then at Audrey, finally back towards the small beechwood from which we'd just emerged.

'It's no good,' he said. 'Better get back. Anyway, Peter might have phoned and left a message.'

'I suppose so.'

Hands plunged deep into the pockets of his sheepskin coat, breath steaming above his head in enormous, vaporous clouds, Upward marched off through the beech trees, disappeared into thickets of foliage, re-emerged, growing smaller by the minute, on the far side.

'I don't know why he came out in the first place,' Audrey said mildly. 'He hates the wet anyway. I told him he'd be better off in bed.'

'Safety in numbers. Everyone else seems to have come out of doors.'

In the distance, beyond the beech copse and the stretch of ground across which Upward's figure could just about be seen walking, perhaps a dozen other people were out taking the Saturday morning air. Some of them were standing on the peacock lawn, on which – as it was early February – no peacocks could be seen. Several were clus-

tered round the back of the house, like Upward probably
waiting for an excuse to get back indoors. One or two more
were inspecting the edge of a large artificial lake. At this
distance I couldn't recognise a soul. Higher up, the roofs
and turrets of the house gleamed and sparkled with frost.

'It's a big place, isn't it?' Audrey said. 'Quite scared me,
the thought of staying here, I can tell you.'

'I know. But still.'

Audrey, Upward's wife of six months, had taken some
coming to terms with. This wasn't because Upward's
getting married was unexpected – for the last few years
he'd talked of nothing else – but simply because Audrey
was so utterly unlike any woman that Upward had previously produced in the two decades that I'd known him.
Supposed to be exactly Upward's age, she looked, if
anything, a good bit older: forty-five, even. Seeing her for
the first time – a fortnight ago when Upward had brought
her to lunch – I'd been irresistibly reminded of the women
Mother knew in Yarmouth: hair going grey under headscarves, preoccupied expressions. In fact Audrey was fairly
cheerful, but she seemed to accept that her youth was
behind her.

'It was all very different when I was a girl,' she said
more than once.

Upward's explanation of why he was getting married
had been relayed in a few sentences: 'Audrey's an old
friend of mine. We've known each other for years. We're
probably even distantly related. I've been thinking of
getting married for a good long time now. I talked it over
with Audrey. We agreed it was the right thing to do.'

There were other ways in which Audrey differed from
the tribes of showgirls and TV hostesses 'done' on snooker
tables and in other places. For a start Upward was
prepared, in fact eager, to be ordered about by her: not to
have extra drinks when she said so, to behave when she
told him to. Also, he told me, he 'didn't want her name in
the paper'. All this was so unlike Upward as to make you
wonder about it. But then Upward, too, was unlike
Upward these days. It was difficult to put this into words:

not exactly quieter, but a bit warier, cross about something. As I later found out, there were reasons for this.

I watched Upward trailing back through the outcrops of trees. He'd found the cigarettes and was smoking one in short, furious puffs. There was another man with him whom I recognised as a journalist on one of the dailies. He was doing most of the talking. Upward stopped once or twice, took the cigarette out of his mouth and said something in reply.

At the edge of the wood there was a kind of rubbish dump, heaped up with dozens of black refuse sacks. They looked, and smelled, as if they'd been there a long time, probably since the start of the current round of industrial disputes. Audrey and I retreated back the way we had come, as Upward and the other man beat a path towards us.

'He's not been well you know,' Audrey said, smoothing her thick tweed skirt further over her knees.

'What's the matter with him?'

'Says he's got pains in his arms. The doctor can't find anything wrong with him though.'

'He looks all right.'

Close up, Upward didn't look so much ill – though his face was certainly a bit drawn – as preoccupied. He would be about forty now, but it was hard to work out how he'd altered in the time that I'd known him. A bit less squat, perhaps. But the essentials – wispy red hair, redder face – were exactly the same.

'Peter hadn't rung,' Upward said, as he came closer. 'Leastways there wasn't any message. I told the girl if he did ring she was to come out here and tell me.'

'She won't like doing that.'

'She watches the shows,' Upward said. 'Gave her my bloody autograph didn't I? Told her she could have yours, too.'

Peter was our agent. Negotiations for the upcoming series, which everyone had previously thought to be going all right, had suddenly stalled. Nobody quite knew why. I suppose, looking back, I should have seen this as a symbol, a pointer to the way ahead. At the time, though, it didn't seem like this. It was just something that Peter, Upward and the TV executives would sort out.

Upward went off to talk to Audrey. I could hear her lecturing him about the cigarettes. It was wet underfoot and there was rain coming through the soles of my shoes. The journalist, whose name was Sexton, came up and shook hands.

'Your wife here?'

'She's in bed with flu.'

'Well, there's nothing much to get up for is there? Do you know they're not even burying the corpses up in Liverpool?'

We stood looking back at the house, while Upward and Audrey started on another conversation, conducted in furious whispers. Most of the people had gone back inside. A few still hung about by the lake, moving this way.

'Always surprises me,' Sexton said, 'that Newsome can afford to keep this place up.'

'I thought he'd made a fortune out of property in the boom. That's what everybody said.'

'Well, everybody said wrong.' Sexton looked as if he got quite a lot of pleasure from saying things like this. 'Look at that pyramid selling scheme of his – Mayflower was it? Stunk to the high heavens, that did. Streets full of people in Birmingham, or wherever it was, paying 40 per cent on loans that the agents had actually fixed up with Newsome's own bank. There weren't many takers next time he went into the City wanting a float. Lost a couple of directorships too, by all accounts.'

'What's he up to now?' I wanted to know this simply as a means of impressing Upward.

'Something to do with the entertainment industry, if I hear rightly. Buying up old theatres or something and leasing them out. Something to do with a bloke called Cooper. That name mean anything to you? I expect you've come across him, doing what you do?'

Sexton went on like this for a minute or two longer, not interested in whatever replies I lobbed back. Upward and

Audrey had stopped whispering and were slapping their arms against their sides. It was definitely getting colder. Probably it would snow.

'I'm going back to the house,' Upward said. He seemed a bit happier now. 'Someone must have put a bloody fire on by now.'

Together we walked quickly towards the beech copse, nearly colliding with two men, until then concealed by the trees, who were coming out of it. There was a flurry of nods and apologies.

'Hello, Sir Gavin,' Sexton said eagerly.

It was the only time I really set eyes on Sir Gavin Newsome at close hand. I'd sat at the same table as him the night before, but been reduced to a fleeting glimpse or two. He was a tall, white-haired bloke of about fifty, apart from that difficult to describe. On the one hand he looked exactly like the pictures of City gents you see in newspapers proceeding in and out of the Guildhall. On the other there was something fantastically alien about him, hard to pin down. This effect was reinforced by the tall Russian hat he wore. The man introduced as Cooper I recognised immediately: a bit older than me, with greasy black hair. If Sir Gavin looked more or less at home here in the middle of a wood on a freezing Saturday morning, Cooper – wearing a white mac and suede shoes that were taking in water – looked completely incongruous. He was breathing heavily.

'Don't think we've met properly,' Sir Gavin said easily. 'Seen Arthur here dozens of times. Looking forward to your thing tonight, of course. Anything new for us, or just stuff we've seen on the box?'

'I daresay there'll be a surprise or two.'

'Well, that whets my appetite I must say.'

There was a faint trace of accent: nothing I could place. Upward had once or twice declared that Sir Gavin was 'a regular northern gent', but then Upward had claimed the same thing about Enoch Powell and a man who turned out to be the captain of the Welsh Rugby XV. What struck you was command of environment. You

got the feeling that if a would-be assassin had jumped
out from behind one of the beech trees Sir Gavin would
have somehow dealt with him, disarmed him, drawn him
into the conversation, asked after his wife. I looked at
the rest of the group. Upward seemed bored: nothing he
wanted to say would have been any use here. Sexton
looked desperate for Sir Gavin to say something to him.
Cooper, muttering faintly, was examining the water-
logged sole of his shoe. Audrey, who had her hands
drawn up under her chin, simply looked worried and
respectful.

Nobody said anything. Sir Gavin looked carefully
around him. 'Excellent,' he said. 'Very good. See you all
later then.'

He and Cooper set off in the opposite direction, where
a path led through waist-high bracken towards more trees.
Sexton looked as if he badly wanted to tag after them, then
thought better of it. As we went back to the house a few
flakes of snow came fluttering down from the darkening
sky. In the entrance hall, making sure that Sexton was out
of earshot, I grabbed hold of Upward's arm.

'Isn't that …?'

'The very same.'

'The one that Captain Groves …'

'Conked on the napper with a soda siphon. I was there.
It just goes to show.'

I remembered it too. The argument spilling out of
Captain Groves's office into the main body of the
Minerva, Groves languid at first, then finally losing his
temper and picking up the first weapon that came to hand,
Cooper – he wasn't badly hurt in the end – being taken
away.

'Still in Soho then?'

'Owns most of Frith Street from what I've heard. And
some other things, too.'

That night we were booked to perform a couple of
sketches for Sir Gavin Newsome's dinner guests. This kind
of celebrity showcase happened quite often. In the past we'd
appeared in front of a roomful of cabinet ministers, the

England football team and the Queen Mother and her entourage. I never enjoyed these occasions: not enough people, forced intimacy, the reminder that you'd have to talk to your audience twenty minutes later. This one wasn't any better except that for the first time – I'd seen it in rehearsals but never taken much notice – Upward unveiled his imitation of Mrs Thatcher. It was unbelievably funny, a kind of humour impossible to convey in words, so funny that I forgot all the professional protocols that had been dinned into me for the last fifteen years and burst out laughing myself. You might not think that a balding, red-faced man waving a finger the size of a saveloy in front of his face could imitate Mrs Thatcher, but somehow Upward managed it. Cigar smoke rising to the ceiling, starched white shirtfronts, fat hands curled round brandy glasses, greying heads thrown back, black air beyond the window – that was the rest of it.

Afterwards I went to bed. Upward stayed downstairs. Next morning when I came down to breakfast I found him hanging about in the hall. He was horribly excited, so excited that he might still have been entertaining Sir Gavin's guests.

'Well, I had a weird evening last night,' he said instantly. 'You want to hear about it?

'All right. Now?'

'Come in here,' Upward said.

To the right of the front door, a dozen feet or so from the stairs, there was a large cloakroom with a row of coat-pegs and a jumble of expensive-looking boots and shoes leading to a lavatory. The room had a sliding door, which Upward now pulled shut.

'If anyone comes I'll pretend I'm having a crap.'

'What shall I pretend I'm doing then?'

'You'll think of something,' Upward said.

Assuming this was a joke, I started to laugh. Upward glared back. Paler than usual, he didn't look as if he had slept much.

'Are you all right?'

'Champion.' He paused for a second and then started off on what was clearly a different tack from the one he'd first intended. 'This is an extraordinary place. D'y' know what I saw last night before we went in to dinner? I was wandering around outside the drawing room where Isla – Lady Newsome – was putting on her gloves. You know them long evening gloves she wears, the ones that come up to your elbow?'

'Yes.'

'Well, get this, Ted. When she'd pulled them on she got out a bottle of cow gum or white spirit from a drawer under the writing table and do you know what she did?'

'Drank some? Started inhaling it?'

'Don't be bloody silly. No, she dabbed a couple of blobs on the inside of each of her arms. So the gloves wouldn't slip down. Can you beat it?' Upward seemed completely entranced. '*Sticking your gloves to your arms so they don't slip down*! Do you suppose the Queen knows that trick?'

'Is that what you wanted to tell me?'

'Of course it bloody isn't.' Upward looked suddenly furious. 'It was just something I noticed. 'Ow the other half lives, that kind of thing. The really important stuff was later.'

'What was that?'

A soft tapping noise had begun on the other side of the sliding door.

'I say,' a well-bred voice said diffidently, 'is there anyone in there?'

'Hold on a minute,' Upward shouted loudly. 'I'm just having a crap.'

There was a noise of footsteps receding.

'Well, after dinner, after you'd gone and that little bloke Sexton had pushed off – said he had to get back to London – there was about ten of us round the fire. Audrey had gone to bed too. Can't stand late nights. Lady Isla as well. Me. Sir Gavin. That chap Cartwright, the MP. The bloke about seven feet tall who looked like an army officer. You know the one I mean?'

'Sort of.'

'Him then. One or two others. What do you think they were talking about?'

'The state of the country I should think. That's all most people talk about these days. Was it the bins not being emptied or "Crisis what crisis?"?'

'Good guess. It *was* that, up to a point.' Upward paused again, winked and bent forward impressively. '*Treason.*'

'Treason?'

'Not in so many words. Nobody said "I've got a file of tanks and I'm going to drive them up Whitehall", or "that Bill Sirs ought to be shot and I'm the man to do it", but take it from me there was some pretty odd stuff flying about. Army committees. Sympathetic newspapers. *Money.*'

For some reason – probably because of the strangeness of the setting – I always remember this as the most unreal moment of my life: the rows of Wellington boots lying on their sides, a ventilator fan whirring in the background, Upward's face nearly purple with emotion, fireside chatter about army committees.

'But Cartwright's an MP isn't he? A Labour MP at that.'

'A solid parliamentarian if the chips were down,' Upward nodded. 'Which I don't suppose they ever will be. Don't you worry, Ted. No one was talking about stringing Jim Callaghan up on a lamp post. I'm just telling you that there was half a dozen blokes – *important* blokes – saying things that, well, you wouldn't want to hear.'

'What did you say?'

'Not a lot. Kept quiet mostly.'

'What are you going to do?'

'Nowt,' Upward said, reverting to stage northerner for an instant. 'But I'm going to ring up Frank' – I knew from hearing the name dropped before that 'Frank' was the Chairman of the Parliamentary Labour Party – 'and tell him about it.'

Someone was tapping at the door again, a bit louder.

'All right,' Upward shouted again. 'Just wiping my arse.'

A moment later we filed out, past a startled-looking elderly gentleman in a tweed suit, into the breakfast room. During the meal I found myself looking at Lady Isla's forearms. On each of them, just beneath the elbow where the bone ran into flesh, there was a small red blotch.

*

Whether or not Upward spoke to the Chairman of the Parliamentary Labour Party I never found out. At any rate he never mentioned it again. There were several reasons why all this might have been driven out of his head. A few days later we heard from Peter that there was to be another TV series, for transmission in the autumn. Then, a fortnight after that, Upward had a minor heart attack and spent some weeks in hospital recovering. Though his face frequently stared out of news-papers or appeared on television, I never spoke to Sir Gavin Newsome again.

Outside Ipswich it began to snow. By Chelmsford the fields were turning white and the flakes were silhouetted against the blue-black sky. From time to time commuter trains whipped by heading east. Here the carriage was nearly empty. No one much travels into London at 5.30 on a Wednesday afternoon. Oddly enough, the train smelled of fish. Perhaps I'd unwittingly brought some of Yarmouth back with me? The only other souvenir was the copy of the *Eastern Daily Press*, with its reports of day care centre openings in Fakenham and sea defence repairs on the North Norfolk coast.

Watching the snow cheers me up, to the extent of making plans about Daniel. Come the weekend, if it's still there, maybe we could make a sledge, head down into Kent somewhere and find a hill. I can see the expression on Daniel's face – that desperate intentness children have – as the sledge comes over the lip of the incline. Tonight, I think, I'll read him *The Hobbit*, which has been lying around in his room for a week unregarded among the video games and the Michael Owen souvenir magazines. The train comes out between a gap in the low hills, and I can see the motorway lights winding away across Essex, down into the deadlands of the east, down into my country.

Back at the estate in Plumstead – four monstrous towerblocks rearing into the night sky – the remnants of Neil's party are still on their way home. As I head towards the lift-shaft the doors opens and a crowd of kids stream out waving balloons and soccer scarves. Up on the fourth floor Kev stands in the hallway, can in one hand, unlit Marlboro Light in the other. He looks a bit puzzled, almost worried, as if seeing me is a contingency he hasn't planned for, wonders how to deal with.

'Yes, mate?'

'I got back sooner than I thought. I hope Dan's been behaving himself.'

''E went off 'alf an hour ago with 'is aunt. Thought you knew.'

'His *aunt*?'

'That's right. Tall woman in a raincoat. Turned up on the dot with some other parents. With some bloke she said was driving them.'

Behind Kev, at the end of a pink-carpeted corridor, I can see Mrs Kev, a friendly-looking woman in goggle glasses, hearing the noise and coming to investigate.

'Let's get this straight. A woman came to collect Daniel from the party who said she was his aunt?'

Kev looks a bit unhappy at this, like someone whose professional judgment has been called into question.

'Wasn't saying nothing,' he says. 'As soon as your Daniel sees her he goes "Hello Aunty Shena". What am I supposed to do? Ask for ID? Anyway, she says she's come to take him home.'

'Kev,' I say weakly. 'She's my ex-wife's sister. She lives in Yorkshire.'

Even now, with my pulse booming away, I can see the excitement on Mr and Mrs Kev's faces as the implications sink in. They know about this kind of thing from the soaps and the tabloids. *Custody dispute* I can see them thinking. *Who'd have thought it eh*? In the kitchen, while Mrs Kev makes tea, Kev replays the events of half an hour before.

'That's right. Bang on the dot of half-past seven. You was in the kitchen, wasn't you, Jen? And there's this bird in a trenchcoat looking as if she's from the Social Security or something, says "I wonder if this is the address where Daniel King is attending a party?" Anyway, we let her in – knew who I was, knew who you were – she sees Dan, he comes running in, that's it.'

'What did he say? What did he look like?'

Kev thinks about this, staring hard at the table-top in front of him. 'He looked like a kid whose aunt's come to collect him from a party.'

'We're dreadfully sorry,' Mrs Kev says, now assuming collective responsibility. 'But what were we supposed to do? Do you want to phone the police or anything?'

'No.' Daniel will be in a car by now, halfway round the M25, off towards the idiot north. 'Seriously,' I say again. 'Thank you. No.'

Something of the gravity of the situation has now communicated itself to Kev.

'Awful thing to happen,' he says suddenly. 'With a kiddie and that. Fucking awful thing to happen. What can I say?'

'Kev!' Mrs Kev says indulgently.

I leave them in the kitchen – the rest of the children are still romping around in the front room bursting the balloons and swearing – and go out of the flat, back along the corridor and into the urinous lift. Outside the snow lies crisp and even on the car bumpers and the tarmac surround. Caught in the sodium glare of the street lamps it looks faintly unreal, like the fake snow we used to use in the carol singers' routine for the Christmas show. I walk up the hill, shoulders hunched against the cold, thinking of Daniel in the car, Shena, the sledge coming up across the lip of the hill that I will never see.

*

Untouched, exactly as it was twelve hours ago, the house seems unexpectedly changed by my absence. There are messages on the answerphone: Lennie telling me that the booker for a chain of south coast pubs will be ringing me; the booker himself telling me that he's just spoken to Lennie; somebody offering voice-over work; finally Shena calling from a mobile – you can hear traffic noise in the background – sounding quaintly formal. *You ought to know that Daniel is quite safe and I am doing this in what I consider to be his best interests. You can expect an official communication in the next twenty-four hours.* Somewhere in the crackle and whine of static I am sure I can hear Daniel's voice. I replay the tape seven or eight times but can't catch it. The dialback facility gives me the mobile number. It has been switched off.

Daniel's room has lost its charm, its invitation. It is just a place where someone has left a wallful of football posters and a few pre-teenage paperbacks, old Mars Bar wrappers and crisp packets. Even the Daniel-smell is fading away, heading up north in the speeding car. I imagine him again, half asleep, with his head pillowed on the armrest, looking out of the window at the drifting snow.

The phone rings.

'Isn't the snow wonderful?' Lucy says. 'You wouldn't believe how I've been enjoying it. How was your trip?'

'Dan's gone.'

'What do you mean "gone"?'

I explain into a silence broken by the intake of breath and tiny sussurations: Shena's raid on the party, the car, the flight to the motorway, details real and imagined. They might not be on the motorway at all, but holed up in some hotel. Halfway through I realise that Lucy's silence is one of immense, sorrowful respect, that, mysteriously, having Daniel removed from my life has somehow confirmed something she likes about me.

'Oh God,' she says. 'That's dreadful. Truly dreadful. Have you called the police?'

'I don't even know where they are. I need to talk to Shena.'

'You ought not to be on your own. Do you want me to come over?'

'It'll take forever. Come tomorrow. Like you were going to.'

'Fuck the script changes,' Lucy says. It is the first time I've heard her swear. 'You must take care of yourself.'

'I'll try to.'

*

Shena, reached by phone at 9.30 a.m., is predictably businesslike.

'I'm sorry to have to do this, Ted, but you didn't leave me any choice.'

'Where is he?'

'Daniel? He's just had his breakfast. Gary's taken him down the park.'

'Gary being the minder you brought along yesterday, I take it?'

'I don't think that's got anything to do with you Ted, really.'

'Seeing he's looking after my son at the moment I think it's got everything to do with me, don't you? When do I get to see him again? I mean, do I have to come up and do a repeat performance?'

'Look, Ted.' Shena sounds unexpectedly worn down by the complex manoeuvring required of her. 'There's a lawyer's letter coming this morning. By registered post. That'll tell you exactly where you stand.'

'I'm impressed by the homework,' I tell her. 'I mean, picking him up from the party. That was a stroke of genius.'

'I could just have met him out of school,' Shena says matter-of-factly. 'It wouldn't have made any difference. I don't know how to say this, Ted, *but he wanted to come*. I wouldn't have taken him if he hadn't.'

'When's he get back from the park? With his escort, I mean. When can I talk to him?'

'Actually,' Shena says, 'I don't think that would be a good idea. In a bit, perhaps. Not now. He's a bit upset.'

'Of course he is.'

'I don't mean that. I mean about the life he's been leading in the past three months. He's told me about it. You leaving him alone in the evenings when you went out. I'm not one to criticise, Ted, but that school …'

'It's just a school.'

'That's as maybe. I'm sorry, Ted, I should never have agreed to let you have him for the three weeks. I knew it would be difficult, that all this would happen. Did you know Daniel used to phone me in the evenings?'

'No.'

'Well, he did. Two or three times a week. Asking when he could come home. How do you think I felt about that?'

'How do you think I feel about this?'

'I shouldn't think you feel very happy. But then – don't mind me saying this, will you Ted? – Paula didn't feel very happy. Not for a long time. You can't just wander back into people's lives when you feel like it.'

'If I find you're keeping him against his will it'll take more than Gary to stop me bringing him back.'

'But I'm not,' Shena says exasperatedly. 'I'm not keeping him against his will. It's not about *owning* him. It's about Daniel. Look, I'll ring you in a couple of days and tell you how he is, all right? But if I look out of the window tomorrow morning and see you there I'll call the police. And from what the lawyers say they'll listen to me, not to you.'

*

Lucy arrives an hour later, her head done up in a kind of Afghan bonnet like the minicab drivers. Meeting in the hallway, we peer uncertainly at each other for a second or so.

'I'm so sorry,' Lucy says fiercely. 'So sorry about Dan. I just wanted you to know that.'

So much of my life has hinged on a failure to accept invitations. This time I don't need any prompting. She falls into my arms in a kind of slow-motion jog, jacketed shoulder coming to rest against my chin. She smells of what? New-mown hay? Expensive toilet-water?

'I thought and thought about it after you told me,' she says. I can feel her fingers digging into my shoulders.

There is no explanation for these things. They happen. They are there. Moving through the hall I see her face caught suddenly in the mirror above the phone: white, sharp-featured, like the other Lucy, the girl in the Narnia books that Mary had by her bedside all those years ago.

The Last Sketch

UPWARD: It's good to see you again.

KING: It's good to see you again.

UPWARD: I thought you'd have changed, but you haven't. Not taken a bath either, by the smell of you.

KING: You haven't changed either. (*reaches over to feel the lapels of Upward's suit*) Still making your own clothes I see.

UPWARD: Huh! My mother was a champion dressmaker y'know … Her and me father in the shop, they knew all about *haute couture*.

KING: I've never heard it called that before.

UPWARD: Listen! Do you want to know what happened when Mrs Thatcher and half the Cabinet had dinner with the European Council of Ministers in Brussels last week?

KING: No, but go on.

UPWARD: They asked her what she wanted to eat, and she said 'I'll have the roast beef of Old England.' And then they said, 'What about the vegetables?' And she said, 'Oh, they'll have the roast beef as well.'

KING: (*admiringly*) You're a one, you are.

UPWARD: (*proudly*) I am. I am a one. That is exactly what I am. So what have you been doing with yourself?

KING: Oh, the usual things. Sorting my stamp collection. Taking the dog out.

UPWARD: I'm surprised at you. With your money you could afford a woman.

KING: I borrowed yours, remember, but it had a puncture.

UPWARD: ...
KING: What's that?
UPWARD: ...

Witham Sports Arena, June 1988

The Comedy Man

Do you know the difference between a cavalry charger and a brewer's nag? Well, one darts into the fray ...

Where did it all go wrong? In all the time that followed I regularly used to ask myself that question. Sometimes I used to believe that it was simply a series of pieces of bad luck, that if we'd somehow managed to push things like Upward's heart attack to one side we'd have been able to jink round the obstacles we found in our way, come bouncing back into the spotlight. What if Upward hadn't been ill? If we'd got the next series, and the one after that? Done the film that Peter wanted us to, but Upward refused? I used to agonise over these mistakes – if they were mistakes – for hours at a time. In the end, though, I realised that there was a perfectly simple explanation. Upward being ill didn't help – he took a long time to recover, and even when he was fit again you could see that it had frightened him, that something had stuck in his mind that hadn't been there before, changed him and chastened him. At the same time – it's something you do when you can feel the ground slipping beneath you – we made some stupid mistakes. Not going back to radio was one, and the two or three films we did around that time were simply diabolical – just girls taking their clothes off and Upward smirking, with me looking hangdog in the background.

But the thing we were involved in, that we'd spent our lives doing, was changing and we hadn't even noticed. Or rather, we had noticed and there wasn't anything we could do about it. I remember once out of curiosity climbing a set of back stairs in Brewer Street of all places around the time of the Falklands to see an outfit called Dogface and Haddock, and thinking that once you took away the shock tactics they were probably quite funny, but that anyone who laughed at them would think twice about laughing at us. Upward, in particular, hated anything that described itself as 'alternative comedy' or anyone who described himself – worse, herself – as an 'alternative comedian'.

'Stupid hair and silly voices and the Tories and no fucking punchlines and bad language and the Tories and jumping up and down,' he once complained. 'Well, it doesn't make *me* laugh.'

Which was accurate, if beside the point.

Naturally enough, none of this happened overnight. As late as 1981, I remember, we were still coming fourth in the polls of 'Comedy Favourites'. But it was all quietening down, fading away. You put out your hand to touch something that you'd assured yourself would always be there and it was suddenly gone. Six million people watched the last TV series we did. Three years before it had been ten or eleven. A TV executive we'd known for years took us out to lunch and explained, politely but firmly, why there wouldn't be another. Upward cried after that lunch – Upward! Who when I first knew him genuinely couldn't care less about anything. I remember sitting there looking at him as he tried to light a cigarette with his hands shaking so much that he could barely hold the lighter, and then issuing a mock-defiant challenge that got printed in the tabloids, towards the back of the tabloids now: WE'LL BE BACK SAYS OUSTED UPWARD! TV BOSSES ARE OUT OF TOUCH – SACKED COMIC'S SHOCK CLAIM! That kind of thing. We did a summer show that year somewhere down in the West Country, and I remember looking out into the stalls a couple of times (the place was still half full – you never lose your audience completely) and thinking that the game was up. Worse, that I didn't care, certainly not as much as I ought to, or Upward seemed to think I should.

After that we started to drift apart. There was no big flare-up or anything. We just saw less of each other, didn't telephone so often. Paula and I had moved to Suffolk by this time, to the big house looking out over the Stour

Estuary, and I suppose that wasn't an incentive. He used to come over at odd times though. I'd get home from a trip to London, back from Manningtree station in a cab late on a dull autumn afternoon and find his car in the drive, Paula and him looking out of the window as the cab swerved into the gravel. You got the feeling – nothing was ever said – that Audrey kept him on a pretty tight rein. Even when he was with us he was always phoning her, worrying about whether it was time to leave. There was always vague talk about plans, reunions, a live video some director was going to shoot in a pub in the East End. Of the pair of us, I'm sure it was Upward who was the harder hit. He was still a bit of a figure in his way – you saw him now and again on the TV gameshows that go out in the afternoon when nobody's watching – and it must have hurt him, the thought that he'd never get back where he'd been before, however much he tried. I remember when Eric Morecambe died he was bitterly upset, not because he'd known Morecambe especially well but because of the symbolism: the good man gone, the toppling over of something you'd thought fixed and irrevocable, the conveyor belt rushing on empty.

And all the while time was moving on. It was 1984, 1985, and we hadn't been on a stage together for four years. It used to puzzle me sometimes, coming back from a walk over the marshes, watching the teal take flight into the winter sky, how you could lose something that had been a part of you and not seem to mind. Once or twice I had offers from other people – younger blokes looking for 'guidance', deadbeats of fifty wanting to head back to the theatre circuit. I always turned them down. I wasn't far off fifty myself if it came to that. And what about me? What did I do? The answer is, I suppose, that I sat tight, read more books, tried to look after Paula. There'd been another miscarriage in the early 80s, after which we'd stopped trying. I used to walk for hours over the flats near the house, all the way down to Shotley sometimes on the furthermost tip of south-eastern Suffolk, watching the birds and thinking about it all, all the way back to Father and Mother and the square, Mary and the old days at the farm, so far away now that it might have been another world, and someone else living in it, not me at all.

As to the life that Paula and I led, I can't begin to describe it. We'd spend whole days together in the house, walking over the wet fields, driving up to Pin Mill on the north side to look at the boats. Everything around the place was to do with water, from the yacht masts passing down the estuary a quarter of a mile away to the smell of the brine which slapped you in the face like a dishcloth whenever you stepped out of the door. In winter huge flocks of geese, two or three hundred at a time, came and camped on the meadows. I used to watch them from the study window upstairs, taking flight momentarily when a ship's horn sounded out in mid-stream, hanging in the air for a second or two then slowly descending to the emerald turf. Sometimes at night you'd be woken by the sound of them flying overhead, a curious rub-a-dub noise like an old-fashioned laundry. What Paula and I talked about over our solitary meals, the summer days we spent out in the water meadows, exploring tiny, forgotten churchyards where the newest gravestone dated from the 1890s, I don't remember. I can recall the substance, but not the words spoken. Was she happy? I don't know. Perhaps I should have asked her.

*

Backstage, you suspected that the dressing room had recently done service as a furniture store. Bits of jumble lay all over the floor. An elderly wind-up gramophone with a rearing loudspeaker. Three or four cane-backed chairs. A case of books. A colour photograph of the Queen Mother dating from the 50s. Stepping past these obstacles, bending to avoid a low-swinging lightbulb, I was reminded of other, similar clutter. It took a second or two to connect it with the shop that Mother and Mrs Moss had kept in Gorleston a quarter of a century before. That was where the memory came from, though: a compound of chalk-dust, mothballs, old dresses hung in rows, Mrs Moss's deathshead face leering from the till.

'Not the bloody Winter Gardens, is it?' somebody said.

In the ten years since I'd last seen him, Tracy Jacks had clearly made some stark decisions about his sexuality. He had lost weight, a great deal of it, and his once curly hair, which in the early 70s had nearly reached his shoulders, was reduced to a savage crew-cut. As a final touch there was a metal stud drilled into his right ear. None of this, it had to be said, was especially convincing. There was a weird sense of someone got up in fancy dress. Upward, who had been reintroduced to him the day before, had taken this transformation about as badly as could have been expected.

'Christ,' he had said. 'It's going to be bad enough already without that little pansy mincing round the changing rooms.'

'You used to like him.'

'Who'd have thought it?' Upward had sighed mournfully. 'Tracy Jacks turned into a bum-bandit.'

Upward sat on a chair at the far end of the room. He didn't look well. Like Tracy Jacks with his short hair, lean face and thigh-hugging chinos, it was hard to say exactly what was wrong. Dressed in a brightly-coloured suit, much more outrageous than anything he'd worn in the past, he seemed unable to work out what kind of mood he was in. Two or three jokes, snapped out on arrival twenty minutes since, had given way to a gloomy silence.

'Bloody hell,' Tracy Jacks said, not quite as respectfully as he'd done fifteen years ago in the studios at Broadcasting House. 'You're not going on stage in that, Arthur?'

'And what if I am?'

'For a start that jacket'll strobe every camera in the hall.'

'I'll wait for the director to tell me that, ta.'

This exchange definitely did Upward some good. He laughed loudly and started to talk to another man who had something to do with the video company. Tracy Jacks watched him for a moment, as if he couldn't quite work out whether or not he'd caused offence, and then moved back in my direction. This too made you feel that what he was dressed in, hairstyle and general appearance, was a kind of disguise. Ten years older and two or three stone lighter, he still gave an impression of lumbering, of being ready to crash into anything left in his path.

'Glad to hear about your missis,' he said, sending a stool skidding across the floor. 'Been a long time, eh?'

'A hell of a long time.'

'When's it due then?'

'Another three months. Two and a half, maybe.'

I was still completely unable to come to terms with Paula being pregnant. Expecting the worst, then finding that the worst didn't happen, was deeply unsettling. Away from her, I used to break into a sweat whenever a telephone rang or someone I knew came purposefully towards me. With her, I'd stare at her stomach, fists clenched, willing the baby to grow. Paula was a bit unnerved by this.

'So no jokes about expectant mothers?' Tracy Jacks said.

'None at all.'

'Fair enough.' Flicking up a finger, he began to massage the earlobe where the silver stud hung. 'Jesus, I'm sure this is infected. I mean, it shouldn't hurt like this, should it?'

'Probably not.'

The reunion concert had been Tracy Jacks's idea. Sacked from, or bored with, the BBC – no one quite knew – he was something to do with an independent production outfit. Tonight's performance would be going straight to video, unless, as had been vaguely rumoured, Channel Four were interested.

'What do they use this place for anyway?' Upward asked. He was taking pairs of spectacles out of his pocket – three or four of them lay on the table top before him – and balancing them one after another on the bridge of his nose.

'Sports hall, I reckon,' Tracy Jacks said. 'There's a couple of basketball nets either side, but I've got the sound boys taking them down.'

One or two other people started to drift into the room, making it a bit crowded: the director, sound men, a security guard. A make-up woman came in and, without speaking, began to scoop up the ends of what remained of Upward's hair into place with the end of a comb. Upward ignored her. He seemed to be floating somewhere, far away from the dressing room throng. With the view obscured by several bodies, I heard Tracy Jacks trying to restart their conversation.

'I read your book,' Tracy Jacks was saying. 'D'you know, I even went out and bought it.'

'Oh, aye?'

Most people would have stopped at this point. Tracy Jacks went on gamely: 'I thought it was a bit, well, *personal*.'

'Of course it was personal,' Upward said with extraordinary savagery. 'What's the point of writing a book like that if it's not bloody personal?'

Whatever Tracy Jacks said in reply was cut off by the director clapping his hands for silence. He was a small, seedy-looking man of about forty with chronically inflamed eyelids. For a moment I tried to concentrate on what he was saying, but it was difficult to take in more than fragments.

'All feeling our way a bit here … Important *not* to play to the camera … Just do your normal act, and leave the technical stuff to us … Language. It'd be a good idea if nobody said "fuck" or "cunt". Anything else we can probably get away with … Same goes for jokes about ethnic minorities … Take a break after thirty minutes, just to make sure we've got the levels right ∴.. All professionals here I know …'

At the mention of the word 'professionals' I stopped listening. Faintly in the distance, as warm-up act gave way to warm-up act, music was playing.

> '*They're playing our tune, by the pale moon*
> *We're incognito, down the Lido*
> *And we like the Strand.*'

It was the same music that had played in Tracy Jacks's studio fifteen years before. I moved forward with the idea of pointing this out to him, but the room was losing its population. Someone said: 'Ten minutes then,' quite loudly. In the distance there was a noise of scattered applause. Tracy Jacks, glimpsed for a second in the doorway, made a thumbs-up sign. I waved back. Then the door shut and I was alone with Upward.

Very slowly, as if they were immensely fragile and expensive pieces of china, Upward was stowing the pairs of spectacles back in the inner pocket of his jacket. This took him several minutes. Doing it he looked a bit decrepit, deflected once or twice by pieces of cloth or his own fingers. When he'd finished he straightened up and said, comparatively normally:

'How's Paula?'

'Very well. She said to say hello.'

'Too late for owt to go wrong now, I suppose?'

'It's never too late. Especially for things to go wrong.'

'That's true enough.'

There was a silence. 'You know,' Upward said, 'I always wanted to have a kid. Too late now, of course. But there's no denying it would have been difficult.'

God knows what Upward meant by this. That it would have been difficult for Audrey to have a baby? That something in Upward's temperament would have stopped him being a good parent? I realised that Upward was in a state that I'd only witnessed three or four times in the thirty years I'd known him: the confidential. While I was working this out there was a knock on the door, which then opened a foot or so, and a voice – owner unseen – muttered, 'Five minutes' and withdrew. Upward seemed not to notice.

'Always fancied it,' he said. 'You know. Taking him out places.'

'It would have to be a boy?'

'Oh I always think you'd want a boy, don't you?' Upward said.

There was another muted burst of clapping in the

distance: the second warm-up act had finished. Upward looked vaguely around him.

'We're not on yet, are we?' he asked.

'Three or four minutes, I suppose.'

People always talk about a light going on in someone's head. That was how it seemed with Upward at that moment. He sat bolt upright, drummed his fingers on the table, squinted at himself in the mirror: tired, maybe, but ready to make a go of it.

'If this goes OK it won't be the last time.'

'You think so?'

'Positive. Shouldn't have left it so long in the first place.'

Coming from anyone else, this would have been taken as an apology. As it was, Upward somehow made the long delay sound as if it was my fault. Then, quite unexpectedly, his mood changed. He looked worried, ground-down, much worse than when I'd first seen him earlier that evening.

'Are you OK?'

'I'll do. Look, afterwards … There's something I want to tell you.'

'Tell me it now if you like.'

'No.' Upward looked appallingly nervous. 'Can't tell you now. Do you understand?'

'I suppose so.'

There was another scuffling noise beyond the door. Upward started indulging himself in another pre-performance ritual I remembered from the old days – tieing and re-tieing his shoelaces. Already we seemed to have got through an eternity of waiting. Upward looked up, nodded, smiled, bent down to reapply himself to his shoelaces. Thirty seconds later we were on stage.

There was a kind of roar of appreciation, scattered applause. Upward, stage-centre, was bowing low, making elaborate gestures with his hands. Still dazzled by the light, I stood on the lip of the stage and stared out into the darkness. The sports hall's immense height – much bigger than an ordinary theatre – made it seem like a huge, dark cavern. There were about three hundred people there,

some empty seats to the rear, but not too many. It was a
fair turn-out. The applause, which was showing signs of
falling away, renewed itself as Upward went into another
of his old routines: sliding forward on his knees with arms
outstretched on either side. Somebody threw a bunch of
daffodils onto the stage. Upward picked them up and
pressed them to his heart. Breathing heavily, scarlet-faced,
he stayed like this for a moment or two, clambered up and
picked one of the microphones out of its stand.

'Ladies and gentlemen,' he bellowed. 'We're not here
today and gone tomorrow.' There was a pause. 'We pissed
off last night.'

There was another roar of laughter. Upward swung the
microphone up in the air, caught it expertly as it fell.

'This is my friend Ted,' he shouted. 'Did you know he had
a Chinese cousin? That's right. Keeps an oriental restaurant
in Walthamstow. It's true. I rang up to order some chow mein
and a voice said "Good evening, I am Fu King the manager,"
so I said "That's OK, I'll call back in a minute." '

I was still looking at the faces: rows of them. Middle-
aged, mostly, but with a scattering of younger people. By
now Upward was prowling restlessly near the back of the
stage.

'He doesn't say much,' he announced, veering towards
me. 'He keeps himself to himself.'

'You should see some of the things *he* keeps to himself,'
I lobbed back.

The laughter was coming in tiny ripples now, important
to play it out.

'I went up to his room the other day and there was this
teenage girl coming out. She said: "I'm a foreign languages
student. Mr Upward's kindly been helping me to brush up
my Greek." ' More laughter. 'I said, "Well, I've never heard
it called that before." '

The laughter reached crescendo. Just as it fell away,
Upward whipped round and tried to do the splits, stuck
half-way and remained there like some grotesque children's toy that had stopped working, needed a prod to set
it functioning again.

Up until now we'd simply been mucking about. All the time, though, I'd been waiting for Upward to launch into the first sketch. The cue for this was that Upward would turn to me and say 'It's good to see you again.' Upward was quite capable of spending five minutes marching round the stage saying anything that came into his head. By this time, I noticed, he'd worked out where the cameras were. There were two, one immediately between the stagefront and the first row of the audience, another on the far right-hand side.

Crouching down now, with the microphone almost vanished between tightly-clasped hands, he murmured: 'They're taping this, you know. That's right … Playing it to the buggers at ITV.'

Three or four people laughed: not many. Upward swivelled round, winked at me lavishly.

'It's good to see you again.'

'It's good to see you.'

The sketch unfolded. An innuendo about *haute couture*. Mrs Thatcher at the Brussels summit. All the time Upward was glancing around him, at the cameras, at the front row of the audience, back at me. Drenched in the bright light, the eyes of the electrical equipment blinking out of the darkness, it was difficult to get a proper sight of his face, but he looked drained, panic-stricken. He'd got the microphone stand in one hand now and was using it as a prop, waving it in front of him, leaning on it as if it was a walking-stick. Halfway through the routine, after the Mrs Thatcher joke, he coughed a couple of times, lost the line, grabbed at it and retrieved it before the audience knew it had gone. I grinned at him but he didn't respond. When it happened, halfway through the joke about the inflatable woman, I thought for a second it was part of the act, some unrehearsed piece of slapstick he'd invented just to spice things up: me feeding him the line, Upward goggling, me feeding him the line again, Upward sinking slowly onto his knees, the microphone stand wedged under his arm like an outsize swagger stick, then rolling over onto his back with his eyes wide open and his teeth bared making little waving motions in the air while the audience laughed and I stood there, looking for a sign that it was all a joke, all make-believe, but not finding it and rushing forward, Tracy Jacks suddenly bobbing up onto the stage from his vantage-point at the side, the laughter suddenly falling away, Upward lying motionless under the harsh, white light.

*

And that's nearly all there is to say about Upward. As it happened he didn't die until the early hours of the next morning, in a hospital out in the wilds of Essex with Tracy Jacks and me prowling up and down the corridors and waiting for the police car that was bringing Audrey up from Kent. I think she got there with half an hour to spare. I was wandering round the grounds anyway, by then, smoking cigarettes and not knowing what to do with myself. Various people lobbied for a proper showbiz funeral, but in the end Audrey put her foot down and there were just a couple of dozen of us at a tiny church in a field near Canterbury, not far from where they lived: Paula and me, some cousins from up north, family of Audrey's. I remember odd things: the wind suddenly sweeping in across the churchyard and dragging Paula's coat tight across her stomach; a couple of youngish women that nobody could identify who sat at the back of the church and left early; Tracy Jacks standing mournfully by the grave after the coffin was lowered into the wet earth.

If I'd expected any great revelation about Upward at that moment – some blinding flash of light about where we stood in relation to each other – then it didn't come. Life stopped for a second or two while I thought about him at Catterick with the PT instructor breaking his collar bone, marching down Bouverie Street, then began again. Going back to the car, Paula and I started a little bickering argument that flared up and absorbed most of the journey home. And that's really what I remember about Upward's funeral: Paula's voice, the endless crawl back round the M25, reaching the big house in the marshes at dusk, switching on lights, wondering what to do with the rest of my life.

I haven't heard from Audrey for six or seven years, but a day or two ago she replied to my letter in search of Upward memorabilia. Even for Audrey, with whom there'd been a fair amount of correspondence in the months after Upward's death, the tone was grimly matter of fact. The fact that I'd known Upward, on and off, for thirty years; that someone wanted to make a radio programme about him; that the whole question of Upward's reputation might be up for grabs: none of this apparently was of much account. In fact the letter – there weren't more than a few lines, but looking as if they'd been much laboured over – and the things that accompanied it seemed to confirm what I'd suspected about Audrey since the evening twenty years ago when the four of us had sat down to dinner in Surrey, that in some respects she was the oddest person I'd ever met, far odder, if their respective characters were ever compared, than Upward.

The package that Audrey enclosed – a largeish brown envelope bound round with Sellotape – had my name written on the front. However, the handwriting was faded in places to the point of illegibility, as if years ago it had been left out in the sun, was Upward's. Had Audrey ever opened it? The tape wound round the seal looked just as ancient as the address. It was possible that Audrey had simply found it at the bottom of a drawer, in a remote attic, under piles of newspapers in a garage, decided to send it on. Perhaps, if it came to that, its discovery explained the chill of Audrey's covering note – Audrey suspecting a secret between the two of us that good manners prevented her from exploring. Perhaps, on the other hand, Audrey had looked at the envelope's contents and then re-sealed it. It was impossible to tell.

For some reason seeing Upward's writing on the corner of the envelope – even an Upward who'd been dead ten years – produced the most tremendous feeling of excitement. It was as if some piece of music, half-remembered from childhood, its cadences hanging tantalisingly out of reach for years, had suddenly poured out of the radio, complete and unblemished. As if, too, it had been magically possible to recreate the sensations you'd experienced on first hearing it. Picking it up, holding it in the palm of my hand, I could hear Upward's voice, wouldn't have been surprised to look up and find him walking into the room. Predictably the contents, turned out and spilled across the table, looked unexciting. There was a bundle of photographs, most of which I'd seen at one time or another, showing the two of us on stage – summer season shots, I guessed, probably dating from the early 70s – a small handful of theatre programmes and several sheets of paper, mostly in Upward's handwriting, occasional additions in my own, containing unfinished sketches. Some of these looked as if they were thirty years old. A crumpled white envelope turned out to harbour half a dozen postcards I'd sent back from foreign holidays in the 70s: France, Venice, Crete. Try as I might, I couldn't remember writing them. Despite all this, despite the poverty of Upward's showbiz leavings – a few photographs, creative tryouts, other odds and ends – the sense of him that these fragments threw up was very strong. Looking at the lines of cross-cut dialogue, unpunctuated, bare stage dialogue printed in capitals (HE PICKS UP HIS HAT/GIVES LOOK OF DISGUST) you got an instant feeling of what Upward was like, how he went about things, the effect he had on people.

There were one or two other things: some fan letters, mostly commiserating with Upward about the end of the TV series; some stuff about Upward's autobiography; finally – the very last thing that fell out of the envelope – a little bundle of foolscap letters tied up with embroidery thread. Something about this parcel drew my eye towards it: the neat bow that held the collection in place; the regular slant of the handwriting. I untied the bow and let them spill out over the table, pushed them apart with my finger. There was no doubt about it. The handwriting was Paula's.

All of a sudden, without warning, a huge amount tumbled into place: Upward's unexpected appearances in Suffolk; Stevens's mistake over Audrey's name; the last conversation in the dressing room. To have what you'd not exactly suspected but worried about, feared, was – what? A relief? Something else? I picked up the first letter – it was dated early 1988 – read the first paragraph – innocuous-enough sounding stuff about the weather as it happened – and then put it down again. Now that the evidence had so dramatically come to light, why read on? I remembered reading Mother's diaries on the train back from Yarmouth thirty years ago. They'd had the power to startle merely because I had no idea what they might contain. Whatever I guessed about Paula writing to Upward would be preferable to what was there to be read. As to how long it had gone on, there was no way of telling. Shuffling the letters back together and carefully ignoring their contents, I glanced at the top right corners of the pages where Paula had scribbled the date. They were all from the early part of 1988, just before Daniel was born. That needed thinking about as well.

I left the letters on the table for a while, came back and stared at them again. The fact that even in death Upward exercised the same influence as he'd done in life wasn't lost on me. For a bit I wondered what Upward would have said had he ever got round to telling me about it. Though he hardly ever talked about his love affairs, Upward had always liked to present them as unavoidable, providential nudges, something he was quite unable to escape from, predetermined by the stars. What had he thought about Paula? What had Paula thought about him? Suddenly it struck me that there was absolutely no point in posing these questions, that they would never be answered, that they were probably best left unsolved. There was nothing left to be done. Separating the letters out from the rest of Upward's leavings, I put them back in the larger bag. Even then it was hard to stop my mind racing, wondering when, and how, and in what spirit Paula had written them, in what spirit they'd been received. Finally, though, I put them in the sink, lit a match and watched them burn. It was a triumph of a sort.

*

'So there's a chance that Daniel isn't your son?' Lucy asks.

'It's a possibility that has to be faced.'

'But what do you think?'

'I don't know. Sometimes I think he is. Sometimes I think he may not be. But it doesn't make any difference.'

'No?'

'Not to anything that matters. I've spent ten years assuming he's my son. He's spent ten years assuming that I'm his father. Pulling that apart isn't going to do either of us any good.'

'Surely you must want to know the truth?' Lucy wonders.

'I don't think there is one, not one I could find out. I could try asking Audrey if she knows anything about it. Can you imagine how she'd react to that? I don't think she even knew about the letters.'

'I think you're being very brave,' Lucy says, a bit uncertainly, the way people say things unthinkingly. *It's tragic. You must be very upset.*

Am I being brave? I don't think bravery comes into it. What do I know about Upward that is 'true' if it comes to that? That I worked with him for a quarter of a century on and off? That he was an edgy, secretive man whom I never really got to the bottom of? That I liked him, admired him, found him funny, whatever that means? That he could be as unscrupulous towards me as to anyone else? It is hard to feel that this amounts to much.

'But what about the practical stuff?' Lucy asks. 'Daniel not being here?'

'I'll sort it out.'

'You must let me help.'

'You are helping.'

This is true. Lennie has reported several flurries in

advance of the radio doc. *Phone 'asn't stopped ringing* was how he put it. Professionally, things are looking up.

*

A week or so later Daniel telephones. It's 3.30 on a grey December afternoon. Outside there are children's voices in the street.

'It's me, Dad, Dan.'

'Does Aunty Shena know you're phoning me?'

'No. She's out somewhere. I just got back from school.'

For a week I've been relishing the prospect of this conversation. Now it's upon me I have no idea what to say, no idea how I want Daniel to respond.

'Are things OK? Are you all right? What's it like?'

Daniel thinks about this for a moment, working out what he can reasonably tell me and what he ought to leave out.

'It's smooth,' he says after a bit. 'Uncle Gary took me to the football last week at Leeds. And there's cable.'

'That's good.'

Silence for a bit. Then: 'Dad … Am I going to be staying here?'

'Probably. Is that all right?'

'I missed Aunty Shena.'

'I miss you.'

'Aunty Shena says …' Another silence. In the distance the sound of a door opening. 'Listen Dad, I've got to go.'

Daniel seems to have settled back into his life here without too much difficulty, Shena wrote in a letter that arrived yesterday. *Gary and I think, however, that the important thing is to disturb him as little as possible while he re-acclimatises himself.*

In English: keep your distance.

*

People In History: *The Comedy Men* went out a fortnight after Christmas. Coming at the dead season of the early

new year, it got some goodish reviews. Half a dozen radio
critics wrote knowledgeably about influences given and
received and what one of them called our 'place in the
English comic tradition, halfway between Miller and
Morecambe & Wise.' Afterwards somebody looked out the
tapes of *The Upward & King Show* and put out a thirty-
minute assemblage on Channel Four. Listening to it, while
Lucy curled up nervously on the sofa ('After all,' she
explained, 'you might not like it') I took some time to
come to terms with the cross-section of professional voices,
the lilt and crackle of the ancient tapes. There was a definite sense of past time, even of past time regained,
simultaneously a feeling that past time had been knocked
out of kilter, reassembled into shapes that bore no resemblance to the landscapes I remembered. As the
programme went on, this feeling of slight bewilderment
hardened into deep unease. Eventually, just before the
end, there was a minute or two of one of Upward's monologues – the one where he impersonated a politician who
wanted to give away free beer on the NHS. Listening to
Upward's voice gradually rising to crescendo, the dutiful
laughter of the studio audience, I realised that I'd become
cut adrift from it, left behind. It was simply a voice
screaming on into the silence.

*

Lucy phones most evenings. We talk about ourselves in the
way I suppose most people beyond their twenties tend to
do: family, heritage, expectations. Sometimes I catch myself
in the middle of one of these conversations and marvel at
it. Once, a week ago, she said suddenly:

'Why did you send me the fish?'

'What do you mean, the fish?'

'I'd forgotten about it until now. Just before Christmas,
I got back from work one day, and there was a dirty great
padded bag with a Yarmouth postmark on the doorstep
stinking of ammonia. When I opened it out came this
rotting fish. It could only have been you.'

'It was what people staying in Yarmouth used to send back to their friends.'

'Well I had to throw this one straight away, I can tell you. But it was a nice thought.'

*

Several times lately I've had a peculiarly vivid and arresting dream. Daniel and I are climbing a hill somewhere. It's a slow and fairly laborious process: through small outcrops of woodland, across a stream, along steadily rising rutted paths, up to a distant prospect of meadows, head-high bracken. Eventually we start running, off through the rising grasslands towards the summit, so high that the flat country stretching out on either side looks like stage decoration rolled into place by scene-shifters who, after we'd gone, would merely roll it away again. Whatever I say to Daniel is blown back by the wind, lost in the endless climb towards the horizon and the shiny sun.

In dreams begin responsibilities.

THE COMEDY MAN

Looking out of the window suddenly
in the midst of the usual chatter, with some arse
or other holding forth about nothing that matters,
I saw, for some reason, the two of them
stuck on some stage, maybe Brighton, or up north,
at any rate somewhere I'd found myself silent and
solitary in an ocean of fools, amused in spite of it all
– idiots with ice-cream, the woman that coughed.
    Well-schooled
in these routines, I note how the tall one, always
    spurned, carries on
regardless, the lessons not learnt in a year,
or a decade, try as he might, and the fat one, toothy
    and slab-faced,
reeling him in like a fish on a hook made of spite.
With the audience pissing themselves, and me
    wanting to shout
*'What in God's name was funny, what on earth were
    you laughing about?'*

                                                    1974

AUTHOR'S NOTE

I should like to thank Justin Cartwright, Jonathan Coe, David Lodge and Auberon Waugh for small pieces of help, about which they know. Many of the showbiz details are drawn from Roger Wilmut's invaluable *Kindly Leave the Stage: The Story of Variety 1919-1960* (Methuen 1985). The lines from Roxy Music's 'Do the Strand' are quoted with kind permission of EMI Music Publishers. Topographical bloodhounds should note that the square in Southtown, Great Yarmouth will not be found on any map. Love and thanks to Rachel, as ever.

MORE DUCKBACK FICTION

Boogie-Woogie
Danny Moynihan   £5.99 Paperback   0 7156 3102 0

Much-praised hilarious satire of the incestuous world of New York's contemporary art scene.

'Moynihan's first novel is spectacular stuff'

Harriet Lane, *Observer*

Intimate Cartographies
Lynne Alexander   £5.99 Paperback   0 7156 3095 4

A beautifully-constructed tale of a mapmaker who comes to terms with loss through the discipline of her work.

'Alexander has created something quite haunting'

Carol Birch, *Independent*

Too Fast To Live
Bidisha   £5.99 Paperback   0 7156 3098 9

A modern-day subversive rewriting of the Arthurian saga.

'Bidisha is clearly a dazzlingly creative writer'

Anthea Lawson, *The Times*

Charlotte
The Final Journey of Jane Eyre
D.M. Thomas   £5.99 Paperback   0 7156 3094 6

An imaginative deconstruction of Charlotte Brontë's *Jane Eyre*.

'a wickedly irreverent antidote to earnest study'

Charlotte Cory, *Independent*

The Comedy Man

D.J. Taylor £5.99 Paperback 0 7156 3157 8

D.J. Taylor's vivid evocation of post-war English life tells the story of Ted King, the 'straight' half of a comedy duo that rose to fame in the late 70s.

'Taylor is utterly enthralling in memoir mode – a rhapsody'

Bob Monkhouse, *Guardian*

Never Trust A Rabbit

Jeremy Dyson £5.99 Paperback 0 7156 3097 0

Twelve surreal stories by one of The League of Gentlemen.

'a stunning debut. His stories nestle in the little chink between Roald Dahl and Borges'

Adam Mars-Jones, *Observer*

Layer Cake

J.J. Connolly £5.99 Paperback 0 7156 3096 2

Contemporary gangland thriller set in London's underworld.

'Layer Cake is a storming piece of work'

Guardian

The Lantern Bearers

Ronald Frame £5.99 Paperback 0 7156 3133 0

WINNER OF THE 2000 SALTIRE BOOK OF THE YEAR AWARD.

Neil Pritchard remembers the summer, 35 years ago, when he acted as a promising composer's muse.

'laced with impending menace from the opening page'

Scotland on Sunday

Valentine's Day
Women Against Men: Stories of Revenge
Edited by Alice Thomas Ellis   £5.99 Paperback   0 7156 3140 3

A brilliant collection of revenge stories by some of the finest contemporary women writers around.

'a sharp anthology, both clever and pointed'

The Times

A Kind of Warfare
Portrait of a Serial Seducer
Deborah Bosley   £5.99 Paperback   0 7156 3139 X

An 'Alfie' for our times is hopelessly addicted to serial seduction and romantic self-absorption, until love hits him.

'crammed with witty and often ingenious observations'

Literary Review

The Undiscovered Chekhov: Fifty-One New Stories
Translated by Peter Constantine   £6.99 Pbk   0 7156 3155 1

Peter Constantine's award-winning translation casts new light on the development of the great playwright's development.

ORDER FORM (BLOCK CAPITALS PLEASE)

SURNAME _____   FIRST NAME _____

ADDRESS _____

_____

_____   POSTCODE _____

METHOD OF PAYMENT (PLEASE TICK AS APPROPRIATE)

☐ Invoice to my Grantham Book Services account
☐ By cheque (payable to Duckworth Publishers)
☐ Please send account opening details (trade customers only)
☐ By credit card (Access/ Visa / Mastercard / Amex)

Card no: ☐☐☐☐☐☐☐☐☐☐☐☐☐☐☐☐☐

Expiry date: ___ / ___   Authorising Signature: _____

POSTAGE (Private customers) Please note that the following postage and packing charges should be added to your order:

UK deliveries: £3 on orders up to £16; £4 on orders over £16
Export surface: £3.50 for first book + £0.50 for each additional book
Export airmail: £7 for the first book + £2 for each additional book

QTY	ISBN	TITLE	PRICE	TOTAL
____	_____	_____	_____	_____
____	_____	_____	_____	_____
____	_____	_____	_____	_____
____	_____	_____	_____	_____
____	_____	_____	_____	_____
____	_____	_____	_____	_____
____	_____	_____	_____	_____

TOTAL £ _____

To: Sales Dept, Duckworth, 61 Frith Street, London W1D 3JL
Tel:+44 (0) 20 7434 4242 Fax: +44 (0) 20 7434 4420
Heidi@duckworth-publishers.co.uk